MW00577344

1919: THE ROMANOV RISING

1919: THE ROMANOV RISING

TOM KRATMAN
KACEY EZELL
JUSTIN WATSON

1919: The Romanov Rising

This is a work of fiction. All the characters and events portrayed in this book are fictional, and any resemblance to real people or incidents is purely coincidental.

A Baen Books Original

Baen Publishing Enterprises
P.O. Box 1403
Riverdale, NY 10471
www.baen.com

ISBN: 978-1-9821-9381-2

Cover art by Sam R. Kennedy

First printing, December 2024

Distributed by Simon & Schuster
1230 Avenue of the Americas
New York, NY 10020

Library of Congress Cataloging-in-Publication Data

Names: Kratman, Tom, author. | Ezell, Kacey, author. | Watson, Justin,
   1983- author.
Title: 1919: the Romanov rising : the winter of sapphire and steel / Tom
   Kratman, Kacey Ezell, Justin Watson.
Description: Riverdale, NY : Baen Publishing Enterprises, 2024. | Series:
   The Romanov reign ; 2
Identifiers: LCCN 2024032472 (print) | LCCN 2024032473 (ebook) | ISBN
   9781982193812 (hardcover) | ISBN 9781625799937 (ebook)
Subjects: LCSH: Soviet Union—History—Revolution, 1917-1921. | LCGFT:
   Alternative histories (Fiction) | Thrillers (Fiction) | Novels.
Classification: LCC PS3611.R375 A616 2024 (print) | LCC PS3611.R375
   (ebook) | DDC 813/.6—dc23/eng/20240716
LC record available at https://lccn.loc.gov/2024032472
LC ebook record available at https://lccn.loc.gov/2024032473

Printed in the United States of America

10 9 8 7 6 5 4 3 2 1

Dedication

Tom's
Sergeant Major Howard Peter—"Pete"—Schetrompf,
9 October 1939 to 4 May 2021
Bruce J. Dyer,
28 June 1957 to 13 May 2020
Staff Sergeant and Foreign Service Officer Thomas J. Wallis,
10 July 1961 to 1 May 2021
James Cochrane,
26 December 1970 to 25 March 2021

Kacey's
For my grandfathers, Major Russell B. Hilton, USAF (ret)
and MSgt William H. Coacher, USA.
And for all the generations of Cold Warriors who held the line.

Justin's
For my grandfather, Master Sergeant Raymond L. Watson, Sr.,
and my father, Chief Warrant Officer Raymond L. Watson,
who spent their adult lives in the decades-long fight
against communism.

And, from all of us, for OTMAA.

1919:
THE ROMANOV
RISING

What has gone before:

Time is a tough fabric, closely woven and very strong.

It was the end of 1917, the beginning of the last full year of the greatest war in human history, to date. All the belligerents were staggering on their feet. Starvation was an ever-present reality, while disease waited expectantly in the wings. In Russia, no longer a belligerent but, instead, rapidly descending into civil war and chaos, a lone family—Father, Mother, four beautiful young girls, and a brave but sickly boy—awaited their own fate, shivering and hungry in the cold and dark, hoping and praying for salvation.

Their relatives in England had turned their backs. The guards set over them did little but torment them. They looked Heavenward, but God gave no answer. The Romanovs knew they were a standing threat to the new regime, a threat that would, in time, be eliminated.

But even the strongest fabric has flaws, weak points. An escaped prisoner of war, caught, injured, and punished, but still highly capable, might become one. An outsized airship, returned and at loose ends after a failed mission to Africa, might be yet another. A German general, taking a wrong turn on his nightly walk and suddenly coming face to face with the reality of the monster rising in the east, *would* prove to be a third.

Thus:

In late 1917, with the Great War raging in the west, but moribund in the east, German General Max Hoffmann took a different turn from the usual on his nightly walk through the wrecked but rebuilding town of Brest-Litovsk. This was where—as a second hat—he was serving as the military observer to the peace talks between Germany and Russia. Hoffmann's first hat, contrarily, was as chief of staff to Ober-Ost, the German High Command in the East, and thus he was effectively the director of the three Central Powers armies in the east—German, Austro-Hungarian, and Bulgarian—even though a mere major general.

In the course of this new path, Hoffmann and his assistant,

Brinkmann, came upon the initial steps in several Bolsheviks' joint attempt to rape a young girl. Hoffmann and Brinkmann saved the girl, killing all the Bolsheviks in the process. This event was also the spark that set alight in Hoffmann's brain a plan to save both Russia and the world from the scourge of Bolshevism.

Taking authority over the German airship, L59, recently returned from a failed attempt to resupply German forces in East Africa, Hoffmann, an excellent Russian speaker, then recruited Daniil Kostyshakov, a captive Guards officer with a penchant for escape, to raise from among trustworthy POWs in German hands a force to travel by airship to go and save the Russian royal family, the Romanovs, being held somewhere in the depths of the Russian Empire.

As portrayed by entries from their second daughter's, Tatiana's, journal, the Romanovs themselves were in Tobolsk, enduring cold, hardship, humiliation, hunger, and rape at the hands of their radicalized guards.

A small reconnaissance team, Strategic Reconnaissance or "Strat Recon," under Lieutenant Maxim Sergeyevich Turgenev, a Guards Cavalry officer with intelligence experience, and Sergeant Rostislav Alexandrovich Mokrenko, a hard-bitten Cossack noncom, set out to pinpoint the exact location where the family was being held, as well as to prepare the way for the actual operation. Strat Recon went out of their way not to be spotted. Even so, some of their actions were too noticeable, ranging from the slaughter of a pirate *cum* smuggling ship's crew to blowing up a Bolshevik destroyer to the massacre of a gang of train robbers.

These things attracted the attention of some well-placed Bolsheviks. They didn't know what was up, exactly, only that something was.

Meanwhile, in spurts and starts, Kostyshakov and his men garnered supplies and equipment, built training facilities, developed a doctrine for rescue operations, organized themselves, trained, and prepared. Men, more than a few, were killed and crippled in the course of the training.

The Zeppelin could not have hoped to carry enough men and supplies in one lift. Instead, five were planned initially, later reduced to four as Strat Recon reported they'd acquired enough horses and sleds for the operation.

Of the lifts, however, only three made it, bringing fewer than three hundred men, before a mechanical failure moored the Zeppelin for a time to its base in Bulgaria.

With only two companies and parts of a third, and with that same fewer than three hundred men, Kostyshakov was confronted with the news that the couple of hundred guards he'd expected had been increased to over six hundred, many of them Bolshevik fanatics, and those with orders to take the Romanovs away to God alone knew where.

With a minimum of soul searching, knowing what was at stake, Kostyshakov decided to go in anyway, no matter the odds. His officers, noncoms, and men supported him in this.

In the subsequent attack, after Strat Recon took out the power plant for Tobolsk, while one company held the largest force of Reds in place, a single reinforced platoon, equipped almost entirely with novel automatic weapons and flamethrowers, attacked and burnt out the barracks for the most fanatical group of Bolsheviks, shooting the escapees down in the street.

The final group, meanwhile, assaulted the Romanov family's quarters, the Governor's House, killing most of the guards. The tsarevich, Alexei, a brave boy suffering from hemophilia, gave his own life in the rescue, smothering a Bolshevik grenade to save his sisters.

Kostyshakov managed to save, after the self-sacrifice of the tsarevich, only half of the remaining Romanovs, after one of the rescue force's own members, a secret Bolshevik, turned his submachine gun on the tsar, the tsarina, and the girls. Two of the girls were saved by their own garments, in which they had sewn twenty pounds of gold and jewels, each. The eldest girl was killed. The eldest surviving Romanov, Tatiana, was saved by one of her former guards turned rescuer, Sergei Chekov.

Repaired, the Zeppelin brought in the missing company, then went back to fly in the replacement company and the spare ammunition. It blew up, due to unknown causes, on 7 April 1918, just as it did in our timeline.

With the tsar dead, the tsarina dead, and the tsarevich and Olga both dead, it fell to Tatiana to take up the vacant throne. Duly crowned in the largest cathedral in Tobolsk, with all the ceremony that could be mustered on short notice, her first order to Kostyshakov was to rescue her aunt, the nun and widow Elisabeth of Hesse and by Rhine, from likely murder at the hands of the Bolsheviks.

Prologue

Imperial House
(nee Governor's House, nee Freedom House) Tobolsk, Russia

The place was warm for a change; absent the Bolsheviks' studied cruelty, the people of the town, who had always, by and large, supported the Romanovs and the monarchy, had brought wood from their own stockpiles, had gone into the woods to cut more, and had ransacked the ruins of the burnt-out Kornilov house to get wood to keep their young empress warm.

It hadn't hurt any, either, that the coronation of Tatiana I, Empress of all the Russias, had taken place in their little town, in one of their cathedrals, with their clerics overseeing what the townsfolk took to be the marriage of their God and their empress, hence their empire.

Currently that empress sat at her late father's desk, reading and signing a stack of paper made up of awards, promotions, transfers, letters patent, regimental recreations, and this, that, and whatnot.

At least they're not death warrants, thought the newly minted empress, with an audible sigh of vast relief. *I don't think I could take any more of those for now.*

The frequent fusillades of the firing squads had been so regular for the last couple of days that Tatiana had found herself flinching in anticipation, approximately every four minutes and ten seconds, awaiting the rattle of musketry that would signal that another Red had gone to meet his maker. Those were done, though; the last of the known Reds in Tobolsk were finished now, even as her newly formed *Okhrana*, or secret police, sought out the few who might remain in hiding.

The air was so cold and dense, the sound carried so well, that I felt every shot. I—

Tatiana's thoughts were interrupted by her youngest sister, seventeen-year-old Anastasia, now serving as an occasional secretary, sticking her head in through the doorway that led to the former tsar's study.

"Yes, Nastenka?" Tatiana asked, looking up from her paperwork. Her sister had a number of nicknames, ranging from that to *shvibzik*, or "imp."

"Guards Captain Kostyshakov is here with his officers and sergeants major," Anastasia announced. "Prince Dolgorukov is standing by, as well."

"Oh, send the prince up first, then give me five minutes and send in the rest," Tatiana said. *There is one good thing about being empress, rather than a mostly useless grand duchess; I can reward my friends and saviors.*

The library, normally rather spacious, was filled to capacity with uniformed men, wearing field uniforms rather than full dress.

Daniil Kostyshakov, chief among the saviors of the remnants of the royal family, made to apologize before the empress cut him off with, "We're at war, Daniil; what uniform could be more appropriate?"

"Attention to orders," announced Prince Dolgorukov. The assembled officers and senior noncoms automatically stiffened to attention.

"The following promotions are announced. To the rank of major general, Daniil Edvardovich Kostyshakov. To the rank of colonel of the guard, Ivan Dratvin, Pyotr Cherimisov, Mikhail Basinets..."

As the names were announced, Tatiana walked down the ranks, shaking each man's hand and saying at approximately every third handshake, "The insignia will follow as soon as we can have some made."

More lists for promotion were pressed into the hands of the senior officers, to take care of those masses of men whom the library could not fit and for whom there was no time to have them promoted personally by Tatiana.

When the senior promotions were done, no man, living or dead, but for two, from the rescue force, had failed to rise at least two ranks. The posthumous promotions would have little importance to the dead, but the higher pensions and honoring of fallen comrades would matter to the living.

The two who were not promoted were the two sergeants-major, Blagov and Nenonen, both of whom considered it a demotion to be commissioned.

Dolgorukov then began with the awards, ranging from Orders of Saint George, at the high end, to Crosses of Saint George, at the lower. Both the sergeants-major were awarded Orders of Saint George.

Tatiana found herself blinking rapidly when the name was announced, "Sergei Chekov." Though Chekov had not been an official member of the rescue force, he *had* been her friend and, more importantly, had saved her life at the cost of his own.

The crowd had cleared out, leaving Tatiana and Kostyshakov alone in the study.

"How go the preparations to save my aunt Ella?" she asked.

He was loath to admit it, but, "I don't know how to, Tatiana. I've kicked the strategic recon section forward to Yekaterinburg to confirm she's there and directed that the telegraph line be repaired but remain silent. But as a logistic matter, I don't know how to move the battalion, or even half of it, so far across the snow and ice to get to her. I was counting on the airship to carry us. We are still trying to think of a way but . . . sorry; it looks impossible. It's a logistic problem, and those are the most intractable. With all the horses and sleighs we can muster, the men would still be starved, hence dead and frozen stiff, before they can reach her."

"Dan, I *must* have my Aunt Ella. I need her to counsel and advise me."

"I understand," he said. "But I still can't do what I can't do."

"Impossible or not," she insisted, "I must have her at my side."

"Tatiana Nicholaevna—"

"Must!"

"It may not be—"

"Must!"

"Then I'll think of a way . . . Your Majesty."

"You must," she said. "Because I need my aunt."

Dan sighed. "We still have to worry about the eventual—inevitable, really—attempt of the Reds to take us here and finish the job they intended for you."

"Then you must take care of both. And there's something else . . ."

"You've finally decided to leave this place, I hope," Kostyshakov said.

"No, of course not. And don't tell me about how silly my parents were in preferring death to escape. They were helpless prisoners, and not in the best shape mentally. But I am free and, thanks to you, have a nice little army—and getting nicer by the day—to fight with. So, no, I'm not going anywhere except forward, forward to Moscow and Saint Petersburg.

"But my sisters; I want them out of here and to safety. And the sooner the better."

"Safety would be a fine thing," Daniil agreed, "but it would be better still if they could go somewhere where they could drum up some help for us. Because, Tatiana Nicholaevna, the operative description for our 'army' is less 'nice' than it is 'little.' Your Aunt Ella would tell you the same, were she here."

Later, still in her father's old study, but alone now, Tatiana had cause to reflect on the future.

Can I win? Sure, I was able to sound full of confidence in front of Daniil and the others. But can I . . . can we . . . actually win?

Moreover, what does winning mean here? What end state am I actually looking for?

Ultimately, I want Russia at peace. I want her prosperous. I want our people educated, our industry built up, our agriculture able to feed ourselves and *a good part of the rest of the world. There's probably no better defense against invasion than that the people who might want to invade you would quickly starve if they tried. Science? I don't know much about it, but whatever it is, I want us to have it.*

I don't know much about government. I do know that ours, our old one, ultimately failed, though it took three centuries. I do know that Kerensky's attempt at one likewise failed. I know that Great Britain has had a stable government, barring a civil war or two, two, if we count the Americans, for about as long as we had an autocracy.

So I think I want a constitutional monarchy, like the British have, almost. Maybe somewhat more actual power to the crown, because we are not British but Russian, and only respect a strong hand. Yes, we are Russians and need a crown that is more than a figurehead.

I also want to make us less of an Empire and more of a federation, if that's possible. I don't know that it is, but Finland, at least, had a pretty good relationship. Why can't Poland and some of the other possessions? I'm going to try.

But equally, some places cannot simply be let go because they think they'll do better without us. Poland, again, is the invasion route from the west and must be held, with or without their permission. Hmmm ... maybe a perpetual alliance, rather than simply ruling over them. This requires thought. Also some insights I know I lack.

But for the time being, we have to fight just to live. The future is going to have to wait to see if we survive.

Chapter One

Wreck of the L59

Ipatiev House, Voznesenski Prospect, Yekaterinburg

Aunt Ella wore a nun's habit, something that could not, even at the advanced age of fifty-three, quite hide that she'd been, in her youth, one of the great beauties of Europe and retained yet a good deal of that beauty.

Ella, Elizabeth Feodorovna, formerly Princess Elisabeth of Hesse and by Rhine, was also quite intelligent and very wise; the future Kaiser, Wilhelm II, smitten with her, had, for example, proposed to her when she'd been fourteen. He'd been soundly rejected.

Following the murder of the man she *had* married by a Red assassin, Ella had sold off all of her worldly possessions, which had been extensive, to found a nunnery, with a school, hospital, dental clinic, and pharmacy to care for the poor of Moscow. Though converted to Orthodoxy for her marriage, her inspiration had, in large part, been the Roman Catholic "Little Sisters of the Poor." Before that, though, she'd gone to the Tsar to beg fruitlessly for the life of her husband's assassin.

Thus, she was also perhaps one of the twentieth century's better candidates for sainthood. Indeed, she was almost too much so for credence.

Even so, she was no weakling or starry-eyed idealist. While she'd begged for the assassin's life, it was because hanging him could only be, she believed, an act of revenge, hence, she thought, unworthy of a Christian state and monarch, and useless besides. But when she'd had good reason to suspect that some patriots were about to do away with Rasputin, she'd kept her own counsel and let the murder happen, because Rasputin had been a continuing and *massive* threat to her sister, the Tsarina, her brother-in-law, the Tsar, and her nieces and nephew, thus to the Russian Empire and to her adopted Orthodox faith, as well.

She'd rarely wept in her life. Indeed, it had only happened when her mother had died, when her beloved husband had been murdered, and now . . . now, on her knees on the rough floor by the rude bed where she'd been praying. Now, when the full weight of the knowledge of the murder of her sister, her brother-in-law, one of her nieces and her dear little *tsarevich*, Alexei, had borne down on her. Now, she wept; now she asked of her God, over and over, "Why? Why? Why?"

South of Tobolsk

Why did it blow up? wondered Signalman Wilhelm Mueller, late of the German Navy, glancing up from the singed field on which lay the charred corpses of his late comrades. He'd been asking himself the same question for days.

The aluminum skeleton of a great airship, L-59, a lost leviathan of the air, lay among the bodies, its mostly skinless frame broken and crumpled on the landscape. Tattered skin fluttered from the wreckage in places, the shreds torn and charred. Amidst the ruin, and all around it, stooped men under armed guards hunted for bodies and whatever military material might be recovered. Some of them appeared to be using brooms to sweep the ice.

All the free men on the field were Russians, Poles, or Finns— Imperial Russian subjects—except for one: Mueller himself, last of the crew of the L59. Teary-eyed and bleary-eyed, he walked among the charred, broken corpses looking for the last remains of his friends. As he discovered them, usually by means of the 1878 or 1917 pattern oval *Erkenungsmarke—metal ovals that had once, in 1864, been called*

Hundesmarke, or "dog tags"—they wore on chains or leather cords about their necks, he beckoned for one of the stretcher teams to come and take the body away to where a separate cemetery for the ship's crew had been laid out.

Mueller came to a corpse, badly charred, with arms and legs drawn into a fetal position. It was impossible to make out features on the blackened, half-melted face. Size was no clue to identity, either; bodies shrank when burnt. Taking one knee, the German aviator brushed aside the few fragments of cloth clinging to the body, then did the same for the bits of cloth and flesh obscuring the tags. He silently read the name: *Gustav Proll.*

Blinking back a new flood of tears, Mueller thought, *What about your wife and children, old friend? We weren't even officially in the navy anymore. Who will care for them?*

Northwest of L59's corpse, a great pyre of what remained of hundreds of corpses—Reds, their collaborators, and sundry criminals—still smoldered between the River Irtysh and a warehouse that normally held those prisoners now engaged in the hunt for recoverable material to the south. The pyre reeked of overdone pork, a stench that had Tatiana Nicholaevna Romanova, Empress of all the Russias, on the verge of nausea. That she'd signed the death warrants for most of those shot and then burnt added an unseemly guilt to the rising urge to vomit.

"Get me out of here, Dan," she said to her escort, Daniil Edvardovich Kostyshakov, late of the Kexholm Regiment of the Imperial Guards as well as of Camp Budapest and Ingolstadt's Fortress IX. "Please, somewhere else, quickly, before I lose the contents of my stomach."

Without a word, guided by perfect understanding, Dan flicked the reins of the sleigh on which he and Tatiana rode, sending the furry Yakut horse that drew it trotting to the south and upwind of the source of the stench. Two further sleighs, bearing armed guards, followed, while a half dozen guardsmen, horse-borne, kept station at a distance. If all else failed, and the guard detail proved inadequate, both the empress and Daniil had machine pistols slung over their shoulders.

The move wasn't quite quick enough; within a dozen of the horse's paces Tatiana had to bend to the side and empty the contents of her stomach onto the ice.

"I'm sorry," she said, recovering in the freer and cleaner air south of the great pyre. "I just . . . the smell . . . and knowing I created it . . . my orders did. Somehow, it's even more real smelling it than it was hearing the firing squads at work."

Dan shook his head in negation. "You did the right thing; none of them would have improved with age."

"Maybe not," she admitted. "But how can I *know* that?"

"If *you* don't know it, Tatiana Nicholaevna, everyone *else* does."

The empress shook her head, doubtfully.

"Where are we going?" she asked, as Dan continued to direct their sleigh in the direction of the monstrous airship.

"There are lots of men with rifles in the town, most of whom are anti-Bolshevik, but a sad dearth of ammunition for them. My quartermaster—"

"The rat-faced one?" she interrupted. "That's not very kind of me, is it? I don't mean it unkindly, but I know no better way to describe him."

"Romeyko; yes, him." Facing her, Dan raised a disapproving eyebrow. "You could maybe try describing him as one of the better quartermasters in the army. Or maybe as a man as responsible as any for the rescue of yourself and your sisters."

Seeing Tatiana flush with shame, Dan looked forward again and continued, "He's trying to salvage what can be salvaged from the airship. I don't have a lot of hope but if he can scrounge enough to give a fighting load to the eleven or twelve hundred men in the town who are armed and whom we can trust . . ."

Maybe trust, he thought, guiltily, remembering that three of the Romanovs had been murdered by a man of his own organization, a man in whom far *too much* trust had been placed.

Romeyko and Mueller saw the escorted sleigh at the same time and began to walk over from separate start points. The quartermaster was considerably closer.

Seeing them, Daniil said to Tatiana, "That's the German aviator who lost all his friends. Given how important they were to saving who could be saved, and how much you've lost, too, you might want to have a private word with him."

"I will then," she agreed.

With the quartermaster now close enough, Daniil asked, "And what have you been able to recover?"

"It's a lot better than I expected," the unlovely supply officer said. "In the first place, the fire, while hot, was short-lived. The wooden boxes are charred, more or less and here and there, but the contents are largely intact. Some of them broke open on impact, which is why I've got men sweeping the ice.

"Better still, I had on my wish list two or three of those British Stokes mortars. Never thought we'd see them but *Feldwebel* Weber or Major Brinkmann apparently came through in the end, sometime after we left. Haven't much of a clue about how to use them, of course, and one of the sights appears to be broken. We might be able to fix it, though; it's very simple. I have two tubes and a few hundred rounds of ammunition. Based on the smell, my best guess is that the ammunition and manuals were stowed somewhere very close to the urine bladder. They stink like it, anyway. It may be that the liquid helped preserve them from the fire, too. The manuals are damaged, mind, but maybe not so much that a clever English speaker can't figure the things out."

Tatiana raised one index finger. "I can read, write, and speak English quite well, Colonel. It was really my first language, since it was the language my parents shared that they spoke best. Give me the manuals and . . . well . . . someone who understands artillery, at least, for terms I won't be familiar with."

Romeyko nodded slowly, using the time gained to collect his thoughts on the subject. *Piss? The Tsarina of all the Russias is going to cover her hands with PISS?* Ultimately, he decided, *Well, her choice, after all,* and said, "That would be a great help, Your Majesty. I'll find an artilleryman for you. Or Corporal Panfil, maybe, who's probably as close as we've got.

"Most of the rifles also made it through," Romeyko continued. "The two spare heavy machine guns have their water jackets pierced, but I think we can fix them locally. Think, not sure. My assistant is out hunting down *some* kind of metalworking shop, or maybe a blacksmith, all else failing, for the job. The pioneer tools are largely intact. Also, one of the Germans sent us nine more Lewis Guns in our caliber, which is certainly helpful. Likewise a few dozen of those Amerikansky pistols, though not much ammunition for them."

Romeyko pointed in Mueller's direction, saying, "There's something

else, too. The German told me about it. We had no clue before but . . ."
The quartermaster let his voice trail off as Mueller had arrived at the
sleigh.

Everyone could see from his red, puffy eyes that the German had
been crying. Tactfully, no one mentioned it.

"The quartermaster tells me you have something for us, *Herr*
Mueller," prompted Kostyshakov.

"Yes, sir. Well, two things. While the radio aboard the airship was
wrecked, there *may* be enough useable pieces and spare parts to
reconstruct it. I'm not sure but I'll try. The other thing is that the ship,
itself, its frame, was different from any other airship ever built. It was
designed to be taken apart and turned into a radio tower."

"Can you still?" Tatiana asked. "I mean, it looks twisted up pretty
badly in places."

"I think so, Your Majesty," Mueller said. "The sections are
aluminum—strong for its weight is not the same thing as all that
strong—so not so hard to twist back into shape, more or less.

"The other thing is . . . well . . ."

"Go on," Tatiana urged.

"Your Majesty, I am concerned about the families of my friends; my
own family, too, for that matter. We were all officially discharged from
the Navy for this mission. That means no survivors' support for the
wives and children. I don't know what to do about it."

"Do you have a list of names and addresses?" the empress asked.

"Not full addresses, Your Majesty, only down to cities and towns,
and I am not one hundred percent about those, not nearly."

"Who could you ask?"

"No one comes to mind," he replied. "If I can find the notebook of
our senior enlisted man, I suspect I'd find their addresses, too. But so
far, I can't find it. It may have burnt."

"Look for it," said the empress. "You find me where to send money
and *I* will support the families of the men killed trying to rescue us. I'll
sell jewelry if I must."

"Does that go for my dead, too, Highness?" Kostyshakov asked.

"Yes," Tatiana replied, "and you should have brought it up to me
sooner. Speaking of sooner—my aunt?"

"Repairs on the telegraph line are complete," he answered. "I am
sending out the first grenadier platoon, less its dead and wounded, under

their platoon sergeant, *Feldfebel* Kostin, first thing in the morning. I don't have another qualified officer to spare and, if they can link up, Turgenev's judgment is sound. On skis, Kostin can probably catch up to Turgenev and Strat Recon before they get to Yekaterinburg. And, Your Majesty, no matter *what* you demand, *that* is the best I can do."

And that's probably the truth, too, thought Tatiana. *Oh, my poor Aunt Ella.*

Fifty Versts East of Tyumen, Russia

The expedition to pinpoint the location of Aunt Ella was making slow progress through the trackless Siberian wastes.

"I wish we'd had time to learn to ski," said Lieutenant Turgenev, leading his little Yakut horse through the snowdrifts of this mostly unsettled and completely un-roaded part of Siberia. Like the rest of the men of Strat Recon, Turgenev now wore winter whites over his uniform.

Mokrenko, walking beside his officer, could only agree. "We'd have made faster time, yes, than we are with having to let the horses spend about half of every day scraping through the snow to graze and half the remainder leading them through things we have enough trouble with ourselves."

Strat—for "Strategic"—recon was a hand-picked group of men, somewhat reinforced now to cover its losses and its previous deficiencies. Beyond the survivors of the first version, Turgenev, himself, Sergeant Mokrenko, Corporal Koslov, also known as "Goat," Cossacks Novarikasha and Lavin, Signaller Sarnof, Medical Orderly Timashuk, and Engineer Shukhov, they'd had added to them another signaller, medic, and engineer, Popov, Gazenko, and Peredery, respectively. In addition, the ranks had been culled for a single Cossack to make up for the loss of Visaitov, killed foiling a robbery on a train. This man was Cossack Bulavin.

Natalya Sorokina and Sergei Babin had been left behind, the former as lady-in-waiting to the empress, the latter as a much-needed staff officer on what was about to become brigade staff.

Those bare twelve had also been reinforced with better arms. A half dozen machine pistols of the killed and badly wounded from the rescue force, plus one Lewis Gun, had been turned over to Turgenev. Moreover, it wasn't quite true that nobody was skiing. The new additions had learnt the skill back in Bulgaria, while preparing for the mission. Conversely, none of them but the Cossack had ever learnt to ride a horse. Hence Popov, Gazenko, and Peredery skied behind the two sleighs carrying the team's supplies, outsize equipment, and the single portable telegraph set.

Suddenly, Mokrenko, his horse, and the lieutenant's, stiffened.

"What is it, Sergeant?" Turgenev asked.

Mokrenko took a moment to answer, eyes closed and concentrating hard. Finally, he said, "Men, I think, sir, numbering between several hundred to as many as two or three thousand, heading this way."

Turgenev listened for a bit, finally hearing a steady *crunchcrunch-crunch* from a great many booted feet.

"Bugger!"

Noise carries in cold, dense air. There was no sense in announcing a change of direction and little more in trying to move as a column; the approaching horde might arrive before the last man had turned.

"Give me your horse, sergeant. Then you walk back the way we came, telling them to turn right immediately, not where I am turning."

"Yes, sir. How far?"

"Half a *verst*, that should be far enough to hide. And for God's sake, hurry!"

Stomping back through the ice and snow, Mokrenko gave the orders and as brief an explanation as possible. "Probable Reds, many, heading this way. Turn right immediately, half a *verst* ... Probable Reds, many ..."

As soon as they'd turned, walked, and then stopped, the horsemen coaxed their Yakuts down to the prone and took cover. Meanwhile, the sleigh drivers and mounted men took out some commandeered white sheets and draped them over the Yakuts and sleighs, before doing the same with their own horses.

Mokrenko trooped the line forward, inspecting the camouflage. "Adjust your sheet, Sarnof; I can see the runners of your sleigh ... get your head down, Bulavin, right after you finish covering your horse; the lieutenant needs to see but you do not ... crawl over behind that snowdrift, Popov ..."

Before he had quite made it to the lieutenant, he caught his first glimpse of the approaching mass. Mokrenko immediately dropped to his belly, then crawled forward over the snow and ice to where his officer and their horses lay, the lieutenant being likewise prone but with his field glasses studying the presumptive Reds.

"I make it about . . . let's see . . . seven . . . eight . . . nine companies, big ones," Turgenev passed on. "A mass of heavy-duty sleighs are following them. They've got their lead company formed up ten across, and about twenty deep, arms linked, just packing down the snow by stamping it down. Clever technique, really. Aha, the lead company has stopped and is splitting up to the sides while the next one moves up to take their place on stamping duty."

The lieutenant went silent then, for a bit, just watching the procession.

One of the good things about this officer, thought Mokrenko; *he's cool in a crisis.*

"They've got a heavy machine gun each on what looks like a dozen sleighs and . . . oh, shit, there are four artillery pieces following. Look like Model 1900s. Could be worse, I guess."

The Model 1900 was an *almost* modern quick firing gun, of 76.2mm, with the recuperator slung in the trail.

"Bad news, then," muttered Mokrenko.

"Yes, very bad," the lieutenant whispered back. "They're not the best guns, to be sure, but they're better than anything we have at Tobolsk. Hmmm . . . there's one good thing."

"What's that, sir?"

"They're moving slow—maybe a *verst* and a half an hour—that way. At that speed they must be carrying a lot of fodder and provisions . . . and it seems they are," the lieutenant finished as a large number of sleighs hove into view.

A *verst* was just a little bit over a kilometer.

"We need to get word back," Mokrenko said.

"I know, but I'm willing to bet you they've got a portable telegraph set, the same as we do. They probably hook it to the wires overhead when they stop for the night."

The sergeant thought about that for a bit. "That means we need to find out two things. One is how many *versts* they're moving per day. I think we can do that by counting off paces between clusters of campfires. The other is when they're moving again, so that we'll know they're not hooked up on the telegraph and we can get a message through to Tobolsk."

Turgenev nodded and then added, "We can probably determine the latter by the distance between the former. But even without that, my guess is going to be that they'll be moving by nine or surely by ten in the morning, probably stopped between noon and one, then stopped again by three so they can gather wood, cook, and set up for the night."

The sergeant did some figuring in his head before announcing, "If you're right, sir, then this lot is moving a bare eight *versts* a day, if that. I wonder what Kostyshakov will make of that."

"That awaits events," answered Turgenev. "In the interim"—and here he lowered his binoculars and took a quick glance at the sky—"we wait for sundown or for them to pass, whichever comes first, and get behind them. I think we might be able to use the road they've created to move faster ourselves."

As the last rays of the sun settled down in the west, Turgenev announced, "I was wrong; there are more of them, at least three thousand in total."

As it turned out, the Reds had encamped not so very far away, perhaps two *versts* to the east.

Mokrenko nodded, somberly. The lieutenant had shared the binoculars with the sergeant over the course of the time it took for the Reds to pass.

"We need to get a feel for how they set up at night," the sergeant observed. "Kostyshakov will need to know, if he's to plan."

"How?" asked Turgenev.

"I'll go, with one other Cossack—reconnaissance is, after all, our specialty—after dark."

"Who?"

"Lavin. And, if we get caught, you will still have a competent noncom with you, Goat."

"All right," Turgenev agreed. "I'll lead the rest of the section westward and set up two *versts* from here, and just off the road the Reds made, quarter of a *verst* to the north. If—God forbid!—there's another large group coming along I'll pull north half a *verst*."

"I think that works, sir. See you there. Sir, I'm going to collect Lavin and we're going to sleep here. The moon won't be up for another six hours or so and, if we don't get some sleep before spending all night on a recon, we'll be useless tomorrow."

"I agree. See you hopefully sometimes before sunrise tomorrow."

✛ ✛ ✛

The sky was overcast, clouds pregnant with snow that could begin to fall at any time. From Mokrenko's point of view, this was perfect, enough light to see by but not so much as to make his and Lavin's movement obvious to any guards posted.

And there *were* guards posted, he found, but none of them especially alert or disciplined. The first one, standing alone, leaning against a tree bordering the new road, was smoking a pipe.

Dear God, thought the sergeant, *smoking? SMOKING on guard?*

They gave the guard a wide berth, skirting his position by almost a quarter of a *verst* before turning inward again. Skulking forward from tree to tree, they actually passed *between* the first guard they'd found and another they didn't suspect, finding themselves essentially inside the Reds' bivouac. By the diffuse moonlight Mokrenko saw men cooking, standing in clusters, joking, a few drinking, and about half of them dead asleep.

Well, this is an unusual state of affairs, thought Mokrenko. *But now that we're inside, the camouflage that got us here makes us stand out.*

He led Lavin to a spot behind a sleigh, out of view of anyone who seemed awake. "Lavin," he whispered, "take your white smock and overcoat off, then put the smock on under the coat. Yes, son; we're going to be very fucking bold, indeed."

Once so clothed, they were indistinguishable from the rank and file of the Red column. Starting near the back, they simply began walking to the east, keeping a mental pace count as they went. The packed snow made a good road; progress was swift.

On the way forward, bits and pieces of conversation floated on the air: "So I told the bitch, either put out or get out . . . No, no, no, comrade, as Ilyich clearly showed in *State and Revolution*, social democracy can never . . . hey, got anything to drink? . . ."

Only once on their forward progress was there a bad moment. One of the Reds stopped them and asked, "Password, comrades!"

"We don't know it," Mokrenko admitted, bluffing, "Ninth Company, don't you know, comrade, and you know what *our* leadership is like. I was hoping to find out the password at headquarters, but I'm not sure where headquarters is."

The Red shrugged, resignedly. "Yeah, I'm not surprised. This is the worst clusterfuck I've seen since the tail end of Brusilov's final offensive. Nobody's really in charge. Nobody knows what to do. We wouldn't even be out here if Sverdlov hadn't threatened Comrade Goloshchyokin with execution if we didn't get on the road. Instead, we'd still be nice and comfortable back in Yekaterinburg."

"So what *is* the challenge and password, Comrade?" Mokrenko asked.

The Red looked down, sheepishly. "To tell the truth, comrades, I was hoping *you* would know. See, I am from the Transportation Company, and if you think Ninth Company has rotten leadership . . ."

"I'd recommend we all desert," said Mokrenko, "but we'd just freeze and starve alone out here." Turning to Lavin, he said, "Come on, Comrade, let's see if we can find headquarters and get the challenge and password."

"If you find them and get them," said the Red, pointing, "I'll be sleeping over by that sleigh. Stop by and let me know, would you? Call out for Comrade Bortnik, or for Konstantin Maksimovich."

"We'll try. Hey, I've got a question; is anyone in the transportation company carrying firewood?"

"Maybe for themselves, but everyone else is on their own."

"So did the Red get his challenge and password?" asked Turgenev, next morning.

"We never could find their headquarters, sir," Mokrenko admitted. "No one seemed to know where it was. Even so, don't totally discount them. They're very well armed and supplied. Well, except with firewood; that, they have to collect daily. Healthy, too. I listened for coughing and wheezing and heard none. I wouldn't expect anything too sophisticated, but if they were lined up and told to charge Tobolsk they could probably take it."

"Right," the lieutenant agreed. "Sarnof? Signaller Sarnof?"

"Here, sir."

"Compose an encoded message to Tobolsk. 'Encountered enemy regiment. Currently fifty *versts* east of Tyumen. Strength roughly three thousand. Yekaterinburg Reds. Marching on your position, not more than eight *versts* per day. Bivouac at night in a long, thin sausage. Security is poor and scouting non-existent. Red commander is Comrade Goloshchyokin. First encountered last night. One dozen machine guns and four artillery pieces, Model 1900. Not well led or disciplined. Collect firewood and cook daily, which slows them.'

"Now are you hooked up to send?"

"Yes, sir," the signaller replied, "but, per your orders, we're waiting for the Reds to sign off and get on the road again before we send anything. In the meantime, we listen to anything they send, but it isn't much. And, yes, sir, we'll take steps to make sure our message goes only to Tobolsk."

Ulitsa Lazaretnaya, Tobolsk, Russia

The eleven remaining men of the first grenadier platoon, reinforced, formed up on the street called "Lazaretsnaya," or Hospital Street, waiting for Kostyshakov to see them off. Six of their number had been detached to form another platoon. To the remainder had been attached a medic, a two-man flamethrower team, the part-Tatar sniper Nomonkov, and his spotter, Strelnikov, and thirty good men skimmed from the ranks and not needed for the newly expanded Guards battalions. He duly marched out from his headquarters about fifty *arshins* to the east accompanied by Sergeant Major Pavel Blagov.

From further to the east there came a steady rattle of musketry as a company of the new recruits—already trained, yes, but not as well as Kostyshakov's Guards—qualified with the rifles. Indeed, the whole area east of the Tobolsk Kremlin had been given over to training and was, bit by bit, coming to represent a close cognate of the training facilities left behind at Camp Budapest, in Bulgaria, some weeks prior. There were enough new recruits to turn both Second and Third companies, with parts of First, into somewhat light battalions, even while filling up the Fourth—Grenadier—company, to nearly a full company in strength and leaving enough for a headquarters and support company for the brigade. They'd eked out the supply of men by adding a couple score strong and healthy-looking women for the regimental mess.

As Kostyshakov arrived in front of the platoon, the platoon sergeant and acting platoon leader, *Feldfebel* Kostin, called the platoon to attention, then reported formally, "Sir, First Grenadier Platoon, all present or accounted for and ready to march."

None of the men wore skis, Dan noted, though these were laid upon packs that looked overstuffed to the point of bursting.

Well, sure, there's not much snow on the ground here and they're going to have to eat only what they can carry.

"Have the men fall out and cluster around, *Feldfebel.*"

While Kostin was taking care of that, a runner from headquarters trotted over to Kostyshakov. "Message from Strat Recon, sir!"

"Sir—?" Kostin began. Kostyshakov held up a palm to command silence while he read. Finally, he told the runner, "Send back to them to continue their mission. Tell that that it would be helpful if they could prevent or slow down resupply of the Red column heading our way. Tell them they may have to—indeed, tell them that they probably will have to—rescue Grand Duchess Elizabeth Feodorovna on their own. Oh, and tell them that Turgenev is promoted to Guards Captain, K7, and Mokrenko to Guards Lieutenant. Then collect the officers and senior noncoms and have them come to headquarters in . . . two hours."

Kostyshakov turned his attention back to the platoon. "*Feldfebel* Kostin?"

"Sir?"

"Dismiss the men to barracks. Orders in two hours."

"Sir. Sir, if I may ask . . . ?"

"A lot of Reds heading our way," Kostyshakov replied. "A *lot.* Not going to arrive all that soon, but since three-fourths of our men are new, we don't have a lot of time to spare. And we can't spare your men, either."

Do we have a prayer of beating this new column of Reds? wondered Kostyshakov.

Ipatiev House, Voznesenski Prospect, Yekaterinburg

"Spare the others, Lord, I pray. Take me in their stead."

Ella made the sign of the cross in Orthodox fashion, up-down-right-left, then repeated the prayer.

Ella was not alone in the Ipatiev House. With her were Grand Duke Sergei Mikhailovich; plus four princes—the three Konstantinoviches, Ioann, Konstantin, and Igor, plus Vladimir Pavlovich Paley—the Grand Duke's secretary, Fyodor Remez, two valets, Dr. Helmersen, and two of the sisters from Ella's convent, Ekaterina Ianysheva and Varvara Yakovleva. That latter, amusingly enough, shared both a first and last name with a rather prominent female Bolshevik.

Word had come from the senior of their guards, Nicolai Govyrin, that they were all to be moved within a week or two. "No, I don't know where," he'd said, "but it's for your own safety."

They told us, Ella had thought, *that the move from Perm to here was to be for our "safety." Of course, they also told us we'd be there at least through May. So much for Red concern.*

Ella did not say their names aloud, but in the silent part of her prayer she said, *Take me, not Sergei Mikhailovich, Lord. Please do not take Ioann Konstantinovich, Lord, but send him back to his lovely wife, Helen. Take me instead . . .*

God remained silent throughout.

Interlude

Commissar Goloshchyokin:

Damn Sverdlov, anyway. What business did he have threatening me with execution if I didn't take this mob on the road, ready or not? He knows everyone and he knows everything important about everyone, but he doesn't know a damned thing about creating a regiment from scratch and moving it.

No more do I, of course; like any good Bolshevik I avoided military service in the swine-of-a-tsar's imperialist army like the plague. Now, I wish I'd listened to Engels and gone in and learned something. Oh, well; too soon old . . . and besides, I might be dead now if I had.

Well, I did what I could with both the column and the town. For the town, before I stripped out the bulk of the forces of liberation, I instituted a brief reign of terror, surely not one hanging more than needed, to make sure that the counterrevolutionaries who were certain to creep out from the sewers in which they cowered would never get a hearing. No doubt many, perhaps most of those, I had hanged were innocent, but one cannot make an omelet without breaking eggs. Moreover, the loss of life would be more than made up by the sheer joys, the utter goodness, of the society we are bringing to life.

As for the column, that was a much less tractable problem. I didn't have any trained leaders—not that would admit it—and didn't entirely trust the rank and file, so I put a couple of comrades of proven worth in charge of each grouping—"companies," they're called—of the rank and file. I found a merchant, one who didn't want his head on a pike, to receive supplies, account for them and forward them to us in convoys, on sleighs, if possible, or *telezhka*, carts, if not.

As it turned out there weren't enough sleighs. There also weren't enough rifles. I was at something of a loss as to what to do, so we waited a dozen *versts* outside of Tyumen—after all, Sverdlov had only demanded I leave by such and such a date; he'd said nothing about when I had to arrive by—while I tried to figure it out.

It was the soldiers who actually figured it out, though the stupid bastards didn't realize it. Without command, a couple of hundred of them linked arms and tramped down the snow where we were camped, to play some game or other. I never found out what they'd wanted to play and I didn't really care. As soon as I saw it and realized it was densely packed enough to support a cart, that was it, I had our way to beat through the snow.

It took almost an entire day to collect the leadership, such as it was, and get things organized. By the next morning, we were ready to march. Progress, yes, was slow when we started, barely five *versts* on the first day. The second day was worse, still, as taut and sore muscles refused to move quickly.

I picked one of the men at random, accused him of being a saboteur, had him tried by a committee of comrades of proven worth and then shot. Speed picked up a good deal after that, though we never have made more than about ten *versts* in a day, even so. I didn't think shooting more of them would have helped any or I'd have done it.

For the first week or so, I found it impossible to sleep. Oh, no, it wasn't that I wasn't tired; I was exhausted. But every five minutes someone would be at my tent asking for instructions about something or other. Eventually, using the excuse of anti-revolutionary forces sniping from trees, I took to hiding my tent—rather, having it hidden—every afternoon and not telling the men where I was. I tried to make up for this by spending a couple of hours daily, walking the length of our encampment, enquiring about the men's welfare, making spot corrections as I saw the need, and talking up the thrashing we were going to give the tsarists with our machine guns, our artillery, and our numbers. And our rifles, once the rest of them showed up. We were and are short about four hundred of them.

I wondered from time to time whether I'd be better off if I abandoned the carts and sleighs as the men and horses ate the contents, then used the horses freed to mount some of the men up for reconnaissance and security duties. In the end, I was afraid to face a court of inquiry on a charge of misusing the revolution's property, so I kept the carts and sleighs, even when empty, up with us.

Did I have anyone who could ride? It was a good question but the only way to find out would have been to ask the men, while in the first place, they'd lie if they thought it would get them out of marching, and, in the second place they might start wondering why we didn't abandon the carts... bad idea, I thought, bad, bad idea.

Eventually, I came to realize that some things, some good things, were happening that I had never ordered, things like a nightly guard mount, designation of places for the men to go relieve themselves. I wondered—I still wonder—if there were some old soldiers, corporals, sergeants, or even officers, in among the ranks. I resolved to sniff them out to try them for counterrevolutionary attitudes.

Chapter Two

Russian sleighs

Twelve Versts east of Tyumen

"Shshshshsh," whispered the leader of Strat Recon, newly promoted Guards Captain Turgenev.

Turgenev could see the foot-stomped path from his perch by a tree and mostly behind a snowbank. The setting sun cast long shadows, which helped conceal him and newly commissioned Lieutenant Rostislav Mokrenko.

Perhaps three hundred meters west, in the middle of a cleared stretch, a small caravan of fifteen carts and sleds formed a circle in the tamped-down snow. These were apparently pulled by horses, large horses, not the sturdy little Yakuts used by Strategic Recon and the Guards Brigade. The animals were tethered to their carts and sleighs, most of them with feed bags covering their muzzles. Smoke from a few fires rose thinly over the encampment. The guard force consisted of no more than two men, walking together, who circled the camp every ten minutes or so.

"Ambush or assault, sir?" Mokrenko asked. "I think our best chance is assault, with a small team to prevent anyone escaping to spread the word."

Turgenev nodded and said, "As it happens, I agree with you, ser . . . Lieute . . . Rostislav Alexandrovich, but mostly because we need to waste no time in getting to Yekaterinburg. An ambush would depend on their timing; an assault on ours. Go back, if you would, and get two men to take over this post. Then we'll go back and prepare to assault with the main force."

"Sir, suggestion?"

"Yes."

"Myself and one other man, using knives and swords only, machine pistols unloaded and slung, to kill the guards and prepare the way. We can signal that the coast is clear with one of those carbide lights."

"Let me think on it."

The moon wasn't quite half-full, and had been shining for the last couple of hours. Even at half-full, it was bright enough to cast shadows from the trees onto the snow-laden ground.

Wearing all white now, and with the hoods of their snowsuits drawn tight to expose little but their eyes, Mokrenko and Lavin moved from shadow to shadow, closing not on the guards, but on a position from which to take out the guards. The guards themselves were on the other side of the encampment now.

Mokrenko's and Lavin's movement was silent, barring only the soft crunching of packed snow under booted feet. From somewhere to the north a lone wolf howled, soon to be joined by an entire pack.

Inside the camp, the fires were either burning low or smoldering on their way to extinction. Though the troops in the camp had started the evening boisterously enough, from the sound of things the boisterousness heavily supplemented with vodka, by nine in the evening all but the two circling guards were apparently asleep.

Certainly, they're quiet enough now, thought Mokrenko. *Understandable if they're exhausted; while we came on the snow road packed down by the Reds' column, they probably had a hell of a time getting these carts through the snow between the railhead in Tyumen and here.*

Interestingly, now that he was almost at the perimeter of carts, Mokrenko could make out several machine guns, carried on top of some of them. How many more might be hidden he couldn't guess.

Grabbing physical control of Lavin, Mokrenko pointed down at the twin paths in the snow made by the two circling guards. Lavin understood instantly. *If they've got an easier path they'll continue to take it.*

With Lavin's understanding nod, the sergeant poked him in the chest, lightly, and then pointed at an evergreen, the full branches of which formed an oval shadow on the snow. He then touched his own chest and pointed again, this time at a different darkened oval, nearby and on the other side of the twin paths. Lavin's nod at that was shorter and shallower.

As Lavin lay down in position, Mokrenko stepped into the nearest of the twin paths. Turning left, he followed the path to the south, looking for a place to cross to the other, inner path. They never did grow close enough to simply step over to the next path. But at some point it was unlikely they would see any trace of a step, so he just crossed over, leaving a marker in the snow. From there he turned right again, heading back towards Lavin. At his own already picked-out shadowy oval, he lay down on the cold snow to await the return of the guards.

The cold will, at least, help me stay awake while I wait. Wish I'd been able to catch up on sleep from the night spent reconning the column . . .

Waiting one hundred twenty meters north of the encampment, and perhaps one hundred sixty northeast of his sergeant, Turgenev understood and expected Mokrenko and Lavin to clear the way with cold steel. To the extent possible, he intended that the rest of Strat Recon would join them in this. To this end, the remaining men who carried unbayoneted machine pistols also had swords, while those with rifles had their bayonets affixed. The exception was the Lewis Gunner, who was crouching next to Turgenev where he could be controlled.

And now we wait for the sergeant's signal.

Mokrenko came awake with a start and with the Red guards' booted feet mere inches from his face. Since he knew where to look he could see that Lavin was still dead asleep.

The further foot moved on, as did one of the other guard's feet, with neither of the guards having apparently noticed Mokrenko's presence.

"So," said one of the guards, "after the landlord put us off our farm for failure to pay our rent, what was left for me but to join the Reds?"

"My story is a different one, Comrade," said the other Red. "We had given up our farm and moved to Moscow fifty years ago. But at what they paid in the factories and what we had to pay for rent and food—heat in the winter was a rare luxury—with no running water and living in filth; well, the words of Comrade Ilyich came through to me like revealed truth!"

"Even so," said the first guard. "My father, of course, would hear nothing against the rotten Tsar..."

Thank God, thought Mokrenko, *for people who don't look for what they don't expect to see. And I must not listen to their words; there's too much truth in them. Or has been too much truth. But the Empress—* Mokrenko felt his heart swell with filial piety—*she will make things right.*

I don't think I can take them both out quietly. Neither do I think that Lavin can awaken quickly enough to stop the other one from raising an alarm. So it's on me—well, you and I, God—to take out both. If I can't make it quiet I can at least give the lieut... err... the captain, a little more time and some degree of surprise.

With no more thought nor time for it, Mokrenko smoothly rose to his feet, drawing his new shashka—the previous one had been given to the new empress at her coronation—and stepped forward. A single swing and the rightmost guard's head fairly leapt off his shoulders in a great cascade of whooshing blood.

The other guard turned his head at the sound, then gasped in horror as the body took another step forward before beginning its slow collapse to the snow. Sensing a movement to his right, he twisted, instinctively pushing his rifle out to guard against the unseen but sensed threat.

Mokrenko's slashing shashka hit the rifle at an angle and then slid down it, neatly removing four fingers and a bit of a thumb. The guard screamed then, twice, once as the shock and pain of missing fingers registered and then again as the slashing sword bit deeply into the junction of neck and right shoulder. He fell to the snow, oozing a rivulet of blood that became a torrent as the sergeant roughly yanked his sword out of the dying body before driving it, point first, deep into the guard's chest.

There was a loud, panicked shout coming from inside the encampment. "To arms! To arms!"

Shit, must have been a duty NCO inside.

Lavin was awake in an instant, sword in hand.

"Fuck the sword," said Mokrenko, "it's machine pistols for us now!" Lavin dropped the *shashka* and took up his MP-18.

Hearts pounding, the pair charged their weapons, not even trying to conceal the slamming of the bolts home after they released the charging handles. Then Mokrenko and Lavin sprinted the few steps to the nearest gap in the wall of carts and sleds. Seeing what had to be a duty NCO or officer bellowing in the center of the camp, outlined by one of the small remaining fires, and directing the awakening Reds to this section of the perimeter or that, Mokrenko took a careful aim.

Brrrrrt. The bellowing man went down, folding at the middle, before plopping onto his arse and rolling over to one side. This, unsurprisingly, didn't slow the rush to arms.

Lavin, standing near to Mokrenko now, and taking cover behind the same cart but at the other end, fired at a running Red, missed, then fired again for the win.

"Insects!" Lavin shouted. "However many you may be, I shall burn you down!"

Turgenev wasn't sure he'd heard a scream. He had his doubts about hearing any shouting. But the sound of two MP-18s firing full out there could be no doubt of. He knew at once, *It's all gone to shit!*

In such circumstances, he did what any sensible officer—well, any sensible Russian officer—would have done. Gripping his own MP-18 firmly in one hand while charging it with the other, he arose to his feet, shouted "Urrah!" and began to charge for the encampment.

"Urrah!" followed him from nine other throats, sounding like two or three times that many. "Urrah! Urrah! Urrah!"

Progress was relatively slow across the snow. At each difficult step Turgenev expected a storm of fire to cut down his little command.

It didn't happen. Between the fire from Mokrenko and Lavin and the sudden confusion, most of the encampment's denizens had hunkered down behind whatever they could find of cover and were not even returning fire. Anyone who had any fight in him had already been dispatched by the MP-18s.

"Fuck this," said Lavin, ceasing fire. "These aren't insects; this is too much like drowning puppies."

Mokrenko agreed. He also ceased fire, made up a quick bluff, and shouted out, "Reds, you are surrounded by two companies of Guards Infantry. Surrender now and you may yet save your lives! Stand up with your hands up and collect yourselves in the center of your camp, by the remaining fires. Drag your wounded with you; anyone found away from the fires will be shot."

By ones and then twos and threes, the men began to come out from cover and gather together. A few bleeding men they carried or dragged. By the firelight, they all looked frightened out of their wits. They also, for the most part, looked very, very young, with only a couple of salt-and-peppers scattered among them for spice.

"Keep an eye on them," Mokrenko said. "I'm going to try to meet Turgenev halfway and stop a massacre."

The new prisoners remained in the center, feeding what remained of the wood to their little fires. Outside, standing atop carts and sleighs, sporting MP-18s, Mosin-Nagant rifles, and a single Lewis Gun, nine of the men of Strat Recon stood guard, while Lavin went through the carts, jotting down what he'd found. Meanwhile, Captain Turgenev and Mokrenko worried and wondered about what to do with their prisoners.

"If we were smart, we'd just shoot them," said Mokrenko. "We don't have the manpower to guard them, and I don't think we can risk letting them go."

"'If...'" quoted Turgenev. "But if there's any way not to ... Well, let's see."

"Sir?"

"I've spent most of my short life studying people, Sergeant. Intelligence is as much about that as it is about terrain, weather, and orders or battle. Let's see what I've learned."

Turgenev turned away, strode over a cart through the ring of guards, and stood inside the circle, perhaps ten meters from the prisoners. He noticed then, in the dawn's light, that none of the prisoners wore complete uniforms. Some wore a few bits of military garb, but not as if they were actual uniforms nor as if they were men used to wearing uniforms.

Interesting.

"Is there anyone here who can speak for all of you?" Turgenev shouted. "Anyone at all?"

Eventually, the other prisoners pushed and prodded one older man forward. Nervously he advanced on Turgenev.

Humbly, the prisoner held his hands clasped in front of him and bowed his head. He looked to be in his mid-thirties, gaunt, balding, and with poor teeth.

"*Gospodin*, I am Denis Denisovich Garin. The men want me to speak for them."

"Tell me about them," Turgenev ordered, though gently.

"Not much to tell, sir. We were, some of us, miners in Yekaterinburg, and others farmers . . . oh, and a double handful of teamsters."

"And you?"

"I was a teamster, sir. Just that."

Having a sudden inspiration, Turgenev asked, "So you all decided to help these counterrevolutionaries against the revolution?"

This apparently startled Garin, causing him to jerk his head and to blink his eyes, repeatedly. "Honestly, *Gospodin*, we never really knew who was who." He gestured at some of the corpses littering the open space, saying, "These men told us *they* were the revolution. They told us this as they herded us to the rail yard to load the horses, sleighs, and carts. We never knew or cared about that; we just didn't want to be shot, bayoneted, or strung up." Garin's eyes grew misty. "Watching a couple of old friends, you know, dancing their lives away under a tree at the end of a rope tends to stifle the urge to argue. Having strange armed men looking at your wives and daughters, with interest, does too."

"Who among these were the men who conscripted you and supervised you on your way?"

Garin looked at the very first one, shot down by Mokrenko, and said, "He was the second in command; Comrade Reznik, he was. And . . ." Garin looked around, then said, "And that one over there was the chief, Comrade Shapiro." Looking around a bit more, the teamster announced, "And that one was Comrade Lopatin. Then there were"— quickly Garin pointed out three more among the slain—"five more. I only see three of them. The other two aren't with us. That's all; just those seven."

"Seven men controlled you all?" Turgenev's voice was highly doubtful. "There must have been thirty of you!"

"There were thirty-four," answered Garin. "They had our families hostage back in Yekaterinburg. They promised to hang them, down to the tiniest baby, if we failed to do our 'revolutionary duty.' We believed them."

Turgenev quoted then, "Ah, 'liberty, liberty; what crimes are committed in your name?'"

Should I take a chance on these, I wonder. No reason not to, I suppose, since we can always shoot them if they fail my test.

"Thirty-four," Turgenev mused. "How many are still alive?"

"Twenty-seven, mostly unhurt, sir. Plus two more I wouldn't expect to live."

"Of that twenty-seven, Teamster Garin, how many are in favor of the revolution?"

"We all used to be, *Gospodin*. Yekaterinburg, after all. Not anymore. You see, there used to be forty of us for the drayage. The Bolsheviks hanged six on the way here . . . for various 'crimes.' And not all of them were content to merely look upon our wives and daughters."

"So, would you rather have the tsar back?" Turgenev asked.

"No," the teamster answered. "But I have heard, we all have, that the old tsar is dead and that his daughter has taken the throne, and promised a new day, a better day, for the peoples of the empire. Do you think it could be true, *Gospodin*?"

Turgenev declined to answer for the moment, instead saying, "Gather them around, Garin; I want to talk to them. In say, one hour,"—Turgenev pointed at a particular cart—"over there."

"So, Lavin," Turgenev asked, "what was the haul?"

"Leaving aside maybe twelve *berkovets* of food and forty of fodder, I count two heavy machine guns, four hundred and eighty rifles, assuming the cases are all full, which they seem to be, and a couple of hundred thousand rounds. The rifles are all Americansky, by the way, *Vestinkhaus*, if I'm reading their alphabet correctly."

"That's a lot of firepower, sir," said Mokrenko. "Even if we trust this lot enough not to just shoot them out of hand, I don't think I trust them with arms."

"No, Serg— Lieutenant, there I must agree with you. But if we don't shoot them then we have to bring them with us, right?"

"Yes, sir, I suppose so. Just cutting them loose is either a death sentence or a lot of loose tongues talking in Tyumen. And Tyumen is connected by rail and telegraph to everywhere."

Rubbing the bridge of his nose with thumb and forefinger, Turgenev asked, "If we have to bring them, they go on foot or on the carts and sleighs, right? And the latter would be faster? And we can't spare a special guard for them?"

"All true enough, yes, sir."

"So I think we take this stuff with us anyway, as long as the drivers need to come."

"One problem, sir," said Mokrenko.

"What's that, sergeant?"

"We have eighteen animals, with the spares. They're not Yakuts, so they'll need to be fed thirty *funt* of fodder a day, each. Do the math, sir; that's only maybe four weeks of fodder, which doesn't take us far enough. And, sir, we can't board the rails at Tyumen, the way these unloaded. I don't like our odds for hijacking a train, either, not without compromising our mission."

"Hmm . . . let me ask."

Turgenev went back into the circle and gestured for Garin to come over. "How were you going to feed the animals, Teamster?" he asked.

"There were supposed to be more convoys of fodder, *Gospodin*. There was a big stockpile of it, building at Tyumen. I saw few enough wagons or sleighs to carry it, though."

"How much more could we carry if we stopped off at Tyumen to fill our load?"

The teamster chewed on his lower lip for a bit, thinking hard. Finally, he answered, "It really depends on how many horses and carts we can find. We were almost full when we left and have only used a bit of that, so there's little room to take on more. But do you really want to go to Tyumen? There are still a lot of people there who would arrest and shoot all of us for desertion."

Turgenev thought for a bit, then asked, "Is there another group of drivers that was supposed to take the next convoy to Tobolsk?"

"Yes, *Gospodin*. There were another sixty or seventy men—I never had an actual count, you understand—who were conscripted with us that there were no carts or sleighs for, yet, and so they stayed back in Tyumen."

"Was there any plan," Turgenev asked, "for sending out more convoys?"

Garin laughed. "You mean that they'd tell *me* about? Hah!" He paused then, scratched his balding head, and then added, "But the truth of the matter is that I don't think they had any plan, but only an ... what's the right word ... oh, I know; they had an *urge*, a direction, nothing more."

"Let me ask differently. If we avoid Tyumen, do we have enough fodder to get to Yekaterinburg?"

"Yes," Garin replied without hesitation, "provided, in the first place, that you are willing to empty out one fodder wagon or sleigh at a time and either cut the horse loose or kill it and eat it, *and* that the cold weather holds but without another dumping of snow on us. If we get stuck out in the middle of nowhere in a heavy snow the horses likely won't make enough progress not to starve and we might starve with them."

"Straight to Yekaterinburg, then," Turgenev said.

"But what do you want to do in Yekaterinburg, *Gospodin*?"

"Among other things, hurt the people who dragged you away from your families and hurt and killed your friends."

"I see," said Garin. "Shall I bring over all the men now?"

"Do."

"Gentlemen," Turgenev began, "after consultation with your spokesman, Mister Garin, I am unsure what to do with you. That having been said, relax; while the convenient thing to do would be to just shoot you, we're not that kind of people. Do you know any people who are like that?" he asked.

"The Reds," answered one of the mufti-clad men, boldly. He was immediately echoed by a dozen others: "The Reds."

"Well, if you haven't figured it out," Turgenev continued, "we're not Reds. Let me ask you another question; what have you heard about the Tsar?"

"The *late* tsar, you mean?" asked that same speaker back. "We heard he's dead and that one of his daughters has taken over. Is it true?"

"It is, friend. The second daughter, Tatiana, is now Tsarina, consecrated before God in God's own house in Tobolsk. She is a remarkable young lady."

"You sound like you know her," that last speaker observed boldly.

"Oh, yes; I was one of those who rescued her." Seeing the men perk up with interest, Turgenev asked, "Would you like to hear about it?"

At the chorus of enthusiastic affirmatives, Turgenev made a patting motion for them to sit down in the snow, and then began to tell the story.

So far the listeners were enthralled at the feat of arms described in loving and gory detail by Turgenev, the smoke and fire, the screams, the desperate hand to hand fighting. They were less enthralled, and a few were moved to tears by:

". . . and then the poor little tsarevich, sickly and weak but brave to a fault, threw himself atop the Bolshevik grenade to save his parents and sisters.

"Even then," Turgenev continued, "it was working well until a traitor in our own ranks shot down the tsar, his wife, and one of the daughters, Olga. All we could save were the three younger girls.

"It was the worst thing, I think, any of us had ever seen, the three beautiful daughters on their knees gathered around the bleeding, shattered mortal remains of both parents and two siblings, weeping like poor lost souls."

In fact, Turgenev had not seen it and didn't actually claim he had, but it seemed like a nice additional touch. He continued through the sequestration of the tsar's remaining family and the combing out of all the Bolsheviks in Tobolsk. Finally he asked, "Do you have any questions?"

That same bold man asked, "What's the new tsarina like? We hear promises—we've *always* heard plenty of promises—but they never seem to get kept."

"Well," Turgenev replied, "she is as hard as she needs to be and as gentle as she can be. She could have shot—have had us shoot—all the men arrayed against us. She said no, she wouldn't permit that. She said there were men there whose only crime was being forced into an enemy army and who deserved forgiveness, could it only be safely given. Those men have almost to a man signed up to fight for her.

"But she is no weakling as, sadly, her father was. If someone needed shooting, she signed the death warrant and witnessed at least some of the executions. No averting her eyes for our tsarina!"

He paused briefly to let both carrot and stick make their impression.

"She's tough in other ways, too. The Reds have custody of all the imperial regalia. In lieu of these—maybe better to say in preference to these—she took a soldier's helmet for a crown, a hand grenade for her orb, a machine pistol like mine"—here Turgenev held out his MP-18—"for her mace, and for her sword a simple army issue Cossack's shashka. It was that man there, Lieutenant Mokrenko's, as a matter of fact.

"This is a girl who means to fight for Russia and intends to win, too. That's important, when you think about your own futures; she *intends* to win. Indeed, she swore, before Almighty God, not to preserve her own power, not to preserve the monarchy, as all others before her have sworn, but to preserve the Russian Empire.

"Finally, I tell you friends, again this is no weakling. In our Tatiana we have the will and strength of Catherine the Great, reborn to us in our hour of need!"

The bold one stood then and began to sing. He spontaneously changed the words on his own: "*Bozhe, Tsaritsu Krani!*"

"God save our tsarina.
"Strong, sovereign.
"Reign for glory, our glory.
"God save the tsarina."

The others likewise stood and joined in, also likewise changing the words. After a short moment, Turgenev joined in as did the guards standing on the carts and sleighs.

"Reign to make foes fear,
"Orthodox tsarina!
"God save the tsarina."

"All right then," said Turgenev, "does anyone have any time in the army or navy?"

"We were all exempt," said Garin. "Critical industries, most of us. There are also a few farmers who would not have been critical except they were critical to keeping Yekaterinburg fed, where Yekaterinburg, itself, was critical."

"Except for me," said the bold one. "I am, I suppose, a deserter. Though what it means to be a deserter from a disintegrating army, I confess, I don't know."

Garin shrugged. "He never said."

"I think we can, under the circumstances, pull a veil over your previous indiscretions," said Turgenev, "provided, of course, there is no repeat. If there is, from you or any of you, you will be shot. Remember, we're on horseback and skis; you will be on foot. And my Cossacks are fine hunters and trappers."

"We understand," said Garin, speaking for all.

"Right. Now, for the bodies. There's no time to bury the Reds; leave them for the wolves. I'll give you a few hours to dig graves as deep as you can in that time for your dead friends. But then we need to pack up and be on the road. It is, after all, a long way to Yekaterinburg."

It *was* a long way to Yekaterinburg, a long way and a hard way. The two wounded teamsters did not, just as Garin expected, make it. They were buried by the side of the trail, with crosses marking the graves and trees hacked to mark the spot, on the theory that simple wooden crosses usually don't last. And they moved out. It was not a simple trek.

There came the time the ice over a river was thinner than believed. One laden cart crashed through it, and the two men on the cart fell through and were washed under the ice to freeze or drown, whichever came first. There was no way to recover the bodies, though it was always possible that the river would carry them to some far lake or sea, where they might have the hope of a Christian burial. With that cart, too, went one horse, thirty-six rifles, roughly eight thousand rounds of ammunition, and a half a ton of food.

Then, too, there was the night a pack of wolves—probably driven to desperation by winter-caused starvation—hit them. The wolves killed two of the horses and ripped up one of the teamsters badly enough that he died the next day and, like the others, was buried on the spot. That cost not only the human and equine life, and not only the time to bury the lost teamster, but also still more time to crossload cargo to make up for the lost horses.

It was after this that Turgenev decided to issue rifles to the teamsters, along with six rounds of ammunition each, doubling the guard as well.

If there was a crossing over the rail line for carts and sleds, they couldn't find it. Instead, the men built a ramp on both sides of the rail, got the horses and vehicles over, then demolished the ramp and camouflaged the leavings. From this they moved west to Yekaterinburg, skirting the town at a considerable distance before setting up camp, northwest of the bridge over the Iset River.

"The men would very much like to go home, *Gospodin*," said Garin, once the circle of wagons was complete.

"Soon," Turgenev promised. "But tell them—remind them—that they're probably all wanted men by this point or, rather, they will be if seen by any Reds who know they'd been drafted for the supply column. Let me and mine go into town and check out the situation. I'll give them leave to go home as soon as it's sensible. Will that do?"

Garin nodded, then said, "It's not ideal, but I think I can make them see the wisdom of waiting."

"I'll leave two men to back you up," said Turgenev.

"No, no need, *Gospodin*. I'll handle them."

"Even so," said Turgenev, firmly, "if there's a problem arising to mutiny it will probably start sooner rather than later. I'm sending a small reconnaissance forward. The rest of us will stay and put a damper on any premature urge to go home."

Interlude

Anastasia:

I know that I'll never really be able to go home. In the first place, even if we win, what was once home to me will be Tatiana's home and I would be, at most, a welcome guest. But in the second place, everything will have changed; Russia and the Empire will have changed. Even the people will have been changed.

I suppose I will have changed, too. So, no, no going back "home" for me.

But maybe I can make a new home somewhere. Maybe. After the needs of the Empire and the War cause my sister to inflict some suitable husband on me. Maybe. If I can stand the idea of a home and a husband when that husband will surely have at least one mistress to entertain him.

Could I stand having a husband I do not love? I don't know; I don't even know what love is. Well . . . girls talk. I know the *mechanics* of the thing. Sort of. But I have no idea of how it feels in the heart.

I wish Olga were still here. She could have told me.

I don't really know how to do anything. Yes, yes; I am only seventeen and not expected to know much. But, for example, Tatiana is going to want me to give speeches someday. I don't know how to give a speech. The very thought terrifies me. And that terror makes it very likely I will not be able to do it.

I feel so useless most of the time. Indeed, I cherish the little jobs Tatiana, our "Governess," gives me, from time to time, because they make me feel useful and alive. Yes, even if those things are only sewing and cleaning and carrying the occasional message.

I would like, someday, to have grown and grown up and to be useful all the time, employed all the time. And good at what it is I am doing.

Chapter Three

Late War Stokes Mortar with highly optimistic Anti-Aircraft sight

Forty-eight Versts south-southwest of Tobolsk

Soldiers will complain; it's in the nature of the beasts. Here and now, one of them was complaining that, "Just when Tobolsk started to feel like home, of course we get rousted out to move out into the snow again."

Somewhere to the south of the town, in a long arc, a dozen riders and the twenty-two ski-equipped men of Kostin's platoon of grenadiers were spread out, screening against the approach of the Red force from Yekaterinburg.

Not sending Kostin to aid Turgenev in the rescue of the tsarina's Aunt Ella had led to something of a row between her and Kostyshakov. He'd finally settled it by pointing out that, "In the first place, Tatiana Nicholaevna, if we don't stop the Reds there won't be anyone left alive for your aunt to advise. But in the second place, with all those

Bolsheviks coming here, Yekaterinburg will have been denuded. There's a better than fair chance that Turgenev can rescue your aunt on his own, and sooner."

The empress was still sulking a bit. He hoped she'd get over it.

Now, while the Exec, Basinets, and Sergeant Major Blagov ran things in the rear, pushing the companies to assimilate and train the new recruits as quickly as possible, Kostyshakov and the Grenadier company, plus the operations sergeant major, the Finn, Nenonen, were out looking for the perfect ambush site to take on and destroy the oncoming Bolsheviks.

"There isn't one, sir," was Nenonen's judgment, a judgment Kostyshakov had come to share. "We've been up and down this area for two days now; there is no place where we can catch the entire Red force, at one time, and destroy it. There are only places where we can catch pieces of it, here and there, and destroy them. That still leaves their numbers and firepower to wear us down and destroy *us*."

"Won't be any better if we try to make a stand at Tobolsk," said Kostyshakov. "Even with the old fortress walls at the Tobolsk Kremlin, they'd just overwhelm us with those same numbers and firepower. And there's no line we can defend from that they don't have the numbers to outflank us at. The rivers aren't even obstacles for another couple of months, they're avenues of approach."

"Yes, sir," the Finn agreed.

"What's that town over there?" Kostyshakov asked.

"Not much of a town," Nenonen commented, "but it's called 'Toboltura' or 'Degtyareva;' I'm not sure which town begins or ends where. Toboltura used to be 'Toboltura Yurts,' I understand, though I don't see any yurts there now. There's another one, Kutarbitka, further southwest.

"Still, even though not much of a town," the Finn continued, "or towns, those dozen or score of houses in Toboltura would be useful to keep our men from freezing at night."

"'Freezing at night...'" Kostyshakov repeated, wonderingly. "'Freezing at night.' Hold that thought."

He had a sketch of the area that had been prepared by one of the Cossack horsemen, Sergeant Kaledin, who did double duty as the unit's equine veterinarian. It showed the river as a sort of unstrung bow shape, running northeast to southwest, with two narrow islands sticking up above the ice. He could see the islands from where he stood, and thought, *You know, if you hadn't been told those were islands you likely wouldn't know.*

"Yes, sir," said the operations sergeant major. "We've another problem if we try neither to ambush them nor to stop them at some line on the ground; if we want to raid them at night we'll have to know where they're set up at night. Sure, Strat Recon told us they move about eight *versts* a day. But eight could mean seven to nine easily enough... or six... or ten. Two to four *versts* is a lot of variation for a target only three or four *versts* long, enough to fuck up the movement from an assembly area to a line of departure to raid them. And that's especially true once the sun goes down."

"So what are you thinking, sergeant major?" asked Kostyshakov.

"We need to be able to make them halt in a particular place we want them to halt, or to take advantage of it if they halt where we want them to, anyway. We can do that if we make a decent guess of roughly where they'll be and set up assembly areas for the two battalions where they can move up by an already reconned route, to already reconned defensive positions that hold the Reds in place."

"Yes, but then what?"

"Then I'm thinking we start chopping them into bite-sized pieces, then pile on and destroy the pieces one at a time. Might take a few days to do it."

"A few days of being under their artillery might be a few days too long," said Kostyshakov.

"Good point, sir, but that means that taking out their artillery is going to be job one."

"No, actually," Kostyshakov said, "Job one is rounding up all the townsfolk and moving them to Tobolsk, so they can't tell the Reds we were scouting here. Job two is fixing the Reds in place and doing so at the right time. Job *three* is the artillery. After that we'll have to play it by ear... although..."

"Sir?"

Kostyshakov faced north, feeling a stinging wind on his face.

"... although we might have a bit of help from Russia's best general. I want tents for our men, in their assembly areas, warming tents, at least. I want firewood cut, turned into charcoal, and brought to those *en masse.* I want the houses of that town reconnoitered, fortified, obstacled, and ready to give the Reds enough of a bloody nose to make them pause and think. And I want enough additional cooks—men, women, I don't really care—collected to give our men at least two and preferably three substantial hot meals every day, plus tea, bread, and soup on demand."

"Sir, I'm..."

"Don't worry, Sergeant Major, this is a job mostly for the quartermaster. I was just thinking out loud. Now let's go look over our future battlefield in more detail, because, yes, this is going to be our future battlefield. And I'll want to know some likely spots their artillery will set up."

The wind began to pick up a little, which made Kostyshakov smile. After thinking about it a second or two, the sergeant major joined him, the two making a pair of lupine grins, dripping with menace.

Imperial House, Tobolsk, Russia

"Your Imperial Highness, you wanted an artilleryman to help..." began Leonid Panfil, going to one knee.

"Stop that!" commanded Tatiana, rising from her cluttered desk "Stop that immediately! If you only knew how I detest all that nonsense, how uncomfortable and embarrassed it makes me!"

"I'm sorry," said the Jewish soldier. "I was told—"

"Don't be sorry," she insisted, "it's not your fault. It's not that well known that I've never liked any of that kind of ceremony—well, to be honest, any of *any* kind of ceremony—and I hope to dispense with it in time, completely... well, maybe for the most formal affairs and those honoring others.

"My father, you see, and his, and his, all the way back to the seventeenth century, thought they owned Russia. *I*, on the other hand, am pretty sure that it's really Russia that owns *me*. The Prussian, Frederick, said it before me; I am just the 'first servant' of the state.

"And, yes, I need an artilleryman to help me with this." She held up a yellow-stained pamphlet, ragged and strongly reeking of old urine.

"What's your name and where are you from?" she asked, noticing for the first time how very, very thin the Jewish noncom was; also that his hair, graying a bit about the temples, was just beginning to thin.

"Panfil, Your Imperial Highness, Leonid Panfil, Corporal for now, though supposedly there are a bunch of promotions awaiting orders to be read off. I'm from Belyov, south of Moscow. But I don't read that language, whatever it is," he said, pointing at the pamphlet. "English, I'm guessing."

"That's all right," she replied. "It *is* English and *I* do. But I don't understand half of what I'm reading, if that. So what I want us to do, you and I, is for me to read the English then explain to you what I think a passage means, then for both of us to work out what it really means. Come," she gestured, "let's make use of those comfortable chairs. And"—here she passed over a pencil and some writing paper—"you get to take the notes while I get piss all over my hands."

Panfil's eyes widened until she laughed and said, "I did that often enough working in the hospital with wounded soldiers. It's not important."

After they were seated, she took the reeking pamphlet and began to translate, "'Light Trench Mortar Drill Regulations.' Then there's some parenthesis with L.T.M.D.R. inside them. I guess ... oh, yes, that just an abbreviation of the title, isn't it? Oh, of course, it is. Then there's a number, '41973.' Any idea what that might mean? No. All right; we'll skip it for now. Okay, the title on the cover repeats itself. So, 'Chapter One, Paragraph One, The School of the Squad'? That's a funny usage. I wouldn't necessarily expect the British ... oh, wait, no, this is an *American* manual. That might make it tougher; their language is English but it's not exactly the *same* English."

Panfil looked contemplative for a moment, then suggested, "We could do this better if we had one of the devices in front of us. Why don't I—?"

"No, not you," Tatiana replied. "Maria!"

A pretty head stuck itself in the door. "Yes, Your Imperial Majesty?"

"Send to Guards' Headquarters that I want one of those mortars brought here, with all its equipment."

"At once!" The head disappeared.

"She insists on being as formal as possible in front of others," the tsarina said, with a minor note of exasperation in her voice. "And now, back to work until the thing gets here."

"Okay," said Panfil, when they were a little deeper into the Amerikansky mortar manual, "we don't have enough guns for a platoon and hardly have enough sergeants and corporals to go around, with all the expansion taking place. I'd say, Highness, that we need to figure out how to write up 'School of the Platoon' as 'School of the Section,' where section means two guns under maybe a sergeant."

"How do we do that?" asked Tatiana.

"I think we need both guns and full crews. I can pretend to be the section sergeant—I'm supposed to be promoted to *starshiy unter-ofitser* in a day or two, anyway—so we'll need a couple of *yefreytor* and eight *radovoy*."

"Why not *starshiy feyyerverker*," Tatiana asked, "These are cannon, aren't they?"

"I'm infantry," Panfil explained. "I ended up in the gun section because I can speak, read, and write good French when the only manual we had for the guns was in French. And these are considered infantry weapons, anyway, as are the 37mm cannon."

"Ah," she said, not really comprehending that but understanding fully that it didn't matter if she understood it or not. "So, anyway, both mortars, two superior privates and eight privates?"

"Probably could use at least one of the shells, too," he said.

"Maria!"

"She obeys you with alacrity," Panfil observed.

"My family didn't call me 'the Governess' for nothing," she replied, perhaps a bit smugly.

While waiting, Panfil stood and walked around the office. He stopped at a bookcase, behind the desk that once had been the tsar's, and began to peruse the titles.

"He didn't much care for Jews, did he?" Panfil asked.

"I'd apologize for him," Tatiana said, "but would it really do any good?"

Panfil shook his head, dismissively, then continued to peruse the collection of books.

Spotting a brass implement of some kind, half seen inside a leather pouch, Panfil began to reach for it. He stopped himself and asked, "May I?"

"Surely."

Picking the thing up, he began unfolding lenses and handles, until he had what looked almost like a pair of opera glasses. Rather, they would have looked like that except for the compass set into the right side.

"Hmmm ... next pair of opera glasses with a compass built in will be the first. This is military."

Walking to the window, he checked the apparent binoculars against a distant target. *Blurry*, he thought, turning a knob he expected would bring them into focus. "Hmmm ... low power. Not really ... well, well, well."

"What?" Tatiana asked.

"It's a Rangefinder," Panfil said. "Not too precise, I don't think, but good enough for, say, riflemen. Or, come to think of it, maybe mortars. What's the range of those things?"

Tatiana began fingering through the piss-soaked manual. "It says maximum effective range is seven hundred and fifty yards. In *arshini* that would be ..." she began to scratch with a pencil onto some paper ... "nine hundred and sixty-two *arshini*."

"Hmm ... this is calibrated in yards, not *arshini*. But, we're the only ones to use the *arshin*. I'll bet you, your highness, that the sight, when we see it, will be in yards, as well."

"Is that useful, then?" she asked.

"Oh, I think it might be."

At that point Maria Romanova returned, carrying the entire mortar on her own. "The shells will be along shortly," she said.

"Your sister is very strong," Panfil observed.

"Always been that way. She used to carry her teachers around, just pick them up from the floor and carry them. When she was little. But I am *still* 'the Governess.'"

The eleven men, including Panfil, along with the empress, took a break in the field south of Imperial House. Panfil was decidedly unimpressed with the quality of the men he'd been given for the task, and more than a little worried that he'd be put in charge of them permanently. Tatiana, still holding her piss-reeking manual, came over to where Panfil was writing down what would become the Russian manual for the Stokes.

"Should we be trying to get a whole platoon of these, Leonid?" the tsarina asked.

He thought for a few seconds before answering, "We should be trying to get a great many more of these, Highness, yes, but I don't think we should be aiming for six-gun platoons, the way the Americansky manual would have it."

"Why not?" she asked. "Seems to work for them."

"It's the range," he explained. "These can only cover about the frontage of a dispersed company. Six guns and thirty-nine men are too much to dedicate to a mere company. The whole company would be doing nothing but carrying ammunition for them, too. But two guns, or a maximum of three, given the rate of fire, are just enough to keep the enemy's heads down, to destroy the machine gun positions of a platoon, or supporting a platoon, or to make a covered and concealed position to the front of a defending company a lousy assault position. And every man could carry one shell, in a pinch, two, which would be a good deal of sustained firepower."

"Why aren't you an officer, Leonid?" she asked. "You're very bright."

"I'm a Jew . . . maybe not much of an observant Jew, but a Jew nonetheless. The Imperial Army wasn't much for Jewish officers, though the Bolsheviks are full of them."

"Then why aren't you a Bolshevik?"

"Because I value both the truth and my soul, Highness, where Bolshevism is nothing but lies, while those who follow it damn their souls."

Tatiana looked skyward, a bit as if consulting the divinity. "The man—a very *dear* friend—who saved me from the murderer who slaughtered my parents and sister, and tried to kill the rest of us, was half-Jewish. He should have been an officer, too." She turned her eyes back to Panfil. "I'm going to fix this problem. I don't know exactly how, yet, but I *am* going to fix this."

Panfil shrugged. He knew bucking culture was about the hardest thing there was to do. Instead of answering the unanswerable, he stood up and said, "All right, you lazy louts; break's over. On your feet and fall in with your mortars."

"What is this thing, Leonid?" the tsarina asked, holding up a glass and steel block, with mirrors inside, a bar that jutted down from the bottom, to which were attached to more bars, ending in a flexible metal yoke that was plainly intended to attach to the barrel. "The box it came in has 'sight' stenciled on it, but I can't find a word or a picture in the manual to suggest any such sighting device."

"I'm not sure, Highness, but I suspect it's an exercise in ridiculously excessive optimism."

"Optimism? How?"

"May I?" He took the sight from her hands and, after fiddling with it for a bit, attached the entire apparatus to the barrel. Two pieces of metal jutted from the top, ending in a ring. One of these stuck out, while another lay against a not-quite-oval shape, marked with roman numerals.

"Hmmm . . . I doubt that's a complete answer. Is there another piece?"

She looked in the box and pulled out another device, this one with a strap rather than a yoke. "Like this?"

"Yes . . . and I think this attaches . . . yes, there we go." Panfil stepped out of the way to show the second device attached to the front of the barrel. He then stepped around the mortar so he could see through the first piece. "Yes, as I suspected; this is to engage aircraft. It's aimed too high to do anything against ground troops or with aiming stakes. If you aimed with it at a target on the ground, the muzzle would be so low that the baseplate would skip across the ground. Aircraft? What could they possibly have been thinking?"

"Wouldn't work, huh?" she asked.

"It would take a miracle," was his reply, "if not even two miracles."

South of Tobolsk

With Tatiana's guards in tow, they'd trudged the mortars, both of them now, down to the open area, south of the town and not all that far from the corpse of the L59. Some of the men carried the pieces of the Stokes, others carried four shells apiece. The quartermaster's assistant had refused to issue even that many until the empress had put her foot down, literally. Now, set up and ready to go, with their translated manual and the original in hand, they waited to figure out the ammunition.

"The manual calls it an 'all ways impact fuse,'" said Tatiana. "What's that mean?"

"I'm not sure," Panfil said, "But I am pretty sure I don't like it. If the thing will go off 'all ways,' what's to prevent it from going off in the tube?"

"Well, neither the British nor the Americans are complete idiots; if they're using these things they're probably mostly safe to use."

Panfil scowled. "Yes, Your Majesty . . . 'mostly.' That's not an especially good word to use around high explosives. It's like being, oh, I dunno, mostly dead as opposed to all the way dead. You're still dead."

"Even so," she insisted, "let's get on with it."

"Let's? Let us? Oh, no, Tatiana Nicholaevna. Here *I* must put *my* foot down. If this thing goes off in the tube, and you are hurt or killed, Kostyshakov won't just shoot me; he'll skin me alive."

He just might, thought the Empress of all the Russias. She considered arguing it anyway, then realized her guards would, without doubt, humiliate her by forcibly carrying her off if she refused.

"All right," she conceded, "where do you want me to go?"

Panfil thought about it. *Fragmenting shell casing? Two and a quarter funt of high explosive?* "You get your imperial . . . mmm . . . self about an eighth of a *verst* to the north. It should be safe there. But . . ." Here Panfil took off his helmet and told her to put it on. She was on the point of refusing when he explained, "At this range, if the shell goes off in the tube, the helmet won't do me any good, but it might do you some at that range. Mind, you need to stay away until I tell you it's safe."

Note to self, she thought, *if dealing with mortars in the future, I have my own helmet; I must bring it.*

"The rest of you lot," ordered Panfil, "get thirty *arshins* away and get on the ground."

Taking Panfil's helmet, Tatiana put it on, adjusted the strap, and began the short trek to the north. Just a moment after she finished turning around, she heard a loud bang and then saw something flying up into the air, end over end. How high it went she had no good basis to judge, but she thought it had to have been at least a few hundred *arshins* in the air. She followed it with her eyes, spinning up; she saw it seem to stabilize in the air, and then she followed it, still spinning, down to the ground, where it formed a large and immensely dirty cloud. Shortly after that she felt the concussion of the blast, not bad at that distance, but still noticeable.

She watched as Panfil brought up two men at a time, then talked them through the process of "aiming" the mortar, estimating range, preparing the shell, and dropping it down the tube. She saw, too, that he switched them off, so that everyone got experience of both.

That seems very sensible. Yes, must do something about commissioning worthy soldiers, no matter their background.

"The Stokes," said Panfil to the empress, on the trudge north back to the town, "is as much a matter of art as science. I need five or ten times the number of total rounds we have to even get them ready to use the things with genuine skill."

"But we don't have that many," she said. "Are there other things you can do?"

"We might be able to make some dummies out of wood to train them in dropping the shell down the tube," he answered. "It's not worth much but is better than nothing. For the rest, just drill, drill, drill, I guess. Well, that and range estimation exercises."

"Best you can do," she said. "It will have to do. But wait . . ."

"Yes, Your Highness?"

"The manual mentioned a practice shell. Could we make some of them in a hurry? Maybe wood filled with enough lead to give the same weight and shape, and a small charge to kick it out."

"We can try," Panfil said, "but I'm not sure what can be done in enough time. We'll be leaving soon to fight."

Ignoring this, Tatiana said, "And as long as you're thinking about training shells, think about making real ones, maybe with fins or something to keep them nose-on."

Imperial House (nee Governor's House, nee Freedom House) Tobolsk, Russia

While the mortar section was back in their barracks, cleaning the systems, Tatiana was at her desk, fortunately without any death warrants to sign for the nonce. Even so, though, her helmet served as a paperweight for some other utterly necessary work. She ignored, for the time being, the short stack of correspondence and forms. Instead she walked to the window to observe one of the companies—it was impossible to tell at this distance which one—drilling in what she had come to learn was called "fire and movement." This involved one or more platoons making short rushes while others kept the enemy's head down with fire. She couldn't hear the men lying on the ground shouting, "Bang, bang, bang," but she could see their lips moving as if they were.

It was easy to tell who was in charge. The older cadre from the Guards regiments all had Adrian helmets just like her own, plus white camouflage smocks. The others were in a mix of uniforms, uniforms mixed with civilian clothes, and even outright civilian clothes.

"Maria!"

Again her sister's face appeared in the door.

"Can you please arrange for the seamstress who sewed our coronation garments to come see me? I have a special job and it's a bit of a rush."

"At once, Your Majesty!"

Tatiana rolled her eyes but said only, "I'll be gone for a bit. I need to track down the quartermaster and the Brigade Sergeant Major."

Brigade Headquarters, near Ulitsa Lazaretnaya, Tobolsk, Russia

Kostyshakov, plus Colonels Dratvin, Lesh, and Cherimisov, stood closest to the terrain model built by one of the headquarters men under the supervision of Sergeant Major Nenonen. They commanded, respectively, the newly formed Brigade of Guards, the First Battalion, Preobrazhensky Regiment, the First Battalion, Semenovsky Regiment, and the First Company, reinforced, Life Guard Grenadier Regiment. Only just further away stood Baluyev, now commanding the rather smaller than battalion-sized headquarters and support. As such, Baluyev had only been jumped up to the rank of senior captain of the guards, a lieutenant colonel equivalent. *Praporschik* Yahonov stood next to Baluyev, in place of the dead Lieutenant Federov.

The Brigade Executive Officer, Colonel Basinets, towered over everyone, so could afford to stand back a bit. Romeyko, though he was only a staff officer, was too important not to have been promoted with the others. Sergeant Major Blagov stood behind Kostyshakov and slightly to his right.

"Sergeant Major, status of the brigade?" asked Kostyshakov.

"The old hands, the ones from Camp Budapest, are as they always were, sir, well-trained, well-motivated. The new men are iffier, frankly. I think they'll be okay as long as they have one of our old hands to lead them, but if they ever lose their leadership don't expect anything but a complete breakdown.

"One thing is good though. Somehow, Her Highness managed to get the women of the town, led by some of the seamstresses, to sew white camouflage smocks for everyone who lacked one. I doubt if there's a white sheet or piece of canvas left within a dozen *versts*."

Kostyshakov nodded. He'd seen it, though he hadn't known where the new smocks had come from and had just assumed Romeyko had seen to it.

"She beat me to it, did our girl," said the quartermaster. "By the time

I got around to it, it was already being done. She's also nagged me for a few rifles and some ammunition. She armed her sisters and servants with them."

Blagov added, "She's also dismissed her guards for the time being. Says the people with her are enough to guard against a possible assassination attempt and we need the fighting men more than she does. Quite insistent about it."

Kostyshakov smiled, decided the Tsarina was wise as well as brave, and shrugged. "Barbed wire?" he asked.

"There's a little barbed wire in and around the town," said Romeyko. "I can certainly commandeer it, but what good will it do? Make the enemy stop in place to laugh for a bit before he steps over it?"

"The two companies I am going to stretch out south of the river need some kind of obstacle," Lesh said. "We're not going to be able to dig them in much."

"Yes, you will," said Dratvin. "Daniil, I don't need to dig my men in at all, given the mission. We can spend a day, maybe two, swinging axes and cutting logs—camouflage, too—to get Lesh's crew dug in well. Myself and the leadership can spend that time reconnoitering, while the men work under the junior noncoms."

"I really can't help there," said Cherimisov. "We're all going to be to the west, screening."

"I'd still like some obstacles," said Lesh.

"Ever hear of abatis?" asked Romeyko.

"No, sir," answered Lesh, who was still not used to his new exalted rank.

"You cut trees down and point the tops toward the enemy. Leave some of them attached to the trunks at an inconvenient height, maybe two *arshins*, or a tad less, so they're hard to clear under fire. Then you cut the branches so they present a sharp point. You can cut them on a line to create killing zones, to channelize, or to tactically mislead the enemy, just like you do with barbed wire, and you can leave gaps to sortie through. You can drag some in from elsewhere to make it a thicker obstacle."

"They're going to be pretty obvious, though, won't they?"

"Cut them almost flat on one side, if you need to make them lower. Also, you can probably cover them with snow to make them blend in. I wouldn't even be surprised if we have some snowfall to help."

Lesh nodded, thinking, *Ought to help some, anyway.*

"Remember, Lesh, you're going to have all four heavy mach-...
hmmm...Romeyko?"

"We got the water jackets patched up, yes, sir. How long the patches
will last, however..."

"Right; you'll have all four heavy machine guns, Lesh, at least
initially. That's a lot of firepower over less than two *versts*. Especially
with terrain that's about as flat as a *blin*. Also, remember, you'll have the
houses of that town...ummm...Sergeant Major Nenonen?"

"Toboltura, sir."

"Right; you'll have the houses of Toboltura for some shelter and
fortification materials, too."

"Sir? Private prop—"

"Fuck that, Lesh; the owners can be compensated...if we win."

"The skis?" asked Cherimisov.

"I want your crew to take theirs," answered Kostyshakov, "if not
needed they can always stash them. But for the rest, they're of no use,
since they'd only take the leadership away from the new rank and file."

Kostyshakov looked around at the faces. "Any more questions or
objections?" Seeing there were none, he said, "Cherimisov takes the
rest of his unit out in four hours. The rest of the brigade will follow six
hours after that, order of march, Lesh, Dratvin, Baluyev. The
headquarters group will accompany Cherimisov to the town of
Toboltura, then establish the initial brigade command post there.

"At my mark, the time will be..."

Imperial House (nee Governor's House, nee Freedom House)
Tobolsk, Russia

The power plant for the town hummed faintly in the far distance.
Both Maria and Anastasia stood in Tatiana's artificially lit office, arms
folded and shaking their heads violently. In front of them, now clad in
a seemingly standard uniform, over the upper part of her bulletproof
jeweled former dress, with a helmet on her head and a white smock
and trousers covering all, stood the Empress of all the Russias.

"You are *insane*, Tatiana," said Maria, who was not remotely
interested in formality at the moment. "Mad as the Mad Hatter,
simply starkers. If you get yourself killed it will be on me to be Tsarina
and, I assure you, I am *not* up to the job. *I* know I am not and *you*

know I am not. Oh, no; my fate, if you live, is a useful dynastic marriage and nothing but. So if you're killed I won't even try. I'll just head as far from the Bolsheviks as I can get and settle down in welcome obscurity."

"Daniil will throw a screaming fit if you do this," said Anastasia, less vehemently than her sister. "Even if you survive, he'll lock us all up under guard and throw away the key. This is worse than insane; it is *dumb*!"

"It's also selfish," added Maria. "You're doing this out of vainglory, out of sheer vanity. Nobody expects it of you. Nobody who would ever know wants it of you."

Under their criticism the elder sister shrank for a moment, then drew herself up to her full height.

"This is none of those things," she said, firmly. "It's that good men died to save us, and more good men are about to. I cannot—not will not but *cannot*—let that pass without voluntarily taking a portion of the risk onto myself, for me, and for you two, as well. Moreover, I don't want to look into another soldier's face with the knowledge that he's a better and braver human being than I am.

"Besides, I'm going to go with the mortars. We'll be out of the line of fire." *Mostly.* "And besides, I'm not nearly the first Russian woman to pick up a gun."

"Have it your own way then!" shouted Maria, throwing her hands up in despair. "I'm going to go pack for my escape after you're killed!"

In the semi-darkness nobody noticed a soldier of average height slip out of the old mansion and begin walking up Great Friday Street. The streetlamps cast a shadow longer than the soldier was tall.

The soldier went northward, with a freezing breeze assaulting from the left, in the general direction of the Kremlin, where the Guards Brigade was forming to march out to confront the Reds. True, the soldier was apparently unarmed, but there were a few men for whom rifles had not been available, and everyone who mattered knew it. True, too, the soldier walked a bit oddly, but that was also fairly common, what with recent injuries from training and older injuries from the war. Also, true, that the soldier's face was mostly covered. Even so, while the days had begun to warm the nights remained bitterly cold, so what did that matter? And the civilian blankets that were rolled and draped over one shoulder? Many of the men of the brigade, both old and new, carried such blankets.

Reaching the long stairway that led into the Kremlin itself, the soldier began the climb. It was long and tedious, but bearable. Others were walking up the same staircase, to the same end. Mostly, they kept quiet and to themselves, saving their breath. Arriving at the flat open area at the top of the stairs, the soldier looked around for a familiar face, then headed in that direction once it was found.

Falling in ranks with the rest, Tatiana Nicholaevna Romanova tried to be as unobtrusive as possible.

Near her, newly minted *starshiy unter-ofitser* Leonid Panfil counted heads.

"Who are *you*?" he demanded of the unfamiliar silhouette. Instead of answering, the Tsarina of all the Russias uncovered just her face and gave a sweet and pleading smile.

"Oh, no," muttered Panfil. "Oh, no. No, no, no, no. Kostyshakov will have my head. Blagov will slice off my testicles before that. With a spoon. No."

Tatiana's smile disappeared. *Let's try the hard approach; it will make the softer one more effective in a few seconds.*

"Keep it to yourself," she said, "or your head *will* be on a pike but by *my* order."

Panfil shook his head. "I know you better than that, Your Majesty. You would never do such a thing."

"Yes, well, maybe that's true," she conceded, "but Kostyshakov *doesn't* know that you know that, so you have an excuse. Besides," she smiled sweetly as she joked, "is it fair of you to take advantage of my sweet nature?"

"What excuse do I have that I can give myself if you are killed?"

"I promise; I'll be very careful. And besides, you might be killed. I know these things as well as you do now. Maybe better. And I *need* to be there for this. I must be."

Now give him the pleading eyes, Tatiana.

Panfil half melted. "I see no end of trouble from this. Well . . . do you promise, too, to do exactly as you're told?"

Crossing her heart, she answered, "I am no more than Private Romanov, T. I will obey my sergeant with my life!"

"Fine; you drive the sleigh. And do you have a rifle?"

Tatiana lifted her smock to show her MP-18 machine pistol, hanging from its sling. A bag full of the odd drum magazines hung down as well. "Will this do?"

"Can you use it?"

"Yes, Kostyshakov showed me and took me out to fire it. Quite a bit, actually."

Panfil gave out the kind of fatalistic sigh one might expect from a French aristocrat, upon looking up and catching his first sight of Madame Guillotine. "I suppose it will be good enough, then. But if something happens to you and I get stood against a wall . . ."

Interlude

Captain Maria Bochkareva:

The first man ever to demand I be stood against a wall and shot was none other than the ever-so-liberal, too pure for words, Kerensky, the same one who lost Russia to the Reds. He was Minister of War then, and knew less about an army than my last pet dog. Indeed, he was worse, since the dog hadn't deluded itself that it knew anything, while Kerensky was sure he knew everything. The idiot.

Why did he want me shot? Because I threw my epaulettes at him and refused to appoint a committee to my battalion, my "Women's Battalion." And why did I refuse to appoint a committee? Because they're nothing but talk, talk, talk, and because the appointment of committees had destroyed the Russian Army.

He wasn't the last one, though, to want me shot. I escaped a Bolshevik firing squad by the skin of my teeth, by divine intervention, and by a Red soldier who remembered that I'd saved his life during the war. Twice it was that I avoided being shot by the Reds. Think of it: *twice*. I doubt I'd escape a third time.

Well, yes, I won the fight with Kerensky, the swine, but events and time saw my dear battalion disbanded anyway. Oh, all right, we were not disbanded so much as dispersed. With an armed mob numbering in the thousands looking for us, the commandant at Molodechno and his staff provided documents and money to let the girls—except for twenty whom the Bolsheviks had murdered . . . no, they did worse than just kill them; I don't like to think about it—scatter in different directions over the course of a couple of days.

They were the children I'd never had. It was hard, so very hard, to see them go.

Some months later, I was in Moscow—this was one of the occasions where the Reds wanted to shoot me—and found thirty of my girls in a hospital, on the verge of being thrown into the street by the Reds. These were sick girls, wounded, shell-shocked, a couple off the deep end, yes, that, too. And some with that nasty illness that seemed to be sweeping the globe. "Influenza," I think they called it. Said it was from Spain. Maybe it was; I don't know.

All I could think of to do with them was to bring them to my home village near Tomsk, in Siberia, and find some place to shelter them. Look, I never liked the Bolsheviks and their rule by committee. But I didn't even hate them when they tried to have me shot. When they started to toss my sick girls out into the street, though, that's when I began to hate them. I begged and borrowed the money I needed to move them. I even went and enquired at the Convent of Martha and Mary about getting a couple of nurses to accompany us.

It was also at about that time that I heard about the daring rescue of the royal family, or a part of it. I'd never cared for tsarism, no, but the tsar and his *nemka* wife were dead, along with, sad to say, two of their innocent children. That much was official.

What wasn't official, but which I believed more than any other word, was that the new tsarina, Tatiana, was duly crowned and promising to end the Red menace, to restore law, to restore the army, and to rule differently than her father.

It was at about this time that I began to hear serious and strenuous rumblings of mutiny against the Reds from the men and especially the soldiers. This was especially true when I went from Moscow to Petrograd to retrieve the medals I'd left for safekeeping. There was no doubt, on that train, that the soldiers had had enough of the Bolsheviks. Whether this was because of the rumors revolving around the new tsarina, or the bungling incompetence of the Reds, along with their greed, viciousness, and venality, I didn't know. Maybe it was part of both. And yet I heard a lot more detestation of the Bolsheviks than I did adoration of the new tsarina. Still, of adoration and hope there was, in fact, some.

And I thought to myself, *How could she be worse than her father or the Reds?* I didn't think it was possible to be worse. And then there were my girls . . . maybe she could help my poor sick and wounded girls.

I sent a telegram to my former adjutant, Princess Tatuyeva, down in Georgia, asking her to assemble whatever she could of the battalion and meet me in Yekaterinburg as soon as possible. Yes, of *course* with their arms; it's a rough world out there for an unarmed woman. On the plus side, when the Soviet was talked and threatened out of shooting me, they gave me a free pass to travel where I wanted to, unmolested.

My own thirty sick and wounded didn't have any of their rifles. How they'd lost all of them didn't matter at this point. I had my pistol still; it would have to do. With my thirty invalids in tow, plus two of the nurses from Martha and Mary, I set out for Yekaterinburg.

In the back of my mind, too, was an idea the soldiers on the train to Petrograd had planted; if I could only get to America, I mind find aid to help us throw the Reds out of power.

Chapter Four

Yekaterinburg

Yekaterinburg, Russia

The Reds are surprisingly thin on the ground in the town, thought Mokrenko.

Having left the captain and the rest behind, newly commissioned Guards Lieutenant Mokrenko and one of the junior enlisted men had found a suitable hotel and stables. They'd then gone back for the rest, where they were camped near the Perm-Yekaterinburg rail line, in the woods a few hundred meters northwest of the railroad bridge over the Iset River.

"It's very quiet in the city, sir," Mokrenko had reported, back at the camp. "Hardly any soldiery or police at all. There were a few—well, all right, a few dozen—frozen bodies hanging by the neck, here and there, which may account in part for why it's so quiet."

"Any sign of Grand Duchess Elizabeth Feodorovna?" asked Turgenev.

"I . . ." Mokrenko hesitated, "I really don't know. There's a house we saw—we saw it before, if you'll recall, on our way to Tobolsk —with a stockade around it, and a few guards, but they're so few I doubt anyone important is being held there any longer. The 'Ipatiev House,' the locals call it, and the locals didn't seem to know anything about what's inside either. It's the only actual house I saw guarded, though there were some guards on the prison, and the Bolshevik headquarters had a couple, as well."

"No chance of renting us a safe house?"

"I thought about it but once I got a feel for the town . . . no, I think we're better off hiding in plain sight. With plainer red armbands."

Turgenev had learned to trust his former sergeant's judgment and insight over such matters; he let it go.

"I've got to warn you, sir," Mokrenko said, "Yekaterinburg seems redder than Lenin. If there's anybody in the city who's not in sympathy with the Bolsheviks, they're being very quiet about it, indeed. Except for the Czechs."

"Czechs? What are they doing here?"

"Yes, sir, quite a few Czechs. Well, Czechoslovaks, but there are more Czechs than Slovaks. There's a contingent of the Czechoslovak National Council staying at the same hotel we are. Some of them speak some Russian and a few speak it well. They're setting things up for a convention of some kind, I think. Pretty optimistic, too, I think. But at least they're not Bolsheviks."

Turgenev chewed on his lip, thinking. "Hmmm . . . I'd bet the reason there are so few guards is that all the Bolsheviks are marching on Tobolsk."

"Yes, sir," agreed Mokrenko, "that was my guess, too."

"And if it's as red as you think, ser . . . Rostislav Alexandrovich, the Bolsheviks might be confident they can hold it without a substantial military force."

"That, too, sir, yes, though the number of people they've strung up by the neck suggests they thought they needed that little something extra."

"Yes," Turgenev agreed, nodding. "Get the men of Strat Recon packed up and ready. We'll go to the hotel you found and, as you say, hide in plain sight. Our story should probably be that we're reinforcements sent from Moscow to the force marching on Tobolsk."

Turgenev signaled for Garin to come over.

"I'm sure you believe that the men will do as they were told, Mister Garin," Turgenev said. "However, they are mostly your friends, yes?"

"Yes, of course, sir," the teamster agreed.

"You will *never* shoot your friends. We both *know* you won't. I am, therefore, still leaving two men here, Bulavin and Gazenko, to relieve you of the burden of having to shoot your friends. They will do the shooting, should any be required."

Outside the town was still strangely quiet as the men of Strat Recon rode, skied, and sleighed toward it. The teamsters, too, had been quiet, after several days of being forced to stay in camp. It had been long enough that Turgenev trusted them to stay there for at least a few more days, provided they had that little extra bit of motivation to do so. Inertia, after all, has a large place in human affairs, too.

As the section rode, the afternoon sun settled down behind them. They all wore the red armbands purchased months before in Tsaritsyn, plus a couple more made in Tobolsk, and, having skirted the town to set up their earlier camp, came in from the west. Even after turning over the bulk of the hoard from their safecracking venture, the section was still quite flush with both cash and gold.

The town itself, once they got inside of it, was noisy and dirty, the latter not from any habit of the people, but from the source of the noise, the factories whose intense pounding constituted an unending assault on the ears, as the smoke pouring from the chimneys assaulted the nose and eyes. An American of the day would have taken one look and asked, "When did Gary, Indiana and Pittsburgh, Pennsylvania open a joint branch office in Russia?"

And yet it wasn't the noise that made the greatest impression. Oh, no; the thing that truly assaulted the mind and heart was a different smell, different from the factory smoke. This was a mix of food poor to begin with and poorly cooked, of garbage long overdue for burning or burial, of rotten meat, some of it likely human in origin, of unwashed bodies, and, above all, of fear.

There wasn't a man in the party who hadn't smelled that very thing already, on the battlefield, in burnt-out towns, in vermin-filled trenches, and in hasty graveyards.

"Chekhov was right," said Turgenev, looking at some of the people in the street. "This is a place where the people were 'born in the local iron foundries and brought into the world not by midwives, but mechanics.'"

They passed a gallows just left of the road that had led them further into the town. On it hung by their necks five men and two women, hands tied, eyes bulging, mouths agape, and frozen solid. Another three women knelt at the uprights holding up the crossbeam, one to one, two to the other, all weeping.

I wonder what their crimes were, thought Turgenev, *if any. I wonder, too, how many people the Reds have had to string up to keep the others in terrified submission. One suspects that the place is less red than Mokrenko thinks, but even more frightened. Maybe . . .*

Shortly after passing the gallows they came to a train station in the Russian Revival style, a mix of Baroque, old Russian, Byzantine, and whatnot, done in a mix of white, brown, and red. On the whole, the effect was not entirely unattractive, but it still wasn't a style designed to calm nerves.

"I'd have expected a bigger station," said the captain, "for a place of this size, importance, and centrality."

"That's the old station, sir," Mokrenko replied. Pointing with his chin, he added, "The current one's up ahead."

"Ah, I see; much bigger. What's that out front?"

What Turgenev saw out front was a collection of about thirty women, or a few more, some sitting on the cold stone steps, some on litters covered with blankets, some staring off into space quietly but a couple who seemed continuously agitated, looking from side to side like frightened mice. A few were in uniforms little different from the one he wore. Two wore the habits of nursing nuns. One of them, the only one standing and fully alert, had on an officer's cap, belt, medals, and epaulettes, and bore a holstered pistol by her side. Shockingly, the officer was a she. Even at a distance, she seemed remarkably unlovely and quite stout.

"Should we enquire?" he asked of Lieutenant Mokrenko.

"If you do," replied Mokrenko, "you'd better be—at least *seem* to be—arguing with and denouncing her. And if you intend to slip her some cash or gold—sure, we can afford it, and we all know you by now—then you had better be subtle about it. Sir."

"What's the name of the hotel we're staying at?"

"Forget it, sir," said the sergeant. "We don't want to be in the same building as, nor identified with, that lot."

"Understood. You do know me uncomfortably well, Mokrenko. In any case, I intended to give it to her to look us up after she finds some place elsewhere to stay, assuming she needs it."

"All right, then; in that case we're in the Amerikanskaya Hotel, on Pokrovsky Prospect. One of these days, sir, your Christian and gentlemanly tendencies are going to get us in trouble."

"You keep going, Rostislav; I'll catch up. I'm going to have a chat with that woman."

"What do you think you're doing here, woman!" Turgenev shouted down at her. This was followed by a much gentler, though much more quietly spoken, "Pay no attention to the words I shout. Those are for the benefit of anyone who might be watching and listening."

As he spoke, Turgenev glanced around and thought, *Some of these are very pretty women. Prostitutes? No, they don't have that look about them. So, I wonder . . .*

It took her a moment to catch on, but then she shouted back, "What business is it of yours?" This was followed by a softer, "I'm waiting for more of my girls to arrive by train."

"These diseased harridans should be in an asylum of some kind!" was followed by a soft, "Do you have a place to stay?"

"To hell with you, you accursed Red!" . . . "We have no money."

"Parasitic drain on the people's resources!" . . . "Gold goes a lot further than cash."

Turgenev dismounted from his horse, then made as if to slap the woman. As he did, he dropped a dozen and a half gold ten-ruble coins on the pavement. He hoped the upraised hand would distract anyone from noticing the opening one, pouring its golden shower to the ground.

"When I strike, cry out and pretend to fall to the ground, stunned. It will give you a chance to grab the gold."

With that, Turgenev brought his hand down. He pulled his slap, though. The female officer did as told, crying out as if in pain and then falling to the ground. He crouched down as if to chastise her further.

"Filthy swine!"

"Thank you so much. To whom do I owe . . . ?"

"I am Maxim Sergeyevich Turgenev, scourge of the capitalist oppressors and exploiters!" . . . "Look for me at the Amerikanskaya Hotel, you alone, early tomorrow. Buy civilian clothes and change into them. I can shunt you a little more money there."

The woman pretended to flinch from the coming blow.

"I'll come after I find a place to settle my girls in. I'm Maria Leontievna Bochkareva." This last was said very softly.

"Bah! Begone with you." With that, Turgenev remounted and spurred his horse to rejoin the rest of the party, further up the street. Once reunited, the party picked up the pace, heading for their quarters.

Ipatiev House, Voznesenski Prospect, Yekaterinburg

An even dozen open-topped carts, each pulled by a lone horse, clattered and swayed up to the stockade's main gate, fronting the street. A senior Chekist, Pyotr Startsev, waited there for them.

Chekist? These were men—and some women—who worked for the Cheka, the newly formed, indeed, less than a year old, Bolshevik All-Russian Extraordinary Commission. Their mission was manifold, but the core was control through sheer terror. You want food confiscated so peasants would starve? Go to the Cheka. A royal family exterminated? That, too, was a Chekist job. You want someone crucified, impaled, burnt alive? All in a day's work for the Cheka. You want to force a rat trapped in a pipe to eat his way through a human victim to escape a fire? That would count as mere. They were rape, murder, agony, terror, theft, starvation, and rape personified; yes, the Cheka really liked rape.

"Things are moving too quickly," said the senior Chekist, Startsev, to his underling, Vasily Ryabov; "too quickly and not so well."

"How so, boss?" asked Ryabov.

"It all stems from the rescue of the Romanov family in Tobolsk. Before that, we were, in the first place, supposed to collect the lesser Romanovs in the Hotel Atamanovska, here, yes? That would have been convenient and comfortable. But then Comrade Sverdlov, I am sure at Ilyich's instigation, ordered almost all the revolutionary troops in the city to march on Tobolsk, leaving not much more than a company here. With so few guards, and so many places needing guarding—do Lenin and Sverdlov have any idea how much precious metal, gold, silver, and platinum is just *sitting* here, waiting for counterrevolutionaries to steal it; I wonder—an open place like the hotel was right out. So we brought them here, to this place, to keep a closer eye on them more easily. The collection of prisoners for this place then speeded up; there are a dozen in there now and only about that many guards, including the ones asleep. And there's hardly enough food even for those, given what Comrade Goloshchyokin took for his column. Nor have the people of the city proven especially willing to cough up more for the cause, no matter how zealously they proclaim their revolutionary ardor and no matter how drawn out we make the hangings of profiteers and speculators.

"And now, before anyone is even settled in, we're ordered to move them one hundred and fifty *versts*, more or less, to Alapayevsk, where nothing has apparently been arranged to receive or feed them."

"I see," agreed Ryabov. "So what are we going to do?"

"Carry out our orders, of course; the Party knows best. But here's how I want it done..."

Ella was awaked by the scream of one of her companion nuns, Ekaterina Ianysheva, as she was unceremoniously dumped from her upturned cot to the floor below.

"Up, you bloodsucking swine!" shouted Ryabov. "Take only one set of clothing, one pair of shoes, one coat, one hat, and two changes of underwear. Anyone trying to take more will be beaten. If women, they will suffer worse than just a beating. 'Up!' I said."

The threat of a beating or "worse" was enough to make Ella leave most of her clothing behind. She could not, however, leave behind a small bejeweled icon, given to her by her late brother-in-law, the tsar, and before which he had prayed before abdicating his throne. This she hid under her coat, knowing she'd be beaten and have it confiscated should the Reds ever find it.

Hustled out of the house, at bayonet point, and through the stockade gate with blows from rifle butts, the dozen prisoners were checked against the roster and then ordered into the waiting carts, two or three per cart. With Ella were her companions, Ekaterina Ianysheva and Varvara Yakovleva. Ella thought the other two looked even more terrified than she felt.

Hoping to calm them, she said, "I don't think they mean to kill us; the basement of the house would do well enough for that." She felt a sudden chill as she said the words, one that even the cold night air couldn't quite account for. She forced the feeling away, then continued, "But if we are to die, let us go to our God with devotion and courage. Join me, sisters."

At that, holding out her hands to the others, for their reassurance's sake, Ella began to sing the old Russian hymn, immortalized by Tchaikovsky in his 1812 Overture, O Lord, Save Thy People.

> *"Spasi, Gospodi, syudi tvoya*
> *I blagoslovi dostoyaniye Tvoyo*
> *Pobedy pravoslavnym khristianom*
> *na soprotivnyya daruya*
> *I Tvoyo sokhranyaya*
> *Krestom Tvoim zhitel'stvo."*

She hadn't gotten past the first syllable when the other two took a hand each and joined her:

> "O Lord, save Thy people,
> And bless Thine inheritance!"

At that point, much to the annoyance of scowling Reds, the men in the carts joined in with:

> "Grant victory to Orthodox Christians
> Over their adversaries,
> And by virtue of Thy cross,
> Preserve Thy habitation."

It was a hymn, a musical prayer, one to be repeated and then repeated, over and over and over again. As such, the musical strains echoed all the way up the long street leading to the train stations.

Princess Tatuyeva, Bochkareva's adjutant from the war and the old Women's Battalion of Death, had finally shown up with another one hundred thirteen women from the battalion. Almost all were in civilian dress, though a few sported scraps of uniforms that could have come from anywhere.

There were only forty rifles among them, most of those bought by the princess from her own means and stored in with baggage. Of ammunition there was a more generous allocation, amounting to roughly ten thousand rounds, plus a few hundred, in a dozen wooden crates.

Tatuyeva, what remained of the battalion being now together again where money could be efficiently spent, had also brought a good deal of money, tens of thousands of rubles, and in gold.

With Bochkareva in the lead, the ragged column trudged south along Voznesenskaya Street. Carrying the ones too sick to walk on litters, or helping those in somewhat better health with a supporting arm or shoulder, the one hundred thirty-four remaining women made slow progress toward a large barn of a house that Bochkareva had managed to rent with a portion of the money given her by that surprising Red, Maxim Sergeyevich. The house had, unsurprisingly, a good Russian stove in it, plus a fair supply of wood.

When Bochkareva had asked about the owners, the realtor had told her, simply, "Gallows, west of town, mother, daughter, father, four sons. The mother-in-law and two more daughters were out shopping; that's how they escaped. I know the dead daughter was raped but don't know about the mother. I am only able to rent it because I paid the Red commissar, Goloshchyokin, for the privilege."

"What did the family *do*?" Bochkareva had asked.

"No one really knows. Maybe they did nothing at all, but the Reds needed some people to suffer and die—and they suffered a good deal before being hanged—to terrorize the town."

"Are the Reds popular here?"

"They used to be, and still are with some. Don't be fooled, though, the terror hasn't won them any friends, just quiet enemies."

Just quiet enemies, Bochkareva mused.

The march south continued. In a bit, over the ragged *crunchcrunch-crunch* of her women's booted and shoed feet on the road, there came the sound of singing. It was soft at first, barely discernable, but the sound grew with every further step south, and every *arshin* the singers moved to the north. It wasn't the sort of tune anybody could really march to. Even so, the girls unconsciously formed ranks, litters to the rear with the nuns and Princess Tartuyeva. When Bochkareva went to both knees and crossed herself repeatedly as the carts passed, the healthy ones, and even some of the sick and wounded, likewise joined in:

"Spasi, Gospodi, syudi tvoya..."

Once the carts had passed, Princess Tartuyeva was the first on her feet, racing to Bochkareva, along with both of the nursing nuns.

"Do you know who that was?" Tartuyeva asked. "I wasn't sure myself, not one hundred percent, until the sisters confirmed it."

Eyes still following the receding carts, Bochkareva answered, "Besides some brave people willing to risk the wrath of the Reds, no."

"I recognized two of them to my certain knowledge," the princess exclaimed. "Grand Duchess Elizabeth Feodorovna was in the third cart, while Grand Duke Sergei Mikhailovich was in the sixth one."

"Yes, Captain," exclaimed one of the nuns. "It was our own dear abbess. Imagine, finding her here!"

"Imagine, instead," said the Princess, "all of us being shot if I hadn't been able to restrain you and your friend from running to her."

The chastised nun cast her eyes down to the road.

"Poor folk," Bochkareva said. "After what the Reds did to us, I can't imagine that those people have even a slight chance."

Hotel Amerikanskaya, Yekaterinburg, Russia

The man at the desk had been very clear, "The only reason I can give your party rooms, Comrade, is because most of your fellow Bolsheviks who were here pulled out, heading east. You have to be prepared to vacate at a moment's notice if and when they return. Indeed, I expect us to be taken over fully as soon as they do return."

"So," began Turgenev, to almost the entire section, in what was the most private and soundproof of the rooms he'd rented. Indeed, it was a lot more soundproof than basic construction allowed, since a thick blanket was hung over the door from the inside frame, every vent was stoppered with bedding, and the integral bath was likewise soundproofed, lest the pipes carry voices.

This was absolutely necessary, as the pounding and grinding of the many heavy industrial workshops all around made speaking well above a whisper utterly necessary. The great Russian writer, Chekhov, when he'd stayed at the same hotel twenty-eight years before, had said the noise had made sleep close to impossible.

"So, Koslov, somebody must remain here to guard our...materiel. That's you. You will have Bulavin with you. The rest of us form four two-man teams, myself and Lavin, the lieutenant and Novarikasha, Timashuk and Shukhov, Sarnof and Popov.

"Anybody and everybody, see if you can find a good, up-to-date street map of the city. The one I was able to get at the front desk was poor and localized only. Also, remember we are looking for information of the whereabouts of Grand Duchess Elizabeth Feodorovna, but we can't ask just anyone—indeed, we just can't ask anyone, not anyone at all—for the information. It all has to be indirect. All else failing, if you just strike up a conversation on unrelated matters you might learn something of use.

"Sarnof, while you're scouting west of here, I want you and Popov to make a thorough scan of the telegraph and telephone system. I also need the exchanges' locations, with an eye to either taking them over or taking them out."

"Yes, sir."

"I don't want us all seen to be leaving at the same time, Sarnof. You two go to breakfast now, eat quickly, then move out. Small talk only in the restaurant. Now don't forget your pistols or your cash, to include the fifty gold rubles for bribes. That goes for everyone. Also, don't leave the hotel without your red armbands on."

"Yes, sir." With that and a nod, Sarnof and his fellow signaller, Popov, stood and left.

"Rostislav Alexandrovich," the captain continued, "look around the train station area. There will be a telegraph station there, too, I am certain. Go to breakfast in about fifteen minutes. Shukhov and Timashuk? Downtown for you. If you do nothing but note where there are guards, that would not be a complete waste. You go to breakfast in thirty. Myself and Lavin will eat last. We're going to scout Pokrovsky Prospect and for the upper-class areas, since those are the only areas I can open my mouth without sounding like an aristocratic spy."

Turgenev and Lavin arrived just as Mokrenko and Novarikasha got up to leave.

He always was a fast eater, thought the captain. No sooner had he and Lavin sat down than an attentive, white-clad waiter was standing by to take their order. *Is this because of the red armbands or because it's just that kind of place? I can't ask directly and I'm not sure how to ask indirectly.*

The waiter laid menus in front of both men, but then said,

shamefaced, "Sirs, I'm terribly sorry, don't pay much attention to those. Most of what's on them isn't available."

"Fair enough," said Turgenev, "what with the . . . disruptions, shall we say? What *is* available?"

"Tea, of course," answered the waiter. "Though it won't have all the spices and juices you might normally expect. Also buckwheat porridge, for which there is at least *some* honey, *syrnicki*"—a cheesy kind of Russian pancake—"black bread, butter, and eggs. We used to have ham but then, just this morning, half a dozen people wearing armbands just like yours . . ."

"It's no problem," said the lieutenant. "We've been on the trail for a long time, coming here, and ate poorly for most of that. We'll take two orders of everything, which is to say, an order each for both of us."

"Very good, sir," said the waiter, turning on his heels and heading toward the kitchen.

The dining room wasn't especially crowded today. Separated from Turgenev and Lavin by an empty table, three men, all rather well-dressed and distinguished looking, and both rather biologically well-insulated against the Siberian cold, talked in a language Turgenev didn't understand or recognize.

"I wonder what they're speaking," he said.

"Don't know, sir," said Lavin.

"It's called 'English,'" said one of the men in question, in perfect Russian, spoken with a bit of a Petrograd accent.

"Indeed?" said Turgenev, thoroughly nonplussed. "Ummm . . . thank you. And who do we have the pleasure of . . ."

"Henry Palmer," said the English speaker, "and these are my colleagues, Seamus Curran and Jay Maynard. We're Americans, by the way, not British. Our accents may account for your not being able to place the language."

"Even so," agreed the captain, though he didn't think the accents would have made a difference. *Hmmm . . . Americans in the Amerikanskaya Hotel. We might be able to gain a little intelligence.*

"Have you gentlemen already eaten?"

"We're still waiting," said Palmer. "Shouldn't be long now."

"Would you care to join us?"

Maynard, Curran, and Palmer exchanged glances. *Why not?* they thought. *We might be able to gather some intelligence.*

Signaling to the waiter that they were moving tables, the Americans moved to the table held by Turgenev and Lavin and sat down.

"What brings you to Yekaterinburg?" asked Maynard, once he'd settled himself down into the cushioned chair.

"We were ordered here by Moscow, supposedly to make up for the comrades who have marched east, to Tobolsk," answered Turgenev, managing several lies in a single sentence. "And why would a trio of Americans want to live in cold and ugly place like Yekaterinburg?"

"I'm the Vice Consul," replied Palmer. "Jay here is with a branch office of one of our banks, which is officially affiliated with one of yours. Seamus is an advisor to one of the mining concerns."

"An American bank, here?" queried Turgenev. "Why—"

"Gold, silver, platinum," answered Maynard. "There is more precious metal pulled from the Earth here than you can shake a stick at. Some Americans—mining experts, like Seamus—help supervise the mines, or rather, did, since they're mostly leaving for . . . ummm . . . health reasons. They need a bank. Or did."

"I suppose I knew that Yekaterinburg is a center of mining for precious metals," said Turgenev, "but I never really thought about it."

"There are, my newfound friend," said Maynard, "*billions* of rubles' worth of refined metal stored here in the town, even as we speak. And that is real value, not inflated paper rubles. I wonder when your colleagues will come for it. I'm sure they know of it."

"There's still more waiting underground," said Curran, himself bearded, tall, and a bit stout.

"Other matters are more pressing, I suppose," said Turgenev. "Notably those matters in the east, Tobolsk, specifically. With the former Imperial family at large, civil war seems unavoidable at this time."

"How *did* that happen?" asked Palmer.

"I know little more than you do, sir," Turgenev replied, being highly economical with the truth. "A force attacked to free them, some lived, some died. This exhausts my knowledge."

Conversation ended then, as the waiter returned, placing bowls and platters of food on the table. Turgenev seemed a little nonplussed; it was much more a Russian custom to bring already filled plates. Noticing this, Palmer said, "I think they take their name more or less seriously here, so distribute their food as it would be done in the United States, at least at home."

Bowls and platters were passed around, while serving spoons flew. Just before digging in, Turgenev crossed himself, Orthodox fashion, while whispering something too low to hear.

Lavin looked at the captain, wide eyed and aghast.

Oh, crap, thought Turgenev. *What if these three are in sympathy with the Bolsheviks?*

But no one seemed to have noticed; the meal continued. The men ate as they conversed.

"What languages can you speak?" asked Palmer of Turgenev, between bites.

"Russian, of course, French, German. My French is better than my German. That's it."

Palmer immediately switched to excellent French, though he looked around for eavesdroppers and still kept his voice low.

"My friend, Jay, here, speaks it too, if not quite so well," said the vice consul. "Seamus only speaks English and effective, albeit maybe crude, Russian."

"What's the town been like since the main column left for Tobolsk?" Turgenev asked.

"In shock, for the most part," replied Palmer. "Before they took most of their men with them, your friends engaged in a reign of terror against the townsfolk, the better for the few Reds remaining to keep control."

Turgenev could only nod somberly and observe, "It does make a certain sense. And has it worked?"

The question had been addressed to Palmer, but it was Maynard who answered. "For a while. Given half an ounce of inspiration, a couple hundred rifles and a hundred thousand rounds of ammunition—maybe less—the townspeople, now, would probably rise in rebellion."

Palmer looked at his friend and colleague as if he were mad. One does *not* tell a Bolshevik that the *people* are set to rise against his cause.

Curran piped up with, "I know my miners would."

Maynard ignored Palmer completely. "There's a lot of gold and silver here, as I mentioned, Comrade Turgenev, along with platinum. Think of something on the order of four billion rubles. About half of that is gold; call it about fifteen hundred tons or nine thousand *berkovets*. The tonnage of silver is simply immense."

"I can see why they didn't try to move it," said Turgenev.

"Indeed," said Palmer. "When I saw the extra troops show up here, I initially assumed it was to move the metal."

"We all did, along with half the town," said Maynard.

"Where is all this gold and silver?" Turgenev asked.

"And platinum," Palmer corrected. "Scattered about the town, in various bank vaults and ore refineries. Your comrades were guarding them but now it's gone back to just civilian guards, mostly older."

"I'll give them this much credit for foresight," Maynard added, "they got an inventory and the names of the guards, for each bank, as well as the addresses of their families before they left. They promised a terrible retribution if anything was missing when they returned."

"Sound, very sound," Turgenev observed. "Who is the senior Bolshevik in the town now?" he asked.

"I've no clue," said Palmer. "They don't wear rank and often issue contradictory orders—sorry, but it's true—so it's very hard to tell. I can tell you where their current headquarters is, though."

"That would help," said Turgenev. "I should be checking in."

"It's on what they call '1905 Square,'" said Palmer. "Go out the main door of the hotel, take a right. Cross over the bridge on the River Iset, then three more intersections and take another right. Go maybe a third of a *verst* and you'll come to a large . . . well . . . a large rectangular open area, to your left. Your colleagues set up shop on the first floor of the lower floor of the building making up the south side of the square. That's city hall. It's still guarded, so you can't miss it."

Turgenev closed his eyes momentarily, engraving the directions directly onto his brain. He then thanked Palmer.

"Well," Turgenev said, "on that note, and breakfast being finished, I'd probably best report in. Gentlemen, I thank you for your counsel. Comrade Lavin?"

"Yes, comrade?"

"Let us be off."

"Stop by my office later," Maynard said, scribbling an address on a piece of paper torn from a small notebook taken from his pocket. "I can tell you where the gold and silver are with rather more precision."

"And I can tell you where the best remaining mines are," added Curran.

"Thank you, comrades."

Maynard and Palmer watched the two of them depart out the front door.

Still keeping to French, Palmer asked, "Are you insane, Jay, giving information like that to a Bolshevik?"

Maynard laughed softly, while Curran said, "Henry, my friend, we have been eating here nearly every morning since the Bolsheviks came. When did we ever see one of them cross himself before a meal? Or show decent table manners? Or fail to use his fork as a toothpick? Oh, no; red armbands notwithstanding, our newfound friends are as much Reds as we three are, which is to say not a bit."

"Oh . . . so what are they?"

"My first guest would be spies, but they may have other goals, too."

"Ohhhhh."

"Yes, Comrade Lavin," said Turgenev as they passed from the hotel to the street, "yes, I *know* I made a mistake. Did they catch it?"

"I'm not sure . . . comrade," answered the Cossack. "It was pretty obvious, so if they didn't see you cross yourself . . ." He left the thought hanging, having no answer for what it might mean.

"Did anyone else notice, do you think?"

"I'm not sure of that . . . hey, comrade, isn't that the woman you were shouting at on the way in?"

It took a moment for Turgenev to recognize the woman he knew as Bochkareva, clad, as she now was, in civilian attire. The civilian overcoat didn't make her look any more attractive, only a bit different.

He and Lavin kept their places, just outside the hotel, as she hurried across the street to them.

"It took longer than I'd expected to find suitable civilian clothing," the female officer told them. "Please forgive my being late."

"As it turned out, it's fortuitous. Come with us . . . Maria? Is that what you said your given name is?"

"Yes, Maria, Maria Leontievna."

"Come with us."

"To where?"

"Bolshevik headquarters, which is to say, city hall."

"I don't want anything to do with the Reds," she said.

"You won't have to have anything to do with them," Turgenev assured her. "But why the hatred I hear in your voice?"

Bochkareva's eyes flashed. "You cannot imagine what your colleagues have done. In the first place, they ruined the Russian Army. It may never recover from their nonsense. In the second place, they raped and murdered at least a score of my women soldiers. In the third, they were in the process of tossing thirty of my sick ones out onto the street in the middle of a Moscow winter. In the fourth—"

"I think that's quite enough," said Turgenev, holding up one hand, palm exposed, to silence her.

"Of *course*," she said, glancing at his armband. "Of *course*, you won't hear any criticism of the Reds. And there I thought I'd found—"

"Shut up, woman; you have no idea what you've found. Now follow along; we can chat as we walk. But no sneering at the Reds, do you hear me?"

Chapter Five

M1900 76.2mm Artillery Piece

Southwest of Toboltura, Siberia

One good thing Comrade Goloshchyokin had to congratulate himself and his side on; it had taken so long to get everything together, and to move the full distance, that spring had almost come upon them. Oh, yes, there was still snow on the ground and likely would be for some weeks, but the weather—that godawful Siberian winter—had mellowed into a godawful Siberian spring, still bloody cold but in every way to be preferred to its less merciful cousin.

Despite the warmer weather, Comrade Goloshchyokin cursed again at the artillery battery leader, reaching out to slap him for the third time that morning.

"Lazy, ignorant fool! Once again, Nikitin, you've let the imperialist swine escape! Why did I even bring you and your monkeys along?"

"Comrade Goloshchyokin," countered the artilleryman, Nikitin, ignoring the blow, "these targets are like phantoms. They appear from odd directions, without warning, fire a few or a few hundred shots, and then disappear. By the time I can get my guns unlimbered they are *gone*! Would you have me waste ammunition?"

Inwardly, the gunner fumed. *Of course, it might have helped if you had given me, as I asked you to, more time to train my gunners. But noooo.*

"Bah," said Goloshchyokin. "Get back to your monkeys and at least *try* to pretend you have value commensurate with the food I waste on you and the oxygen you breathe."

At the mention of "oxygen" the artilleryman paled. He'd heard Goloshchyokin refer to "wastes of oxygen" before, before one of his sham trials and genuine hangings.

"Yes, comrade!"

Dismissing the artillery from his mind, Goloshchyokin turned his attention to the northeast, the direction from which so much harassment had come.

And that's all it's been, so far, the Red mused, *harassment, clearly intended to slow us down. Well, it won't work.*

"We press onward!" he said, loud enough to be heard a hundred *arshini* or more away. A few men of the two companies spreading out to the front turned to see who was shouting.

"Pay attention to your front, you dogs!"

Young Colonel Georgy Lesh, crouching low behind one of his camouflaged heavy machine guns, itself encased in a strong bunker composed of logs, stone, earth, and ice, watched what looked to be about four hundred Reds, in two groups, one north of and one south of the little hamlet of Degtyarevo, spreading out with perhaps two *arshini* per man between them, or slightly more. They advanced confidently. The platoon from the Grenadiers that had been harassing them passed through Lesh's lines with well-rehearsed ease, before turning south, then west, to join the rest of the reinforced Guards Grenadier company and Dratvin's First Battalion of the Semenovsky Regiment.

Not much experience of war, then, have you? thought the new colonel, watching the carefree Reds approach. *Well, we'll fix that soon.*

Lesh was dirty and unshaven, like his men, and his hands were, also like theirs, blistered from sawing logs and abatis and cutting down into the frozen ground. Behind him stood several messengers and a bugler.

There were four heavy machine guns along the line of stream-fed woods west of Toboltura. Their arcs of fire were intermeshed across the front. Out further, abatis lay in long, straight lines, some forming triangles along the lines the machine guns were sighted on, with others to hide just where those lines of sight were.

The first line of Reds reached one of the line of abatis. They peeled around it, filing into gaps in the line, before coming upon a longer and still more solid line.

"Hold your fire," said Lesh. "Wait for them to build up."

"Yessir," said the guardsman sitting bent over behind the Maxim, peering intently through the rectangular vision port in the gunner's shield. The gunner's thumbs twitched incessantly with anticipation.

"Sir," said the gunner, after a few minutes, "there must be forty of them lined up."

Lesh, who had a better point of view than that of the gunner, replied, "Oh, surely more than that. Ready?"

"Yes, sir."

"Fire!" said Lesh, slapping a palm down on the gunner's shoulder for emphasis.

Instantly, the gunner's thumbs depressed. With only an imperceptible delay, the water-cooled Maxim began spitting out bullets at the rate of about ten per second. This was no light machine gun, either, where one had to ration out the rounds to avoid overheating. Rather, as the water in the barrel shroud turned first hot and then to steam, the gun kept firing, spitting out six hundred bullets a minute, a constant stream, more of an obstacle, on its own, than a mere barbed wire fence.

Lesh watched with satisfaction as the Reds bunched up along the line of abatis began to fall, some knocked directly to the ground and others spun like tops before sinking slowly. Even over the rattle of the gun he could hear their cries of pain and fright.

Close to four hundred rifles, an even dozen Lewis Guns, four per company, and the other three heavy duty Maxims, joined in.

That first probe was simply crushed, leaving from seventy to eighty Reds littering the field, either dead or writhing in pain while crying for aid. How many less grievously wounded may have run away or been dragged off was anyone's guess. They'd also made no impression on the defenders nor even on their wooden obstacle system.

Hardly any return fire, either, thought Lesh. *They went down or scampered off too fast.*

Artillery should be next, I think. This he thought while watching the shattered remnants of those two Red companies running for their lives. *Not a lot active that I can do about that, on this end. Everything we can do has been done.*

Lesh shouted out to the men standing behind him. "Bugler, blow 'stop.'" This was one of only four tactical bugle calls in the Imperial Army. "Messengers, get the word to the companies to take shelter; we're about to take a pasting."

The machine guns and their crews, along with Lesh, however, would remain in their bunkers.

"Get your guns into action without delay," ordered Comrade Goloshchyokin.

"Yes, Comrade," Nikitin said, before trotting off to give the orders. He knew there would be a lengthy delay and knew there was nothing to be done about it.

There'd be no indirect fire here; he himself was the only one who knew how to compute it. *And I don't have any observers, anyway, nor field telephones for them to give me observations, nor wire to connect us. Maybe someday I'll have the time to train some. Besides, that silly turd, Goloshchyokin, hasn't actually given me any instructions on what he wants my guns to actually do. "Destroy, Comrade Goloshchyokin? Suppress, Comrade Goloshchyokin?" And I'd ask, too, except that he can be very dangerous when someone asks him a question to which he lacks an answer.*

The horses pulling the four cannon and the caissons weren't any better trained than the men. Getting them into a position, some twenty-four hundred *arshini* southwest of where the fire had come from, was an exercise in sheer frustration.

They eventually formed a battery of four guns, pointed generally in the right direction, albeit not perfectly aligned.

But that doesn't matter, thought Nikitin, *I'm going to have to talk them through direct lay anyway. Fortunately, I've at least been able to drill them on setting sights and fuses.*

Nikitin put his French-made, range-finding binoculars to his eyes. Unfortunately, this set depended on seeing a horse or upright man to determine the range by matching either to a silhouette inside the binoculars. But; *No, not a damned thing to see. Still, I can make a good guess as to the range. But they could see me, I think, if they were trying. I'm guessing they knew we had artillery and have pulled back mostly into bombproofs for shelter. There's something wrong with that theory, though. I can't quite put my finger on it but . . . Why would they . . . ? Aha! They couldn't have built bombproofs if they'd only had the time between our first skirmish and now, or even several days ago. So they either don't have them or they've been watching us for some time.*

What can I do about that? They could still be on the line and just waiting for another infantry assault. In that case, if I fire, they'll fire back. So . . .

After consulting his firing table, Nikitin shouted out, "Battery, at my command, one round, shrapnel. Combination fuse. Set your fuses for one and one quarter seconds. Elevate your guns to ten degrees. Your target is the center of the wood-line twenty-four hundred *arshini* to your front."

After waiting for some seconds while the fuses were set, the guns loaded, the guns trained to bring them on target, and the gun chiefs announced, "Ready!" Nikitin raised his binoculars back to his eyes and ordered, "Fire!"

Snow on the ground billowed out, forward of the guns, while trees shook and evergreens deposited white fluff and needles. The guns' barrels leapt back, compressing both the oil cylinder and the forty India rubber rings in the trail. A bit over a second later, four small dark clouds materialized in Nikitin's view. *Crappy sheaf,* he thought, sourly. *Well, to be expected.*

Any reasonably experienced observer, and Nikitin had a good deal of experience, could spot where the shrapnel balls struck the ground by the soil, water, or snow they cast up. He gave the guns a new elevation and fuse setting.

"Fire!"

Except for two shrapnel balls that came into the firing port, hit the gunner's shield, and then ricocheted off to bury themselves in the dirt, the shrapnel pattered harmlessly around the mostly abandoned line.

"I don't know about you men, but the sound of rain on a tin roof always helps me to fall asleep," Lesh joked with the gun's crew. Rank hath its privileges so, even though it was a fairly old and weak joke, it still raised snorts of laughter from the crew.

There was one louder bang; a shrapnel shell's fuse apparently failed, causing it to revert to impact detonation. However, the explosive charge inside a shrapnel shell was usually trivial. (There was a German shell, the *Einheitsgeschoss*, that contained more explosive and fewer balls, but this tended to do a fairly poor job with each, so had not been copied by the Russians. Or anyone else.) After the noise of several hundred machine gun rounds inside a tight bunker, the men with Lesh barely noticed.

"How long before they try another assault, do you think, sir?" asked the chief of the gun crew.

"Your guess is as good as mine, corporal. I don't think it will be all that soon, though."

Daniil Kostyshakov, Ivan Dratvin, Pyotr Cherimisov, Sergeant Yahanov, and Corporal Panfil crouched in a tight group on the safe side of a low ridge south-southwest of the hamlet of Degtyarevo.

Cherimisov's entire company of grenadiers, now brought up to strength with nearly one hundred sixty men, were arrayed likewise along that friendly side, forbidden to look over the ridge. Further southward, hidden in some woods, was Dratvin's First Battalion, and for now only battalion, of the Preobrazhensky Regiment, among which were mixed the 37mm infantry guns under Sergeant Yahanov, plus Panfil's mortars. The same shallow ridge concealed the lot from the gunners trying to ply their trade, south of the town.

Panfil and Yahanov were already well known to the company from the steady support provided by the 37mm gun section during the rescue in Tobolsk.

"Can't range that far, sir," Panfil told Kostyshakov. "We can do a little over nine hundred and sixty *arshini*. Little more with a tailwind, sure, but not even that with a headwind. You've got to get us close to do the job."

"Just that? Nine hundred and sixty *arshini*? I can almost get more range out of our machine pistols. Well, I *can* get more from the Lewis Guns and a good deal more from the heavy machine guns."

"Probably, sir," Panfil agreed, "but will a round from your machine pistols or Lewis Guns scour an area free of healthy life within a radius of thirty or so *arshini*?"

"No, I suppose not," Kostyshakov admitted. "Can you fire at night?

We can get you close enough once the sun goes down. There's a very low ridge between us and them."

"We still going to have about half illumination for most of the night, sir?" Panfil asked.

"Yes, should have better than that, if no clouds roll in."

"Then, yes, probably I can. The cannon should be pretty obvious, after all."

"I get a lot more range out of the 37mm guns," Yahanov offered. "The problem is we don't get nearly as much effect on the target. Not much explosive in those little shells, after all."

"Sir," asked Cherimisov of the short and dark Colonel Dratvin, "can you take out the guns tonight with both of these supporting you?"

"Probably," the colonel replied. "My problem comes in in holding the space against the anticipated counterattack. Yes, even with the guns. It might not be a problem, mind you, if Lesh sends me two of the heavy machine guns as he is supposed to, tonight."

"I'd trust Georgy to follow orders," said Kostyshakov. "Why do you ask?" he demanded of Cherimisov.

"Well, sir," Cherimisov answered, "My scouts report that the Red field trains are located in the town to our west, Kutarbitka. Maybe I can take and hold their trains and maybe I can't, but I'll bet my life I can at least hold them long enough to burn everything."

"Daniil," said Dratvin, "I can hold on here with two companies and give Pyotr one company of rifles to help. Frankly, even a threat to their trains will likely thin them out enough to make it a lot easier to get to those guns."

Dan raised a quizzical eyebrow at Cherimisov.

"Yes, sir. Moreover, after we beat off the inevitable counterattack, I can probably ski back here to help Colonel Dratvin attack the guns. Even moving in a wide circuit, we're a lot faster on skis than they'll be in boots."

"When do you want to hit them?"

"As soon as I can get there. These will be rear echelon types, even less ready to die for Lenin than the ones in front. The company Colonel Dratvin gives us needn't be there for the assault, only to take our place so we can come back here."

Kostyshakov thought about the proposal, which was only really an opportunistic modification to the original plan, itself full of places to be modified.

"All right, with one proviso: swing a little further out and drive as many as possible of their support personnel into the mass between Kutarbitka and Toboltura. You can ask why."

"Thank you, sir; why?"

"Food, blankets, and panic, but especially food. If you push them into the main formation, the Reds' infantry and gunners—they don't seem to have any cavalry—will be forced to share what they have with those support people. This will shorten the time before they all start going hungry. It will also, if you don't burn anything, increase our stockage of food and ammunition. Yes, I'll understand if you must burn it all, and I expect you to prepare to burn anything that can't be moved quickly, but I'd rather we get to shoot and eat everything available, as well as get the horses, sleighs, and carts.

"Oh, and Cherimisov?"

"Yes, sir?"

"Cut the telegraph line as you pass, but not in any way we can't fix easily."

"Yes, sir."

That they weren't spotted while moving Cherimisov attributed to the snow camouflage and the slight but important undulations in the ground, all greatly enhanced by the apparent lack of any real reconnaissance capability on the part of the Reds.

In any case, moving four or more times faster than Dratvin's foot, the Grenadiers covered the roughly seven miles to southwest of Kutarbitka in a little over an hour, which was nothing especially impressive for an athlete but by no means bad for a laden infantry company.

They were still out of sight of Kutarbitka, which was discernable only by virtue of the smoke rising from the chimneys of buildings abandoned when the Guards moved the people out, and now full of Reds trying to keep warm without working.

Cherimsov stopped, turned around, and made a signal with his hands for the company to get on line, First Platoon on the left, Second in the middle, and Third on the right, as they faced the town. The newly formed weapons platoon, which included the sniper teams, of which there were two, as well as the twelve-man engineer section, which ported two flamethrowers, and the Lewis Gun section, fell in behind Cherimisov.

He'd seen the town before, during the period of reconnaissance and set up, so he knew where he wanted the Lewis Guns to go. He called the section to him and, as he drew in the snow, gave his orders. "I want number one gun on the road that runs southwest to northeast, orienting its fire to the northeast, and I want number two gun on the road that runs northwest to southeast, fire orients to the northwest. Kostyshakov wants us to drive them all to the northeast, but there's too good a chance of some of them rallying in that part of the town, so listen carefully; nobody escapes across those roads. When we reach them, I'll toss a grenade into the crossroads. That's your signal to back off the roads into the area already cleared by us, and race to rejoin us at the crossroads. Don't shoot anyone wearing white camouflage like us. Understood?"

"Yes, sir . . . yessir."

"Good, move out."

"Snipers?"

"Here, sir," answered the best of them, Corporal Nomonkov, the short, stocky part Tatar with the best eyesight anyone in the brigade had even heard of.

"Cut northwest toward the Tobol River. Spread out. Prevent *anyone* from escaping to the north."

"Yes, sir. Both teams, sir?"

"Both, yes; I think it will take both. Let them escape to the northeast or east, though, if they seem to be heading that way."

"Yes, sir."

"Now, for the rest of you, kick off your skis and remember that the same rules apply as during the rescue of Her Majesty: no prisoners; no quarter. Platoon leaders, limit of advance, the far side of town. Now back to your men."

After a few minutes' wait to let the platoon leaders get back, Cherimisov gave the command, accompanied by his right arm rising and then cutting downward, "Forward!"

Konstantin Maksimovich Bortnik warmed his hands by placing them, palm to the front, near the fire-fed Russian stove in one of the houses in the northeastern part of the town. Yes, yes, he was supposed to be on guard, and, for the most part, he was. Surely this didn't prevent a man from taking a break and warming his hands and feet.

Glass was not unheard of, even for peasants, even in small towns in the hinterland. Bortnik's current house had three windows of six panes each facing to the southeast. He could almost perform his duties as guard from inside it, where it was warm. If the windows could have been opened he could have done more watching, of course, but this was Siberia where windows did not open and where fresh air was let into a house in the winter via the mechanism of pulling a plug from a round hole or pipe in the walls.

"And what's the point of guarding, anyway?" Konstantin muttered aloud. "It's not like I have a rifle or anything. Sure, sure; we were supposed to get rifles with a resupply. But that hasn't shown up and isn't likely to now."

The fixed windows shook with the blow of another salvo from the northeast.

"I'd best get outside anyway, I suppose."

Opening the door, Konstantin was hit by the expected wall of frigid air. Then his eyes were hit by something completely unexpected, the sight of half a dozen white-clad men, maybe eight or nine hundred *arshini* away, bearing some strange-looking firearm along with a number of rifles.

"Holy shit, those are not ours!"

The leader of First Platoon, *Feldfebel* Kostin, was actually the first man in the company to reach one of the houses. There was no smoke coming from the chimney—not that a big Russian stove gave off a lot of smoke—so he took a chance on it not being occupied. Instead of kicking it open and throwing in a grenade to smooth over awkward introductions, he kicked it open and burst in. Furiously he swept the muzzle of his MP-18 from left to right, holding his fire though for lack of targets.

"Chalk it," he said to the two nearest men outside the house. "Chalk it and leave the door open. As for the rest of you, who told you to fucking stop?"

From about four hundred *arshini* to the east, Kostin heard the first grenade explode, followed by the rattle of a machine pistol, both sounds full and loud in the dense, cold air.

Konstantin Bortnik stood frozen in the doorway. He was no fanatical Red; he was just a teamster who could keep his horses going and his cartwheels turning.

They didn't even give me a damned rifle, he thought, once again.

What got him moving was the sight of a half dozen or so of his colleagues of the field trains, reaching the road that ran roughly south, stepping out into it at a run and being cut down by the weapon—*A machine gun; it must be a machine gun, but so small and light?*—and left lying and bleeding out on the icy road.

Even then he stood frozen, as the shock of what he'd seen warred with the realization of what it meant. *They're killing everybody. No prisoners! Oh, God that the Reds tell me I'm not supposed to believe in, help me now!*

Instantly, leaving the door swinging behind him, Botkin bolted for the northeast, shrieking his lungs out, "Run! Run! Run for your lives!" His shrieking was loud enough and sincere enough to start a panic, with streams of Red support troops abandoning everything from horses and carts to their field kitchens and aid station.

There was little fighting and the only casualty—fortunately a non-fatal one—in the Grenadier Company was from a friendly fire incident arising from the confused clearing of a house. One private stood over another one, the stricken one, apologizing in a profuse stream.

At the far side of town the troops stopped, whereupon the platoon leaders turned matters over to their seconds and went looking for Cherimisov.

Kostin was the first to find his company chief. "Go secure that little hamlet up north, Khudyakova," Cherimisov ordered. "Take one of the Lewis Guns with you, the one on the left. Watch out for our snipers who may or may not have gotten into position."

"Yes, sir," said Kostin, saluting and trotting off to rejoin his platoon and round up his light machine gun.

Third platoon leader arrived next. The was Guards Senior Lieutenant Molchalin, doing double duty as company exec and Third Platoon leader. There was a promotion for Molchalin, the orders had been cut and signed, as soon as the unit grew enough for a second company. Taciturn as always, Molchalin said, "Area cleared, sir."

"That wood line, Lieutenant. Take the other Lewis gun. Orient your fire to the northeast."

"Yes, sir. Sir, we passed by the Reds' field kitchens on the way. There's a good deal of bread and soup there to pass out to the men."

"I'll have Mayevsky"—Mayevsky was the grenadier's first sergeant, for whom a promotion was also waiting—"see to it."

"Also, sir, the supply sergeant ought to do an inventory. There are a *lot* of horses and vehicles we passed by."

"Ordinarily, since you are the exec," said Cherimisov, "I'd tell you to worry about it. But platoon leading is more important at the moment. Mayevsky can handle this, too."

"Sir."

"Second Platoon Leader?" called Cherimisov.

"Here, sir," said *Feldfebel* Pasternak, the new platoon leader of the platoon formed from parts of the old First and Second Assault Platoons, with fill from the rest of the original force. "Lost one man, friendly fire. Don't really know how. He'll live but is out of the fight."

"We'll figure it out later, Pasternak. For now, I want . . ." Cherimisov pointed out the arc he wanted defended, north of the town.

"And now we wait for Dratvin's boys to catch up to us."

Degtyarevo

The blast of the guns was sufficiently unpleasant to Comrade Goloshchyokin that he'd retired to nearly half a *verst* behind the firing line and *still* felt the need to cup his hands over his ears. Thus, he didn't immediately hear the firing from the rear, in the vicinity of Kutarbitka and Khudyakova. Even the occasional blast of a grenade didn't quite reach through, possibly for the beating his hearing had already taken from Nikitin's first salvoes.

Thus it was that the first warning Goloshchyokin had of the disaster in his rear was the pell-mell flight of several hundred of his support troops from behind him, heading for the front. Indeed, the *very* first warning was Comrade Konstantin Bortnik. It was only after that one had passed that Goloshchyokin turned around to see the rest.

He may not have had military experience before about a month and a half prior, but the Red had enough experience of protesting crowds fleeing the Tsar's cavalry to know panic when he saw it. Goloshchyokin identified one particular man, even now veering slightly to his right to avoid smashing into him. Moving a few steps, the Red leader straight-armed the panic-stricken soldier, taking him across the throat and dropping him, choking and gagging, in his tracks.

Before the felled soldier could arise, the Red Commissar dropped to one knee, grabbing the collar and shaking the man like a rat in a terrier's mouth.

"What in the name of Ilyich is going on?" Goloshchyokin demanded. Getting no immediate answer he shook the man again, then released the collar and slapped him hard across the face several times.

"Next time I ask a question and don't get an answer I shoot you," said the Red, putting his hand to his pistol for emphasis.

"The . . . the . . . thousands of them . . . killing everybody . . . came out of nowhere."

"Thousands of *what*, you fool?"

"Imperialists! Imperialists, sir! We've got to get away. They've overrun the trains, the field kitchens, ammunition, food, and fodder. They've got everything. And there are THOUSANDS of them!"

Uh, oh.

Of course, Comrade Goloshchyokin was not a soldier. If he had been, he might well have studied Clausewitz. In that study, he might have come across the military pearl of wisdom: "Many intelligence reports in war are contradictory; even more are false, and most are uncertain."

Being an amateur, however, he took the report at face value. *There are,* he was instantly convinced, *thousands of Imperialists in my rear. Thousands of them. I should have expected treachery. Did that bastard Jew, Sverdlov, set me up? What must I do? What can I do? I know what I can't do; if I cannot break through the thousand or so I am told, I must stop the attack forward and set up a perimeter! Yes, that! And I must get control of whatever ammunition and food we have remaining. I'll search the men . . . have them searched, rather. Lifeboat rules, those are all that can save us. And I must get a message back. I must be relieved. Lenin must know how the Imperialists have grown, the new threat they present.*

Kutarbitka

Cherimisov could hardly believe it. He expressed his shock and amazement to the commander of the company from Dratvin's First Battalion of the reborn Semenovsky Regiment.

"I don't get it, Pavel," the grenadier commander said to the man leading his relieving company, Pavel Aminoff. "There aren't even two hundred of us here. We're not dug in. The enemy outnumbers us twenty to one and has artillery, to boot. Yet no counterattack. By now they could have turned around everyone attacking Lesh's Preobrazhenskys, if that was all they had, and reached us. But it isn't all they had. I should have been talking to you now while hiding in some peasant's basement. And yet here we stand, in the open and unmolested. It just doesn't make any sense."

Aminoff shrugged. "No matter, we've got a lot more firepower than you do; nine Lewis Guns, after all. We can hold."

"Good man," Cherimisov said. "And now, if you please, I'm going back to Dratvin to do our next job of the day."

Aminoff looked at the sun, now fairly far down in the west. "I doubt you can get there in time, Pyotr, despite the skis."

"Then we'll attack at night," said the grenadier. "It's not like we haven't done it before, and in worse circumstances."

Southeast of Ushakova

It was not long before nightfall when the truth dawned on Comrade Goloshchyokin. He'd spent the last few hours reorienting the troops to the northeast to a defense, the troops to the southwest, the same, and the artillery, with two companies of foot, to all-around defense in the center. At the moment, he was in the center, with the artillery.

"Comrade Goloshchyokin," asked Nikitin, the artilleryman, "How do we know that there were thousands of imperialists who overran the trains?"

"Because the ones fleeing told me so," answered Goloshchyokin.

"Indeed? How many did you ask?"

"Well...one," Goloshchyokin admitted, "but they were all running."

"I'm sure," said Nikitin, "I'm sure."

Both went silent then as Goloshchyokin went over the matter in his mind. At length, with what he knew was a death sentence if he couldn't fight his way out and to victory, the truth began to dawn.

"No," he said aloud, when reality finally hit him. "This is not possible. If there had been 'thousands' of imperialists overrunning our supplies and transportation, they'd have kept coming. They didn't so there couldn't have been nearly so many."

"No, there couldn't have been," agreed Nikitin. Not wanting to be shot or hanged for counterrevolutionary attitudes, the artilleryman added, "I am sure whoever told you this made for a creditable presentation. They always do."

The likely death sentence, as Samuel Johnson once observed death sentences tended to do, concentrated Goloshchyokin's mind "wonderfully."

"So what is there, do you think? A few hundred?"

"Might even be less. These were rear echelon types, not combat soldiers, and mostly unarmed, to boot. They could have been routed by a cattle stampede."

"What do I *do* then?"

Nikitin thought aloud, "I doubt they've had a chance to move more than a few of the wagons and sleighs. And if they'd burnt them we'd have seen smoke and fire. Also, while they may be in the buildings, the ground's too hard for them to have done much digging in. A strong counterattack in the morning might yet retrieve our fortunes. Get as close as we can with fixed bayonets and no chambered rounds and then assault at first light. Why don't you arrange a counterattack? With very little reorientation I can support with my guns from near here.

"You might also, comrade, start sending out patrols to find a way out of this treacherous imperialist trap."

"You say we're trapped?" asked Goloshchyokin, his voice heavy with suspicion.

"Not if we can find a way out," answered Nikitin. "Because we're not going to fight our way through the Maxims."

Chapter Six

Illustration from an early manual for the Model 1910
Water-cooled Heavy Machinegun

Outside the Amerikanskaya Hotel, Pokrovsky Prospect, Yekaterinburg

"So where do you intend, finally, to go?" asked Turgenev of the stout, now mufti-clad, female captain. The pair of them, Turgenev and Maria Bochkareva, plus Lavin, generally trailing slightly behind, walked the cold streets of the city, seeking out the Bolshevik headquarters, thought to be on 1905 Square.

"Tomsk," she replied. "That was my original plan. I am from there, have family there, and there I could have seen to the care of my sick troops."

"What changed your mind?" he asked. "You *have* changed your mind, yes?"

She shook her head, but not exactly with negation. "Only to the extent of wanting to keep as many of my girls together as possible for

103

what I expect to be some very bad times to come. I changed my mind," Bochkareva added, "when I heard that the imperial family had been rescued. That, so I thought, surely means civil war."

"You're a militarist," said Turgenev, feigning a sneer. "You want to be in on the civil war you predict will come?"

"Maybe," she admitted. "Maybe I would, if I knew what side to be on."

Turgenev grinned. "And what side would you be on if you could pick that side's political platform?"

"The side of democracy... though ... not if that idiot Kerensky were in charge of it. And that's even leaving aside that he wanted me shot."

"This is Russia," Turgenev said. "Democracy is probably not suited to us."

"Maybe not," Bochkareva admitted, "but we can get closer than either a tsarist or a Red autocrat."

"Funny you should say that..." The Guards Captain let the thought trail off. "Sometimes, you know, the proper thing is to pick the least-worst solution, over the most worst."

Now it was Bochkareva's turn to sneer. "Are you suggesting the Bolsheviks are the least worst?"

Turgenev answered this with a noncommittal shrug. Instead, he changed the subject to, "And how did you become a captain?"

"I don't know who made me one," she replied, "only that I was told of the promotion by General Valuyev."

"It's a low rank for a battalion commander," he observed.

"My battalion was only the size of one big or two little companies," she said. "And I wasn't really a trained officer, though I think I was a pretty good sergeant. I know hardly anything about machine guns or artillery, for example, and have only a woman's natural grasp of logistics. But those things can be found in others, while Russia's army needed what I was really good at, strict discipline."

She changed the subject abruptly. "You ask a lot of questions, Maxim Sergeyevich. I have answered yours, so answer one of mine. Why in the name of all the saints are you even *here*?"

I have gotten too used to lying to accomplish my mission, thought Turgenev, *but then, what's one more lie... or one more shading of the truth?*

"My superiors are concerned for the safety of the Abbess of the

Convent of Saints Martha and Mary, and wish me to ensure her safety, especially as the Reds of this town are unusually extremist in their views."

"Funny you should say that," she said, "for my girls and I saw her just last night..."

"Where?" Turgenev demanded, stopping progress, spinning the stout woman to face him, and grabbing her by both arms.

"She was...she and about a dozen others were in carts, moving north from a stockaded house south of the train station. I don't know the name of the house nor its address, but it was at the intersection of Voznesenski Prospect and Voznesenski Lane. You really can't miss it; there's a not-quite-complete stockade around it."

"Come on, this way" he ordered, changing direction.

"Where are we going?"

"To the intersection of Voznesenski Prospect and Voznesenski Lane."

"But the abbess isn't there, I told you."

"I know, but the men there will know where she was taken. Come on!"

The remaining guards on the Ipatiev House hadn't said a useful word. All they'd admitted to was that the prisoners were "Gone, comrade. Spirited off in the middle of the night."

Currently all of Strat Recon, except those with the wagon and sleigh train northwest of town, and one on guard outside the door, were crowded into Turgenev's room in the hotel. With them was Maria Bochkareva. They'd been discussing matters for a half an hour, at this point, and the general tone of the discussion led Bochkareva to an unavoidable truth.

"You're no Bolshevik!" Bochkareva accused. "I don't know what you are but a Bolshevik you most certainly are *not!*"

"Shshshsh," said Turgenev. "What I am and what I am not is not germane to the discussion at hand, which is finding out where the Grand Duchess and the others were taken."

"It *does* matter," the woman insisted. "You brought me here to enlist my aid in something. Whether I help you, whether you get that something, depends on what you are."

The leader of Strat Recon blew air through his lips, sighed, and decided. He answered, "I am Guards Captain Maxim Sergeyevich Turgenev, and my mission is to rescue Grand Duchess Elizabeth Feodorovna from captivity.

"As to what I want from you...I could attack the house with the stockade and take the remaining guards prisoner. But that might be noisy and might therefore alert the remaining Bolsheviks in the city. I think, if you could send one or two of your more seductive women..."

"Get that right out of your mind," she said, eyes flashing indignantly. "My girls are all good girls. A fair percentage of them were aristocrats and royalty, too, like my Adjutant, Princess Tatuyeva... Well, there was that *one girl,* but she isn't with us anymore."

"I'm not saying they must sleep with anyone," Turgenev said. "Maybe they could just chat up the guards, take them to lunch when they get off duty. I can always attack if I must, and take the risk. But I'd really rather not."

"Do you have a couple of very friendly and pretty women?" asked Mokrenko. "They needn't do anything immoral, but if they could pretend they would and lead a couple of guards down a dark street or alley, we can handle the rest."

"I doubt any of my girls could convince anyone of any such thing."

Mokrenko tilted his head quizzically and asked, "Do you have a couple of pretty ones who are also smart?"

Turgenev shot an inquiring glance at his sergeant.

"Sir," replied Mokrenko, "in an industrial town like this, finding a whore to teach them the ropes should be no problem at all. But I'll need a couple of ten-ruble pieces. And we'll need a safe house after all, someplace soundproof to cover up the inevitable screaming."

Bochkareva looked from man to man to man, taking the measure of all the men in the room. *These are real soldiers,* she thought. *The kind of soldiers I haven't seen since maybe a year after the war began. Admit it, too, Maria, that if Turgenev lied to you about what he was, you lied to him, equally, about the side you were on... would be on. You don't really care about the form of government, do you? Oh, noooo, don't lie, especially to yourself. You care about the form of army you're in.*

"I used to work in a brothel...no, get that disbelieving look off your faces, you swine!" Bochkareva laughed and shook her head, ruefully. "Look at me; even when young I was no prize. Why, two years ago, when I was in the hospital for frostbite, we put on some amateur theatrical play;

they had to use a young male officer to play the girl's part. Why? Why because *he* was prettier and more feminine than *me*. No one was going to pay good money to screw me. I just kept house for the madam. Well, yes, okay, and was an occasional bouncer. But I watched the working girls. *I* can teach a couple of my girls how to act. That's *if* any of them will volunteer, because this is a mission for volunteers."

"Why makes you sign on so readily?" Mokrenko asked.

With a deep sigh, Bochkareva answered, "Because first and foremost, Lieutenant, I am a soldier. That's all I am and all I want to be. My girls are the only family I want. Speaking of which, the quarters I found for my girls will do for your safe house. As you say, there will be a lot of screaming to cover up, yes? Well, my girls are out of singing practice. Remedying that should help.

"I think I'll need a couple of your men, Maxim Sergeyevich, to test my candidates against. But then what? What are your ambitions, Guards Captain Turgenev?"

Bochkareva's Barn, Yekaterinburg

Though large, the place wasn't really a barn. Rather it was a two-story log cabin, with a basement, and something on the order of five thousand square feet, not counting the basement. It was warm, toasty warm, had a few windows for light, and even a number of beds for the sicker among the women. For the rest, a good deal of hay had been found in an actual barn on the property.

Mokrenko and Timashuk were there, while Shukhov, the engineer, was off collecting one of the sleighs and one of the Yakut horses.

All of Bochkareva's women, even the sick girls, had volunteered. By this point in time, too, they all had their hair back. She selected by having each of them walk past Mokrenko and Timashuk, the medic, in as seductive a manner as possible. Most had failed, and failed *miserably*.

Only two seemed shapely enough, pretty enough, and—the real discriminator—brazen enough for the job, Anna Petrova and Lada Kusmina. The former, tall, blonde, and naturally slender, had a little amateur theatrical experience, while the latter, shorter and darker, and with the most impressive breasts, just seemed to have the instincts for the job at hand.

When Bochkareva asked her about it, though, Lada answered, shame-faced and staring at the floor, "After we split up, I decided to stay with the sick ones. To nurse them as best I could. We had no money so..."

Bochkareva was shocked speechless. Everyone present and within earshot was.

Ah, good, thought Mokrenko, pragmatic as always; *we won't have to find a local whore to teach the rules of the game.*

It was Timashuk who offered, "Whatever you had to do, to save another human being, and especially a comrade in arms, and whatever"—here he looked directly at Bochkareva—"anyone might say about it, it was a holy act, insofar as you did it for others."

"Thank you," Lada whispered.

"Yes, thank you," Bochkareva echoed. *Well, he only spoke the truth, a truth I was a bit blind to.*

"Okay," said Bochkareva, "the rest of you are dismissed for the evening. Don't forget your prayers. Lada and Anna, we're going to work with these two men until we have everything properly planned out and rehearsed."

"I'll need to make a few modifications to the house, too," said Mokrenko.

Ipatiev House, Voznesenski Prospect, Yekaterinburg

"Ten rubles," said the guard, "it's all I have."

"Ordinarily, love," said Lada, the vastly more experienced of the two women, "I'd take you up on that, even eagerly. But this is Yekaterinburg, in the winter, and there's little or nothing to buy. And what about my friend, here?"

"I have a friend... but he won't have anything I don't..."

"Surely there's a kitchen in that fine old mansion," Lada said. "Find two large sacks and fill them with bread and meat and butter and cheese. Add in some cabbage and potatoes. We'll show you a very good time for that, and cook you a good meal, too."

"I'm still on duty," said the guard. "but... I'll be off in three quarters of an hour. Can you wait?"

"Can you get the food?"

"Yes."

"Then," agreed Lada, "we'll walk around the block a few times. We'll be back in... well, it will take you some time to fill the sack... let's say in one hour?"

"One hour works," agreed the guard. "And, God knows, I use a good screw right about now . . . as well as a good meal."

Timashuk, being the most harmless looking of the three, had the reins of the sleigh.

"Wish to fuck they'd hurry," complained Shukhov, shivering with a large piece of canvas wrapped around his shoulders. The fact that his boots were off made it all the worse, despite his feet being wrapped in cloth.

"These things, I suppose, take some time," said Mokrenko patiently, without turning around. Instead, Mokrenko lay on his belly, slowly freezing solid, with the top of his head just barely around the corner of a building, at ground level. "Though, yes, it's been a while. I wonder if . . . aha, never mind, here they come."

With that, Mokrenko slid back, then stood, stiffly, and hurried to the sleigh. He slipped his hand through a loop in a short piece of rope then checked to ensure that Lavin had done the same.

"Cover us up, Timashuk," the Cossack ordered, while taking his boots off, "then turn the corner toward the girls."

Covering the men and taking control of the reins had been rehearsed several times. Both acts took Timashuk considerably less than a minute. Then the medic gave a flick to the reins to get the horse going before pulling on one rein to turn the sleigh to the right.

The two couples, two Red Guards plus Anna and Lada, swayed together down the street, making suggestive small talk and giggling with mutual arms around waists. As rehearsed, both girls leaned heavily onto their presumed customers as the sleigh pulled by the little horse clattered down the street.

Once the sleigh was past, the driver pulled on a single cord. The cord split somewhere under the concealing canvas, leading to grasping hands, to tell both men riding hidden that it was time to come out.

Silently, Mokrenko and Shukhov flipped off the canvas and rolled out onto the street. Each man had an Amerikanski pistol stuck in his belt and a sheathed dagger hanging from the same. But the weapon of choice for tonight's festivities for each was a cosh, a long sock, purchased on the civilian market, filled with sand and gold coins, and double tied below the filling.

They should feel privileged, thought Mokrenko, padding up on half frozen unshod feet. Up came the cosh. Another two steps and Mokrenko reached out to yank his target's *ushanka* off of his head. Then down it came, fast, striking the Red's skull, dropping him almost silently to the ground.

To Mokrenko's left, Shukhov had been as successful.

"Fine work, girls," Mokrenko congratulated. "Now take the legs of your would-be clientele and let's get them loaded into the sleigh."

With the Reds loaded, face down, Mokrenko and Shukhov bound their hands behind their backs and then their legs at the ankles. The prisoners' mouths were stuffed with bunched cloth and tightly gagged. They were then covered with the canvas. Lada took a seat next to Timashuk, while Shukhov sat atop the two silent bodies, cosh in hand and ready for reapplication as needed.

"Off with you, then," Mokrenko said, pulling on boots. "I'll walk with Anna to confuse matters and meet you at the girls' quarters in about twenty minutes."

Bochkareva's Barn, Yekaterinburg

"Gentlemen," said Mokrenko to the two bound and gagged prisoners, "we are going to play a little game together. Now, before we begin to play, I want you to understand a couple of things. One is that the irons are already being heated; indeed, they are red hot by now."

The lieutenant's eyes twinkled as he smiled broadly. The smile, more than anything else, terrified the two prisoners.

"Another is that the flaying knives are sharpened. A third is that down in the basement, where you will be brought in a minute, are ropes tossed over beams to haul you up by your wrists, which, you may have noticed, are behind you. You know that really *stings.* I have hammers for your toes, fingers, kneecaps, wrists, and elbows."

He paced a bit in the space between the two prisoners, before continuing, "Those, however, along with your bodies, are the pieces of the game. The game itself is called 'information.' I win—and so do you—if I get all the information that I want. I lose—*and so do you*—if I don't get it.

"The way the game is played is that you two will be separated into rooms where you cannot hear each other. I will ask each of you the same question. If I get answers that match, we move on to the next question. If I don't—and this is the really *sad* part—I inflict a great deal of pain upon you both until the answers match.

"Now think about that before you try to make up a lie; your comrade isn't going to know the lie and so cannot match it. Therefore you will both suffer until the one of you who's lying realizes the pain will never end until he tells the truth. Oh, and the one who *is* telling the truth; stick to it. If you start to lie too then the pain will not end. That would be how *everyone* loses, and we don't want that, now, do we?"

Nodding at Shukhov and Timashuk, Mokrenko said, "Move them to the rooms that have been prepared." To Bochkareva he suggested, "Captain, I think you should begin choir practice in about five minutes."

While the women upstairs could be heard doing a very heartfelt rendition of *Ahk Vy Seni, Moi Seni,* both prisoners were sobbing, separately but about equally. Mokrenko muttered, "Alapaevsk? The school in Alapaevsk? I suppose it makes a certain sense."

"What about this one?" Shukhov asked, pointing with his chin at the bound, sobbing, trembling ruin of a man, broken toed, somewhat burnt of skin, hanging by his wrists with his feet above the dirt floor, the rope running behind him and over a beam. The man lacked the strength and will anymore even to have his feet flail for purchase on the ground below. Some quantity of fecal matter ran down the prisoner's foot and dripped off his toes.

"Put him out of his misery?" Mokrenko said. "No, I offered a chance to live if he cooperated. Besides, Timashuk's a gentle soul." Noticing Shukhov's doubtful grimace, Mokrenko added, "You're wondering why I am reluctant after seeing my conduct on the train, yes?"

On the TransSiberian Railway, Mokrenko had once held a man's face to a red-hot iron stove to extract information, then killed his victim without pity.

"You didn't show the slightest reluctance or mercy then, Sergeant."

The lieutenant shrugged. "There's a difference, Shukhov, between what you feel you can do when your blood is up, with bandits who had tried to rape a young girl, when you owe your life to that young girl, and . . . well . . . soldiers not a lot different from ourselves, really, not at core.

"So help me get the rope and we'll lower this one gently. Then let's see if Bochkareva or her girls have some vodka for their pain."

Amerikanskaya Hotel, Yekaterinburg

"Worse and worse," said Turgenev at the news. The news? Sarnof, hanging around the telegraph office as if in search of a job, heard a telegram come in telling of another eight hundred Reds coming to Yekaterinburg to fill in, partially, for the ones gone to Tobolsk.

"What do we do?" asked Bochkareva.

"I'm not sure. Eight hundred Bolsheviks hunting for us as we try to spirit away nearly a dozen royals is about seven hundred and ninety more than I want to deal with. And it's still almost the dead of winter, we can't survive out there indefinitely."

"What if . . . ?" The woman hesitated.

"What if what?"

Making a sudden decision, she asked, "What if we could keep them on the other side of the river from the town? It's not as if my girls have any reason to love the Bolsheviks after what was done to them."

"A hundred of you? Against eight hundred Reds? I don't think so."

Mokrenko asked, "But what if we can change the odds?"

"What do you mean, ser . . . lieutenant?"

"The captain's women are not the only ones with no reason to love the Reds. We've got a couple of dozen more men, plus whoever in the town can be recruited . . . lots of rifles and two heavy machine guns. Those, plus whatever can be captured."

"We don't know how to use machine guns," said Bochkareva.

"So we leave a couple of men here who do," said Mokrenko.

"Who?"

"Me . . . and . . . mmm . . . Novarikasha, I think. We can drill an adequate if not great couple of crews in a few days."

"How much time do we have?" Turgenev asked of Sarnof.

"Four or five days, sir. Or maybe a little less, to be on the safe side."

"How many Reds went with the royals?" he asked of Mokrenko.

"The Reds we interrogated said eight guards went with them plus their commander, Startsev and his assistant, Ryabov."

Turgenev had gotten a good deal more decisive since he and Mokrenko had first met. "That means I go on the rescue, because I've a better chance of bluffing the Reds with Startsev. *That* means that you and Novarikasha stay here to aid Captain Bochkareva. You'll need one man to oversee the teamsters, either *Bulavin or Gazenko...*"

"Bulavin, sir," said Mokrenko, "though Gazenko's a competent medic and probably ought to stay here with Captain Bochkareva. Some of her women are still sick, after all."

"And you, but not on a machine gun. Oh, wait—silly of me to forget. You're a *Guards* Lieutenant now; Rostislav Alexandrovich. That makes you rather senior."

Mokrenko said nothing since he was pretty sure he could do the forthcoming job better than the woman. *No shame to her; I've just had more time in, more training, and more experience.*

"Then... Lavin can use a machine gun. He's not a fully trained gunner but I know he's had to take the place of a trained gunner a couple of times."

"Captain Bochkareva?"

"Sir?"

"Do you have any problem taking orders from Guards Lieutenant Mokrenko? He does outrank you."

"None, sir."

"Good. Now let's start planning to take over the city, tonight. I'll leave in the morning for Alapaevsk. Mokrenko, send someone to the teamsters to bring in them and the weapons. No, on second thought, it has to be you in order to enlist them and take their oath."

Got to love having a decisive superior officer, thought the Cossack.

"Also, before you go, send someone to round up the American consul and the banker, Maynard, as well as that miner, Curran." Turgenev reached into a pocket. "Here's his address."

"Why the banker and miner, sir?" queried Mokrenko.

"Because right after we polish off the Reds, I want to get our hands on that gold, silver, and platinum for Her Majesty's war chest. And they know where it all is."

Ipatiev House, Voznesenski Prospect, Yekaterinburg

There were a number of targets. Not all of these had to be hit in the initial strikes; some could be picked up later. The banks fell into the latter category, as Jay Maynard explained: "There are no Bolsheviks guarding the precious metal, just the civilian guards that were there before."

"The miners," added Curran, "are the most Bolshie men in town.

But they're not armed, and the precious metal will wait there until someone digs it out."

Of the targets that mattered, there would have been two popular bars, if they were not closed, while there were three well-staffed brothels that *never* closed. Both of the latter classes having been revealed and confirmed by the kidnapped Reds, who still wallowed in misery in the basement of the house. There was also one central barracks, mostly empty, the Bolshevik headquarters on 1905 Square, the main train station, which included the telegraph, and the stockaded Ipatiev House. Also, two two-man teams were dispatched to sever the phone and telegraph lines leading out of town.

Bochkareva drew the Ipatiev House. For the task she kept twenty of her women, rifles loaded, but with filled magazines only; no rounds in the chambers, and bayonets fixed. These double-timed up Voznesenski Prospect until splitting up just before reaching the stockade. Ten of them raced for the rear of the house, on the side facing the river, where the fence was not nearly complete yet, while ten and Bochkareva, herself, went for the guards on the gate.

The shocked and surprised guards on the gate didn't get a shot off before finding themselves pinned to the log wall by three or four bayonets each. These were of the old-fashioned sort, spike bayonets, basically. The girls had to stab several times each to make sure the men were quite dead. Blood welled around the impaling spikes, but these were hardened women, who had already seen something of war. None of them wilted at a little spurting crimson.

The guards being dispatched, Captain Bochkareva and nine of her women stormed through the gate with the former in the lead.

There *was* one woman left behind, not as rear security, as one might expect, but because she'd driven her bayonet so hard into the Red's body that the damned thing was stuck into the rough, unsawn wood behind it. When the other ten charged, she was still struggling to get it out, to the extent of lifting herself up by the stock of her rifle to plant both booted feet on the Red's upright corpse. Cursing communists and bayonets with equal fervor, she pushed and pulled and twisted. And the thing *still* refused to budge. Finally, in disgust, she left her own rifle where it was and took up the dead Red's weapon. She emptied the chamber while holding the next round down with her thumb to close the bolt, and then ran after her sisters.

At the door, Bochkareva threw her own not inconsiderable bulk against it. It wasn't quite enough to break the wooden crossbeam that held the thing shut, no, but it was enough force to half break it and splinter the wood. Another foray and the door sprung open.

Into the upper floor of the house drove Bochkareva and her girls. Down below, in the basement, she could hear cries of shock as the dozen or so men still down there were awakened to gleaming, spiked bayonets and rifle butts.

In not even a full minute from the first bayonet thrust the house was secured.

There were no prisoners.

"Come on, girls!" exclaimed Bochkareva. "We've got a hot date at 1905 Square!"

Elsewhere in the city, three groups of a dozen women, each reinforced by one of Turgenev's men, stormed each of the three bordellos on the list. Oh, the shock, oh, the embarrassment, as Reds and innocent—for certain values of innocent—customers alike were hounded out into the street at bayonet point, huffing and cursing all the while, carrying their clothes and their tattered dignity before being searched and allowed to dress...in the street. Any that were left, hiding, two of the girls and their attached man from Strat Recon went through to club and bayonet to death. No shots had been fired, to date.

The remaining women, now freed up, began to trot to 1905 Square to join their captain in a siege.

Main Train Station, Yekaterinburg

The teamsters, led by Bulavin and Gazenko, drew the train station. It turned out to be not much of an event. They charged in and burst through the main door, to find the dozen or so Reds present being caught at breakfast and largely disarmed. Teams of four and five fanned out to make sure the station was clear, and especially to grab the telegraph, but found no one who wasn't already at breakfast. Even the telegraph was, oddly, unmanned.

Leaving a small garrison under Gazenko, Bulavin began marching the rest, under threat of bayonet, toward the designated POW collection point, which was the basement of Bochkareva's Barn, now cleaned of blood.

✛ ✛ ✛

Main Bolshevik Barracks, Yekaterinburg

No one was quite sure how many Reds were in the main barracks. Estimates ranged from a low of fifty to a high of two hundred fifty. One thing could be ascertained, however; this was that no more than four were on exterior guard at any one time.

The building itself, generally northeast of the center of town, was of about three thousand square feet on a floor, and of two floors, plus a basement. It was this size that made the high-end estimates of the troops billeted there at least plausible.

The building was oblong, with the short walls having relatively few windows and no doors, while the longer walls—front and rear, basically—had many windows and two doors each. One each of the heavy machine guns, therefore, was hauled into place at opposite corners, set back into the streets, with wagons pulled up to provide a modicum of cover. The machine guns' fires were oriented to prevent escape out those windows and doors by anyone fleeing to and through the open areas to the front and rear.

There was no call to surrender. Instead, some of the men and women took up positions facing the front and rear and, at a preset time, opened fire to kill the guards shivering outside of the doors or, at least, drive them back inside.

At the sound of the opening of fire, Mokrenko, at one corner, and Novarikasha, at the other, each supported by one other man, respectively Peredery and Shukhov, the engineers, bounded up before pressing themselves against the blank walls. Each also carried about four *vedro*, or roughly six and a half gallons, of kerosene. Their backups had, each of them, a sledgehammer, matches, a couple of kerosene-soaked rags, one container of two *vedro*, and a section of hose.

Looking around the corner to make sure the coast was clear, Mokrenko calmly walked the few *arshini* to the nearest basement window, put down his heavy buckets of kerosene, and pointed at his backup's slung sledgehammer. A quick strike and the basement window shattered inward. Then it was toss the open-topped buckets in, one after the other. When he was done, his supporting man did likewise.

Then it was strike a match, torch off a couple of kerosene-soaked rags, and toss them inside. *Foooshshshsh!*

"Come on," said Mokrenko to his backup, "let's get out of here and back to the Maxim!"

Build a man a fire, thought Mokrenko, as he and Peredery trotted for cover, *and keep him warm for a night. Set a man on fire and keep him warm for the rest of his life.*

The heavy machine gun wasn't far away. Novarikasha and Shukhov had plenty of time to settle in and become bored before the Bolsheviks began pouring out of the building on the side they covered, half dressed, half armed . . .

But utterly screwed, the Cossack thought, as he opened fire and began slapping his machine gun with his left hand and then right to sweep back and forth across the open space. In his view, Bolsheviks went down by rows. A few tried raising their arms in surrender but, in this context, a Maxim became practically an area fire weapon and lost the ability to distinguish. Even with that, many of the Reds decided that bullet was a better way to go than flame; by fours, fives, and sixes they bolted out, only to be cut down on the reddening snow.

Soon enough, there was fire blazing from every window and no more Bolsheviks trying to flee.

1905 Square, Yekaterinburg

Forty women under Princess Tatuyeva had taken positions around the Bolshevik headquarters on 1905 square. Their signal for opening fire was simply: "When you hear shooting, commence firing yourselves."

The return fire was brisk but, on the whole, the women were better trained than the men inside the building. Moreover, they were continually reinforced by Strat Recon, with the heavy machine guns and Lewis Gun, the teamsters, such as were not guarding the rail station, and several score more women from their own battalion.

As the volume of fire coming in began to beat down the resistance, little white flags likewise began showing at the windows and doors. "Quarter?" came the cry. "We ask for quarter."

Turgenev started to walk forward but was stopped by Mokrenko.

"I'm more expendable than you are," said the latter. "I also bluff better." With this, Turgenev couldn't argue.

"Moreover, sir, you need to make sure the narrow-gauge train you ordered prepared is ready."

"Can't argue with that, either, Ser . . . Rostislav Alexandrovich. Even so, even accepting all you've said, get the surrenders started; I'll leave after that."

"Yes, sir."

Mokrenko then walked right out into the open space. "There are nine hundred soldiers surrounding this place," he claimed. "Right now they're under control. But if you shoot me, there will be no holding them back. You will all be killed. Probably in some lingering and disgusting fashion.

"If you want to save your lives, you must subdue anyone who still wants to fight, then come out with your weapons held over your heads. Drop them to the side as soon as you exit the door and then walk toward me.

"You will be well treated."

Turgenev, freed of the need to even suggest he was a Red, was busy pumping the three Americans for information.

"No, Captain," said Maynard, "there's no rail to Alapaevsk. There's a rail line, to Nizhny Tagil, but that only gets you a little bit closer. It's not enough difference to even be worth the effort."

Turgenev indulged himself with a very rare, "Shit! It will take three or four days to get there on horseback and I don't know that we have that much time. Honestly, I don't even know that we have any time at all, but I have to assume . . ."

"There are automobiles and trucks," Maynard suggested. "I have an automobile. The consulate—"

"No," Palmer interrupted, "until the U.S. government recognizes what's going on in Russia, the consulate's hands are tied. We can neither side with the Bolsheviks nor with the Royals. Well, not in any way that can be officially tied to the United States."

"No matter," said Curran. "This is an industrial town; there's no shortage of drivers and trucks, and the gasoline stocks are still ample."

"Mr. Maynard," asked Turgenev, "You know the town and the people. Could I prevail on you to . . ."

"Do you want to bring your horses?" Maynard asked.

"If at all possible."

"Give me . . . oh, call it four hours for Seamus and myself to round everything up."

"Thank you!"

"No sweat," Curran assured him. "Wouldn't do to try to walk there, after all."

"And can you spare us a rifle each?" asked Maynard. "Never know if we might need one."

Interlude

Saint Petersburg, Russia

Maxim Ippolitovich Ganfman, walking this brisk late winter morning to his law office, was a very worried man.

Rumors flew constantly. Who could know what was really happening? Even Max couldn't, and he was a lawyer by training, as well as a man of vast intelligence. Indeed, he sat on the board of the prestigious Saint Petersburg magazine, *Pravo*. He had a flair for literary and newspaper editorial work.

The rumors? Oh, that the royal family was dead, on the one hand, that they were alive, on the other, or that they were some of them dead and others alive.

Me? thought Maxim, *What do I think? I think some are alive and others dead. I also think that the Reds' reaction is a lot more consistent with that than with anything else. Why else dispatch a column to a solidly Red city like Yekaterinburg unless they had reason to worry about it? Indeed, why crack down on us here, in barely less red Saint Petersburg, except that the Reds are running very scared, indeed.*

Max stopped at a street stand to try to pick up a copy of one of the local newspapers. Unfortunately, all the real papers were gone—and he didn't think they'd been sold out—so the only one available for purchase was the Saint Petersburg edition of *Pravda*. He picked up today's edition with an audible sigh, a sigh of longing for better days, either in the past or still to come.

And Pravda, of course, means "Truth," thought Max, putting his folded copy under his arm. *And, indeed, you can find the truth there . . . provided you assume every word printed in it is a lie, then the real truth, the opposite of what Truth claims, will stand revealed.*

With no other sign beyond that perhaps ill-advised sigh, Maxim continued on his way to work.

Here in Saint Petersburg was far beyond the Pale of Settlement, the area first decreed by Catherine the Great, and since modified from time to time by her successors, where Jews were allowed to live. This didn't affect Maxim; he was a convert to Orthodoxy. As with many or even most converts, Maxim deeply loved his church and its faith.

He didn't need any conversion, though, to be Russian. He'd always loved Russia, to include even the Empire, could it have been reformed, along with the Russian language and the Russian people. Thus, his devotion to Russia's laws, and to his editorial work in the Russian language.

He also loved the truth, even when he had to gain it by reference to the lies.

Entering the warm, tiled hallway from the windy and cold street, Maxim walked the single flight of stairs to his office. There, taking his chair and putting his feet on his desk, he began to read today's "Truth."

He read the whole paper, end to end, and, when he was finished, said softly, "We are in serious trouble. I've got to get Ekaterina and our children out of here. Trouble? What a gift for understatement I have! No, don't fool yourself, Maxim; Russia is going to have a civil war.

"But where can I take them? No place inside of the rump of the Russian Empire left by the Germans will be safe. Finland is already showing signs of breaking out in civil war. Germany? The next time I'll trust the Huns will be the first.

"Go back to the United States with Ekaterina? She knows the place, after all. But, no, too far from my own country, which is this one, and my own people, who are also these. From someplace closer, like the new Baltic states, I could hope someday to visit.

"Tallinn? Vilnius? Kiev? Maybe Kiev. I wonder if Milyukov is still planning to start a newspaper there? I could do that. And Ukraine is not so very far after all. Maybe Kiev."

Maxim's wife, Ekaterina, was Orthodox, which probably had a good deal to do with his claiming to be Orthodox in University. As to whether he'd ever been baptized, the Russian Orthodox church thought he had, but his family was not so sure. This may have been a bone of contention between Max and Ekaterina.

In any case, she was waiting for him at home, cooking dinner, with her daughter, Eugenia, in attendance. Cooking was not a skill Ekaterina's upper class background had imparted to her; she was still learning the techniques, one culinary faux pas at a time. Max had promised her a servant when it became possible again She remained skeptical.

The girl ran to her father as soon as she recognized his footsteps. Her mother called out a "Welcome home," but was otherwise too employed.

Maxim entered the kitchen and said, "Mother, I've been thinking."

"A dangerous pastime," she replied, while stirring a bright copper pot.

"I know," Maxim agreed. "But it's important. After dinner, you and I need to sit down and discuss getting away from the Reds."

"I don't want to return to New York," she insisted. "It's warmer than here but a colder place all the same."

"No, no; I agree. Kiev?"

"Maybe Kiev."

Chapter Seven

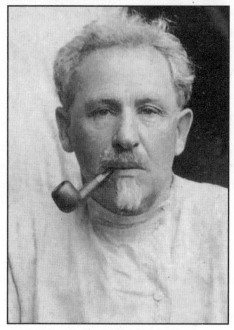

Comrade Goloshchyokin

Southeast of Ushakova

If they had a competent commander, thought Kostyshakov, *they'd go through us like crap through a Christmas goose. Or maybe he is competent, but being held in check by someone who is not. It's not like we've never seen that before, during the war. Or maybe we're just that good... nah, we're—three quarters of us, anyway—hastily trained militia with a sprinkling of semi-trained conscripts.*

I confess, if only to myself, it worries me. Eventually, given time, they're going to figure out how light is the net we've cast around them. Then there'll be Hell to pay. Unless, of course, we can drive them in closer and make the net a good deal tighter and heavier.

In fact, the Guards Brigade had only three adequately held sectors.

The strongest was the one to the northeast, in the vicinity of Toboltura, which was held now by two heavy machine guns and two thirds of Lesh's battalion. Lesh's other company was strung out—*thinly* strung out—along the northwest side of the Tobol River, in little patrols who could not have hoped to prevent a breakout but who could, and so far had, prevented the Reds from discovering there was a way to break out.

They had two chances at this: one was finding and engaging a Red patrol on the way out. The other was finding and engaging it on the way back in.

There was another one to the southwest, held now by a single company of Dratvin's battalion. That company was depleted, since beating off two Red attempts to retake their trains, and then having to launch a vicious and bloody counterattack to retake Khudyakova. It mustered perhaps eighty-five still healthy men, though it retained a good complement of Lewis Guns and a preposterous amount of ammunition, courtesy of the Reds' carts and sleighs.

Southeast of the Red sausage, in a line running from Kutarbitka almost to Kostyshakov, and then from just past him to Toboltura, four of Dratvin's remaining six platoons did the same thing the people on the other side of the river were doing: preventing Red patrols from finding a way out.

Only in the center did Kostyshakov have a maneuvering force, this consisting of Cherimisov's company of Grenadier Guards, two platoons under Dratvin, the 37mm gun section, the mortar section, and a section of two heavy machine guns.

Under three hundred men; it wasn't a lot to try to split a brigade in two, then hold the pieces apart, and that at the place where that Red Brigade's firepower was greatest, right at the battery position of their four pieces of artillery.

But the mortars, thought Kostyshakov. *Tatiana, who saw it, told me they put out a surprisingly powerful blast . . . if they can get close enough.*

The grenadier company, borne on their skis, had passed perhaps an hour and a half before. The moon was down and would not rise for another three hours. That was three hours to get those three hundred men into position before there was enough light to attack by.

Though, at least, it will be a pretty bright moon, thought Private Romanova, sometimes called "Your Imperial Majesty." Bright enough to see the enemy by and, as important, to see each other, despite the white camouflage.

There was one carbide-fueled light Tatiana could make out clearly, though. Backed up as it was by snow between it and the enemy, and turned down as was the feed of water to the carbide, she thought it unlikely anyone on the other side could see it. To left and right, too, were others, but giving even fainter light. She hoped no one who wasn't supposed to be able to could see those, either.

Tatiana had been assigned to drive the ammunition sleigh for the two mortars. It was a larger than normal sleigh, pulled by two sturdy Yakut horses. Waiting and bored, the horses hooved the snow in front of them to get at the still-green grass beneath.

There were actually two sleighs of ammunition. One load of one hundred twenty rounds was here, being driven by Tatiana. Another one hundred twenty were in the field trains with Romeyko. The remainder, some forty-four rounds, in total, was on the backs of the men of the mortar section, along with their disassembled mortars, and their own personal gear. It was a prodigious load for each.

It was also a noisy load, even leaving aside the grumbling of the men. There was just a lot of metal there to clang against other metal. Tatiana doubted, what with the still, cold and dense air, that they'd get within what the manual had called "effective range" before being heard.

Lost in her thoughts, Tatiana didn't hear the approach of Panfil, the mortars' chief.

"Your Majesty?"

She recovered quickly. "Please, Leonid, for now it is only 'Private Romanova.'"

"In a few hours," he said, "it's our big day, our premier performance. I'd be a lot happier if you would give this one a miss and go back to Tobolsk or, at least, to the field trains."

"So would I," she said, "but I can't. Funny, though; if I'm too afraid to go back, I'm also pretty afraid of the coming day."

Panfil made a sort of brushing gesture. "Well," he said, "as to that,I can tell you from my own experience and what I've seen from hundreds of others over the course of the war; you're really afraid that you won't prove up to it. You're afraid of being too afraid to perform."

He shook his head as a light, humorous tone entered his voice.

"Don't worry about it. Least likely thing to happen because you're going to be too *busy* to be afraid."

"Is that the truth?" she asked.

"Gospel . . . well, Torah truth, Private Romanova."

"Oddly, you know, that *does* make me feel better."

"Sound theology," Panfil joked, "has a way of doing that."

Tatiana smiled then, saying, "Thank you, Leonid."

At that time, a ski-borne messenger from Cherimisov came up. "Sergeant Panfil?"

"That would be me."

"We've cleared to within about nine hundred *arshini* of the last spot we know the Red artillery was seen. I'm here to guide you forward to a position the commander found. It's not a great one, but the best we could find for you."

"Lead on."

The mortar section was demonstrably *not* borne on skis. Thus, they were actually quite slow, struggling through the snow under their weighty packs.

Panfil noticed a slight rise, then asked his guard, "How much further?"

"See the lights ahead?" asked the guide. "They used to look like just one to you, yes? Well, when you can see them as distinct lights it means you're maybe two hundred and fifty *arshini* away."

"Two hundred and fifty? I see. Private Romanova?"

There was a witness who wasn't in on the scheme. "Here, sergeant," she said in as deep a voice as she could muster.

"He's very young," Panfil counseled the guide. "But we were scraping the bottom of the barrel in Tobolsk to field this brigade so . . ."

To Tatiana, Panfil said, "I see a slight rise to our right. I want you to settle the sleigh in there and keep it, the horses, and yourself under cover."

"Bu—yes, sergeant."

Nikitin and his gunners didn't hear it. One thing that can be said of artillerymen the world over and since the invention of the first big guns: they tended to be deaf as haddocks.

Instead, it was Konstantin Maksimovich Bortnik, the displaced and harried teamster, who first heard the jingle of metal on metal, to the southwest of the battery's firing position.

He sought out Nikitin and, having found him, said, pointing to the southeast, "Comrade, there's something out there and it sounds both deliberate and dangerous."

Nikitin knew his hearing was rotten. He wasn't shy or defensive about it, either; it simply came with the territory. He listened, even so, for several minutes, hearing nothing.

"Are you certain, comrade?"

"As certain as I am of anything," Konstantin replied.

"How close, do you think?"

The teamster thought about that, then listened some more. "Less than half a *verst*," he finally said, "but not a lot less. Maybe...six hundred *arshini*?"

"Right. Well done...who are you?"

"Konstantin Maksimovich Bortnik," came the reply. "I attached myself here, from the field trains."

"Glad you did, Bortnik. And now, if you will excuse me?"

Nikitin then walked to the nearest gun. Kicking the crew until he found the chief of the gun, he said, pointing to the southwest, "Get your men up and swing the gun as quietly as possible *that* way. Get half a dozen shrapnel shells and set them for a tenth of a second, then another half dozen set for a second and a quarter."

"Yes, comrade."

"I'm going to bring the other guns on line with yours. If there are a bunch of imperialists waiting out there to attack, they're going to be in for the surprise of their lives. When I give the command to fire, I want you to traverse your gun left to right between shells and then right to left again."

Cherimisov, like the men of his company, waited, crouching low above the snow. In the east, when he looked, he saw the first faint rays of light from the sun, now climbing but still just below the horizon.

It was time. The commander stood, as did his men, in twos and threes, and just as he was about to give the order to assault, he heard from the Red battery, "*Ogon!*" Fire!

Instantly, four double red blossoms bloomed. Each of these were composed of the muzzle flash of the guns and then the shrapnel shells' bursting charges. The air was filled first with the shocking blasts, then with the whizzing sound of hundreds of projectiles lashing through the air, and then the far more ominous sounds of dozens of men screaming in pain as they were hit.

For now Cherimisov was not hit. *The bastards were waiting. One chance... only one...* He stood and shouted, "Urrah!" then charged for the guns.

He got maybe fifty or sixty *arshini* before he felt his legs knocked from under him by the passage through his flesh of one or more shrapnel balls. Though the bones were not broken, the flesh was badly mangled. Cherimisov fell to his face, trying to keep from crying out. With that, the assault collapsed. Men took what cover they could and hid from the searching fire of the guns.

Nikitin laughed aloud as, for once in this battle, his guns had had a chance to show what they could do.

The laugh died quickly, though. What killed it was twin flashes from almost a *verst* away, followed at length by two unusually powerful explosions, much more so than from his own three-inch shells, a hundred or so *arshini* short of the battery's position.

"What?" Nikitin asked himself. "How did they get artillery this close? No matter; they *did*!"

"Aim for the flashes!" he cried out to his gunners. "They're the only things that can harm us now. Aim for the flashes."

By the faint light, Panfil and his mortar crews worked frantically to adjust the range to bring the battery under fire. Neither group was especially well trained, but the Red artillery was just *that* much better. Before a second volley could be launched from the brace of Stokes, the artillery put four rounds of shrapnel into the air just short of the mortars.

Panfil took a ball to his helmet, which prevented his brains from being splashed out onto the snow, but didn't stop the energy of the ball from knocking him senseless. One of his ammunition bearers, on the other hand, was literally eviscerated by a chunk of shrapnel casing that tore through the flesh of his belly, allowing his guts to spill out in a stinking bloody mass onto the snow-clad ground. Though the light remained dim, it didn't take high noon to see the sudden discoloration of the snow, to smell the contents of raped guts, or to hear the pure agonized shriek of the dying victim.

The remaining men bolted for the last covered place they knew of, the little hollow in which the bulk of their ammunition was secured.

"Hah, you bastards!" Nikitin exulted. "How do you like taking some of what you've been dishing out?"

After half a moment's reflection, Nikitin called out, as loudly as possible, "Cease fire! Cease fire! But load another round of shrapnel set for muzzle burst: zero seconds."

Tatiana was close enough to feel the blast from the cannons' muzzles rippling her internal organs in a way that was more disgusting than anything she'd ever felt.

How much worse for the men who've been hit? she asked herself. In a lull in the firing, she risked a peek over the ripple in the ground behind which she sheltered with the sleigh and ammunition. When she looked, she saw eight or nine men fleeing in her direction.

She felt her fear surge at this show of disaster . . . surge and then drain away, as if it were someone else's. For now, she had a job to do. And that mattered. *And besides, they don't call me "the Governess" for nothing.*

Taking up her machine pistol, Tatiana stepped out into the open.

"And just where do you people think you're going?" she demanded.

"Everyone's dead!" exclaimed one of the privates, coming to a halt. "The Reds . . . the cannon . . . Sergeant Panfil . . . dead . . . Ivanov . . . dead . . ."

"Which explains perfectly why there are . . . let me count, *nine* of you running like rabbits. Now, let me tell you what is going to happen. You are going to turn around and go back to the mortars. I am going to follow you with the ammunition. If we're lucky and quick, we'll get there without being seen and fired up. But seen or unseen, fired upon or not, we *are* going and we *are* going to smash those cannon."

She pointed the MP-18 menacingly. "Now turn around and get back where you belong."

Nikitin looked around until he found the one man with his battery that he really didn't need at the moment. He called over Bortkin.

"Konstantin Maksimovich," Nikitin said, "I need to you carry a message to Comrade Goloshchyokin. I think he's settled into Degtyarevo. Find him and tell him what has happened here, that we've broken the attack by the imperialists completely. Tell him that I think if he could get in a counterattack while they're pinned, he could reap large. Now go!"

The bright moon peeked over the trees at almost exactly the time that Tatiana managed to bring the sleigh in behind the fold in the ground that sheltered the mortars. From somewhere behind her she heard the faint sound of what she supposed were the 37mm infantry guns, trying to take on the cannon.

Glancing down, Tatiana looked at the eviscerated man, lying in a pool of his own guts, shit, and blood, and managed—barely—not to throw up. He, at least, was mercifully dead.

But what of Leonid?

She cast her eyes around. There was only one other body lying on the snow. The mortars themselves were one standing and one knocked over by something, possibly one of the fleeing troops.

"Get both of them set up and ready to fire," she ordered, then raced, keeping as low as possible, for Panfil's supine form.

Kneeling down next to him, she was relieved to see that he was, in the first place, still breathing, and, in the second, not bleeding out.

She shook him by the shoulder, insisting, "Leonid! Leonid? Leonid, wake the hell up!!!"

"Go away," Panfil said, groggily. "Can't you see I'm dead?" He opened his eyes and saw two beautiful angels, crouched above him. "See? Even the Christian angels—or maybe Valkyries—have come to take me away."

"You're not dead," Tatiana insisted. "I wonder what . . ." She picked up and examined the badly dented helmet, then matched the dent to a large goose egg now visible on Panfil's head. "Oh, I see.

"Sergeant Panfil," she said, more gently this time, "I assure you that you are not dead. However, if we can't take out those cannon we most certainly *are* going to be dead, and very soon."

The contemptible pops Nikitin heard from somewhere to the south were followed by two small explosions just behind his guns. He scanned across the horizon—his artilleryman's eyes were in much better shape than his artilleryman's ears—but couldn't see where the shells had come from. Even his binoculars failed to help.

Then he heard another two shots, and saw two small columns of snow, slush, and ice arise, off in the distance.

"Don't bother to unload the guns! Fire what you have and then load shrapnel with the fuses set for three seconds!"

Lieutenant Molchalin, Third Platoon Leader and executive officer of the company, usually said little. This time he was at a loss for words. He didn't know what had become of the CO, Cherimisov. From where he lay, he couldn't see more than three of his own men. He supposed he could have seen more and done more if he'd been able to lift his head more than a foot above ground level but the scything Red cannon to the front had ruled that out.

From behind he heard a couple of not terribly loud pops, the second such pair he'd heard. From ahead, half a minute later, he heard four much more powerful blasts. The passage of artillery shells overhead, sounding more like passing freight trains than anything else, was followed in less than two seconds by four more blasts behind him. After that he heard the tell-tale whiz of scores of shrapnel balls, heading away.

As long as the Red artillery is concentrating on the two 37mm jobs— and God look over them please—we can at least crawl forward. Get enough of us into small arms range and we still have a chance.

With that, and without raising his head more than six inches, Molchalin shouted out, "Third Platoon, Grenadier Guards Company, forward, after me, *crawl!*"

"Leonid, what's the range?" Tatiana asked. "I'm not good at doing math in my head."

"It should be . . . should be . . ."—Panfil turned to the side to retch— "something like max range. Seven-fifty on the clinometer."

Tatiana adjusted the setting on the clinometer, the device for measuring angles when placed against a mortar tube.

"Wait! Are you sure that's the range?"

"No," Panfil replied. "It was too dark to be sure."

"It's not too dark now," she said.

"No, but I can't see well enough. Here," he said, handing over the small collapsible range finder she'd given him from her father's collection.

"I don't know how," she said. "You never showed me."

"It's not complicated. Look inside ... no, the other way, with the little lenses up to your eyes and the big ones toward what you want to see. See the little curved line with the cross bars?"

"Yes, I see that."

"The space between cross bars is an average man's height." Panfil stopped to throw up again. "Gah. Frame an upright man inside those and look to the left; that will be the range in the British system of yards, which is also the system on the clinometer."

She'd led a sheltered life before the war, but Tatiana was no dummy. Taking the rangefinder and crawling up the little embankment to the front, she framed one upright Bolshevik who seemed to be in command of the guns. On the side of the line in the sight she read, "725."

Good enough.

Sliding back down the embankment, she set the clinometer at seven hundred and fifty, then placed it against the tube. Holding it there with one hand, she manipulated the mortar until the bubble in the clinometer was between the lines. Then she went and did the same thing with the other mortar.

But aim where? I can't see the guns from here.

"Get over here," she told one of the privates. "I'm going to stand up and tell you when to move the mortar. Ready?"

"Yes, your—"

"Private Romanova," she corrected him. "I am Private Romanova."

With that, Tatiana stood to her full five feet, nine inches, looked over the embankment to the front, glanced down at the white line painted on the top of the mortar barrel, and said, "Left ... little more ... little more ... no, back ... and that's good."

She checked the mortar again with the clinometer, then went the thirty *arshini* to the next tube and did the same.

"All right, everybody, get two shells and remove the safety pins ... got it? Let me see ... good. Make sure they each have four rings of charges. Now when I say 'fire,' we're going to drop ... no, wait ... instead, keep an eye on me. I'll point to who I want to drop a shell and then into which mortar. Ready?"

Tatiana pointed to one man, then to the tube to her left, and said,

"Fire!" She turned to another and, before even the first shell had been dropped, pointed again and then to the other mortar, saying, "Fire."

Before she could turn back, there came two blasts in rapid succession as the first man dropped both shells down the tubes, one after the other.

"You! Fire!"

"Fire!"

"Fire!"

"Fire!"

Nikitin knew instantly what the first muzzle blasts from his front meant. *Crap; they've got those other guns, whatever they are, back in action.*

"Cease fire!" he exclaimed, "Target, left front, some kind of heavy gun, maybe mortars. Load shrapnel and set your fuses for one second."

He didn't need to watch the gun crews as they went through their drill. Instead, Nikitin watched by moonlight the slow-moving shells, spinning end over end, now descending from on high.

"Not going to be quite quick enough," he muttered. "Oh fucking well."

At the end, not really ever having been a Bolshevik but just a man caught up in the web of fate, Nikitin crossed himself and asked the Almighty to see to the souls of his men. *They did their best for what they believed in, Lord, and you cannot ask for more than that.*

"Yes!" Tatiana exulted, as the shells began falling on and around the Red battery. "Yes!" she repeated at the best part, which was when one shell apparently went off right underneath one of the Red cannon, also touching off some unfired propellant that really should have been moved elsewhere, and sending the entire gun—along with diverse bits of the crew—into the air a good fifty or sixty *arshini.*

"Yes!" she repeated, throwing her arms around one of the crew and spinning him like a child.

"Yes!"

Molchalin decided to risk his head to look forward when he heard the mortars come back into action. He saw the Bolshevik battery deluged with a storm of shells. When he saw one of the guns lift, he knew it was his time.

Standing erect, Molchalin shouted, "Grenadier Company; *Urrah! Urrah! Urrah!* Charge!"

By ones and twos, and then, inspired by those, by the mass, the company arose to its feet and began running forward. The Lewis Guns, held at an angle to prevent stoppages, were the first to begin marching fire. The rifles joined in shortly after that.

Ah, but when the machine pistols kicked in, slaughtering everything in sight and setting the Reds still living and hale to running for their lives...

Dratvin, too, saw the gun fly up, spinning. The two platoons he had left to himself, having detached everyone else in his battalion to a different mission, were comparatively unscathed, as were the heavy machine guns sent to him by Lesh.

Standing up, he said, "All you men of the Preobrazhensky, on your feet. Machine guns?"

"Here, sir."

"Get ready to wheel your guns fast."

"The grenadiers will cut to the river. It's our job to make sure they aren't taken in the rear as they do, and to prevent the enemy from linking up again."

"Now, let's go!"

Degtyarevo, Siberia

Konstantin Maksimovich Bortnik hadn't yet found Comrade Goloshchyokin even a few minutes after the explosions behind him said that the artillery battery to which he'd attached himself was no more. Indeed, he turned around in time to see the gun that had been launched skyward crash down to Earth.

He stopped for a moment, before continuing his search, to contemplate what they meant.

What it means is that my alibi is gone. No Comrade Nimikin to vouch for me that I was doing my duty when I left the line. Now what will that very unreasonable communist make of this? Oh, I know, I'll be strung up to a tree before I can utter my first explanation.

So, this being the case, why don't I get my revenge for my upcoming murder, in advance?

With that, Bortkin spent a few minutes hunting for a club. He found a piece of wood that would do, picked it up in a gloved hand, and went looking for Goloshchyokin.

Southwest of Ushakova

"It's only a matter of time, now," said Kostyshakov. "We've got them herded into two small perimeters, no bigger than a thousand *arshini* across, either of them. They've got no food, no tents. And we can keep them from building any fires, too. While the days have turned warmer, the nights remain rather bitter."

He looked at Romeyko and asked, "So how do we get them to surrender? I don't want to lose another man here if we can help it."

"Speaking of which," said Romeyko, "there are a couple of points of interest. I think we can set the field kitchens upwind of the trapped Reds, first one, then the other, and tempt them to surrender by the smell of good hot soup cooking and some bread being baked. Another is they say Cherimisov will live and will not lose his legs, though we shall lose the use of him for probably two or three months. The final matter, however, concerns just who was in charge of the mortars when they silenced the Red battery..."

Of course no good deed goes unpunished...

"You did WHAT?" Kostyshakov stormed at his empress. "Are you out of your imperial *MIND*? Yes, I know inbreeding has made you royals dumber than the general run of mankind, but this is really beyond the pale. WERE YOU INSANE?"

"I was trying to help," she sniffed, softy. She wasn't a girl given much to crying but a tear rolled down her face even so. "And I didn't want to feel anymore that I wasn't doing my part and—"

"ENOUGH! And, Your Imperial Majesty, I have *had* enough."

With that, Kostyshakov removed his epaulettes and threw them at her feet. "If you're going to go around me like that then you don't need me for a commander. Find someone more interested in putting up with your spoiled little girl games. I am *through!*"

With that, the former commander of the Brigade of Guards turned on his heel and stormed out.

Interlude

Empress Dowager Maria Feodorovna (Dagmar)

To: Tatiana, by the Grace of God Empress and Autocrat of All the Russias, of Moscow, Kiev, Vladimir, Novgorod; Tsarina of Kazan, Tsarina of Astrakhan, Tsarina of Poland, Tsarina of Siberia, Tsarina of Tauric Chersonesus, Tsarina of Georgia; Lady of Pskov, and Grand Princess of Smolensk, Lithuania, Volhynia, Podolia, and Finland; Princess of Estonia, Livonia, Courland and Semigalia, Samogitia, Bielostok, Karelia, Tver, Yugor, Perm, Vyatka, Bogar and others; Sovereign and Grand Princess of Nizhni Novgorod, Chernigov, Ryazan, Polotsk, Rostov, Jaroslavl, Beloozero, Udoria, Obdoria, Kondia, Vitebsk, Mstislav, and Ruler of all the Severian country; Sovereign and Lady of Iveria, Kartalinia, the Kabardian lands and Armenian province: hereditary Sovereign and Possessor of the Circassian and Mountain Princes and of others; Sovereign of Turkestan, Heir of Norway, Duchess of Schleswig-Holstein, Stormarn, Dithmarschen, and Oldenburg, and so forth, and so forth, and so forth...

✢ ✢ ✢

My Dearest Tatiana,

Oh, my darling girl. Words cannot express the sorrow and pride in my heart. When I received the news about your poor parents, sister, and brother, I confess that my own breath nearly stopped. I wept for three days, unable to rise from my bed for the thought of my poor, poor Nicky.

And yet, within the storm of my grief, there remained a kernel of hope and pride in my heart. For the very messenger who delivered the sad news of your parents' murder informed me that you had been saved! You, Maria, and Anastasia yet live by the miracle of God's grace and the bravery of our Russian patriots. I have been told that you have been crowned with a helm of war, and that even now you shoulder these burdens for which you were never prepared.

Darling, shall I come to you? The Hun surrounds us here in the Crimea, but I am certain I can find a way if you need me. I have nothing but faith and pride in you, my dear one, but you must know that this role you have so bravely stepped into is an extraordinarily difficult one.

What I shall write to you now brings me great pain, but you need to know it. My son, your beloved papa, knew he would one day become Tsar. He was raised with the knowledge from birth. My husband and I—indeed, our entire household!—did our best to prepare him, to train him for the burden of leadership. We had great hopes, but ultimately, we failed. We failed Nicky, and we failed Russia.

For my son was *not* prepared for the life he was fated to lead. He was not strong enough, decisive enough. He was too concerned with minute affairs and too focused on the intense love he bore for his family. Your papa was the very best of fathers, I cannot deny that. But the traits that served him so well in fatherhood were ultimately his downfall as a ruler.

My dear, you must understand, my heart has been shattered, and to write this to you, so bluntly, so cruelly ... it takes the shattered pieces and burns them to ash. But it must be written, for you must know. You must understand, as your father did not, that if you wish to survive ... the crown must come before all else. You shall marry, and may it praise God bear healthy heirs, but you must cleave to the throne of Russia before all others. Your first obligation *has* to be there. Your father loved your mother above even his own life. He was blinded to anything but her happiness, and that blindness ultimately killed them both.

You must be strong, my Tatiana. You must be stronger than poor Nicky, than your poor sickly mother. You are an intelligent girl, and you will need every bit of that wit to see you through to the days ahead. Choose wise advisors and listen to them, but you must never, ever forget who you are and what you have now become.

    With the greatest love, I remain your loyal subject,
    Maria Feodorovna
    Dowager Empress of Russia

P.S. Please pass to your rescuers and, especially, their commander, my personal gratitude for the safety of yourself and your sisters.

Chapter Eight

Major William Donovan

Nearby to U.S. Army Field Officer's School, France

Major William Donovan showed his guest into the restaurant, then signaled for the maître d'.

Many of the U.S. Army officers attending the Field School organized by the French Army took every opportunity for furloughs in Paris, nights out drinking and eating in the local bars and restaurants, as well as any other opportunities for pleasure and ease, but Bill Donovan was not one of them. He'd kindled a friendship with a local doctor with whom he took frequent meals and practiced his French, but beyond that, Donovan focused mind, body, and spirit on absorbing everything useful the French veterans had to give so that he could get back to his battalion even better prepared to lead them into the trenches.

Tonight, though, he dined at the finest restaurant available—ascetic preferences aside, it wasn't every night the son of Theodore Roosevelt looked you up for a social call before heading to the front. Captain Archibald Roosevelt was a young man, with prominent forehead and elongated nose—not a terribly handsome lad, but possessed of an infectious and enthusiastic manner. A bottle of Andrew Jameson's private stock Irish Whiskey sat between them.

Donovan had experienced the pleasure of Theodore Roosevelt's company once in the officer's mess during his deployment to the Mexican border, and again back in New York when Roosevelt had been canvassing National Guard units for likely officers to command his volunteer regiments "Over There." The former president had lived up to the legend, and he suspected the apple had landed well within blast radius of the tree.

"So, how is your father, Archie, have you heard from him lately?" Donovan asked.

"As frequently as the mail comes," Archie said, swirling the whiskey in the glass a bit. "He's still furious with Wilson for ordering him to stand down on his volunteer divisions. He was ready to give you your own regiment, you know."

Donovan nodded. The official reason the War Department gave for ordering Roosevelt to stand down was that too many promising National Guard and Regular Army officers wanted to join. The official reason made sense as far as it went, but Donovan suspected at least some petty jealousy and paranoia on Wilson's part.

"I know, and it would've been an honor commanding a regiment in Roosevelt's Volunteers," Donovan said. "But at least we're here, ready to get into it. Are all the Roosevelt boys in France now?"

"We are indeed," Archie said. "Ted has a battalion over in the 26th, Kermit was in Mesopotamia with the Brits but now he's got an artillery battery here, and Quentin," Archie shook his head, "Quentin is a fly boy. I'll be honest with you, sir, my kid brother is so damned bold, he's the one I'm worried about getting his tail shot off."

"I'll make sure to include him, all of your brothers, in my prayers," Donovan said, draining his glass and pouring another measure. He held the bottle inquiringly, and Archie nodded, holding out his own glass for a refill.

"What do you make out of all the noise in Russia?" Archie asked.

"I don't know, Archie," Donovan said. "It'll certainly be a damn bad turn if the Kaiser gets forty divisions freed up from the East. But all I know about Russia is what I read in the papers. I've never made it as far as Russia in my travels, and I doubt I ever will."

69th (165th) Infantry Regiment, Near Luneville, France

When Donovan and the men of the 1st Battalion of the 69th Infantry (now labeled the 165th Infantry on the American Expeditionary Force's Table of Organization for consistency with the numbering of other federalized National Guard units) reached the front, they found their trenches in ill-repair.

The parapets were higher than the parados in several places—meaning that a man sticking his head and shoulders out of the trench to fire upon the enemy would be silhouetted rather than having a backdrop of earth to break up the outline of his Brodie helmet. For long stretches there was no fire-step to stand on when engaging the enemy, so his men would have to crawl further up the forward berm to put their rifles into action. The duckboards that were supposed to keep his men's feet out of the mud and muck were either rotted through or nonexistent and he hadn't seen so much as a yard of corrugated iron to reinforce the sides of the trenches. The sandbags they had were mostly ripped and leaking their contents to create yet more sludge to traverse.

Donovan, with the aid of a helpful French captain named Mercier, searched for the commander of the French battalion they were relieving in this sector. After an hour of traipsing around, he found the man at a command post situated under cover of a culvert in the road. In contrast to the conditions in the trenches, the dugout for the battalion CP was solid, reinforced with both timber and intact sandbags. The interior was relatively free from water.

The French battalion commander was a short, sallow major with a thick black mustache and sunken eyes. He did not offer to shake hands and his possessions were already packed. His eagerness to join his men departing the front was readily apparent in his distracted expression and the way he leaned toward the door. As they talked, the French battalion staff officers and NCOs departed one by one after hastily exchanged words with Donovan's own staff.

At the end of a frustrating conversation, Donovan's counterpart shrugged with Gallic nonchalance and said, "Listen, friend, this is a quiet sector. The Germans over there don't want to get their heads blown off this close to the end and neither do we. No heavy fighting means we're not on the priority list for any of that shit.

"If you're smart, you'll hold the line quietly here. If you're stupid, you'll get your men killed trying to make a splash. That's your affair."

Mercier's tone and expression were somewhat contrite, but he said nothing to contradict the French major before the man turned and walked away, summarily ending the conversation, the final word being the squelch of his departing boots in the mud. Donovan glowered at his back. Mercier quickly followed the French battalion commander, giving Donovan some room to stew.

"My, isn't he a helpful fellow?" a lilting voice asked.

Donovan stuck his head out of the dugout. The regimental chaplain, Father Duffy, stood regarding him with a smile that mingled sympathy and amusement. Duffy had such a reputation for character and courage that, despite being a chaplain rather than an infantry officer, he'd been considered for command of the 69th.

A mustachioed, shorter, and heavier, but still fit, man stood next to Duffy; this was Corporal Joyce Kilmer, one of the regiment's intelligence section NCOs. A poet of no small renown before the war, Kilmer had been offered a commission twice. He'd refused each attempt to promote him because becoming an officer would have necessitated a transfer to another regiment, and Kilmer, with a devout faith in the martial virtues of his fellow Irishmen, wouldn't be persuaded to fight with anyone other than the 69th.

"Well, if I was at this for four years, I imagine I'd be a little short on patience with the man standing between me and the rear, too," Donovan said with all the good grace he could muster. "Come on in, Father, Corporal Kilmer."

"Gracious of you to say so, sir," Kilmer said as they joined him in his new command post. "But no one believes it for a second."

Duffy chuckled. Donovan didn't respond, save for a deprecating wave of his hand.

"Sir, if it's all right, I'd like to accompany a reconnaissance patrol tonight, if you're going to send one out," Kilmer said. "I'd like to start developing our own picture of the German positions. I'm thinking perhaps our allies haven't been terribly eager to head out for a looksee…"

Kilmer shot a meaningful glance out the door of the dugout whence the French had departed.

"Couldn't agree more, Corporal." Donovan gestured to where his adjutant, a handsome young lieutenant, was poring over a topographic map laden with red and blue operational graphics depicting German and French—now American—positions and suspected positions. "Get with Lieutenant Ames, he's plotting our patrol route for the evening."

"Our? Sir?" Kilmer asked. "Are majors supposed to be crawling around no-man's land?"

"Kilmer, if you refrain from asking if battalion commanders need to crawl around in no-man's land, I'll refrain from asking the same of regimental staff NCOs." Donovan quirked an eyebrow.

"Point taken, sir, I'll go talk to Lieutenant Ames."

Once Kilmer was engrossed in conversation with Ames, Donovan turned back to Father Duffy and offered him a seat on one of the camp stools. Duffy accepted gratefully. Seated, he removed his wide-brimmed Brodie helmet and ran a hand over his shiny bald pate.

"How are your men settling in, Bill?" Duffy used Donovan's first name with confidence, speaking, as he was, to a member of his flock as much as a brother officer of the same rank.

"Well enough, Father," Donovan said. "A, B, and C companies are on the line, I've got D in reserve back in Camp New York. I wish we'd had more time for maneuvers as a battalion, especially more live fire exercises, but Lord knows the men are eager for a fight."

"And they trust you, Bill. I recall, back at Blooey," Duffy referred to the town in France where the 69th had done its final train-up, "I heard two of the lads talking after one of your cross-country runs. The first boy said, 'Major Donovan is a man among men, he ought'a be the King o' Ireland.' The second, one of the pudgier privates, said, 'Major Donovan is a sonofabitch!' A third piped in, 'Wild Bill's a sonofabitch, aye, but he's a game sonofabitch.'"

Donovan laughed from his gut for the first time in weeks. He clapped Duffy on the shoulder with a grin.

"Father, if my luck should fail on this adventure, I want that as my epitaph."

Donovan and his reconnaissance party crawled on knees and elbows through the grass and mud, under skeins of barbed wire, into and out of the craters made by hundreds of cannons and mortars over the course of the war. Many of the craters already had grass creeping back into them, indicating that his French predecessor had been correct, this sector had seen less shelling in recent days.

A waxing moon shed adequate light to move by, but that was a double-edged sword. Adequate light to see by was also adequate to be seen in. Thus, they traversed nearly two miles of no-man's land with agonizing slowness. They were exhausted and caked in dirt when Sergeant Kilmer, traveling at the point, held up a hand for a halt. They all froze, lying flat on the ground in a deep ravine.

Donovan and his men lay still and silent for several minutes, looking, listening, even smelling for any sign that the enemy had observed them. Once Donovan was fairly certain they were uncompromised, he low-crawled forward, dragging himself up the side of the trench, body pressed to the mud; his party followed, holding their long, Enfield 1917 rifles just off the ground by the slings.

He sidled up shoulder to shoulder with Kilmer, close enough to hear the other man's breath. Bathed in moonlight, a series of jagged gashes ripped through the field before them, dotted here and there by occasional dull gray domes—German steel helmets.

The German forward firing trenches were separated from one another laterally to prevent the fall of one trench from precipitating the collapse of the entire firing front. Each firing trench connected with narrow, perpendicular trenches that led back to a more extensively interconnected support trench system. Admittedly, Donovan could only make out so much detail in the moonlight, but the German positions appeared deeper and better maintained than the French ones they'd inherited.

"All right, Kilmer," Donovan breathed. "We got our looksee, time to head back."

Back at his command post under the culvert, safe from direct enemy observation, Donovan and his men sighed in relief and exchanged exhausted laughter. Lieutenant Oliver Ames, Donovan's adjutant, was awake and perked up like a loyal puppy when his boss walked into the dugout.

"Did the recon go well, sir?" he asked.

"It did." Donovan nodded. "We got within sight of the German firing trenches. Kilmer and I are going to update our enemy situation maps."

Father Duffy joined Donovan and Kilmer as they sat around a table, transferring their new knowledge of the German trenches onto the map provided them by the French.

Does the man ever sleep?

"Good evening, Father," Donovan said.

"Good morning, actually," Duffy said, sidling up to the map table. "The sun's well up, lads. I hear the patrol went well."

"Yes, Father, thanks to Sergeant Kilmer's daring and intrepidity," Donovan said.

"I thought it was my sins, sir," Kilmer said, yawning through the sentence. "Not my boldness."

"It can be both, after all, Aquinas told us to sin boldly, did he not, Father?" Donovan turned to Duffy.

"Yes, but I'm not sure that's what he meant, Bill," Duffy said, settling down onto a camp stool across from them.

"In any event, I think we've got it all down now, Sergeant," Donovan said, turning back to Kilmer. "I think you can go get some sleep, we can look this over again after we've rested and you've updated regiment. Thanks for helping us out."

"My pleasure, sir," Kilmer said. "Looking forward to the next patrol with 1st Battalion."

Donovan, with the regimental commander's support, implemented a consistent program of sniping and harassing artillery fires. The Germans responded to the Americans' violation of the informal truce with heavy artillery bombardment every morning for the rest of the time the 1st Battalion stayed on the line. This ritual, so the French had informed them, already had a name, "The Morning Hate." They lost a few men wounded and killed to fragmentation from the shelling, but the most devastating impact of the consistent shelling was likely psychological.

Being under artillery fire was as close a thing as Donovan could imagine to experiencing the wrath of God firsthand. The eardrum-shattering blasts, the waves of concussion that loosened bowels, and the utter lack of control as men were occasionally maimed or eviscerated about him hammered at his calm. Only his duty and responsibility kept a sane, banal smile on his face.

Forcing his own terror aside, Donovan trooped his line between volleys, calmly extolling his men to keep their nerve and watch their sectors, and not to worry, the American artillery would be giving Jerry much better than they got. Sure enough, the American 75 mm and 6-inch cannons opened up in a cacophonous retaliation every morning like clockwork.

The Germans supplemented the shelling with occasional forays by their riflemen and light machine gunners just far enough into no-man's land to pepper the American lines with direct fire. For his part, Donovan ordered his men on an even more aggressive patrol schedule, killing and capturing more Germans night by night. Day by day they repaired and replaced duckboards, filled sandbags, ensured the field phones were operational and deepened the communication trenches leading back to the support trenches.

Finally, it was 1st Battalion's turn to rotate off the line. They were replaced by the 2nd Battalion of the 69th. It was a fine unit, and Donovan was satisfied with the hand-off his company commanders conducted with their counterparts, but he was less enthused about the 2nd Battalion commander. The man had always been a bit too remote from the action, even in training, and willing to ride on the accomplishments of his junior officers and NCOs. In fact, Donovan thought it the regimental chaplain's only failing that he seemed to overlook the 2nd Battalion commander's numerous iniquities.

Donovan stayed on the line for several days after his battalion had already departed back to Camp New York, encouraging the 2nd Battalion commander to give rational orders, and occasionally exceeding his authority to ensure that 2nd Battalion's troops were making proper preparations against German shelling and harassing direct fires.

During stand-to on the fourth day after his battalion's departure, the German shelling was particularly vicious. The German shells were landing in thick, gut-wrenching volleys, punctuated by the lower-pitched *thunk* of *Minenwerfer* mortar rounds. Donovan observed from the command post, his teeth gritted, preparing to go forward to encourage the 2nd Battalion's men as their own commander appeared content to stay in his command post dugout.

The American troops had reacted to the GI Cans with disdain at first, thinking the short, fat rounds a pale imitation of genuine, high-explosive artillery rounds. That disdain had evaporated the first time they'd seen what a direct hit from a GI Can did to earthworks and fortifications—and the men inside them. Rarer than standard high-explosive rounds, the fact that the Germans were expending so many *Minenwerfer* in today's shelling was concerning.

They wouldn't be using so many if they didn't feel like they'd zeroed in...

A direct hit on one of the platoon dugouts sent earth and stone into the air in an ugly brown and gray fountain and basso *crack-THOOM*. Donovan watched, horrified as the structure fell in upon itself. He turned back into the command post.

"One of the platoon dugouts took a direct hit," he said.

"We know," the 2nd Battalion commander said, not bothering to look in Donovan's direction. His executive officer was on one of the field phones.

"Collapsed?" the captain was saying. "Understood, we'll send help. Do what you can—"

"I'm going to help," Donovan announced, turning to leave.

"Donovan, majors are not expendable, you will stay here," the 2nd Battalion commander snapped.

Donovan turned slowly back toward his counterpart, fists balling at his sides. He advanced on his fellow major, eyes glacially cold. The command post was suddenly quiet.

"Major, you are going to give me permission to go help those men, and you're going to do it right now," Donovan said, his voice low, lethal.

Under Donovan's flint-hard gaze, staring at the fists that had dismantled the regiment's toughest men in the boxing ring, his fellow commander quailed. Clearing his throat, he took a step back and spoke.

"Major Donovan, I would appreciate your assistance with the emergency at C Company's position," he said, voice cracking on, "emergency."

Donovan stormed out of the CP without a reply.

As he sprinted through the communications trench to reach the front, he saw a soldier who was supposed to be on guard huddled at the bottom of his trench, his rifle gripped in white-knuckled hands. All along the line he saw the sentries shying back from their posts.

Damn it, if the shelling creates a gap for the Germans...

Donovan leapt to the first boy and shook him by the shoulder.

"What's your name, son?" Donovan shouted over the barrage.

"Kelly, sir!" the lad shouted in reply.

"Well, Kelly, are you going to let those goddamned Krauts rattle you?"

The boy couldn't have been a day over nineteen, but his hazel eyes hardened, his chin jutted forward, and he dragged himself to his feet.

"Hell no, sir," he said, settling in on the firing step, his rifle pointed across no-man's land once again.

"Good boy!"

Donovan repeated the process up and down the line for a few minutes, making sure the boys were ready to meet any German assault. Any rescue attempt at the collapsed dugout was sure to fail if their lines collapsed under enemy assault.

Once he was satisfied that the men were bolstered, Donovan ran to the collapsed dugout and dove in among his soldiers shoving aside earth, stone, and shattered timbers. They could all hear cries and shouts from men still under the rubble. Donovan grabbed and flung another chunk of stone out of the way, then a segment of log, ignoring the splinters that dug into his hand deep enough to draw blood.

"Hold on," he screamed. "We're coming for you!"

A hole, just narrower than Donovan's shoulders, appeared in the ruins. Duffy appeared next to Donovan.

"O'Malley, you and Malloy grab my feet," Duffy said, addressing two of the privates. "I'm going in there."

"Father, you can't, it could come down on you," the young soldier protested. Both looked at Donovan, who was the only infantry officer present, for guidance.

Donovan considered for only a moment.

"Do as he says."

With a man grasping each ankle, Duffy crawled into the crevasse. Donovan schooled his features to stern impassivity as Duffy emerged with one man clinging to his arms, then returned to the narrow passage to retrieve another, and then one more, gasping and wiping debris out of his eyes as the men pulled him and Duffy clean. Duffy took only a few seconds before he made to return again.

Before Duffy could return to the narrow passage, the ground shifted dangerously beneath their feet. Donovan struggled to remain standing as the narrow passage collapsed, along with the skeletal remains of the dugout. Within seconds, only flat, debris-strewn ground marked where the dugout had once been.

They dug for several more hours, to no avail. Nineteen men remained buried, with no way to reach them. Donovan called for the engineers. Long after the wounded had been evacuated, Donovan stood with Kilmer and Duffy, staring at the impromptu tomb.

On his way back to the command post, Donovan saw another body in the trenches—it was young Private Kelly, missing his helmet, along with a chunk of his skull. Donovan's lips pressed firmly together and he shook his head, uttering a quiet prayer. He continued on his way as Kelly's mates removed the boy's remains.

Damn this bloody business, but if I have to go, I at least hope it's that quick.

Interlude

Tatiana's Journal

I don't know what to do. I am lost, lost, utterly *lost*. The weather outside has turned so warm and yet I feel so cold and dead inside.

Daniil refuses to speak to me. Even his sergeant major, to whom he always listens, says he will not discuss me and refuses to resume command.

So we sit here in the Governor's House in Tobolsk, and in the town itself, and do nothing but train and guard the two thousand or so Bolshevik prisoners taken at the Battle of Toboltura. But for the food captured in the battle I doubt we could even feed them.

On the plus side, the river is free enough of ice now for water transport between Tobolsk and Tyumen. Tyumen is still under the Reds, of course, so we get no messages from Yekaterinburg. I have no idea of what is happening with my dearest Aunt Ella.

I don't understand Daniil's actions. Before he resigned and threw his epaulettes at my feet, he mentioned me "in dispatches" as "Private Romanova, T." This is supposed to be a very good thing. Why would he do that and then resign? Maybe Ella can explain it, if we're ever reunited.

I know Dan's in love with me. That was obvious years ago, when he was an invalid at the hospital at Tsarskoye Selo. What I didn't know, not until he turned his back on me, was that I feel the same way about him. I don't even mind that I'm taller than he is. Had someone asked me five years ago if that would even have been possible, I'd have laughed.

I can't laugh anymore, not about that or about anything.

But what can I do now? You can't beg someone who refuses to be in the same room with you. Could I send him a letter? Would he bother to read it?

What is left to me but to try?

Chapter Nine

Dugout for the Field Telephone Exchange
of the 1st Battalion of the 165th Infantry

U.S. 42nd "Rainbow" Division Headquarters, France

The German newspaper's headline read in massive font, TSAR AND TSARINA MURDERED—GRAND DUCHESSES ALIVE AND FREE! Standing in the corner of the division headquarters, Second Lieutenant Sigmund Abramovich puzzled out the text of the paper. Unlike English, the language of his homeland, and Russian, the language his parents brought with them from the Old Country, German he'd learned the hard way in high school and at West Point, so reading it took more of his concentration.

It was well past midnight, but the divisional command post was a buzz of activity under the lantern light. Officers and NCOs answered

155

field phones, dispatched runners, and updated the cellulose acetate overlaid on their French maps with grease pencils. Sigi wasn't idling amidst the bustle by reading a newspaper. The intelligence section had more open-source enemy intelligence—newspapers, propaganda pamphlets, novels, journals, and the like—than they could ever hope to process. The fact that Sigi was semi-literate in German meant that, when not on other taskings, he was expected to help filter the written materials for military relevance.

"What's it say, Sigi?" A familiar Texas drawl drew Sigi's eyes from the paper. A tall, muscular lieutenant with sandy blond hair, a jawline straight and firm enough to plough an acre, and cheerful brown eyes stood before him.

"It looks like the Bolsheviks murdered the Tsar and the Tsarina, Hank. Shot their little boy and one of their daughters," Sigi said, still scanning the text. "But three of the girls were rescued by the Imperial Guard, now I guess they're trying to rally the anti-communist forces."

Hank Thornton was a sharp contrast to Sigi, who was short, bespectacled, and slight of build—though wiry and much stronger than he looked, as Hank had learned during Plebe boxing four years earlier at West Point.

Ultimately, the tall Texan linebacker had still beaten the little Jew from Queens to near unconsciousness, but the task had taken every round of the match and been challenging enough to earn Hank's respect. A good thing for both parties, as Hank's popularity fast-tracked Sigi past his classmates' antisemitism into social acceptance. Without tutoring, Sigi was fairly certain there were three, maybe four classes Hank would've flunked.

"Do you think they'll be able to win, Sigmund?" Another voice cut into their conversation; this one was also familiar in its clenched-jaw formality. "And will they win in time to rejoin the struggle against the Hun?"

Sigi and Hank both snapped to attention and saluted as the 42nd Division chief of staff, Colonel MacArthur, approached. MacArthur returned their salute with a casual familiarity that belied the fact that he would've torn Sigi and Hank new anal orifices had they shown anything less than the most punctilious military courtesy.

"I don't know, sir," Sigi said. "The *Berliner Tageblatt* is collating second- and thirdhand reports here. They seem pretty certain as to which Romanov children escaped, but I don't think they have a handle on the military situation in Russia at all. We should probably have Sergeant Bauer read this one as well, though."

"Of course, but I trust he'll come to much the same conclusion," MacArthur said. "In the meantime, we'll just have to rout the *Boche* ourselves."

"Yes, sir," Sigi and Hank chorused.

"Henry, Sigmund, I have an important task for you," MacArthur said, waving them over to a situation map. He picked up a grease pencil and indicated the 42nd Division's forward line of troops. The division's infantry strength was distributed in two brigades, the 83rd and the 84th. Each brigade was comprised of two infantry regiments and an independent machine gun battalion to supplement direct firepower. The division was manned largely by National Guard troops mobilized from all across the country, thus the symbolism of the division's rainbow patch. U.S. Army divisions were larger than any equivalent enemy or allied formation in human history, largely because of an appalling shortage of trained officers.

MacArthur's pencil tracked to the 83rd Brigade's sector, then rested on the symbol depicting the center of mass of one of its subordinate regiments, the 165th Infantry, whose troops were drawn from Sigi's native New York. He'd hoped to wrangle a platoon in that regiment, but God and Douglas MacArthur had seen fit to execute other plans.

"At last report, the 165th had crossed the River Ourcq but is just shy of their first objective, Meurcy Farm." MacArthur's pencil rested on a small green patch on the map; within the patch a few black blocks indicated buildings. "We need them to push through and take the farm to solidify our lines. I want you two to find Colonel McCoy, relay the urgency to him. While you're there, look around, get a feel for the situation, then meet me back here at the command post. If I'm not here, report to the commander or deputy commander."

"Yes, sir," Hank said. "Why wouldn't you be here?"

"The 84th Brigade's advance has floundered far worse than the 83rd's," MacArthur said, a grim expression darkening his face. "I'm going to their sector to help straighten things out."

Sigi kept his features impassive, but he groaned inwardly for the poor hapless bastards about to be graced with MacArthur's presence. As a couple of rare West Point graduate lieutenants in the exponentially expanded U.S. Army, Colonel MacArthur had snatched up Hank and Sigi for the divisional staff literally moments after they'd reported in to the 42nd Division.

Working for MacArthur had been quite the experience thus far. His vanity and ambition alike were prodigious, and anything in his way was likely to be shoved ruthlessly aside, including the career of any peer or subordinate who could not keep up with MacArthur's ambitions.

"We understand, sir," Hank said. Sigi nodded in agreement.

"All right, gentlemen, here's a written order with General Menoher's signature," MacArthur handed over a large envelope. "Along with copies of the reports of the 12th Aero Squadron. Take a couple of horses to ride down to 83rd Brigade headquarters, but I'd dismount after that if I were you. Knowing Colonel McCoy, he's probably got the 165th's command post too close to the front to go galloping around against the skyline, especially once the sun is up."

Per MacArthur's order, they drew two chestnut brown mares from the Headquarters Company stable. Sigi was no judge of horseflesh, but from the size of the beasts they seemed more draft animal than riding steeds.

Standing a mere 5'4" *in* his boots, Sigi considered his mount, its saddle and stirrups, and his own kit, all with a baleful glare. Hank must have noticed his expression, for the tall Texan checked his own movement, removed his foot from the stirrup and walked over to Sigi with a mischievous grin on his face.

"Can I give you a hand there, Sigi?" Hank said.

"Yeah, thanks," Sigi muttered, the indignity of the admission outweighed by their need to complete their journey to the 83rd before sunrise.

"Leave your pack on the ground, I'll hand it up to you after you're settled," Hank said.

Sigi leaned way back to get his left foot into a stirrup that was level with his shoulder. With a grunt and a shove from Hank on his butt and lower back, he pulled himself up and swung his right leg over the saddle to end up in more or less the right position. With the stirrups shortened to the greatest degree possible, he was just able to get both feet secure.

Hank handed Sigi's pack up to him, grin back in place.

"You know, Sig, we could've asked them if they had any ponies," he said.

Sigi accepted his pack with a scowl, looped his arms through the straps and tightened them while his friends held the reins.

"Sometimes I wish I'd let you fail calculus, you shitkicking dingbat," Sigi muttered, snatching the reins away from his friend.

Hank addressed his horse with confidence, one hand on the saddle, left foot in the stirrup, and vaulted up onto the beast's back with a grace Teddy Roosevelt in his prime might have envied. Sigi glared in disgust.

Hank's grin widened and he laughed good-naturedly.

"Temper, temper, Sigi," he said. "If you'd let me flunk out of the academy, you'd be *walking* to the front."

The front.

They'd survived some shelling since arriving in-country, but neither of the lieutenants had actually seen real battle yet. Neither had fired their pistols, nor had they been forced to take cover from enemy rifle or machine gun fire.

Hank wheeled about on his horse and stepped off at a canter. Sigi guided his horse around and gave it a prod with the heels of his boots. His horse followed Hank's easily, but whether because of Sigi's guidance or simply following her stablemate, Sigi couldn't say.

As the miles to their destination dwindled, Sigi settled into the saddle and allowed himself to enjoy the ride. The city boy actually liked the novelty of horseback riding much more than he was willing to admit to his Texan friend.

Even in the gray predawn, the French countryside was beautiful, with verdant hills and copses of trees dominating the landscape. This stretch of it even had remarkably few craters. They were still some miles from the front. The distant chatter of machine gun fire and occasional thunder of artillery inspired some trepidation, but mostly excitement. Little Sigmund Abramovich was finally going to be with the real soldiers.

Finally, he faced the moment of truth. He'd proven himself clever enough, and strong enough to become an officer; would he be brave enough to deserve his commission? Would he crack up under fire, end up a shell-shocked wreck like some of the men he'd seen coming off the line? Sigi was young, but he wasn't stupid. He knew his ambitions were no shield against an exploding shell or a sniper's bullet.

Shaking his head as if warding off a fly, Sigi shoved his doubts aside and spurred his horse to catch up with Hank. Side by side, they crested a rise in the undulating terrain, and picked up a little speed on the downslope.

Brigadier General Lenihan, the 83rd's commander, wasn't at his headquarters when Hank and Sigi galloped up to their position, so his chief of staff reviewed the orders given them by MacArthur, made facsimiles of all the intelligence they'd brought, and gave them permission to leave their horses at the 83rd's Command Post.

On foot, Hank and Sigi reached the 165th's command post just before dawn. The post was nestled in a low, wooded area. Much smaller than the divisional CP, only a handful of NCOs and officers operated field phones or stenciled upon the single, acetate-covered map.

The 165th's commander met them. Colonel McCoy was a tall, thin man with a genial face, prominent ears, and a carefully trimmed mustache with the ends just slightly upturned past the corners of his mouth. Accepting the envelope from Hank, he read the order therein rapidly and let out a short bark of laughter.

"We're already on it," he said, handing the order to one of his staff NCOs to file while he examined the reports from the aerial reconnaissance. "1st and 2nd Battalion attack in two hours."

"Sir, General MacArthur charged us with observing the front," Sigi said. "With your permission, we'd like to accompany the attack."

"Boys, I don't think any of my battalion commanders need extraneous shavetail lieutenants touring around their sector in the middle of an operation," McCoy said, his tone kind. Sigi's heart sank in his chest.

"Sir, we'll stay out of the way, or do whatever we're told," Hank said. "But we can't report back to General MacArthur without completing our mission."

McCoy looked at them, visibly measuring them for a long moment. His eyes flicked to Hank's right hand, then Sigi's. He quirked an eyebrow.

"Class of '17?" he asked.

"Yes, sir," both lieutenants chorused.

McCoy raised his own right hand, palm inward. The make was a bit different than their rings, but there was no mistaking the Class of '97 West Point ring glinting on his third finger. A hopeful smile crept across Hank's face, and Sigi caught his own breath, leaning forward just slightly. McCoy stared at each of them in turn for another ten seconds.

"Oh, all right," McCoy said. "You'll need the experience. You can join 1st Battalion. But listen closely—"

McCoy leveled a finger at Sigi's nose, then Hank's, forestalling their happy grins.

"You keep your heads down, and you damned well do what Major Donovan tells you," McCoy continued. "If he sends you back to the rear, you come back to the rear. Otherwise, feel free to make yourself useful. Sergeant Kilmer—"

McCoy called over his shoulder, a man of moderate height and thicker build with a long, bristly mustache stepped up behind him.

"Yes, sir?"

"Since I know you were over there concocting an excuse to get down to 1st Battalion before the attack anyway," McCoy said, "copy down the flyboys' information for Major Donovan and his staff, and then you and these young men can head down together."

"Yes, sir," Kilmer said, grinning.

Equipped with the copied reconnaissance reports and a new guide in the form of Sergeant Kilmer, plus two boxes of grenades for 1st Battalion, they set off at a jog. Artillery, machine gun, and small arms fire boomed, chattered, and cracked louder with every step forward.

Something odd occurred to Sigi as they left the road and wound their way through a patch of conifer forest.

"Sergeant, are you *Joyce* Kilmer?" Sigi asked.

Kilmer didn't even glance backward.

"Yes, sir," Kilmer said. "Guilty as charged."

"It's a pleasure to meet you," Sigi said. "I enjoy your book reviews in the *Times*, though I think you were a little hard on Ford Madox Ford."

"Lieutenant, if you find Ford's drivel more penetrable than I, I'd love to discuss it," Kilmer said, looking over his shoulder and smiling as if to take the edge off his words. "But we should probably table the debate until after the attack, hmm?"

"Of course, Sergeant," Sigi said.

Presently they stood before a broad-shouldered, square-jawed major with a handsome, rugged Irish face who regarded them with a mixture of amusement and annoyance.

Sigi and Hank both saluted and introduced themselves.

"I'm Major Donovan, gentlemen," Donovan said. "I command the 1st Battalion. Sergeant Kilmer, do you mind telling me why you're bringing replacement officers to my Command Post minutes before an attack?"

"Well, sir, there were these two fine specimens, from the United States Military Academy, no less, sitting forlorn and abandoned at Regiment. So, I said to the Colonel, send these gentlemen with me, lo, and I shall find them gainful employment," Kilmer said. "And to their credit, they brought gifts with them."

Kilmer handed over the copied aerial reconnaissance reports to Major Donovan, and nodded for each of the lieutenants to deposit their box of grenades on the floor.

"Kingly gifts, indeed," Donovan agreed. "Sergeant Major, get me some runners and get these grenades down to C Company, they'll need them for the assault on the farmhouses."

Donovan began to scan the aerial reconnaissance report, nodding along with the pilots' observations.

"Sir, we're not actually replacements," Hank spoke up. "Colonel MacArthur sent us down to observe the attack and we'll have to return to Division after the operation is concluded, but we're at your disposal until then."

Donovan gave them a look very similar to the skeptical examination McCoy had given them at the regimental command post, only Donovan was no West Pointer. Sigi could see their dismissal forming behind Donovan's eyes.

"Sir, Lieutenant Thornton and I both speak French," Sigi volunteered. "And I'm conversant in German as well. Perhaps we can be of some use to you as linguists, at least?"

That gave Donovan a moment's pause. He removed his helmet and ran a hand through his close-cropped hair before replacing his headgear and nodding once.

"All right, Thornton, you can go with C Company, they have a French battalion on their flank," Donovan said. "Should coordination become necessary you can assist Captain Bootz."

"Yes, sir," Thornton said.

"Abramovich, you will shadow my adjutant, Lieutenant Ames," Donovan said. "Do what he tells you to do, keep your head down. If we take any prisoners, you can help sort them."

"Yes, sir."

Interlude

London, England

George V, by the Grace of God, of the United Kingdom of Great Britain and Ireland and of the British Dominions beyond the Seas, King, Defender of the Faith, Emperor of India, stepped out into the unceasing mistiness of the English morning. Despite the damp (it was always damp!), George felt a lightness in his being that translated to a spring in his step. Even the deep, chesty cough that plagued him couldn't diminish the cheer in his mind as he turned to offer his hand to his wife as she followed him out.

"My love," he said, with a smile for his Queen. She returned his greeting with a small, dignified nod. As always, Mary presented herself as the pinnacle of elegance and decorum. Only the tiniest of glances, a secret gleam of a deepening smile indicated that she, too, shared his good mood this morning.

Not for the first time, George V thanked the Lord above for a wife who loved him. It was a rare enough thing in his social circle.

And she has, too, he thought, *grown more regal and still better looking with the years. I am a lucky man and perhaps, given recent history, the luckiest of kings.*

George tucked his wife's hand into his arm and started walking toward the path that would lead them to the estate's chapel. Mary squeezed his forearm gently, another secret reminder of her love.

"Your Majesty!"

George paused at the sound of his private secretary's voice. It wasn't like Bigge to be flustered, but here he was, rushing up with gravel crunching under the army-style boots he still wore.

"Why, Stamfordham," the queen said, her voice light and musical despite the gentle rebuke in her tone. "On the Sabbath morning?"

"My apologies, Your Majesty," Bigge said, coming to a halt and executing a bow with military precision. "I am afraid this news cannot wait."

163

George let out a sigh and smiled gently at his wife. "Go on, my dear," he said. "You know Stamfordham wouldn't interrupt us if it were not necessary. I shall join you presently."

Mary met his eyes, a question in her gaze. He smiled, hoping she'd draw reassurance from his calm expression. She gave him a tiny nod and turned to continue walking toward the chapel. George watched her go, taking one more moment to admire her graceful, elegant form before turning his attention back to his private secretary.

"All right, Stamfordham," George said. "What is so earth-shattering that you had to interrupt me on my way to church?"

"Your Majesty," Bigge said, "I have . . . terrible news. Your cousin, Tsar Nicholas is dead."

"The Former ts—what did you say?" The correction had come automatically before George had fully processed Bigge's words. Nicholas had been forced to abdicate by the revolutionary forces currently enflaming Russia. Fear of those same forces in England had kept George from acting to retrieve his cousin and his family from their suddenly dangerous homeland. An icy tendril of fear snaked through his gut at the thought. Had he condemned Nicky to death with his inaction?

"It's true, sir. I've just had the report this morning. Apparently there was a rescue attempt made by monarchist forces in Tobolsk. They stormed the house where the former Tsar and his family were being held. Casualties were quite high, among them the former Tsar and his wife, and Tsarevich Alexei and one of the daughters."

"*One* of the daughters? So the others still live?"

"Yes, sir. The former Grand Duchess Tatiana has been crowned Empress of all the Russias by the monarchist faction."

"Tatiana? Was Olga the one killed, then? And what is happening with the other two?"

"According to the report, Grand Duchess Maria and Grand Duchess Anastasia were both present at their sister's makeshift coronation, sir."

"And where are they now?"

"We don't know exactly. The foreign office suspects that the Russian monarchists may have them on the move—likely for their own safety. But we don't really know for certain."

"They must come here!" The King felt his face flush as he straightened his spine and met his private secretary's eyes. "I was wrong not to do it before. Poor Nicky . . ."

"Sir, I'm not sure—"

"Damnit, Stamfordham! I know you're worried about sending the wrong message to the socialists here at home, but they're just little girls! And they're my family!"

Lieutenant Colonel Arthur Bigge, 1st Baron Stamfordham, rolled his shoulders back and nodded. "Yes, Your Majesty."

George stared at his private secretary for another long moment as he recalled an earlier conversation they'd had about his Romanov cousins. After Nicky's abdication, Bigge had been the one to persuade him of the folly of extracting the former tsar and his family. As George continued in silence, Bigge's shoulders slumped infinitesimally, showing that he knew he carried a portion of the blame.

"I don't care how you or the Government do it," George said, his quiet words throbbing with intensity. "But bring them here. If not Tatiana, then at least Maria and Anastasia. And find out what's happened to the rest of the family. The Dowager Empress is the Queen Mother's sister, for God's sake! She must be protected!"

"Yes, Your Majesty."

"Very well," the King said, and drew in a deep breath. He nodded once at Bigge, who stood still as a statue under his monarch's scrutiny. "I will leave you to it. I must to church. Poor, poor Nicky!"

With that, the King of England turned his steps toward the house of the Lord God, where he hoped he might find solace . . . and forgiveness.

Chapter Ten

Chauchat in Action

Near Meurcy Farm, France

Sigi hit the ground just as an unforgiving shell exploded near enough that dirt and rock clattered against his helmet. His inner ear was set wildly askew as the concussive force of the blast rippled over him. The dizziness and nausea yielded to Sigi's will after only a brief struggle, and he turned his attention back to the battlefield before him.

Donovan, Ames, Kilmer, and Sigi lay in the prone below the forward crest of a hill overlooking Meurcy Farm. Amidst the fields of the farm stood half a dozen buildings facing a courtyard encompassed by a large wall, all constructed of hard, gray stone. The windows of the buildings occasionally sparked with the muzzle flash of a rifle; the Irishmen's return fire pinged and ricocheted off the stones of the wall.

"I told them we needed more artillery," Donovan said. "Damn."

Sigi shoved his fear aside and focused on deciphering the chaos of the battle. Three hundred yards short of their objective, the men of the

A and B Company were stalled. The preparatory fires had apparently been insufficient. From within the farmhouses, and amongst the trees on the ridges south of the farmhouse, the Germans winnowed the staggered line of advancing Americans with devastatingly accurate rifle and machine gun fire.

Men perforated by bullets dropped like marionettes with their strings cut, the screams of the wounded audible even at this distance. Driven to hide behind what scant cover was available in the green fields between the stream and the farmhouses, the German artillery barrage caught the battalion stationary and practically in the open.

With three companies deployed abreast in the attack, Sigi couldn't pick out the men of C Company on their extreme right, advancing through the wooded hills to their East. He saw only vague shapes and flashes of fire moving between the trees. Glancing at Donovan's expression, Sigi marveled at the man's apparent calm. Only a scowl of concentration betrayed Donovan's frustration and worry at having hundreds of men, many of them out of his sight, pinned under German direct and indirect fire.

A few minutes into the attack, a brown-uniformed figure sprinted out of the woods from C Company's position. The runner zigged and zagged, occasionally dropping to the ground. Sigi wondered what he was doing for a moment, then as puffs of dirt from impacting rounds followed his progress, he realized that the soldier was running in erratic patterns and getting up and down to make himself harder to hit.

Huh, they should probably be teaching that at West Point . . .

"What is it, Mills?" Donovan shouted as the man crawled the last few feet to join them.

"Sir, Captain Bootz is wounded, bad," the man said between panting breaths. "The *Boche* sure have lot of machine guns here for a rear-guard action, and they're dug in and camouflaged real good. We can't see 'em 'til they open up."

Donovan looked over to the woods, then to the field where his other two companies were stalled out. His brow furrowed for only a few seconds, then he nodded.

"Here's what we're going to do," Donovan said. "Mills, go back and tell Thornton to take charge and hold his position for now. Abramovich, head back to the CP and get us some more artillery support. Oliver, you, and Kilmer stay here and coordinate. I'm going to go pull A and B Companies back out of range of the farmhouse and have them set up a base of fire against the woods."

Donovan pushed himself to his feet and ran toward his beleaguered men. In contradiction of his orders, Oliver Ames likewise shot up and began to follow.

"He'll get himself blown away if no one's there to watch out for him," the young lieutenant shouted.

Sigi stood and turned to leave but as he did a *crack-hiss-thunk* split the air, a rifle shot so close that it was gut-wrenchingly audible even amidst the din of battle. Terror gripped Sigi, a quick, chilling thrill, but it was Oliver Ames who crumpled to the ground perhaps a dozen yards from where they'd all been lying.

The realization that he was still alive, but unlikely to stay that way if he didn't get down, hit Sigi's brain just in time. He dropped to the ground, just as another near miss kicked up a small geyser of dirt a few feet behind him. Sigi crawled to where Oliver lay, unmoving. Donovan met him there, put a hand to his adjutant's neck and shook his head, a fleeting twist of sorrow contorted his face, but his expression hardened immediately.

"Carry out your orders, Abramovich," Donovan shouted. "Get us that goddamn artillery!"

"Yes, sir!"

Hank darted to the next tree, drawing a hail of rifle fire as he did so—but no machine gun fire. The New Yorkers responded in kind, their bolt action Enfield 1917 rifles flinging hefty .30-06 rounds through the trees at the Krauts who had just tried to shoot their new lieutenant. The initial bloody flurry of automatic fire that had greeted C Company upon entering the woods had died down now, as both sides sought to preserve their precious machine guns until they could be most effective.

Hank hit the ground next to an automatic rifle team.

"Remember, hold your fire unless you can see one of their MGs, or if you see a cluster of four or more infantry," he said.

The man behind the automatic rifle was solidly built and appeared to be in his thirties under the dirt layered on his face. He looked at Hank with unrecognizing brown eyes, but seeing Hank's lieutenant's bars, the brim of his helmet dipped as he nodded acknowledgement.

"Yes, sir."

Hank continued his harrowing circuit through the woods, sprinting, crawling, sprinting again, hiding behind trees and rocks until he was sure he'd reached every automatic rifleman alive in the company. That done, he lay down and shouldered his rifle, a thick tree between him and the direction of the enemy. His breath came in shuddering gasps as his mind raced furiously for something else to do, but Mills had relayed Donovan's orders.

Hold your position.

Another rattling chorus of rifle fire shattered the stillness in the forest, and a scream of agony from his own lines let Hank know the Germans had struck true somewhere on that volley.

I hope you're faring better than me, Sigi.

The spool of wire strapped to Sigi's pack weighed damn near as much as he did, but he struggled with it all the way back to the front despite the ponderous weight. The only saving grace was that the spool got steadily lighter as he unrolled it over the hundreds of yards of his journey.

Finally, he reached the reverse slope of the hill where Sergeant Kilmer and two junior enlisted runners maintained the battalion's forward CP. Realizing that a highly visible spool of wire on his back would make him any sniper's favorite target, Sigi dropped the spool before he started to crawl up the hill and unwound enough wire to make it the rest of the way over. He cut the length, looped the smaller coil of wire over his right shoulder and continued the agonizing crawl uphill, careful to maintain the connection as he did so.

Kilmer started when the young lieutenant crested the rise and started rolling down the forward slope, but he relaxed upon recognizing him.

"Welcome back, sir," Kilmer said. "Would we be receiving any artillery support, and what is it you've got there?"

Making sure to stay low to the ground to reduce the chance the Germans could see what he was doing, Sigi retrieved the field phone from his pack and hooked it up to the telephone wire.

"Working on your artillery now, Sergeant," Sigi said, as he cranked the handset.

Kilmer's eyes widened.

"You do know anyone with a field phone this far forward is a magnet for sniper fire, do you not?"

"Well, then you better stay in front of me," Sigi said. "Because I can't very well adjust artillery if I'm dead, now, can I?"

"You're an artillery observer?" Kilmer asked.

"Well, no, but I did really well when we trained on it at West Point," Sigi said, then held up a hand as he heard the other end of the phone line come to life.

"Major Ericson, 149th Field Artillery."

"Major Ericson, this is Abramovich, 42nd Headquarters," Sigi said. "I'm forward with the 165th Regiment, we need a concentrated fire mission on Meurcy Farm while we readjust our lines, then we'll need a creeping barrage to support the attack."

"Abramovich, I need proper release authority from the division commander or chief of staff—"

"Major, the chief of staff is forward with the 84th Brigade, and by the time you get a hold of General Lenihan, this attack will have failed and the 165th will have lost half its strength. Can you hear what's going on here?" Sigi held the receiver out for a moment then brought it back to his ear. "We need artillery support right goddamn now or you're going to be responsible for a dead regiment."

Kilmer glanced sidelong at him, with eyebrows raised. Sigi just shook his head.

"Send it, Abramovich," Ericsson said.

Sigi relayed his position and angle to the target, as well as the target's coordinates and estimated elevation. The first round landed well north and west of the farmhouse.

"Drop five hundred, right one hundred," Sigi said. The artillery fire direction center acknowledged the adjustment, and a minute later another round landed, quite a bit closer. Sigi made two more adjustments before a round detonated amidst the stone farmhouses.

"Target, Fire for Effect!" Sigi shouted into the phone.

Sixty seconds later, massive blasts from six-inch shells shook the farmhouses and took chunks out of the stone wall surrounding it. The German fire slackened as it was their turn to experience the closest facsimile to God's Wrath yet conceived by man. Sigi grinned as the steel rain continued and the Fighting Irish were able to pull back out of effective range. Kilmer gave him a nod of approval.

"Well, sir, you may have questionable taste in books, but there's no denying you're a fair hand with a call for fire," Kilmer said.

"Why, thank you, Sergeant Kilmer," Sigi said. "I'll try not to let such compliments go to my head."

Donovan found his way back to them, covered in mud and no small amount of blood, but grinning nonetheless as he clapped Sigi on the shoulder.

"Damn fine work, Abramovich," Donovan said. "I'm going to take D Company through the woods with C Company. We'll clear out the woods, then D and C can form a base of fire against the farm itself while A and B Company renew the attack."

"Sir, if you can figure out some way to mark your position that will show up through the woods, I can adjust the artillery ahead of you," Sigi said.

Donovan looked thoughtful for a long moment.

"There were some smoke grenades in the crates you brought," Donovan said. "We'll use them to mark our forward position. Keep the artillery two hundred yards in front of the smoke. We'll advance about a hundred-fifty yards, then pop another smoke grenade for you to adjust off of."

Sigi looked at Donovan with raised eyebrows.

"Sir, with the circular error probability, two hundred meters could put you within the burst radius of any short shells..."

"And if the shells land too far behind the Germans, they'll stick it out, keep their wits about them and cut us to shreds. We found out the hard way that the Spirit of the Bayonet only gets you so far," Donovan said. "These are hardened veterans; we're not going to dislodge them from prepared defenses by playing it safe."

Sigi nodded and started cranking on the phone again.

"Yes, sir, one creeping barrage coming up," Sigi said.

In an hour, Hank lost four more men killed and seven more wounded too badly to keep fighting. Perhaps later it would bother him that he didn't know the men's names, but for the moment he was too busy with his inherited command responsibilities.

The ranges at which they were engaging were too long and the trees between them too densely arrayed to have a good idea of how many Germans they'd shot in return. His men were already digging shallow fighting positions per doctrine, but the relative stability of their position over the last sixty minutes gave Hank no comfort.

It was only a matter of time until the Germans brought their artillery to bear on his newly inherited company. A cavalry officer by training, moreover a horseman since his sixth birthday, Hank's instinct was to maneuver, and this was the exact opposite.

Rustling leaves and underbrush from behind signaled the approach of D Company. Hank reached out to tap the man on the other side of the tree from him. The soldier looked back at him, and Hank gestured for him to head back, away from the Germans.

"That's D Company. Head back and tell them to stay low," Hank said. "Don't want our reinforcements cut to pieces just getting here."

The man obeyed, running back toward the approaching troops at a crouch.

As the men of D Company started to take up positions amongst C Company, Donovan crawled up to Hank.

"Thornton, what's our situation?"

"Sir, we've been holding this line for more than an hour. We have eighty-three effectives left and we're running low on ammunition."

"We brought some more for the rifles and machine guns. More importantly, your friend Abramovich has a line back to the artillery." Donovan pulled six smoke grenades from his pack and handed them one by one to Hank. Hank accepted them with some confusion.

"I don't think we have enough smoke grenades to screen our advance, sir."

Donovan shook his head.

"They're not for screening, they're for marking. I'm going to go to the extreme right flank, you're going to take the left. We're each going to toss smoke to visually mark our forward line for Abramovich."

Hank began securing the grenades to his person.

"Understood, sir. Umm...sir...these are Mk. II grenades, phosphorus. Hard to throw them further than the burst radius."

Donovan paused a moment; he hadn't thought of that. Finally, after half a minute's reflection, he said, "Tie cord to them and use it to sling them ahead of you. Pull the pin; release the spoon; one complete twirl above your head, two at the most, and let fly."

"Yes, sir," Hank agreed. *Clever, if it works.*

"Make sure your NCOs understand how important it is to dress their lines properly," Donovan said. "In between each bound, troop the line until you meet me in the center, then we'll head back to the flanks to pop smoke. Godspeed."

Two plumes of gray blossomed out of the treetops. Sigi peered at them intently, estimating distance and direction from his position to each smoke cloud, from the clouds to Meurcy Farm, and from the clouds to the top of Hill 137. He plotted his estimates on the map and cranked the field phone again.

"We need a linear sheaf between the following coordinates," Sigi said. "Adjust each successive volley 200 meters along a line orientation 6100 mils."

The Fire Direction Center acknowledged his mission data and sent a time of flight of two minutes. Sigi held his breath as a ragged line of sixteen explosions ripped through the forest, shredding trees, and sending black clouds of smoke and frag into the air. The concussion of the volley washed over him even hundreds of yards away. The rounds were north of the marking smoke, but without the ability to talk directly to the troops in contact, he was still operating on faith.

Kilmer must have seen Sigi's worried expression.

"Looks like you've landed another well-plotted fire mission, sir," he offered by way of comfort.

"I hope so, Sergeant Kilmer," Sigi said. "Because if I screwed this up, I could've killed them all."

In between the earth-tremoring impact of the artillery, the forest came alive once again with rifles and machine guns. Sigi watched and listened for several heart-wrenching minutes until two new plumes of gray smoke emerged from the treetops. Sigi groaned in relief; a knot of painful tension unclenched in his shoulders.

On their third bound forward, one shell burst short of the rest in the volley. The explosion was a mere fifty yards from one of C Company's squads, peppering them with metal shards and splintered tree. Two men fell to the ground clutching wounds, their mouths open in screams that were barely audible over the thundering detonations of the barrage.

"Hang on, C Company," Hank screamed at the top of his lungs. "Get down and wait for the volley to shift forward. GET DOWN."

Three men from first platoon started to run south, away from the friendly shelling and the enemy, but Hank ran up to the lead man, grabbed him by the shoulders and forced him to the ground. Kneeling on the man's back, he pointed his pistol at the other men who had run.

"Get down, but stay *here*," Hank shouted. "We'll need to hit the Germans while they're still rattled!"

The remaining two men shared a quick glance between themselves. Apparently deciding that the crazed lieutenant pointing a gun at them was more dangerous than their own artillery, they dropped to the ground, rifles pointed north again toward the enemy.

"Good boys! Stay here until you hear the whistle!"

Hank ran up and down C Company's line, repeating the order, ignoring the watery sensation in his gut every time a tree was shattered by an artillery round. Only after he was sure his company was down, neither retreating nor advancing until the barrage moved farther north, did Hank find a piece of cover for himself, lying down behind a wide, low rock.

Duty accomplished for the moment, Hank squeezed his eyes shut and prayed silently as the world shook and heaved about him under the pounding of the guns.

Lord, deliver us. Bless me, bless these men, and bless Sigi's big ole brain. Put the Boche *under our bayonets... and if I could live to see Lubbock again, that'd be right nice, too. In your Son's name and for his sake, Amen.*

Finally, the shelling stopped, the guns needing to adjust to their new linear target further north. Relative silence fell over the wood and the smoke and dust began to clear. There, no more than fifty or sixty yards away, lay a line of German machine gun nests. Many of the gray-clad troops lay dead or wounded, but more were dazedly returning to their firing positions.

No time to wait for Donovan to order the attack.

Hank pulled the whistle Captain Bootz had given him, pressed it to his lips and gave a long loud blast, then dropped it to dangle on its chain and screamed, "FOLLOW ME!"

Hank sprinted forward, not daring to look behind to see if the men were following him.

Ten yards. The Germans were rallying, machine gun bullets began to kick up dirt and chip away at the bark of trees about him. The bursts filled the air with sonic cracks and a vicious buzz akin to a hornet's nest.

Twenty yards, and thirty, return fire from C Company's automatic riflemen flew past him toward the enemy.

Forty yards, the muzzle of a German machine gun, flashing fire, tracked toward him. He dropped to a knee, took aim, and fired. The powerful .30-06 round kicked the rifle butt into his shoulder. A clean miss, a searing pain in his left thigh. Hank worked the action on his Enfield furiously, but it was too late—

Two rifle shots from his right, and the German fell away from his machine gun. Hank glanced right; it was the man he'd thrown to the ground and one of his comrades. No time to celebrate—another German dove for the machine gun.

Hank covered the remaining ten yards faster than he'd ever managed back at West Point's football field, adrenaline dulling the reports of pain in his left leg. He fired from the hip, taking the man behind the machine gun in the shoulder. The man fell back, his hand scrabbling at his belt for a pistol.

Without time to work the action on his rifle, Hank drove forward, ramming his bayonet into the German. The blade pierced cloth and flesh and sawed against his victim's ribs with a sickening, grating sound. The German let loose a guttural scream and writhed violently to the left, wrenching the rifle from Hank's hands.

From the right, three more Germans charged. One went down to a rifle shot, a C Company man intercepted the second with a bayonet into his guts, but the third closed the distance. He swung a short-handled shovel in a vicious overhand arc at Hank's head.

Hank threw himself to the right and tugged furiously to free his holstered pistol. The sharpened shovel whistled through the air past Hank's face and buried itself in the mud where he'd been a split second before. Hank tripped and fell on his back against the side of the German machine gun nest behind his assailant. The German pulled his shovel free from the earth and turned to continue his assault.

Instinctively, Hank raised his left hand to ward off the blow even as he raised his pistol in his right hand. He jerked the trigger, momentarily forgetting everything he'd ever been taught about shooting a pistol, but at this range the round still took the man in the knee, breaking the German's momentum as he screamed in pain.

The shovel fell with far less force than before. Hank clamped down on the tool's haft with his left hand and ripped it out of his enemy's hands. Hank punched the muzzle of his pistol into the German's chest, eliciting from him an inarticulate cry of pain. He yanked the trigger and nothing happened; the slide being pushed back by the German's chest, it was incapable of firing. Pulling the pistol back slightly, enough to let it go back into battery, he jerked the trigger four times. The shovel-wielding attacker fell to the ground, limp, but Hank's pistol jammed on the fourth round, a cartridge caught and deformed by the slide-action.

Before he could drop the shovel to clear the malfunction on his weapon, another German charged, bayonet leveled at Hank's chest. Hank swung his new shovel in an awkward up-stroke parry. The impact reverberated through the handle into Hank's arm as the haft intersected the rifle's barrel. It was enough to knock the point of the blade off target.

In the gap, Hank swung the jammed pistol in a lateral arch, smashing the slide of the pistol into the German's teeth as violently as he could in the confines of the MG nest. The weapon connected with a crack and a squelch; the German spun around from the blow, a shower of blood and teeth spurting from his mouth onto the corpses of his dead comrades.

His pistol now further fouled, Hank dropped it, took up the shovel in a downward grip with both hands and drove the point down with all his might into the back of the German's neck. Spine, esophagus, and windpipe gave way, leaving the German's head attached by only threads of flesh and sinew.

The sound of more bootsteps squelching through the mud, snapping twigs and brush sent Hank scrabbling for his pistol. He brushed away the tissue caught in the ejection port then yanked back on the slide. The jammed round still didn't eject so Hank slammed the palm of his left hand into the weapon repeatedly, finally knocking it free. The slide flew forward, chambering another round, but as Hank raised the weapon to address the new threat, he realized that he was surrounded not by field gray, but by doughboy brown uniforms.

The men of the 69th surged past him, shooting and stabbing, bludgeoning and slashing. Finally, the Germans broke, running from the murderous Irishmen or throwing their rifles down in surrender.

Hank smiled dazedly for a moment, but the adrenaline was fading and suddenly his left thigh was screaming in pain.

"Oh, hot darn," he said between gritted teeth. He slid to sit against the side of the MG nest. His left pant leg was soaked in blood.

The big familiar face of Major Donovan, medals on his breast, smoking M1911 pistol in his hand, filled Hank's vision. Donovan took one look at his condition and shouted for a medic.

"Sorry I didn't wait for you, sir," Hank said. "There wasn't time—"

"No need, son," Donovan cut him off. "You did just right. Lie still and let Doc work on you. A and C Company are taking the farmhouse as we speak. It looks like a win today, lieutenant."

A boy younger than Hank appeared next to Donovan. He cut away Hank's pant leg with a pair of scissors and examined his wound with a frown of professional concentration. He prodded around it, eliciting a hiss of pain from Hank.

"You're lucky, lieutenant." The medic began to clean the wound. "An inch left, and this would have broken your femur, two inches and it might have severed the artery and you'd already be dead."

"Well, I gotta give these German fellers credit, they die tough," Hank said.

Donovan looked around at the carnage in the hole, gave a short, sharp laugh and clapped Hank on the shoulder.

"Not tougher than a Texan, it appears."

Hank gasped as the medic started packing the wound. The boy stopped and looked up at him.

"You need some morphine, sir?"

The pain in his leg was stabbing and throbbing at the same time, but a memory of the boys who caught a piece of the artillery flashed in his mind. Hank shook his head.

"Nah, save it for someone really dinged up. I'll manage."

The medic shrugged and went back to work. "If you say, so, Lieutenant," he said. "Major Donovan, sir, we do need to get him back to a field hospital so they can give it a better cleaning and sew it up. And he'll need to stay off it for a while."

Hank's heart sank.

"Is that necessary? Just give me a couple days off the line—"

"If you want to lose your goddamn leg, Lieutenant, then yeah, a couple days off the line," the medic said, laconically. "If you'd like to avoid infection and amputation, then you'll shut up and go back to the hospital. You also probably need a pint of blood."

"Easy, Doc," Donovan remonstrated before turning to Hank. "It's all right, Thornton. Go to the hospital, get patched up. When you're ready, if you can escape Colonel MacArthur, you're always welcome back here with the 69th."

Chapter Eleven

A Younger Aunt Ella in a Happier Day

Yekaterinburg, Siberia

Turgenev and the bulk of Strat Recon were gone, leaving Mokrenko in charge and on his own.

I hope to see them all come back, thought the lieutenant.

At this point, Mokrenko had six heavy machine guns, nine hundred thirty-seven rifles, including a couple of hundred which were privately owned, brought in by volunteers, and about a thousand troops, sixty percent of whom were untrained and an eighth or so of whom were trained, but female.

He had no other officers but from the women's group, and the women, he decided, really needed their own to stay with them.

Imagine, then, the former sergeant's relief when an elderly colonel, fat, bearded, and dark gray, walked into his headquarters and said, "I know you, sergeant . . . you were the one who stopped the train robbery."

"Well, hello, Colonel Plestov," replied a beaming Mokrenko. "Wonderful to see you, sir. By the way, it's Lieutenant of the Guards now, sir. No chance to change insignia . . . no insignia to change *to*, for that matter."

"Lieutenant of the . . . you were one of those who rescued the royal family, weren't you?"

"What we could save of it, yes, sir. I was part of a group sent forward to determine and send back their precise location to the people who actually launched the rescue, and to prepare the way. We participated after that, yes, but were not central to the operation."

"They also serve, Serg—Lieutenant; they also serve. Speaking of which, could you use whatever help an old man can give you?"

"I don't need an old man's help," replied Mokrenko, "but I could use an old and brave soldier's hand, yes. I just wish I had some artillery to put you in charge of. Let me ask you, sir: what can you do for us? We're expecting a strong column of Reds to show up in a few days, and all I have—well, all except for the women—is well-meaning but untrained rabble, half a dozen machine guns, and no other officers . . . again, excepting the women."

"Women? Women? You're shitting me, right?"

"Yes, sir, and no, sir; I have about a short company's worth of women under their own captain. They're actually pretty good girls and better than half decent soldiers. Couldn't have liberated Yekaterinburg without them, sir."

"Indeed? Well, I'm too long in the tooth for active combat and I know it. If I didn't know it, my wife—who, you may recall, is altogether too honest, in her own way—would surely tell me. I could take over logistics for you."

Mokrenko's head and eyes rolled ecstatically as he breathed a sigh of nigh unto infinite joy. "Sir, that would be an *immense* relief. I'm nearly lost, logistically, without my usual boss, Guards Captain Turgenev. Let me tell you what we've got going so far . . ."

✤ ✤ ✤

Alapaevsk, Siberia

They could have ridden, of course, ridden and skied. And perhaps that would have been less difficult and more comfortable. But to Turgenev and his men, the safety and comfort of their party came in a distant second to finding and rescuing the Imperial prisoners in the hands of presumptively murderous Reds.

Thus, instead of trying to ride their Yakuts and glide on their skis, for days on end, the seven men of the group not left behind in Yekaterinburg—Turgenev, now Sergeant Koslov, "Goat," Sarnof, Timashuk, Shukhov, Peredery, and Popov—rode in an open truck, driven by Curran, and with the top down on Maynard's auto. In two trucks behind them rode the Yakuts, covered by blankets against the wind chill, with a couple of men in back likewise bundled against the cold. Further behind, after the Yakuts, was an empty truck, on the theory that the captives might be hurt badly enough they'd need to stay prone. The vehicles and drivers had been commandeered by the senior teamster, Garin, though he remained behind to lead the teamsters seized earlier.

The road . . . well, it wasn't actually much of a road, a mix of mush, snow, rock, and dirt, all intermixed with potholes, ridges, and lonesome bumps. Moreover, the vehicles' suspensions, while just barely up to the demands of keeping the car and trucks from falling apart, were in no way up to keeping the passengers from taking an awful beating.

If it hadn't been for the time, thought Turgenev, cold and miserable, with aching chest and kidneys, *I'd rather have ridden the horses. No, that's not exactly true, I'd rather have walked! These things are the devil's contraptions. . . .*

Maynard, conversely, was having a very good time, laughing as he wheeled over and around all manner of misery-inducing impediments.

Man, thought Turgenev, *was never meant to move at*—he spared a glance at the shifting needle that told the speed, then did some mental calculations—*my God! Fifty* versts *an hour! And not on a nice smooth railroad!*

A sign flashed by: *Alapaevsk.* Then it was onto a bridge, crossing the Nevya River, with the bulk of the lake-like river to the west and the steep-sided bluff of the main industrial area to the northeast.

The road in the town was substantially different from the road leading here from Yekaterinburg. Pothole, rock, ridge, and ditch disappeared in favor of sheer mud. Maynard's auto bogged down up to the axles within a hundred meters of leaving the bridge behind.

Turgenev looked north and decided. *Not a chance it's any better through the town. Horse time.*

"Koslov?" the captain demanded.

"Here, sir!"

"Get the Yakuts off the trucks."

"Peredery and Popov?"

The latter stuck his head out. "Here, sir, both of us."

"You two stay here to guard the vehicles. The rest of us are moving forward by horse."

An old woman, bent and worn with the cares of years and decades, came out, carefully keeping her feet from the sea of mud that fronted her little wooden porch.

"Madam," Turgenev asked, "can you direct me to the Napolnaya School?"

"Do you mean the one where they've locked up the royals?"

"The same; I bear important dispatches and orders from Moscow. Lenin has decreed they are to be brought to him." *This continuous lying really doesn't sit well with me.*

The woman passed over the directions, adding, "You had best hurry, then. I've heard a rumor they're all to be shot."

Lower Selimskaya Mine

"I'm not going any further," said Grand Duke Sergei Mihailovich. "Not one step."

The grand duke was a cousin of the late Tsar, Nicholas the Second. It would have been easy to mistake one for the other in a dim light, provided they were wearing some kind of headgear, since Sergei was more or less bald. He'd never married, finding in his cousin's ex-mistress, the beautiful Polish ballerina Mathilde Kschessinska, all the family he wanted or needed. This had remained true even after Mathilde had also taken up with his cousin, Andre. No one really knew to whom the resultant child belonged, but Sergei had taken the boy up, raising him as his own, anyway.

He'd led and loved the military life and, if he was no great shakes as a soldier, it still could be said that he was honest, brave, and tried to the best of his ability.

"So you're not going to follow orders?" said the Chekist, Pyotr Startsev. "Have it your own way then." At that, Startsev drew his pistol and shot the grand duke once through the head, dropping him to the ground like a sack of meat. At six foot three the grand duke's corpse was large enough to make an audible *thump* as it hit, despite the soft ground.

"I trust," said the Chekist, after the women stopped screaming, "that I won't have to be as harsh with the rest of you."

It was with that shot that Elisabeth Feodorovna knew that her prayers to offer herself as a sacrifice to save the others had been ignored, and that they were all doomed.

"Move them on," Startsev ordered the rest of his party. They were all still blindfolded, with their hands bound behind them, as they had been since leaving the school, hence there was a good deal of stumbling and several complete falls.

"Oh, take their blindfolds off," Startsev ordered, "but leave their hands bound."

"Hey, Boss," asked Startsev's assistant, Ryabov, "could I have a word with you? Sort of privately?"

"Just move them on once they can see," said Startsev, before turning to ask, "What is it?"

In a low voice, Ryabov asked, "Just this; since we're going to kill them anyway, is there any reason the boys shouldn't have a good time with the women before we kill them?"

"We're not in that much of a hurry," Startsev mused. "Yeah, sure, why the hell not? It's not like they'll suffer overlong for it, and the boys will have a nice memory to warm them on a cold night. Yeah, go ahead and fuck 'em."

"Great, Boss, and thanks!"

"Keep them tied and toss the men in first though."

"I think we ought to rough them up a bit, too," said Ryabov. "They'll be more cooperative that way."

"Sure, go ahead."

"I brought a couple of bottles, too, Boss, if you don't mind."

"*After* the men are in the mine!"

"Sure thing, Boss."

✣ ✣ ✣

Napolnaya School, Alapaevsk

The half dozen prisoners taken by Turgenev and his men knelt on the cold floor in a simple line, with their feet bound and their hands bound behind them. Turgenev had been able to take them during their meal, without a shot being fired. It remained to be seen if shots would still be fired, though.

"No one in the revolution outranks Ilyich," said Turgenev. "No one has the right to deny him anything. I don't have time to play games. So I am going to ask you each, once, where did they take the prisoners Ilyich wants brought to Moscow. If you refuse to answer, that will be the last thing you refuse. And you had better hope there's no God or Devil, no Heaven or Hell, but Ilyich will still revile your names."

Give them the excuse they need to talk.

"Where did they take the prisoners? One . . . two . . . three."

And a good reason to.

On "three" Turgenev discharged his pistol into the head of the man to the extreme right of the line. His brains, along with a good deal of blood and a number of skull fragments, flew out onto the floor in front of him, even as the limp body flopped forward.

Turgenev took a step to the left, while thinking, *Mokrenko has perhaps been a bad influence on me . . . or maybe a good one. Maybe a good one in this world.*

As soon as warm muzzle of the M1911 touched the back of the head of the next man, he blurted out, "There's a mine to the north of here. Take the north road to Nizhnaya Sinyachika. It will T-out on an east-west running road. Take a left, maybe one or two *versts* and south of the road a little, there's a mine. They're taking them there."

"To kill them?"

"Well, yes, of course. Those were the orders from the Perm Soviet."

"Very good, thank you. I can't spare a man to guard you, sorry, and, since you are a party to a kidnapping and what we hope is only an attempted murder . . . Koslov, have these men shot then meet me outside to saddle up and race!"

Lower Selimskaya Mine

All but one of the rifles were stacked in tripods together.

One by one the men in the group had been clubbed and beaten half unconscious or even dead and then tossed into the mine. The number of splashes, however, did not equal the number of men tossed. Moreover, lighter splashing suggested that someone had gotten free of his bonds and saved himself. That promised more trouble later.

But later was later; for now it was the turn of the three women. Their faces were left alone, other than for a few hard slaps each, so that the men could enjoy their looks. Neither were they clubbed, so that they wouldn't simply be lying there, as if dead. Instead, they were, each of them, brutally punched in their abdomens until they wept with the pain.

"Leave the others alone," Ella begged. "Please! . . . *oof* . . . They're just . . . *aiaiaia* . . . simple women . . . *oof* . . . . . . oh God! . . . I'm the aristocrat here . . . *aiaiai* . . . I'm the one you want revenge on." Weeping then, tears flooding down her elegant face, Ella began to vomit from the beating. This earned her another, harder slap.

The Reds didn't listen, anyway. Once the women were beaten into pure helplessness, their clothes were roughly torn away, leaving them stark naked but for rude socks and worn shoes on their feet. Somebody—Ryabov, she thought—used her underwear to wipe the vomit from Ella's face.

She'd never borne a child. Her body retained almost all of the beauty it had had in her twenties. The Reds, almost as a single man, licked their lips in anticipation.

"Don't worry, Princess," Ryabov said. "We're *all* going to have you and then we'll take turns with the other two, as well." With a show of contempt he ripped from Ella an icon—a "not made by human hands" image of the Savior, given her by the late Tsar—and tossed it contemptuously to the ground. Then, with a one-handed shove he knocked her flat on her back.

"Hey, two men; get over here and hold the bitch's legs apart!"

One of the other men, not so detailed, said, "I'll get the aristocrat later. For now, I'll make do with this nun." At that, he pulled Varvara Yakovleva up by her hair, lowered her to her knees, and said, "Open wide!"

Ella couldn't get a decent count. It had started with Ryabov, of course, thrusting like a pig while two men held her legs far apart. That should have hurt . . . and had.

It hadn't hurt merely because she was dry. Nor because Ryabov was anything special, in the stallion department. Rather, she'd never had much sex in her marriage and none at all, with anyone, since the murder of her husband. Vaginally speaking, she was almost a virgin and had torn, much as a virgin might.

It should have hurt more than it did, both physically and emotionally.

It hadn't. In a way, the beating had been a bounty, causing an endorphin surge and insulating her against the pain and some of the humiliation. But drugs wear off. By the seventh or eighth rape—she had lost count—the pain in her vagina was far worse than the beating had been. This was so, even though she was no longer dry but well-lubricated with a mix of semen and blood.

With a grunt and a hard thrust her current rapist finished and climbed off of her. He'd smelt abominably; they'd all stunk since the second, reeking of cheap vodka, harsh tobacco, and filthy, rotten teeth.

The next one squatted on her chest, waving a monstrous penis in her face. At first, she thought he was going to do what she thought she'd seen one or maybe two of them doing to Varvara. But no. This one said, "You may think you're all high and mighty and aloof, Princess. But when I stick this in you, you *will* scream; I guarantee it."

I will not scream. Nothing they can do can make me scream. My God stands beside me, even in this hour. Nothing they can do to my body can matter...

Oh, God, she wanted to scream when the Red forced himself into her, to scream, to cry, even to beg... *But I will* not, *no, no, no, not ever. But, oh, my dear God, it hurts, it hurts sooo much.*

That went on for a while, every second and every thrust a new torment. Still, she would not cry out or show anything but indifference.

The Red stopped for a moment. "You're a tougher cunt than I thought. But you'll scream now, I guarantee it, bitch."

With that he pulled out, got to his knees and roughly flipped Ella over onto her stomach, before lowering himself onto her back. She felt him groping to line himself up. Then she could feel the head of his penis beginning to push into her from behind and steeled herself for what she knew would be the worst tearing of all.

But it didn't come. Instead, she heard a fusillade of shots and then the Red rolled off her back and flopped to the ground on his own back, moaning.

✛ ✛ ✛

Dismounting, Turgenev left one man, Timashuk, to hold the horses. Then he led the remaining three to the north side of the road and began following the wood line west. It hadn't been hard to figure out where the mine was; a dozen or so wagons were clustered in a little open area just off the road. And then there were the screams, female screams of utter pain and degradation. As they got closer, they could hear male laughter interspersed with the screaming.

Even without seeing it, Turgenev and the men with him knew what was going on. Still, he and they resisted doing what they wanted to do, to charge at full speed with their machine pistols and Lewis Gun blazing.

A bare fifty meters from the mine, Turgenev signaled the others to halt. He crawled forward himself, on his belly, until he could take in the scene. Barely, he resisted the urge to vomit. When he had a good idea and, more importantly, could articulate what was going on and explain what he wanted, he crawled back to where the men waited.

There, whispering, he sketched out a map on the ground with his left index finger and gave his orders.

The Lewis gun barked, spilling the blood, guts, and brains on the only rapist obviously armed on the site. Turgenev and Sarnof bolted to place themselves between the stacked rifles and the rapists, while Koslov and Shukhov, the latter bearing the Lewis Gun and swinging it menacingly, stepped out from the wood line. Meanwhile, Koslov butt-stroked the Red who was trying to jam himself into the anus of one of the women, freeing her of his weight. The corporal made a point of not looking down at her.

Startsev drew the pistol with which he'd murdered Grand Duke Sergei. He was not nearly fast enough. Before he could properly aim at anyone, Shukhov had put half a dozen bullets into the Bolshevik's lower abdomen and legs. One of those—by luck or by divine providence—had torn away Startsev's penis and testicles. He screamed and moaned without surcease as he lay on the ground. When he realized what he was now missing, Startsev added a good deal of weeping interspersed with the screams.

Covered by Turgenev and Koslov, Sarnof and Corporal Koslov first retrieved some rope they'd noticed on the wagons, along with half a dozen blankets. Looking away, they passed the blankets to the naked women and then tied all the men's hands and feet together. When that was done, they went back to Turgenev and asked, "What do we do with this lot, sir?"

Turgenev looked around the site and said, "There's plenty of lumber here to crucify the lot, but I see no nails and we lack enough rope to make crosses. There's plenty of wood to impale them all, too, but we lack the time to sharpen them enough, while the ground's too hard to dig proper support holes."

His eyes came to rest on a long section of fence. Nodding, and remembering what had been done to the nuns, and with what almost happened to Ella deeply in mind, he said, "Stick a bayonet five or six times up each of their arses. Then untie their hands and tie them to the fence so their arms are at about forty-five degrees. When they're all tied, smash their legs."

To Timashuk, who had arrived leading the horses, Turgenev said, "See what you can do, if anything, for the ones in the mine."

Nearby, Bolsheviks were screaming as cold steel was rudely shoved into the rectum of each one, twisted, then shoved in again, and again, and again, and again. Fresh blood flowed with each jab, running across unwashed buttocks and down hairy legs.

The nuns, Varvara and Ekaterina, hadn't been quite as badly abused as had Ella. Blanket-wrapped, they were able to make their way to her. On the way, Varvara stopped to pick up one of the bottles abandoned by the captive reds. She took a swig, swished it around her mouth several times, then spit it out on the ground. She did this five times before she actually took a healthy slug of the not particularly healthy distillate.

Then she and Ekaterina framed themselves to either side of Ella, sitting her up. Varvara held the bottle up to Ella's lips, but she batted it away and let out a single, horrible, piercing shriek containing everything she'd felt over the course of the entire, vicious gang rape. Only then did she start to cry.

After their anal bayonet-rapes, the Bolsheviks had been, one by one, dragged to the fence and had their hands tied to the top rails. Indeed, so tightly were they tied that, within the hour, deprived of blood, the flesh of those hands would die anyway. Already they and the wrists were monstrously swollen around and above their bindings.

If there had ever been an iron bar on site it was nowhere to be found. No matter, shitty and bloody bayonets notwithstanding, the four rescuers used the Reds' own rifles to break the legs of each. Their screams redoubled now. The ones whose legs hadn't yet been broken screamed and begged for mercy.

"Too late for mercy," said Turgenev. "You should have shown mercy to your victims."

Moreover, with broken legs, none of them could stand any longer. Instead, they had to drop—something which further damaged their already ruined legs—to where only their swollen, dying wrists supported them. Within a mere ten minutes breathing had become quite difficult. After that, to breathe they had to pull themselves up by those same dying wrists. This further agonized their broken legs, eliciting further screams.

They still begged for help, for mercy, and none more than the now-dickless Startsev. Nobody listened, though Turgenev, who seemed to have been changed by what had been done to the women, laughed at them.

It's not strictly necessary to wait, thought Turgenev. *They're going to die or be utterly crippled no matter if they die or not. But I want the nuns to know, deep down, that they were avenged.*

By the end of two hours, the Reds were just cooling meat, all life having fled.

Walking along the fence, Turgenev drew his knife across the throat of each. Blood leaked; it did not gush. "For my little Natalya," he whispered, as he slashed every throat.

By this time Timashuk, working with Shukhov, had rigged a tripod over the mine and recovered the victims. All but two were dead to split skulls. The exceptions were Grand Duke Sergei's secretary, Remez, who was expected to die, and Vladimir Pavlovich Paley, the illegitimately born Prince, who somehow managed to avoid the split skull and leaking brains of the corpses, but was still largely incoherent with a large knot on his skull.

"Get the women and wounded into the wagons," he said, finally. "Take the horses that aren't needed for the wagons with us, too. Let's go."

"What do we do with the bodies, sir?" asked Koslov.

"Leave the Reds hanging for the birds to eat. Put the innocents in a wagon and bring them with us."

❖ ❖ ❖

Hotel Amerikanskaya, Yekaterinburg

"When you took the town," said Tomas Masaryk, head of the Czechoslovak National Council, "I dispatched two riders to find the legion and bring it here." The "legion" was the Czechoslovak Legion, composed of tens of thousands of Czechs and Slovaks, some born in the Russian Empire, other deserted or defected or recruited from POWs in Russian hands, fighting for freedom from Austria-Hungary. Masaryk himself had been en route to the United States when he'd heard of the rescue of the Romanovs and doubled back, sensing greater opportunity right here in Russia than in distant America.

"Chances of them getting here with troops anytime soon?" asked Mokrenko, briefly halting his back-and-forth pacing.

Masaryk, an old, gray man, goateed and heavily mustached, shrugged his shoulders and shook his head. "There's no real telling. I sent good men, but it is a difficult and uncertain world."

Mentally, Mokrenko dismissed the possibility, thinking, too, *If we'd left all the gold and silver here for the grabbing I'm quite sure they'd have managed to turn up.*

He resumed pacing. *Good thing, I suppose, that that Slovak Minister of War and French Army general, Stefanik, hasn't shown up yet. That would be more complications that I would prefer to deal with. After all, would he listen to a former sergeant and jumped-up Guards lieutenant? Nah.*

Captain Bochkareva and her assistant, Princess Tatuyeva, stood by silently while Mokrenko paced. Likewise did a few older veterans not from Strat Recon, and two prominent citizens of the town who probably could *command*, but hadn't the first clue as to what they should be doing or why. One of the veterans, a lieutenant, seemed mildly ill. He shook slightly, too. There were also a couple of men in suits, with top hats, who didn't look remotely Russian, representing the Czechoslovak delegation.

I don't have a battalion, thought Lieutenant Mokrenko. *I've got five distinct mobs plus a support mob plus the women, who are not a mob. Thank God, at least, for Colonel Plestov, who has brought a degree of order to the support mob. More importantly, he's getting the precious metals out of town so that if . . . no, be honest, when I lose here at least the Reds won't have that. Rather, they won't if I can buy Plestov enough time. Which is probably all I can do.*

For the rest . . . well, there are "prominent citizens" in charge of two of my mobs. For three I have two former sergeants and a former lieutenant, the latter with only one arm and an obvious drinking problem.

With twenty heavy machine guns and crews for them, this wouldn't be hard. I'd outpost them in the cellars of buildings around the town with interlocking grazing fires and then put the mobs, by platoons, under the command of the gun crews' leaders to defend the guns.

But I don't have twenty. I have six. And I don't have six good crews. I don't even have one good crew. I've got two men from Strat Recon, who trained the others a very little, and can somewhat manage their own guns.

And the Reds are supposedly coming by train. I'm actually surprised they're not here yet. I wonder what will be in the follow-on echelons. Ten thousand? Twenty? I'm too weak to defend against those kinds of numbers. I'd be too weak if all my soldiers were well trained.

And then, too, let's not delude ourselves. There's an anti-Bolshevik element in the town that has stepped forward to fill the ranks. That doesn't mean there isn't also still a significant pro-Bolshevik element in the town, ready to rise at the first opportunity. They probably don't have much in the way of arms, but would they need much?

So that is actually job one and, moreover, a job my civilian-led mobs are suited for.

Mokrenko stopped pacing and looked directly at the two civilians in charge of the almost two-hundred-man mobs. They were late middle-aged, prosperous and well-fed, and appeared to Mokrenko, the both of them, to have earnest and honest faces.

"Mr. Smirnov and Mr. Kuznetsov," Mokrenko observed, "this town was, until quite recently, very pro-Red. What are your opinions on it today?"

"Still mostly Red," shrugged Kusnetzov, stocky and with a red beard.

"Less than it used to be, after the terror inflicted on it, but there's a strong stream of sympathy for the Bolsheviks," the thinner and beardless Smirnov added.

"I want you two to each take half the town, divided along . . . let's say . . . the Ulitsa Malysheva. Smirnov, take the north; Kuznetsov, the south. Compile lists of likely Red sympathizers who could organize a counter-counterrevolution. A few hundred for each of you. More if you think it's necessary. Arrest them and lock them up in . . . well, why not be a little poetic; stick them in the Ipatiev House and provide a score or so of armed guard from each of your groups."

"Shoot them?" asked Smirnov.

"Not yet," Mokrenko said. "We'll keep them alive as hostages for the good behavior of the rest."

Mokrenko waited a few seconds, then asked, "Well, what are you waiting for? Those internal threats won't incarcerate themselves."

Wordlessly, the two men left to see to their new duties.

"Captain Bochkareva?"

"Yes, Guards Lieutenant?" Maria Bochkareva tended to the formal.

"We are too weak to defend, as we are right now. Therefore, we are going to attack. That is to say that *you* are going to attack.

"I want you to take your healthy women, plus two heavy machine guns, plus a good deal of explosive demolitions and a detonating machine, and ambush the train lines to the west. Do so at least eight *versts* away from the western edge of the town, and twelve would be better."

"How am I to know," she asked, "if an oncoming train is full of Bolsheviks or full of civilians?"

That stopped Mokrenko cold. There was, indeed, no good way to tell what was inside a train from the outside, unless there happened to be artillery on a flat car or a number of cavalry horse cars visible.

Finally, he answered, "Find your ideal ambush position and blow up the tracks there. Make it really obvious that they've been blown, so the train has time to stop . . . but only *just* enough time to stop. The Reds will dismount then. Ambush them when they do."

"Fair enough," Bochkareva replied. "Come on, Princess; we've a lot of work to do and a lot of *versts* to cover.

"I'm going to need to find a miner who knows something about explosives," she added. "Neither I nor any of my women had time for any training in that."

"Do," Mokrenko said. "There's a fair chance Colonel Plestov may be able to help you there. Look him up. Also, after you ambush the train, I want you to be able to break contact and race back here. You, as the only trained group of soldiers, are going to reconstitute here as my reserve. If you can ride, you have my authority to seize any cavalry or riding horses that may be found. The colonel can probably help with that, too.

"And, as mentioned, I'm going to attach two heavy machine guns to you with carts to move them."

"Now, as to the other three companies . . ."

Bochkareva's women, with half a dozen one-horse carts, two heavy water-cooled machine guns, and two miners alleged to be both skilled in demolitions and none too fond of the Reds, left Yekaterinburg. They left, marching west, before Mokrenko could finish making sure his three "companies" that had at least some military leadership were deployed into position.

She stopped at the station to ask how long it took a train to stop and how long a train carrying eight hundred men would be. The answers were, "It depends." Finally she managed to get an answer that sort of worked: "A passenger train, moving sixty or so *versts* per hour, can usually be stopped in about ninety seconds, or about a *verst* and a half. 'Usually' . . . if they're at that speed . . . and they see a blockage up ahead . . . if."

"As for the length, assume twenty cars for eight hundred men, plus another two for officers, plus a dining car and a cooking car. Then there will be at least one but probably two fuel and water tenders. Probably another pusher car and its tender or tenders, too. All in, call it maybe four tenths of a *verst*."

Knowing there wasn't a lot of time for anything fancy, she called a halt as soon as she found a length of rail line that would do. It was situated just on the other side of a bridge over the River Iset, not very far from where Strat Recon and the teamsters had encamped. There were good, thick woods to the north of that section of line, which would provide cover and concealment for her troops, and a river, the Reshetka, meandering along to the south, more or less in parallel.

Where the Reshetka joined the Isets was too swift flowing and churning to be fordable. Instead, Bochkareva had a single span of rope stretched across the stream about one hundred fifty meters southwest of the junction, in a bend that would provide her troops some cover as they pulled themselves across.

Her two machine guns she ordered into positions about one hundred meters north of where she intended to have the rail line blown. In rethinking what Mokrenko had told her, she'd decided,

That makes no sense. If I want them to stop then they have to see the blast that cuts the line. They'll never see a few lengths of twisted steel rail.

The spot she chose to blast was where the Reshetka came closest to the line.

Her troops she had already divided into three platoons. One of these she stretched along the woods to the north, the other in the sparser woods to the south. The elevated rail bed would keep them from shooting each other. The third she stretched out to either side of the Iset, along its eastern bank, to cover the withdrawal of the rest.

Then she, and they, sat down to wait while the miners prepped the line.

Mokrenko found the lieutenant already drunk and his men milling about without direction. He had the man arrested and escorted to Colonel Plestov for disposition.

And I have neither an officer nor a sergeant to take his place. I think that means I am now the commander of this grouping. Shit.

Before he was marched away, the one-armed lieutenant said, "I wasn't always like this, a drunk. It was the arm . . ."

"I suppose everyone can find an excuse," Mokrenko said, not entirely ungently.

Then, turning to the milling troops, he ordered, his voice ringing for entire city blocks, "Entire company to assemble on me, NOW!"

Whether she'd timed the explosion properly was something Bochkareva would never know.

First, before the train even appeared, she heard the whistles repeatedly. This, she understood, was not for the sake of pedestrians on the tracks, but to let the other cars and locomotives know that a turn or halt was coming, for them to begin their own braking.

Ah, hell, she thought, as the implication dawned on her, *they're not going to be coming at sixty* versts *an hour, are they?*

Captain or not, she had little education. Quickly changing her calculation for when to detonate the explosives on the line was beyond her. Even if she had been able to do the math in her head, the skill would have been useless since she didn't know how much the train would slow for the curve. Nor could she hope to judge the speed of the train that would soon be visibly oncoming from the front. She really couldn't have judged it from the side.

If you survive this, Maria, you need to see about schooling. As is, you're a decent sergeant who got bumped to captain without any qualifications but a fighting heart.

She spared a glance at the miner on her right, manning the blasting machine that would send a locally generated jolt to the blasting caps in the charges.

Understanding her look, the miner said, "I truly don't know, Captain."

The locomotive, already sensed from its smoke and the sound of the whistle, made its first appearance coming about the bend to the southwest. *No, I can't tell what the difference in speed is.*

Watching more and more of the train emerge into view, she wondered about whether it was civilian or military. This doubt, at least, was dispelled when she counted a number of cars equal to about what the railway man had told her would be needed for the force supposed to be coming.

"Are you ready?" she asked the miner.

"Yes, Captain," he replied.

"Then . . . blow it!"

The miner pushed the plunger. Nothing happened.

"What the hell is going on?" she demanded.

He shook his head rapidly while pulling the handle of the plunger back up. Again he pushed it and, again, there was nothing.

Suspecting treason, Bochkareva began reaching for her pistol. Cursing a storm, the miner pulled the plunger back and, once again, shoved it down.

Khawammmm! This time it worked. A substantial cloud of dirt, rock, gravel, spikes, and wooden ties began to climb skyward, leaving a growing cloud of explosive smoke and dust below. Almost immediately came the sound of shrieking and squealing steel tires trying desperately for purchase on steel rails. A frantic whistling accompanied the sound of the tires on the rails.

At no time did this cacophony end until the first locomotive reached the twisted, ruined rails, a hundred meters to the southwest of Bochkareva, the miner, and number one machine gun. At that point, it began to tip over to its own left while sliding off the remnants of the tracks and onto the dirt on that side. The tenders and at least two passenger cars followed. Once the locomotive was perpendicular to the track, instead of sliding it began to roll, then spin, all the time coming closer to Bochkareva.

Like deer in headlights, all were transfixed by the approaching multi-ton machine of doom. It spun. It bounced. And all the time, the whistle kept screaming.

Expecting death and too much in shock to avoid it, Bochkareva crossed herself. Ever after she credited that religious act with saving her life, since the locomotive spun to a stop a bare fifteen *arshini* from where she stood. She and those around her were pelted with clods of dirt and rocks.

Thank you, God.

Almost immediately, rifle fire erupted from both sides of the track to her southwest. Then the machine gun on the other side of the tracks added to the symphony. She immediately realized that the dead and now half-sunken locomotive blocked any fire from the machine gun near her.

She ran the few steps to the gun. "Snap out of it!" she ordered the crew who sat there, mumbled prayers on their lips. Lavin, of Strat Recon, was one of them. "STOP IT, YOU MORONS! Bring the gun to the nose of the locomotive and set up there to sweep that side of the train. And then, for the love of God, shoot!"

"I'm not dead?" wondered Lavin.

"You will be if—"

"We're moving, Captain, we're moving!"

Bochkareva ran ahead of the gun crew. Climbing up the side, she looked inside the cab to where the dead engine crew lay, broken and twisted by their train's ordeal. Looking out and past them, the train, itself, she saw, was mostly a ruin, with the passenger cars a twisted rope and most of them off their tracks and on one side. The rifle fire from her women and the machine gun, the latter more effective for its sound at the moment than for its fire, kept the Reds inside with no ability to shoot back.

"Lavin!" she shouted, "forget the machine gun for now. Get up here and tell them to show a white flag if they want to live. Then to come out with no weapons, not even a pistol or bayonet, or they'll be shot. Tell them that if they don't surrender now, the *brigade* they're facing will take no prisoners."

✢ ✢ ✢

Mokrenko wasn't really overly given to vulgarity, but when he saw the column of something over seven hundred disarmed, hobbling, bleeding, and thoroughly shocked Reds being marched forward under the guard of about seven women and a cart-mounted machine gun front and rear, he could only say, "I don't fucking believe it."

"Where are we going to put them?" Bochkareva asked, when she drew abreast of the Guards Lieutenant.

"I don't know yet," Mokrenko answered. "I think I'll dump it on Colonel Plestov." He counted heads. "Must have been a hard fight if you lost a third of your women," he said. "And Princess Tatuyeva? I'm so sorry."

"I didn't lose a single girl," she replied. "I just left one platoon back there, with most of the carts, plus the machine guns, to move the Reds who were too badly hurt, to collect the guns and ammunition, and to inventory the loot. The princess is in charge of that."

"Holy shit!"

"Something, at least, was holy about it."

Chapter Twelve

Douglas MacArthur, in one of his more humble moments

42nd Division Headquarters, France

Sigi returned to division headquarters with mixed feelings. Unquestionably, he'd helped the 69th win their battle at Meurcy Farms, but he felt oddly dissatisfied. At first, he'd chalked it up to worry for Hank. Sigi had few friends and having one shot up was a new experience. But hearing that Hank was recovering well in a field hospital only a couple miles away alleviated those fears.

The men of the 69th who had died in the attack weighed on him professionally, but he hadn't had time to get to know them as individuals, except for, perhaps, Sergeant Kilmer and Donovan himself.

Perhaps it was because his contribution had been largely based on geometry. He'd only needed map reading skills and an understanding of artillery procedure. What he'd done hadn't really required that much courage, or any real leadership. He'd just done some quick calculations, then refined the math to keep the artillery coming in on top of the enemy.

Donovan had farewelled him warmly, commended him, and assured Sigi he'd recommend the newly established Citation Star for Sigi's quick thinking and skill in coordinating the artillery. Hank he was recommending for the Medal of Honor—but expected to secure only a Distinguished Service Cross. Donovan made it clear that should either, or both, of them escape durance vile up at the 42nd, he'd find places for them in the 69th.

No jealousy tinged Sigi's thoughts. Hank's own matter-of-fact account plus the word of those who had seen in him action left little doubt in his mind that his friend deserved the higher award. It was just that Sigi, somehow, *still* didn't feel like a real officer, and now, here he was back up on division staff, well away from the action.

I've got to escape.

Sigi checked in with the duty officer in the foyer of the chateau which was serving as the 42nd's headquarters. The harried captain told Sigi that *General* MacArthur wanted to see him ASAP. Sigi made his way through the building to the richly appointed study that MacArthur had secured as the Chief of Staff's Office.

Inside he found a sergeant and two privates packing up MacArthur's books, liquor collection, and other sundries. MacArthur himself stood, directing them with sharp words and his swagger stick.

"No, no, wrap the decanter more carefully, Cartwright, I don't want that crate smelling like brandy when we arrive!"

Sigi cleared his throat politely. MacArthur turned to see who had interrupted his packing. The shiny star of a brigadier general did, indeed, grace MacArthur's lapel. Sigi came to attention, saluting MacArthur crisply.

"Sir, Lieutenant Abramovich reports to the general as ordered," Sigi said.

MacArthur waved his swagger stick in the general direction of his forehead.

"Ah, Abramovich, I see you interpreted my orders in the broadest possible sense," MacArthur said with an arched eyebrow. "And took some liberties in arranging support from the divisional artillery."

"No excuse, sir," Sigi said, feeling his stomach drop and a bead of sweat roll down his neck. If MacArthur was annoyed or embarrassed by his actions, his career was about to take a nosedive.

MacArthur's expression remained inscrutable for another three heartbeats, then the man smiled, an ironic quirk of his lips.

"I think you'll find that results almost always provide adequate excuse, Lieutenant," MacArthur said. "Well done."

"Thank you, sir."

"Now, as you can see, I have been promoted." MacArthur paused, expectantly.

"Yes, sir, congratulations. Will you remain as chief of staff?"

"No, I have been given command of the 84th Brigade." MacArthur's smile was sublime. "I had hoped to bring both you and Thornton along with me, but needs must and with Thornton in the hospital, I have decided to name you my senior aide-de-camp. With that comes a promotion, of course."

Sigi attempted to conceal his reaction, but MacArthur must have seen some of his discomfort.

"Is something wrong, Lieutenant Abramovich?" MacArthur's voice cooled, and he tapped his swagger stick lightly on one of the crates.

Oh, shit, I better lay it on thick.

"Sir, it has been an honor serving with you. I cannot begin to tell you how much I've learned and how appreciative I am for the opportunity to benefit from your mentorship," Sigi said. "But with the war winding down, I have to request a chance to lead troops in battle. The 165th has several companies shy a commander."

Sigi used the 69th's Table of Organization number, 165th, rather than its traditional numbering. MacArthur frowned, but it seemed a thoughtful expression rather than an angry one. Perhaps Sigi could avoid a patented MacArthur tantrum after all.

"I appreciate your desire to command your own unit, Sigmund, but I must be frank with you; officers of your faith and race face more fearsome social and professional obstacles than we gentiles. Outside my influence, I'm afraid you may find your career unfairly stagnant."

Bilious bastard, though he may have a point.

This time, Sigi did manage to keep his reaction internal.

"You may be right, sir," Sigi said. "But what kind of career is it if I never get the chance to lead men in battle? Major Donovan told me how you kept him from being reassigned to the field school so that he could command his battalion. I'm asking you to help me the same way."

For a moment MacArthur said nothing, the only sound in the study the wind outside and the rustle of the enlisted men packing his things away. Sigi waited, silent, while MacArthur considered his point. Finally, the general whacked the edge of a crate with his stick once, decisively.

"All right, Abramovich," MacArthur said. "I fear you may be ruining your career, but I won't hold a man back from the front lines. See the adjutant, tell him I approve your transfer to the 165th. Good luck."

MacArthur turned his back on Sigi, his attention back on ensuring his baggage was packed correctly for his new assignment. Sigi smiled ruefully as he left. The abrupt dismissal didn't bother Sigi—he'd gotten what he'd wanted. The fact that he'd merited as much as "good luck" from Douglas MacArthur after the man had no further use for him was noteworthy unto itself.

Mobile Field Hospital, France

A young woman helped Hank into the tent. The green canvas was set up around the back of a French truck. Hank knew the French called them, "Little Curies," but had no clue why. The young woman was dressed in the bulky uniform of a French Army nurse, her black hair tied tightly away from her face. Her large, dark eyes were hazy with fatigue, but she managed a smile for the wounded young American as she gave him instructions in heavily accented, but easily understood English.

"All right then, Lieutenant, please to lie down on the cot, there."

Hank gave the canvas rack and the black panel underneath it a skeptical glance.

"Pardon my accent, miss," Hank said in French. "But could you tell me what this contraption does?"

The girl laughed.

"Your French is quite good, Lieutenant," she said, her drawn features brightening into a smile. "This device is called an X-ray machine. It is a relatively new invention—or at least the portable version is. It will allow us to photograph the inside of your leg to ensure there is no shrapnel or fragmentation left behind without any need for an incision."

"For real?" Hank was startled back into English. The girl smiled indulgently and nodded.

"Just lie down there." She gestured to the cot again. "Do not worry, this should not hurt at all."

Hank complied, easing himself onto the cot. His thigh throbbed where the scar tissue in his quadricep shifted, but the pain was manageable. The girl began to move the film tray and other apparatus into position over his leg.

"About how long will it take?" Hank asked.

"Fifteen to twenty minutes to get an exposure. As long as you do not toss and turn, you may nap."

Hank settled down to wait, and maybe catch a short siesta, but then a question reoccurred to him.

"Miss, why do they call these trucks, 'Little Curies'?"

The girl's smile shifted from one of indulgence to one of pride, her shoulders squaring against her fatigue.

"They are named after their inventor, my mother, Marie Curie," she said. "I am Irene Curie."

"Your momma is Marie Curie?" Hank whistled. "Even out in Podunk, Texas, we've read about Marie Curie. She won the Nobel prize, right?"

"Twice," Irene said, fiddling with some instrumentation on the machine. "And she offered to melt both down for their gold in order to finance these 'Little Curies' when the government said it didn't have funds to do so."

"That's noble," Hanks said, then realized his unintentional pun. "Sorry, it's admirable. I imagine being able to peer into a fellow's body without cutting him open has been right useful."

"I think so, yes. I don't have the exact numbers, but we've conducted at least hundreds of thousands of X-ray exposures, and we have to have saved tens of thousands of lives. Now, if you'll lie still as you can, Lieutenant, we'll see how you're doing."

The X-ray found no fragmentation or bone splinters, but the doctors insisted Hank needed at least another week in hospital to allow the wound to fully heal before putting it back into field conditions. Hank sulked at the news; he was bored out of his mind in the field hospital and, if he was being honest, sitting amongst the amputees, the shell-shocked, and the dying ate at him harder than the shelling, the bullets, even the blood-soaked brutality of the melee.

Despite the pain in his leg, he spent as much time outside the hospital tents as possible, fulfilling whatever light duty requirements he could for the hospital staff away from the hacksaws and needles and the necessary butchery of the surgeons. Two days after his conversation with Irene Joliot-Curie, Hank was charged with censoring the American doctors' and nurses' mail.

The willingness of some of the young women to write to their sweethearts and husbands in graphic and titillating detail, even knowing their mail had to be censored, shocked the naïve young Texan. It also gave him an unpleasantly voyeuristic thrill. Hank had grown up on his family's ranch with little interaction with girls who were not kin. He'd attended Lubbock High School, but he could count his female classmates there on the fingers of one hand.

West Point, naturally, had been populated entirely by men. The normal schedule of debutante balls and mixers with proper young women's educational institutions had been one of many things omitted in order to rush the next class of lieutenants to a war front which was desperately short of officers. Hank was still, like most of his peers, whatever their stories to the contrary, a virgin.

Thus it was that a letter from one particularly libidinous young nurse so thoroughly engrossed the young man's imagination that he failed to notice his best friend entering the hospital staff tent until Sigi was standing right in front of him.

"Hank, you with us?"

Hank started and stood up from his camp stool, dropping the letter. Recognizing Sigi, he wiped a hand across his flushed face.

"Oh, Sigi, it's you," Hank said. "Sorry, old boy, I was just caught up—"

Sigi reached down and snatched up the letter. He started scanning it, then whistled.

"I can see why you were focused," he said, handing it back. "Aloysius there seems a lucky man."

Hank snatched back the letter, scowling at his friend.

"Sigi, that's private, darn it."

Sigi laughed.

"Hank, they know the letters have to be censored for security," Sigi said. "If she wanted privacy, she wouldn't have put it to paper."

"Even so, Sigi, it ain't polite to go talking about it out loud," Hank said, glancing around the staff tent. It was mostly empty, but here and there a few doctors scribbled out reports for the 42nd Division, or penned letters to home—letters they knew would have to go through the same censorship process to maintain security.

Sigi held up his hands.

"You're right, of course, Hank. Sorry. I'd apologize to the lady in question, but I'm sure that would only make it more awkward."

"Forget it," Hank said, sealing the letter in its envelope and putting it in the OUT pile. "How are you? How are things back at Division?"

Sigi grinned, then his expression took on a more sober tone.

"That's why I came to see you," Sigi said. "MacArthur got his star and command of the 84th Brigade. I managed to wrangle a transfer down to the 69th."

"That's great news," Hank said. "Well, you getting out of Division is great news, not sure how I feel about *General* MacArthur. As soon as I'm out of the hospital, I'll try to get down there and join you."

Sigi looked a little sheepish.

"We're moving out, tomorrow," Sigi said. "I think there's a big push in the works. It may be a while before you can catch up with us."

It might be forever. A hell of a lot of men had been killed in their first battle. Hank found his throat thickening. Surprised at the sudden emotion, he coughed loudly into his hand and blinked rapidly. They stood there for several seconds. Sigi looked as unsure what to say next as Hank felt. Finally, Hank broke the silence.

"Well, Sig, you give 'em hell for me, you hear?"

"Will do."

Hank coughed again and chuckled.

"And don't get your head blown off, while you're at it, all right? I'm going to need you when we get to Leavenworth someday," Hank said.

Sigi laughed.

"Well, I'm a much smaller target than you, so I should be all right," Sigi said. "I better get going. See you around, Hank."

Sigi stuck out his hand. Hank grabbed it and tried to put his emotions into his grip, simply unable to say it out loud.

"See you, Sigi."

✣ ✣ ✣

The day before Hank's release from the hospital, a tall lieutenant colonel with a long, thin nose and narrowed eyes, wearing an immaculate uniform with brightly polished knee-high boots under his jodhpur pants walked in. In a loud voice he announced, "I'm looking for a lieutenant named Thornton."

Hank took one look at the man's scowling face and parade-ground-sharp uniform and a flash of anxiety hit him.

Oh, Lordy, what does this guy want?

"That's me, sir, how can I help you, Colonel?" Hank said, standing up, his left leg barely twinging under the weight. The starched and pressed lieutenant colonel looked him up and down clinically.

"My name is Patton, I command the 1st Tank Brigade. You're the Texan cowboy who killed three Germans with a shovel? The same man who played linebacker for my beloved alma mater?"

Hank chuckled nervously.

"Well, sir, I only killed one German with a shovel," Hanks said. "I shot one and bayonetted another."

Patton laughed from his gut and slapped Hank on the shoulder.

"Well, I'm glad you cleared that up, Thornton, can't have a captain who doesn't report accurately. Pack up your kit and come with me."

"Pardon me, sir?"

"You've been reassigned, son. And promoted." Patton pulled out a small box and opened it, showing Hank the twin-silver bar captain's rank therein. "I need company commanders, your reputation indicates I might not have to relieve you or shoot you, so you're it."

"Sir, I don't know the first thing about tanks," Hank protested.

"I can teach a man tanks, Thornton. I can't pull good combat leaders out of my ass. Now, come here, boy."

Hank stepped forward. Patton released his lieutenant's bars and replaced them with the captain's insignia.

"Not as grand as when Pershing pinned my railroad tracks, I'm afraid," Patton said. "But the pay'll spend just the same. Welcome to the 1st Tank, Captain Thornton."

69th (165th) Infantry Regiment, France

It was late afternoon by the time Sigi found his way down to the 1st of the 69th's bivouac area. Passing the line for chow, Sigi didn't see Sergeant Kilmer or any of the men he'd worked with a few days ago.

Plucking up his courage, he picked out a man with sergeant's stripes on his sleeves and walked up to him.

"Excuse me, Sergeant," Sigi said. "I'm Lieutenant Abramovich, could you tell me where the battalion command post is? I need to talk to Major Donovan."

The sergeant was of medium height but beefily built with blue stubble on his jawline and a bored expression that looked permanent on his blunt features.

"Well, Lieutenant, it's actually Lieutenant Colonel Donovan, now," he pointed west. "And his command post is about half a mile that way. Big tent. Can't miss it."

The sergeant turned back to jawing with a corporal with flaming red hair. Sigi muttered his thanks and turned to leave. He pretended not to hear their murmured commentary as he departed.

"Man, lotta jewboys in the army, these days," said the corporal.

The sergeant grunted. "You got something against Jews?"

"They're all so damn smarmy," he said. "And there's the fact that they killed Jesus."

"Higgins, you know what Father Duffy says about the blood libel shit," the sergeant cut him off.

"Well, I don't know about you, Sergeant, but I don't fancy following a Hebrew midget through a cloud of mustard gas, why couldn't we keep that cowboy—"

Sigi moved too far away to hear what the beefy sergeant said to Higgins in retort. He merely shook his head and kept walking. It wasn't the first time; it wouldn't be the last.

The tent was relatively quiet and calm compared to the last time he'd been at the 1st of the 69th's command post, but still busy. Senior Staff NCOs and officers carried on phone conversations with regimental headquarters or supporting arms like the artillery and engineers. The junior NCOs applied graphics to maps with grease pencil and metal stencils. Donovan himself was bent over his field desk, writing on the top sheet of a thick stack of paper.

Sigi approached Donovan and coughed politely. He looked up, his eyes unfocused, mind clearly elsewhere for a moment until recognition dawned. Sigi saluted.

"Sir, Lieutenant Abramovich reporting as ordered."

Donovan returned the salute and smiled.

"Ah, Abramovich, I'm glad you're here," he said. "Willis, where is that citation?"

Over at a desk with a white-painted wooden sign reading, "S1-PERSONNEL," a reed-thin NCO looked up from his stack of papers.

"Just a second, sir," he said, shuffling through a few different piles, before snatching up a document. "Here it is."

Donovan accepted the paper.

"Abramovich, this should've been cleared already, but the French pushed back on it," Donovan said. "I'm walking this over tomorrow with some other citations to have a word with them, but we weren't, well, we weren't actually sure how your last name is spelled."

Donovan handed the paper over. Sigi read it rapidly. Seeing phrases like "tactical acumen rare in an officer so young," and, "instrumental in securing victory," and, "Lieutenant Abramovitch's skill and intrepidity reflect credit upon himself and the Service," made Sigi a tad uncomfortable. But the facts of his actions were represented accurately, not inflated.

Hell, maybe I do deserve a medal...

"There's no T. It's just I, C, H at the end."

He handed the paper back to Willis. The personnel NCO looked long-suffering but accepted the correction with a "Yes, sir, we'll fix it right away."

"Wait, Sergeant," Sigi said. "You probably need a copy of these as well. They're my transfer orders."

Willis took Sigi's orders as well and Donovan grinned again. He reached out and shook Sigi's hand.

"You did manage to escape. Congratulations, Abramovich, and welcome to the 1st of the 69th, we're glad to have you."

"Thank you, sir, I'm happy to be here."

"I'm actually in the market for a new adjutant." Donovan's expression sobered rapidly. "I'm afraid I've lost two in short order. You were here when Oliver Ames was killed. I'm afraid we lost Sergeant Kilmer to a sniper on a leader's recon the day after you went back to Division."

A melancholic sensation washed over Sigi. That he'd had a brief chance to know a favored writer as a man and a soldier before his death made the loss sharper, but also hallowed.

"I'm very sorry to hear that, sir," Sigi said. "I didn't get a chance to know him well, but I respected his work here and at home very much."

"Me too, Abramovich." Donovan took a deep breath. "So, what do you say? Would you like to be my adjutant?"

Sigi hesitated, unsure how to ask for what he really wanted without sounding ungrateful. Donovan must have misread his expression.

"If you don't want the job, I can understand," Donovan said. "I'm not superstitious, but it does seem to have a low survival rate. We have staff primary positions open in the Operations and Intelligence shops if you'd prefer one of those."

Sigi straightened, indignation forcing a louder protest than he'd intended out of him.

"It's not that at all, sir!"

Donovan raised an eyebrow at the outburst. Sigi looked at his boots for a second, chagrined.

"What is it, then, Lieutenant?"

Sigi hesitated for a moment to consider his phrasing.

"It's just that I know you have company command positions vacant," Sigi said. "I was hoping for one of those."

Donovan nodded, sympathy and understanding appearing in a fatherly smile.

"You've been stuck on staff since you got to France, you finally escape only for me to make you a staff officer again. I can understand why that is less than you hoped for."

He paused, tapping his pen on the desk three times, then shaking his head.

"The trouble is that we are headed back into the line too quickly for a company to get adjusted to you and vice versa. We've already got a passel of replacement troops we're breaking in. I'm loath to reshuffle the leadership on top of that; especially this close to a major attack."

Sigi should've known his escape from Division had been too easy. Well, being Donovan's adjutant would be far from dull. At least he'd be at the front. He opened his mouth to say so, but Donovan continued—

"Here's what I'll do for you, Abramovich. Take the adjutant job for three weeks, the war is unlikely to be over by then. That will give the battalion time to get used to you, time for me to figure out which company would be the best fit. Do a swinging job, and I'll give you one of my open companies; and the captain's bars to go with it if I can swing it. Square deal?"

"Yes, sir!"

"By the way," Donovan asked, "how's your pal Thornton doing?"

Chapter Thirteen

Renault FT17s, moving up

344th Tank Battalion, France

As he ground-guided tanks off of railway cars and into the battalion's assembly area, Hank knew one thing for certain. He was damned glad his company was comprised of Renault FT-17s instead of those enormous land-battleship jobs like the Brit Mark IV or the French Schneider. The little two-man contraptions were still finicky and required constant maintenance, but they really weren't all that more mechanically complicated than his Uncle Jim's Model-T. Furthermore, they were less likely to get stuck in the late fall mud of the French countryside, and when they did get stuck, they were a hell of a lot easier to break loose.

Actually, *two* things he was sure of, come to think of it; Hank was also grateful he wasn't expected to actually *crew* a tank in combat. True to his word, Patton had gotten Hank up to speed on tanks in a matter of days. Days that had been more packed with study than he'd experienced since West Point, but mere days, nonetheless.

Standing well over six feet, Hank had contorted himself into the driver's compartment and the gunner's turret in turn just long enough to get an appreciation for how his men did their job. Then he emulated his superiors and led his men either on foot, or riding crouched on the back deck of one of the tanks. With a maximum speed of only four miles per hour, Hank had no trouble keeping up with the tanks even over rough terrain.

The tanks' engines combined with din of battle made verbal orders impractical, nigh on impossible from anywhere but right next to the crewman's head, so he'd been practicing directing them with hand and arm signals. It was a frenetic method of leadership, having to run back and forth amongst the tanks, pounding on their hatches with the butt of his pistol or a handy rock to get crews' attention, but at least he always had somewhere to take cover.

Once all sixteen of his tanks were lined up and ready, his battalion commander, Major Brett, approached. Brett was a young man, Hank guessed he wasn't yet thirty, with thick brown hair with a slight widow's peak and strong, regular features. He wore his normal, calm, unassuming expression. Hank found Brett's quiet, professional aplomb a relief in contrast to Patton's bombast. He was glad Brett was between him and Patton in the chain of command.

Hank saluted.

"Sir, Company B is assembled. All personnel accounted for."

Brett returned the salute, looked over the assembled company and nodded.

"Gasoline trucks will be up soon; we've got a longer road march than I'd like to the line of departure so tell the boys to pay attention to their fuel levels. The brigade commander went up to the 42nd Division headquarters to try and get more smoke and artillery support for us a few hours ago, he should be back soon for the final mission brief."

As if summoned by the mention, a truck lumbered around a corner mere minutes later, stopped on the road behind their assembled tanks and deposited their brigade commander on the field. Hank and Brett snapped to and saluted as Patton approached. He returned the gesture sharply.

"Sereno, Hank," Patton said. "Your boys and tanks ready?"

"Company C is falling in now, sir," Brett answered. "What did the 42nd say about the augmented artillery and smoke request?"

Patton snorted in disgust.

"That dumb sonofabitch Major Murphy won't allocate any more assets because, according to him, 'There's no time to make new stencils.' I swear, our own laziness and incompetence is more dangerous than a German division.'"

Hank recoiled a bit at the language. Oh, he was inured to the troops' profanity, but Patton's willingness to throw such epithets at a senior officer in front of juniors still shocked him. If Patton noticed Hank's discomfiture, he gave no indication of it. Hank retrieved his canteen and took a swig of water to cover his momentary lapse.

"Sereno, your battalion is going to be supporting the 84th Brigade," Patton continued. "The French and Compton's heavies are going with the 83rd. Since the 84th is the main effort, I'll accompany you, at least for the first phase of the operation."

Hank choked as a bit of water slipped down the wrong pipe. MacArthur was commanding the 84th now. Patton turned a knowing smirk on the younger man.

"Not eager to see your old boss, Thornton?"

"Well, sir, I didn't exactly get a chance to tell General MacArthur that I'd been reassigned..."

Patton laughed. "You're worried MacArthur will have taken your defection to the Tank Corps personally? Heh, well, he probably will."

Hank frowned. "Thank you, sir, that's very comforting."

"Not my job to be comforting, Thornton, and you better get used to the idea that you can't do this job without pissing off a few people. Isn't that right, Major Brett?"

"Well, sir, not all of us are quite as efficient as pissing people off as others," Brett answered in a lighter tone. "No sense worrying anyhow, Hank, the *Boche* might send you West, and then General MacArthur won't be able to touch your career."

1st Battalion, 69th (165th) Infantry Regiment, France

The blackness of night coruscated with sheets of rain and the glow of headlights. The heavy precipitation drummed on Sigi's Brodie helmet and soaked through his uniform, making the early French autumn *much* colder than the mercury would indicate. The mud caked his boots and weighed down his every step, making the art of dodging mule cart and motor truck alike that much more perilous. The constant low drumming of the rain was accompanied by a thunderous chorus of artillery. Their preparatory fires had already begun. American and French artillery screamed overhead to rain steel and fire on the German positions to their front.

A cocktail of adrenaline from the near misses with vehicles, anticipation of the upcoming battle, and exhaustion from the long slog mingled in Sigi's bloodstream as he peered through the rain-soaked night. The 1st Battalion led the 69th in order of march, which led the division, which led the attack. But even as the vanguard of the 42nd Division's attack into the St. Mihiel salient, they were relegated to the side paths off the road.

While the doughboys trudged through the mud of the forests and swamps framing the road, the road itself was choked with supply wagons and trucks, artillery caissons, and tanks. Irritated beasts and finicky engines brayed over the sound of the pouring rain.

As Colonel Donovan's adjutant, Sigi ranged up and down the column, such as it was, helping his commander make sure all his companies were still on track, not having gotten lost in the woods or delayed down the wrong path. Despite the relatively straight direction of travel and the large road nearby, the pitch-black conditions of night and severe weather made getting lost a real threat.

For hours they continued the march. The rain didn't slow in tempo until the gray predawn, when it finally subsided into a lighter drizzle. In contrast to the chaotic forward lurch through inclement weather and seemingly endless caravans of mismatched vehicles, the 1st of the 69th arrived to find their pre-assault trenches neatly taped off and marked by the engineers down to the platoon level.

Sigi consulted his pocket watch; it was not quite 0400, still more than an hour until their step-off. Sigi counted the last platoon of Company D into position then jogged to find Colonel Donovan who'd been, naturally, marching near the front of the column. He found him between Company A and Company B's sections of the line.

"All units in position, sir," Sigi reported, forcing himself not to shiver.

"Good, let's troop the line," Donovan said. "Does the men good to see their officers calm and relaxed before the fight."

Calm. Relaxed. Right.

Sigi trailed Donovan, taking mental notes—any attempt at writing things down would've been a mess amidst the deluge—and trying to look unconcerned vis-à-vis the impending battle.

"Don't worry boys, won't even be as tough as a cross-country run back at Blooey," Donovan said as he slapped shoulders and grinned at the lads in 1st Platoon of Company C. "The Germans know they're done, sooner or later. Let's finish them off sooner."

The shelling continued as Donovan and Sigi walked the battalion line, bolstering the troops for the big plunge. Sigi mostly hovered in the background. The company commanders and platoon leaders either acknowledged his presence with a polite nod or ignored him. The enlisted troops were too busy talking with their much beloved battalion commander to pay any attention to the diminutive lieutenant trotting along at his heels. It wasn't racial bigotry; the handful of Jewish boys in the battalion were just as oblivious to his presence as the gentiles.

At least not for the most part. The redheaded corporal who had made the smartass remarks about Jews the day he'd transferred to the battalion gave Sigi a look only a hair's breadth away from, "Silent Insolence," as defined by the Manual for Courts Martial. By and large, though, the New Yorkers of the 69th were used to their "Irish Jew" comrades, and neither Donovan nor, just as importantly, Father Duffy, accepted open antisemitism in the ranks.

Maybe if I learn a few of the songs, thought Sigi.

With mere minutes to go before the attack, twenty-four French Schneider tanks painted in swirling camouflage patterns lumbered off the road and churned their way to the front of the infantry. The Schneider resembled nothing so much as a great metal box on tractor treads, with one side of the box sharpened to a knife edge prow with a 75 mm cannon protruding from it.

According to the Operations Order, the French tanks would precede the 83rd Brigade in the advance, providing mobile cover and fire support as well as tearing gaps through enemy wire. Hank's unit, the American 344th Tank Battalion, was supporting the 84th Brigade. Sigi hoped there would be a chance to say hello after this operation.

Donovan's meat hook of a hand on his shoulder interrupted Sigi's reverie.

"Ready, Sigi?" Donovan said. "It's almost time."

Sigi removed his M1911 pistol, checked that a round was chambered, and gave his commander a firm nod.

"Yes, sir."

Donovan put his right foot on the first rung of the ladder out of the trench. All about them, eager young privates and stone-faced veterans alike gathered, bayonets fixed, ready to go *Over the Top*. Donovan consulted his pocket watch, his eyes visibly tracking the path of the second hand. He snapped it shut.

"Time." Donovan secured his whistle and gave a long, high blast that was echoed by the company commanders' whistles all up and down the line.

Sigi followed Donovan up and out of the trench. The artillery continued to shriek overhead whilst the French tanks lumbered out ahead, mechanical heirs to the ancient world's war elephants. Low in the sky, a formation of biplanes bearing the hat-in-the-ring insignia of the famous 94th zoomed over the advancing armies, noses pointed at enemy observation balloons, only to be intercepted by German triplanes. Sigi paused, fascinated, as a flaming warplane plummeted into the trees less than a hundred yards away.

A shove sent him stumbling a few steps forward. Ryan, one of the company commanders, looked over his shoulder.

"Keep moving, Lieutenant, sightseeing will get you killed."

Sigi shook himself out of the awe the spectacle of the battle had struck, reacquired Donovan, and ran to catch up, focused on his part again rather than the terror and majesty of the whole affair.

Interlude

Woodrow Wilson (D) was President of the United States. An academic progressive and state governor before his election, he retained a considerable degree of ivory tower aloofness as well as an uncanny conviction in his own inherent rightness, intelligence, and sheer all-around wonderfulness. The first Southerner elected to the office of President since Zachary Taylor, in 1848, and the only one ever to have been a citizen of the Confederacy, he retained in vast measure the racial attitudes of his parents, themselves having been ardent secessionists and believers in and defenders of the institution of slavery. Indeed, so completely in accord with his parents' views was Wilson that one of his first acts as president was to resegregate the federal bureaucracy.

It was little surprise, then, that highly progressive President Wilson had screened the film, *The Birth of a Nation*, which lauded the KKK and demeaned black Americans, while in the White House. This was, in fact, the very first film screened at the White House. Wilson had also been quoted or misquoted three times within the film. He never objected to either. To the director of the film, whatever public sentiments he'd professed, Wilson had called the work a "splendid production."

Wilson was, again, a staunch "progressive."

Ice clinked in whiskey glasses while cigar smoke swirled. The President of the United States was holding forth and had the rapt attention of all.

"They've a limited attention span, you know," said the president, jovially. Why not, too, since he was among friends, men of similar outlooks and backgrounds?

"Why we had one servant, back in Augusta, and she would regularly become impossible, just impossible. Not just lazy, but also sloppy, sassy, and useless. Well, she'd been with the family a long time, and her people had been with the family for generations. So, when she got bad my mother would take her out to the woodshed and give her a good thrashing. Oh, not enough to draw blood, of course, but there would be welts and bruises a-plenty. And then she'd be a perfect housemaid for a week. In another week she'd get a little lazy. And then in the third week she'd become impossible again, and it would be back to the woodshed for her."

The men laughed. Some of the laughter was sincere, since humor can also be found in the completely expected. As much was due to the fact of the President of the United States condescending to joke with them. Some too, was habit, since the President had a thorough repertoire of what he called "Darky jokes," as well as a penchant for imitating an exaggerated form of the speech of southern blacks to raise a laugh.

"Mr. President," asked "Colonel" Edward House, "what are we going to do about this Russian matter?"

House, it may be noted, had never seen a real day's military service, his rank being more or less honorary. House was also at least as virulent a racist as his chief.

"What about it?" asked the President.

"Well, sir, the papers are full of the news of a daring rescue of the Romanov family, or at least a part of it."

"I haven't had time to read them, Edward. Can you summarize for me?"

"There's a good deal we don't know, Mr. President. And some reports are contradictory. What we do know is that a group of loyalists, members of the various Guards regiments, it's said, launched an attack in a little city in Siberia. Most of the family was killed, including both parents, one sister, and the little crown prince. But the oldest remaining sister has taken up the duties of empress and seems determined to carry on the fight."

"The fight against Germany and German militarism?" asked Wilson.

"No, sir," came the answer, "the fight against Red Bolshevism."

The president considered this and then asked his usually ignored secretary of state, Robert Lansing, for his opinion.

"In the long run, Mr. President, democracy isn't suited to Russia, while Bolshevism is suited only to ants. I think we should recognize the Imperial Regime and send an ambassador."

"Where is our current ambassador?" Wilson asked. "For that matter, *who* is our current ambassador?"

"David Francis, Mr. President, was our ambassador. But since, so far as we knew, the old regime was gone, as was its replacement, Kerensky's government, and insofar as we have not recognized the Bolsheviks, he's been hanging on as de facto chargé d'affaires. Last I heard he was in a place called 'Vologda,' a few hundred miles north of Moscow. With the apparent resurrection of the imperial government Mr. Francis would, I suppose, be ambassador again.

"Do you have any instructions for Mr. Francis, Mr. President?"

"Not at this time, Robert. Let me think upon it."

Chapter Fourteen

Captured German 7.7cm Cannon

Company B, 344th Tank Battalion, Near Varennes, France

The German artillery battery was dug in, with a clear field of fire all the way to the wood line. About a company's worth of German infantry, in full retreat from their original positions minutes ago, were getting organized in and around the guns. Hank thought furiously as he examined their fortifications through his field glasses. He and an infantry company commander named Toliver from the 167th Alabama lay in a thicket near, but not right at, the edge of the forest, careful to stay concealed as they reconnoitered the enemy position. This was the third angle from which they'd viewed the howitzer emplacement.

With earthworks and sandbags surrounding each gun they would have good cover against even his tanks' 37 mm cannons. The German 75s would have a distinct range advantage, though they'd be slower to traverse and thus have a harder time targeting the moving tanks, hopefully, than his gunners could traverse to engage them. The tanks were going to be moving much slower than a man could run over this terrain, though, so their mobility advantage might or might not be enough to counter the protection afforded by the enemy defenses.

Normally, the smart thing to do would be to halt the advance and send a runner back up through the chain to call in artillery on this strongpoint. The only drawback was that it might take an hour or more to get shells landing on target. Thus far, they'd advanced through the St. Mihiel salient at breakneck speed and all across the line the Germans were showing signs of rout, even panic. The Americans had all the momentum; this was their battle to lose.

Hank tapped the Alabaman captain on the elbow and raised his eyebrows questioningly. The infantry company commander nodded, indicating he'd seen as much of the enemy position as he needed as well. They crawled their way more than a hundred yards back into the woods through thorns and twigs and brush. Even this far back they didn't stand straight up but rather kneeled to have a hasty conversation.

"What are you thinking, Thornton?" Toliver's Alabama accent was a bit slower and syrupier than Hank's own Texas drawl. The man was of medium height and thickly built with dark stubble covering his cheeks, lip, and jawline.

"I'm thinking they've got a great field of fire," Hank said. "And those guns can definitely knock out my tanks. We're going to have to be clever."

"I've found that hollerin' for as much artillery as you can get is just about the cleverest thing you can do for most tactical situations," Toliver volunteered.

Hank snorted and gave a low chuckle.

"I would normally agree, but I don't want to give them the breathing room it would take. We're more than two miles from the nearest field phone to the artillery." Hank gestured eastward. "When we traveled the woods in that direction, the trees were too close together in most places but there was a dry streambed just big enough for one of my Renaults to travel until it opens up on the enemy's left."

"You're thinking we bypass their position?" Toliver asked.

Hank started drawing in the dirt with his finger. He traced one big oval to represent the enemy position, then a series of lines for Toliver's infantry platoons and boxes for his tanks.

"Not exactly, just an envelopment. You keep two of your platoons and half my tanks, the ones carrying the Hotchkiss MGs. You form a base of fire against the enemy—the trees are lighter here so the tanks can play peekaboo—drive forward, pepper the enemy, then reverse back into the trees. While you're fixing them in place, I'll take one of your platoons and the other half of my tanks, those equipped with 37 mm cannons, up the streambed and envelop the enemy."

Toliver nodded as Hank swept his right index finger through the dirt, indicating the maneuver.

"All right, your tanks will likely draw the artillery's fire, so I'm going to put some lateral separation between them and my infantry."

"Probably smart. Make sure everyone keeps their fire to the left of the lead tank in the flanking force, I'll have your men follow behind my tanks so they don't get nailed by friendly fire."

Toliver nodded.

"Let's get it done."

With riflemen out to the flanks for security, Hank led his tanks up the streambed. The relative serenity of the sun-dappled forest was in sharp contrast to the staccato pops of machine guns and the basso booming explosions of the artillery resounding from their west. Listening to half of his command exchanging fire with the Germans without being able to see for himself how the fight was progressing wracked his nerves.

The shriek of an artillery round split the air, punctuated by the screech of shearing metal and a louder explosion than previous impacts. A moment later, a gray column of smoke rose over the woods to their west.

Hank fought the urge to break into a sprint. There was no point, as the Renaults couldn't get through this forest any faster than the quick march. Showing up by himself, or with only the infantry who would be cut to pieces in the open terrain between the woods and the enemy position without the tanks, would do no one any good.

A few more agonizing minutes of travel brought them to the place where the streambed widened out into the plain. This angle on the German position revealed howitzer crews feeding rounds into their cannons at breakneck speed while their riflemen frenziedly worked the bolts on their rifles and their machine gunners cleared feed trays and swapped belts and drums of ammo.

They were focused on the woods to their south, where the wreck of one Renault FT17 smoldered amidst dozens of muzzle flashes from rifles and machine guns. The remaining tanks in that element were pulling forward to fire, then reversing back into the trees between bursts as planned, making it harder for the German artillery to score another direct hit.

Hank and his element hadn't been spotted yet. He held up a hand signaling for the column to stop, then he straightened his arms out to his sides, parallel to the ground, indicating that the tanks should come on line as soon as they cleared the woods. He indicated with two fingers that they should bound in sections of two, one section advancing while the other kept up fire on the enemy from a stationary position.

As the tanks spread out for the attack, the Alabaman infantrymen fell in behind them, using the armored vehicles as mobile cover in the terrifyingly open terrain. Hank took up a perch atop his lead tank, crouched behind its turret where he could talk to the gunner commanding the vehicle. By the grace of God and carefully rehearsed maneuvers, they were in formation by the time the Germans saw them and shifted some of their firepower to the flank.

Rifle bullets ricocheted off steel and the German howitzer crew nearest them put their backs into the piece's trails, swinging its muzzle around toward the new threat posed by Hank and his men. Hank shouted through the open hatch of the tank turret.

"Kowalski, kill that howitzer!"

Kowalski already had his eye to the gunsight, training it on the enemy, so Hank stood back up and shouted at the top of his lungs to be heard over the gunfire and tank engines.

"Concentrate fire on that howitzer!"

The Alabamans shot down three men of the howitzer crew, but the Germans must have known getting the piece into action was their only chance because each dead or wounded artilleryman was replaced on the trails by another soldier until the howitzer was pointed their direction.

Kowalski's tank and his wing tank each belched fire and smoke, sending projectiles into the German lines. Hank rocked with the mild recoil of the Renault's 37mm cannon. Both rounds landed beyond the howitzer, wounding a handful of German infantrymen but leaving the artillery piece untouched.

The German cannon answered the higher-pitched chorus of American small arms and tanks with a full-throated roar as it returned fire. The High-Explosive 77mm shell impacted behind the trail tank in 2nd Section with a bone-rattling *BOOM*. The gray burst of its fragmentation enveloped one of the rifle squads, sending several men to the ground screaming and clutching jagged-edged wounds.

The artillery piece was unquestionably more powerful, but the tank cannons were quicker. Four 37mm shells flew towards the howitzer; two landed astray again, but two struck home, blasting the breech of the cannon into wreckage and shredding the crew who had been trying to clear the breech for their next round.

With that artillery piece out of play, the Alabamans poured more fire onto the Germans, willing to poke their heads out from behind the tanks now. Hank leaned forward to talk to Kowalski through the hatch again.

"Great shot! Advance to that dip in the terrain, two hundred yards front-right."

Hank held on tight as the tank treads churned the French field beneath him, bringing him closer to the enemy. While the ride crouched on the back deck of this contraption was about as different from a saddled horse as one conveyance could be from another, the cavalry officer in him was suddenly right at home.

The Alabamans were following his tanks unhesitatingly, stopping only briefly to fire at the Germans now and then. Back over Hank's left shoulder, the other two tanks in the platoon fired two more high-explosive rounds every four seconds, supplemented by rifle and machine gun fire from the infantry that were traveling with them.

With their attention now split between two axes, the Germans were losing fire superiority in both directions. 1st Section halted in the depression in the ground, securing the defilade Hank had been angling for. At much closer range now, their first volley claimed another howitzer. Kowalski's victory whoop was audible even over the din of battle.

By the time second section was on line, the Germans were flinging their rifles to the ground and throwing their hands up. The Alabama boys surged forward, urging their newly captured prisoners into neat rows on their knees with their fingers laced behind their heads. Captain Toliver brought up his other two platoons from the support-by-fire position. The surviving Hotchkiss-equipped tanks rolled up slowly behind him.

"Well done, Thornton," Toliver grinned. "Your rattletraps are pretty darn useful."

Hank chuckled.

"I'll admit I had my doubts at first, but yes, I think you're right," Hank said. "We better push a security element north into the woods, just in case the Germans get their act together for a counterattack. We'll need some more fuel and ammunition before we continue the advance."

Hank dispatched one of his junior NCOs to find Major Brett or Colonel Patton to relay Company B's situation and request fuel and ammo resupply. In the meantime he took stock. One of his tanks was a total loss, but miraculously both crewmen had survived, seriously wounded and a little crispy, but both had been conscious and intact as the litter teams carried them back to meet the ambulance. The rest of his tanks were fully intact and combat capable, provided they were fueled and rearmed soon.

Hank did a quick estimate counting the rows and columns of the captured Germans. There were at least seventy enemy POWs kneeling on the ground, Enfield 1917s leveled at them. A like number of German dead lay in and around their howitzers. Toliver's Alabamans had lost nine killed and sixteen were wounded badly enough to need evacuation.

Nine dead and sixteen wounded Americans and one tank out of action in exchange for an enemy artillery battery and nearly ten times their casualties in enemy dead and captured. Hank couldn't call it a bad day's work.

Colonel Patton agreed wholeheartedly when he showed up. Surveying the captured Germans and cannons, he clapped Hank on the shoulder.

"Damn fine work, Thornton. Major Brett has A and C Companies rallied about a mile northwest of us. Meanwhile your old friends in the 69th have taken Essey with some help from the French."

I hope Sigi is doing well.

"Yes, sir," Hank said. "Our men did extremely well, the Alabamans, too. This is the first time I've seen the Germans break like this."

Patton nodded, his expression turning thoughtful.

"We're close to the end, Hank," Patton's tone was wistful. "We know it; the Germans know it. We've only got a few more weeks, maybe a couple of months, to really get it stuck in. This war may be over soon, but it won't be the last. The reporters were full of shit when they labeled this The War to End All Wars. There isn't a War to End All Wars until Kingdom Come. In the meantime, the tank is going to be vital to ground maneuver warfare, and if our brass aren't convinced to invest in them, we'll be caught behind when the shells start flying again."

Hank hadn't thought much about what came after the Great War. Hell, he hadn't counted on surviving it. Much was made of Patton's eccentricities, and Hank had witnessed them himself in the short time he'd served in the man's brigade. Here he was, though, already contemplating how to win the next war. The man's harsh leadership style and considerable ego aside, Patton was committed to the art of war more deeply than most men committed to anything.

Their conversation was interrupted by the arrival of General Douglas MacArthur. He appeared from the wood line south of the artillery emplacement, several nervous-looking staff officers trailing him as MacArthur walked, unconcerned, toward the front.

"Would this be his royal nibs, Hank?" Patton asked, sotto voce, while MacArthur was still several dozen yards distant.

"Yes, sir, that's General MacArthur."

"Well, let's go say hello." Patton marched toward MacArthur and Hank fell in step just behind and to Patton's left. They came to attention a few paces in front of MacArthur and his party and saluted crisply.

"Good morning, sir," Patton said. "Lieutenant Colonel Patton, 1st Tank."

MacArthur returned the salute with a touch of his swagger stick to the brim of his cap. MacArthur would not deign to wear anything so mundane as a helmet.

"Patton, I'm MacArthur, I command the 84th. Your tanks have been very helpful in our advance," MacArthur said.

"Thank you, General," Patton said. "With your permission, I'd like to get priority for my gasoline and ammo trucks to move forward to refuel and rearm my tanks to continue the advance."

Before he answered, MacArthur's eyes rested on Hank and his expression went cold.

"Henry, I see you've been promoted. Congratulations." MacArthur's tone was glacial. "I'm glad to see you've found gainful employment, though one thinks you might have rendered me the courtesy of a visit before departing my service."

"I meant no offense, General," Hank said, trying not fidget under MacArthur's glare.

"I'm afraid it's quite my fault, General," Patton interjected. "You see, I got word of a young fire-breathing Texas Cavalryman about to be released from hospital and I had to snatch him up. I got his orders cut, got him trained up and in command of one of my companies so fast he had limited time for the courtesies you would normally expect."

To Hank's relief, MacArthur's cold glance returned to Patton, who seemed utterly unfazed by it.

"Of course, I understand." MacArthur's voice was devoid of sincerity. "Exigencies of the service. I'll see about your fuel and ammunition, Patton. Carry on."

MacArthur strode away, off to spread joy to some other corner of the battlefield. Hank exhaled and slumped as soon as the man was out of earshot. Patton glanced at him and laughed.

"It seems General MacArthur is a mite peeved with you, 'Henry,'" Patton said, imitating MacArthur's tone on Hank's Christian name. Though he'd been grateful that Patton had defended him, Hank was now annoyed with Patton's mirth at his expense.

"He didn't seem to like you very much either, sir."

Patton shrugged.

"I've known MacArthur's reputation for years, Hank; I'm not surprised," Patton said. "I may be a prima donna, but do you know the difference between Doug MacArthur and God?"

Hank snorted.

"I can think of several, sir."

"Certainly, but chief among them is that God doesn't think he's Douglas MacArthur."

Chapter Fifteen

German soldiers with grenades and machine gun,
doing the best they can

Company B, 344th Tank Battalion, The Argonne Forest, France

The sun dawned on a thick fog blanketing the Argonne Forest. Hank had to lean close in to make out the details on their French map, fighting both the poor light and his own fatigue. It had been a long complex operation just to get the battalion out of the St. Mihiel salient and into the vanguard of the 35th Division for the beginning of the Meuse Argonne offensive.

Between combat losses and tanks broken down or inextricably mired in the mud endemic to France's rain-drenched autumn, Hank could only field eight tanks. The surviving crews of lost tanks joined the cobbled platoon they'd commandeered from a disorganized battalion.

Now they advanced through heavily forested and hilly terrain with visibility down to conversational distance, pausing every few hundred yards to verify their location and direction of travel.

Unless Hank was mistaken, they were within a mile of their next objective, the village of Cheppy, which meant the chances of meeting resistance approached certainty. They'd spread out from their column formation into a wedge an hour ago. Their lateral dispersion had made controlling movement a greater challenge, especially with the vegetation and intervisibility lines of the hills and ravines. However, the formation mitigated their chance of taking mass casualties from concentrated artillery fire.

Three other men stood at the back of Hank's lead tank with him. Major Brett, Colonel Patton, and Patton's orderly, a PFC named Angelo, all gathered around the map.

"We're headed in the right direction, Sereno," Patton said, confirming Hank's own estimate. "You head back and grab the rest of your battalion and see if the 35th will cut us some more infantry for the attack. Hank and I will continue to reconnoiter."

Major Brett headed south, back to where Companies A, C, and D were waiting. Hank and his men pushed onward in their tanks, gasoline engines sputtering, treads churning French grass and mud as they wove in and out between the trees. And always the tall, ramrod straight figure of George S. Patton marching before them through the fog.

As they advanced, the sun rose, extending Hank's field of view deeper into the fog. Twenty minutes into the march the straight lines and right angles of man-made construction, or at least the remnants of it, took form in the distance. As they drew closer to the hamlet it became apparent that most of the structures were dilapidated, roofs caved in, walls missing, glassless windows staring like empty eye sockets amidst the stones and rotting timbers.

Hank peered intently, searching for any movement, any sign of life, but nothing stirred amongst the ruins. No protruding rifle barrel or glinting binocular lens betrayed the presence of Germans. It couldn't be . . . Cheppy controlled one of a handful of crossroad intersections in this section of the Argonne—surely the Germans had left some kind of force to contest it—

The dark recesses of the stonework sparked with dozens of muzzle flashes. German machine gun rounds lanced out at Hank's company, pinging off the armor of the tanks, sending up splashes of mud and water. Hank crouched low behind the Renault's small turret. Most of his dismounted troops hit the dirt and started returning fire.

Colonel Patton wasn't one of the lucky ones. He doubled over as if taking a hammer blow to his abdomen and crumpled to the ground. From behind one of the Hotchkiss Machine Gun tanks on the right flank, the skinny figure of PFC Joe Angelo sprinted out through the sheets of German machine gun fire to where Patton lay. The brigade commander had his 1911 out now and, though sprawled on his back, was firing away at one of the machine gun nests. Angelo got his arms under Patton's armpits and dragged the tall officer back to a shell crater.

Hank banged on the turret with the butt of his pistol. Sergeant Kowalski popped the hatch on the rear of the turret, the gray-headed NCO looking askance at Hank.

"Kowalski, get us between the colonel and those MGs!" Hank shouted.

Kowalski nodded and rebuttoned the hatch. The tank rolled forward, but fifty meters shy of Patton's position it plunged into an unseen bog, burying its tracks. The driver gunned the engine to try to break free, sending up a shower of mud that coated Hank instantly and only buried the tank deeper. Hank managed to keep his perch and banged on the turret hatch again.

"TELL HINES TO KNOCK IT OFF," Hank screamed. "And get out of there, we'll dig the tank out later!"

The treads stopped, and even over the machine gun fire, Hines banging on the inside of the driver's compartment was audible. Hank jumped off the back deck and was instantly calf deep in mud. He waded around to the front where Kowalski was already struggling against a hundred pounds of mud to pry open the driver's hatch. Hank joined him on the hatch, muscles straining to pull it open wide enough for Hines to escape.

Rounds pinged off the turret and hull of the bogged tank. One uncomfortably close miss sent a spall of metal shards across Hank's face, slicing his right cheek open. Hank cried out in pain and his grip slipped on the hatch just as it started to give with a massive sucking noise. He flopped backward into the mud.

Hank's left hand shot to his cheek involuntarily and came away bloody. The cuts burned but his face didn't seem to be sliding off his skull, so he ignored the wounds and pushed himself out of the muck to a crouch—he did not stand straight up with rifle and machine gun bullets flying back and forth across the field.

He stumbled toward the tank to help Hines out of the tank but motion out of the corner of his eye drew his attention. He whirled to see two men in muddy field gray uniforms tromping as fast as they could through the mud toward him. Each had a bundle of grenades lashed together under their arms—improvised anti-tank charges. The massed grenades would be enough to punch through the Renault's light armor plating, and more than enough to reduce Hank and his men to scattered viscera.

His 1911 cleared leather in a heartbeat. Hank aligned the pistol's front sight post on the chest of the nearest man and—*BLAM*—miss, he'd yanked the trigger rather than pressing. He realigned, taking a deep breath to try and steady his hand—*BLAMBLAM*—the nearest German dropped into the mud, two .45 caliber rounds punching holes in his thoracic cavity and blowing blood, bone, and lung tissue out his back and into the mud. Hank tracked right with the pistol and fired again, emptying the remainder into the man.

The German fell, but not before he hurled the conjoined grenades like an Olympic shotput. As the bundle of high-explosive arced toward him, Hank turned and dove to tackle Kowalski and Hines.

"DOWN!" he screamed.

The linked grenades detonated in the mud next to the tank's right track, throwing up a geyser of mud. The concussion rippled through Hank's bowels and reverberated painfully off his eardrums, but the mired tank's hull blocked the grenades' killing fragmentation. Hank rose unsteadily to a crouch, grabbed a handful of Kowalski's tunic and shouted at him and Hines to follow. He led them around to the back of the tank as German machine gun fire resumed.

With shaking hands, Hank changed the magazine in his pistol while he assessed the situation. Without artillery, the German fire wasn't having much effect on his tanks, but their stone emplacements were holding up against his tanks' 37mm cannons and Hotchkiss machine guns. His own dismounts seemed to be huddled behind the tanks, providing only sporadic rifle and light machine gun fire against the Germans. In their stone redoubts, it was impossible to estimate German casualties so far.

Boy, we could really use some of those 75 mm guns right now. Note to self, mixed teams in the future?

The action on his 1911 slid forward with a clack, chambering a round. Hank grabbed Kowalski's shoulder and pulled him close to speak.

"I need you to get back to Major Brett. Tell him we've got German infantry and machine guns in at least company strength fortified in stoneworks at the crossroads, we're down one tank and Colonel Patton is wounded. Tell him we need reinforcements fast. Low crawl until you hit the wood line, then move as fast as you can, got it?"

"What are you going to do, sir?" Kowalski asked.

"I'm going to see if Colonel Patton is still alive, then I'm going to focus on killing these Germans. Go."

Hank didn't wait to see if Kowalski and Hines obeyed, but instead started crawling toward the shell hole where he'd seen Angelo drag Patton. Along the way, he snatched the cluster of grenades the dead German had intended to throw at his tank. He sprinted in zigzag patterns, then dropped to crawl for a few feet, only to hop up again, then slid like he was stealing third base into the crater.

Angelo was packing a bleeding hole on Patton's left butt cheek. The colonel looked over his shoulder at Hank as he dropped down into the muck with them.

"You look like hell, Thornton," Patton said, in between grunts of pain.

"Yes, sir, you seem to be having a day yourself."

Patton chuckled.

"Apparently the *Boche* decided I wasn't a big enough asshole so they blasted me a second one. What's our status?"

"Seven tanks operational, one man wounded, sir—you," Hank said.

"Two wounded, Hank, it isn't like you cut yourself shaving."

"Right, sir, the Germans don't appear to have anything heavier than machine guns and grenades, but they have some improvised anti-tank charges." Hank held up the grenade cluster.

Angelo finished securing the bandage to Patton's rear.

"All right, sir, best I can do," Angelo said. "I wouldn't go trying to ride a horse or nothin' any time soon."

"Thanks, Joe," Patton said. "Help me up."

Hank and Angelo helped get Patton off of his stomach, then propped him up so he could see over the lip of the crater to evaluate the battlefield. Patton was a heavy man, but between them, Hank and Angelo managed.

"All right, let's get back down," Patton said. They slid back down to the bottom of the hole.

"Hank, that MG nest at the southeast corner of the hamlet—concentrate fire on it, close in with one of the tanks, then clear it out with grenades, then work your way east to west across the village."

"Here, give me the grenades," Angelo said, reaching to take them from Hank.

"It's all right, I can—"

"Captain, no one's questioning your guts, but throwing grenades into machine gun nests is private's work." Angelo grinned. "Don't worry, you'll have plenty of chances to get your ass shot off running around telling everyone what to do."

"Listen to the man, Hank," Patton said. "I can't run around giving orders; command your company, boy."

Angelo wasn't wrong. Machine gun fire kicked up plumes of black mud in his wake as Hank sprinted from tank to tank, and from man to man, relaying the plan and repositioning them to execute it. It took him nearly thirty minutes running around under enemy fire to get his men organized for the attack.

Finally, he and Angelo fell in behind the rightmost tank with the bulk of the company's dismounts. This time, discretion tempering his valor, Hank walked behind the tank as it advanced rather than riding atop it. The tank's Hotchkiss machine guns were deafening; it kept up steady bursts of fire as it approached the squat stone MG nest.

Even with the tank closing and pouring 8 mm rounds into their position, the Germans continued to shoot back. Two of Hank's men went down, wounded. He dared not stop the tank's advance, though.

"Keep it tight behind the tank, men!" Hank screamed. "We'll come back for them after we've cleared out the *Boche!*"

The rounds sparking off the Renault's armor came slower and fewer as they approached within fifty yards. The stone building they were assaulting now obstructed the enemy's field of fire from the other MG nests. At less than ten yards, the tank stopped, continuing to fire. Another German sprinted from around the back of the stone building, clustered grenades in hand. Hank leveled his pistol and fired twice, dropping the grenadier cold.

"Angelo, you're up," Hank shouted. "Everyone else, covering fire."

Hank leveled his own pistol again and started sending .45 rounds into the nest's firing slit alongside his riflemen and the tank's Hotchkiss. They kept their fire to the left side of the bunker as Angelo ran up to the right side, stripped a stick grenade from the rig Hank had given him, paused for four heartbeats, then chucked it into the stone building.

The grenade detonated a half second later with a *THOOM*. Fire from inside ceased immediately. Hank led his men to the entry door on the rear of the position. They found only dead and horribly wounded Germans inside the nest. One gut-wounded man screamed as his blood and intestines oozed through his fingers. Hank's men stripped away weapons and ammo quickly and brutally. Without a medic handy, the Americans allowed the Germans to perform first aid on their wounded men with rifles leveled at them.

Hank grabbed a dirty and shredded linen blanket from one of the German's cots and hung it out the firing slit to visually confirm that they'd cleared this bunker so his gunners could shift fire to the next objective.

Two more men went down, one dead, one wounded, clearing the next bunker, but mere seconds after Angelo's grenade detonated inside the second nest, the remaining Germans in Cheppy ceased firing and started to stagger out of their fighting positions, hands held high, weaponless, shouting, "*Kamerad!*" at the top of their lungs.

Major Brett arrived with the battalion's remaining twenty-six tanks mere minutes after the surrender. After assuring that his own wounded were receiving treatment and that his dead were being gathered for movement to the rear, Hank went to Patton's stretcher where Major Brett was conferring with him as he was loaded into the field ambulance.

"Sereno, you're in command of the brigade," Patton said. "Stay on Compton, he's too damned passive. Thornton, damn fine work today, son. Don't let the brigade go soft while I'm gone, I'll be back soon as they sew up this extra orifice!"

As the doors closed on the ambulance, Brett turned to Hank, looking with frank appraisal at the slashes the spalling had left across his cheek.

"Looks like you're going to have some fine dueling scars, Hank," Brett said. "Go get them cleaned out and patched up. We've got a solid hour before we get refuel and rearmament. Don't want you going to down to infection."

Hank complied, searching out the brigade aid station. He thought back to the comparative ease of their attack into St. Mihiel. Hank still thought that Patton was right, the war was nearly over, but if this is what the Germans were like in the last minute of the fourth quarter trailing insurmountably, what had they been like in 1914?

The young officer looked at his dirty, exhausted, but determined men. They'd fought like wildcats today.

Ole Jerry was probably a lot like us.

Chapter Sixteen

Father Francis P. Duffy

165th Infantry Staging Area, France

Less than a week in, the offensive into the Argonne Forest had already tallied the highest butcher's bill of American lives of any operation in the Great War to date. The untested divisions of the AEF's V Corps had fought valiantly, but inexpertly, in the vanguard of the attack, and every yard of progress was costly. The region's wooded hills were littered with German fortifications. Terrain and weather slowed and disrupted support from the French and American tank units assigned to support the offensive.

Worse, the American sector of advance was flanked by the unfordable Meuse River, the heights beyond which offered clear observation and fields of fire for artillery and machine guns all along the American axis of advance.

The closed terrain and ubiquitous wire obstacles made maneuver so slow going that many infantry units found it difficult to keep pace with the creeping barrages meant to support their attacks. The shelling passed over German defenses before the Americans were ready for their assault, thus allowing the defenders to engage advancing American infantry at the maximum effective range that visibility and their weapons allowed, without hindrance from suppressing indirect fires.

The forwardmost units in the attack had no way to communicate directly with the artillery's fire direction centers, so American commanders at the front faced a brutal tactical problem. Halt the advance and wait the hours necessary for a runner to find a field phone tied back to the artillery and convince them to adjust fire, or attack in the face of rapidly mounting piles of dead and maimed men to maintain initiative.

General Pershing knew that just beyond the main German line of defense between the towns of Landres and Landres-et-St. Georges lay open terrain and lighter defenses—and the Germans, however hard they fought, were weary from four years of war. The enemy did not have inexhaustible reserves of fresh troops. So, with a bloody-minded determination that would've done credit to Ulysses S. Grant, Pershing pressed the attack. He committed his reserves—including the 42nd Division.

The Rainbow Division roused from her bivouac near St. Mihiel and marched forth under cover of night into the abattoir. The Fighting 69th led the way. Sigi joined Colonel Donovan and Father Duffy on a promontory to watch the procession of the regiment toward the front.

Shiny new captain's bars glinted in the night on Sigi's collar across from the brass crossed rifles of the infantry. He'd been promoted but did not yet have command of a company. Donovan promised it was coming but seemed to keep putting off the reassignment. Donovan said it was because Sigi was vital as his adjutant to help him stay organized and free of niggling details so that he could command the battalion effectively.

Sigi knew that was true, as far as it went, but it rankled him deeply. He hadn't been manning a typewriter during the St. Mihiel Offensive, but had been right beside Donovan, running messages between companies and back to higher headquarters and doing anything Donovan needed to keep command and control of the 1st Battalion.

Donovan had recommended him for two more Citation Stars. But Donovan knew how badly Sigi wanted a chance to command, and neither Sigi's intellect nor courage had been found wanting—so why was Sigi still on the bench?

Father Duffy was praying over the advancing troops as Sigi approached him on the hilltop, so Sigi stayed quiet and bowed his head. In the midst of Father Duffy's eloquent prayers, though, the troops started singing out a cadence.

"Ohhh, Lulu has a bicycle,

"Her seat runs back to front,

"And every time she sits on it,

"It goes right up 'er—BANG BANG LULU!

"Lulu's gone away!

"Who's gonna bang on Lulu?

"While Lulu is away?"

A peal of laughter escaped Sigi before he was able to lock it down and reestablish his bearing. Donovan shot him a reproving glance, but Duffy merely finished his prayer. But as he walked away, shaking his head, he muttered, "Never such a group of ruffians in need of *Jay-sus* as our lads."

There was no raucous singing during the next night's movement into the Argonne sector. Residual green clouds of German gas prompted the regiment into their gas masks, making the night movement even more confusing and dangerous than normal. Ranging up and down the column while having to breathe through the gas mask filter exhausted Sigi rapidly. Only sheer terror at the idea of appearing weak in front of the men kept him on his feet.

As they neared the jump-off point it became apparent that there hadn't been time for grave details to sweep the area since the last wave of American attacks. The brown-uniformed bodies of doughboys were strewn throughout the woods like broken toys as they approached the front. Distended and bloated, mangled and eviscerated, each corpse was a unique horror. One man's abdomen lay wide open with his entrails splayed over a nearby log. Another looked whole, save for a grim rictus on his face. A third sat as if merely resting, but a second look revealed a gaping, bloody hole where the right top quadrant of his skull should have been.

242 *Tom Kratman, Kacey Ezell & Justin Watson*

Sigi steadfastly turned his eyes away from the corpses and shut out everything except putting one foot in front of another and checking his mimeographed map and compass at every intersection to verify they were on course. Through an act of will, he confined his universe to the map, the route, the men, shielding his sanity for the fight ahead.

Setback and slaughter, advance and retreat; the Argonne ground upon Sigi in a way he hadn't imagined possible until now. Planned tank support failed to arrive. Only a pittance of grenades, vital in assaulting bunkers, found their way to the attacking battalions. And Bangalore torpedoes, equally necessary for cutting wire obstacles, were in even shorter supply. Without tanks or Bangalores, the men were reduced to manually cutting through the triple-strand obstacles employed by the Germans, a process entirely too lengthy while under fire.

Coordination in the woods under constant fog and rain, not to mention enemy shelling and long-range machine gun fire, was a nightmare. Messages to and from higher headquarters and flanking units arrived out of sequence—when they arrived at all. The dispatch runners and junior officers entrusted with those messages took some of the highest casualties per capita.

At one point the 69th overextended and lost contact with the unit to their left, the 167th Alabama. They'd had to withdraw under fire to reestablish their lines and avoid being surrounded and cut off by a German counterattack.

It was only after days of battle and hundreds of men killed and maimed, that the men of the 69th finally reached sight of the German main defensive line between Landres and Landres-et St. Georges. But the 1st Battalion, more than a thousand men strong by table of organization, had fewer than two hundred officers and men combat effective.

Sigi huddled next to Donovan and a combined team of their own infantrymen and some engineers from the 117th. Another volley of fire from the regimental Stokes mortars impacted on and around the formidable, concrete-reinforced German machine gun positions before them. Donovan, resplendent with Distinguished Service Cross and Croix de Guerre pinned to his tunic, waved his hand forward.

"Follow me, 1st Battalion!"

Donovan leapt from their crater and ran toward the German wire.

Sigi followed close on his heels, looking about to ensure the men were keeping up. A German artillery barrage that dwarfed their own mortar fire landed all around them, but still Donovan pressed onward as if the steel and fire falling from the sky were of no more concern than the autumn showers. And his men followed.

A burst from a German machine gun sent one of their engineers spinning to the ground. Sigi grabbed the wire cutters out of the man's pack. A line of machine gun rounds kicked up spurts of mud behind him as he dove for cover behind a thick tree, just shy of the wire.

Amidst the chaos, Donovan stood tall, urging his men onward. Sigi sprinted to catch up, tossed the wire cutters to one of the soldiers, then tried to remonstrate with Donovan.

"Sir, you've got to get down, you're going to get your head blown off!" Donovan shook off the caution.

"If I don't urge them on, the boys will break," Donovan shouted to be heard over the artillery and machine guns. Then he grinned, a mad glint in his eye. "This is why we get paid the big bucks, Sigi!"

The German wire was arrayed in multiple rows, each in triple strand. A hundred yards away, one of Company B's breach teams disappeared in a cloud of orange and gray as an artillery shell landed squarely among them. The man Sigi had thrown the wire clippers to fell back, streams of blood pouring out exit wounds on his back as the German MGs claimed another victim.

Sigi looked around desperately, but none of the breach teams were making progress, and every minute more men fell dead and dying among the wire. Another burst of fire impacting mere feet away sent Sigi diving for cover again. Donovan cried out, and when Sigi looked back, his commanding officer was clutching his leg, blood welling from multiple bullet holes.

"Mullaney, Riley, help me get him back," Sigi shouted.

"No," Donovan shouted through gritted teeth. "I'm not leaving my men."

Sigi motioned for the men to start dragging Donovan against his will.

"We're just getting you to cover, sir," Sigi shouted.

Back in the relative safety of the shell hole, Mullaney started tying a tourniquet around Donovan's leg. Examining the stalled attack before him, Donovan's expression grew grim.

"Goddamnit, pull the men back," Donovan said. "This slaughter isn't getting us anywhere. Riley, get back to the regimental CP and tell the Mortar Company to lay down fifty-fifty HE and smoke to cover our withdrawal. Sigi, go tell the remaining commanders to pull their men back."

Most of the company commanders were dead or missing, but the NCOs Sigi was able to find were only too happy to abandon the doomed assault, except when he tried to reach the remnants of Company D on the far right flank, there was no way to get to them—and no way for them to get out of their positions huddled down at the edge of the wire behind rocks and stumps of trees.

When he relayed the message to Donovan, Donovan frowned, lost in thought for several seconds. He looked to the far right.

"All right, Sigi, here's what you're going to do," Donovan said. "Take command of Company C. Rally them and as many machine guns as you can find, take up position in that patch of woods," Donovan indicated the spot he was talking about with a knife-hand. "It's not a viable position for more than a few minutes, but from that point you should have an angle to provide enough suppressive fire for Company D to withdraw."

"Yes, sir," Sigi said. "Sir, we need to get you evacuated, you could lose that leg."

"Hang my leg, Abramovich, I'm not leaving until the battalion is safe. Now carry out my orders!"

Sigi sprinted to where a group of men lay, back in the tree line, exhausted and looking shellshocked. He couldn't see an officer, so he scanned as rapidly as possible until he spotted a senior sergeant, a big fellow with black hair and a boxer's nose. Sigi knew his name—he knew almost all their names at this point.

"Sergeant Hanrahan, gather all that's left of Charlie Company," Sigi said. "D Company is pinned down. We're headed to the tree line five hundred yards that way to provide them covering fire so they can pull out, too."

Before Hanrahan could answer, Corporal Higgins, the ginger bastard who'd been making snide remarks since day one, cut in. "Hey, Captain, you ain't our CO, we're not going anywhere for you—"

"Higgins, shut your fucking mouth," Sigi snapped. "Colonel Donovan just gave me command of this company, he's in that shell hole, you can go ask him but do it *after* we rescue Company D. If you give me any more of your horseshit, I'll have you tried for insubordination and if your squad isn't ready to move in thirty seconds, I'll throw in misbehavior before the enemy and have you FUCKING SHOT. Now, MOVE."

Higgins snapped his mouth shut. Hanrahan grinned.

"Yes, sir," Hanrahan said. "You heard him, Higgins, get the other NCOs and let's move."

With the help of his NCOs, Sigi mustered fifty-five riflemen, a Chauchat machine gun team, and one of the new Browning M1917 gun teams. Sigi led his new command through a ravine that gave them cover and concealment from nearly all angles of fire. Only occasional near misses from machine gun bursts and rifle fire marred their journey, but they lost no one getting to their new firing position. One by one, Sigi positioned each of the ad hoc sections amidst the trees, assigning hasty sectors of fire. He told them to hold their fire until the Vickers machine gun team that anchored the company's center opened up.

"After you open up, I'll sprint out and tell the Company D boys to pull back," Sigi told the NCOs, well aware that he would be running out into the open, not only exposed to enemy fire, but in clear view of an NCO he'd just threatened to have shot.

Fortune favors the bold . . .

Instructions given, Sigi returned to the center of the line, took a deep breath, and slapped the Vickers gunner on his shoulder.

"Fire!"

Two machine guns and almost three-score rifles opened up. Concrete chipped away at the firing slits of the German bunkers and their fire slackened. Sigi dashed, covering the ground in great bounds. His men's rounds snapped over his head as he pushed as fast as his legs would carry him, shouting at the top of his lungs the whole way.

"Pull back, boys! We've got you covered!"

The men of Company D, having been under fire and taking heavy losses for the better part of the morning, stirred slowly. Sigi reached their lines before the bulk of them were on their feet and moving to the rear. Sigi put his shoulder under the arm of a man hobbled by a mangled calf. He continued to shout encouragement to the company to move.

"Come on, Colonel Donovan gave the order to regroup! Move it!"

The Germans must have seen their quarry escaping, for their fire increased in intensity and accuracy; six more men fell, but the bulk of what was left of Company D made it to the relative safety of the woods. NCOs counted off their soldiers and checked their ammunition and water supplies. Sigi found there was one lieutenant still alive in Company D, a man Sigi's own age named Reid.

"Reid, as soon as you have accountability, get your men ready to move back," Sigi said.

"Yes, sir," Reid said. "Thank you for coming for us, I thought we were all dead men."

"Thank Colonel Donovan, it was his idea," Sigi said, grinning. "Come on, we need to regroup with the others."

The 1st of the 69th limped out of range of the enemy's machine guns and out of their artillery observers' field of vision, back to their jump-off point. True to his word, Donovan refused to be carried from the field until all his men were accounted for and retreating with him.

While Donovan received medical treatment in his command post, Sigi rallied the remaining company officers and reported to the battalion operations officer to coordinate their dispositions. Only after his men were set with security and priorities of work and rest did Sigi head back to the command post to check on his CO.

Major Anderson from Regiment was in the CP, talking animatedly to Donovan, who was still having the bullet wounds in his leg bandaged.

"Sir, Colonel Mitchell insists the next attack has to go as scheduled," Anderson said. "It will disrupt the entire division's scheme of maneuver—"

"Anderson, our artillery prep failed," Donovan said. "Their machine gun emplacements are entirely intact and fortified. We don't have enough Bangalores or tanks to cut their wire, and I am down to one hundred eighty-six effectives. The 1st Battalion never hesitates to fight, but I'm not ordering my men into a useless slaughter."

Anderson paused.

"Sir, I understand your objections, but are you refusing a direct order from Colonel Mitchell?"

"Tell Colonel Mitchell that with the proper artillery and engineer support, and a resupply of ammunition and grenades, the 1st Battalion will take Landres et-St. Georges by dinner, but without it, we'll accomplish nothing but littering the German wire with more American bodies no matter how many times we throw ourselves against their lines."

Anderson nodded gravely, and he saluted. Donovan returned it. The staff officer left and returned to his car without another word. Sigi looked at Donovan, torn between admiration and anxiety.

"Sir . . . You could be court-martialed."

Donovan gave Sigi a hard look, his blue eyes piercing.

"Sigmund, an officer who puts his own career ahead of the mission or the men is the worst kind of bastard," Donovan said, then his tone and expression relaxed. "Besides, they're not going to take me to trial. Then they would have to put why in the records, and that's too many generals recorded for posterity as having done damn foolish things."

"I suppose you're right, sir."

"Of course I am, and speaking of promotions— Willis! You got it typed up?"

"Yes, sir, right here, hot off the press!" The personnel NCO brandished a sheet of paper.

"And his name's spelled right?"

"Uhhhh." Willis stopped, looked at the paper and looked at Sigi. "No T in Abramovich, right, sir?"

"That's right, Sergeant," Sigi said, a little confused.

"Ah, yes, then it's spelled right," Willis said, his tone happier. He handed the paper to Sigi, along with a fountain pen. The header included the date and the battalion's official designation—the 1st of the 165th. The body of the memorandum read:

The undersigned hereby assumes command of Company C, 1st Battalion of the 165th Infantry Regiment.
Abramovich, Sigmund T.
Captain, Infantry

Despite the blood and terror of the last few days, despite the misery and the errors that cost lives, a wave of pleasure washed over him. He'd led men in battle and done well—and now they were *his* command, officially.

Donovan smiled at him and held out his hand.

"Congratulations, Captain Abramovich," Donovan said. "I know you're assuming command under some damned challenging circumstances, but I never met a man who worked harder to earn his guidon."

Donovan then fixed Sigi with an icy stare. "That said, young captain, the next time you abandon your own company to run a message to another company will be the last."

Gulping, Sigi answered, "Yes, sir."

Chapter Seventeen

Tatiana Nikolaevna, Empress of all the Russias

Imperial House, Tobolsk

"Natalya." Tatiana looked up from her correspondence as the young girl who'd become her close friend and confidante entered the room.

Natalya was a pretty girl, though still a bit thin, and one who'd been through more female-specific atrocities than any young girl in a fairer world would ever have experienced. Coming from minor nobility, she'd seen her parents, mother and father both, murdered in front of her by Bolsheviks. That same group of Bolsheviks had then turned her into a sex slave before trading her to the crew of a smuggler for some cheap rotgut.

She'd done as much as, or perhaps more than, anyone for the rescue of the three remaining members of the Royal Family, from saving the group sent to pinpoint their location for a rescue, to spying out the exact floor plan of their Tobolsk prison. And every step of that had been at the risk of her own life.

Tatiana had come to love her as another sister, not least because, after all that suffering, she remained whole and clean inside.

"Your Imperial Majesty," Natalya said, dipping into a curtsey. Tatiana exhaled audibly through her nose, but allowed no other sign of her impatience to show as her friend straightened up with an impish smile.

"You know I want you to call me Tatiana when we're alone."

"And you know that I will, once I've greeted you properly at least once," Natalya fired back. "I'm sorry I didn't come right away, but your message said it wasn't urgent and I needed to finish some things."

Tatiana waved a hand to dismiss the apology and pointed to the chair next to her. She sat at a large table in front of a wide window that looked out on the snow-covered landscape and provided plenty of natural light. Letters and reports lay stacked in neat piles all around her, along with a bottle of ink and one of the precious fountain pens they'd been able to keep in good repair.

"It's fine," Tatiana said. "But please come sit. I need your advice."

"Of course." Natalya smoothed her day dress and sat on the edge of the chair. She didn't lean forward to look at the papers in front of Tatiana, but simply folded her hands in her lap and waited.

Tatiana let out a sigh.

"So. I have been informed that I must secure the succession. What are your thoughts?"

Natalya's eyebrows shot up. "On the succession? I quite agree. You must secure it as soon as possible."

"Obviously I must, minx. The question is, how?"

"That is the obvious part, I should think," Natalya allowed herself a smile. "You must marry and have children. I rather think General Kostyshakov might—"

"Natalya. Stop." Tatiana's voice cracked with a bit more harshness than she intended, so she hurried to continue before Natalya's infernally keen mind could fixate on why. "We are not talking of him. That isn't what I mean, and you are well aware of it. If I marry, it must be for the political gain of Russia, and that cannot happen until this war is won. No, I'm talking about in the meantime. Should something happen to me—"

"—Such as, for instance, if you were hurt or killed while serving as part of an artillery battery?" Natalya's sweet tone did nothing to hide the barbs of her question. She'd made it very plain that she disapproved of Tatiana's actions in the recent battle.

"Yes. For instance," Tatiana said. She took the jab, but her tone held a warning. She was still dealing with the fallout of her actions, and she wasn't about to rehash her decisions now. "I must put some provision in place."

"Well, your sisters come most immediately to mind. Though I suppose we could find you a cousin or two if needed."

"It must be one of my sisters," Tatiana said. "If I am hanging my legitimacy on the fact that I'm the eldest surviving child of the Tsar, then I cannot in good conscience pass either of them over without reason . . . and therein lies the problem."

"Why?" Natalya asked, her eyes narrowing slightly. Tatiana suddenly realized that her clever handmaid very likely knew exactly what she was about to say. But she knew that articulating her thoughts would help Tatiana come to a decision . . . and so she let her sovereign speak first, like a wise courtier.

"Maria," Tatiana said slowly, dropping her voice down. "She is the next eldest but . . . I worry for her. She cries, every night, for Mama and Papa. I miss them too—of course I do! And Olga and little Alexei. It's like an ache in my chest that never really goes away . . . but I cannot afford to fall into tears every night. A Tsarina has too much to do. And truth be told, the way she speaks of our parents leads me to believe that she is almost . . . canonizing them, in a way. In her mind. The other day, she questioned me quite sharply when I mentioned changing a policy that my father put into place. It was a nothing policy . . . something silly about etiquette. Not even the kind of thing we can reasonably support in this environment, and yet she acted mortally offended that I would even think to tamper with what she termed 'his legacy.'" Tatiana snorted and pressed her lips together, then turned and looked out the window as a formation of her troops marched by, singing, on the road that led past her front door.

"This war is his *legacy*," she said, speaking lowly enough that Natalya might not even have been able to hear her. "The unrest, the violence, the Reds . . . all of it. *He* might have prevented it, had he been a better ruler. If Maria cannot see that, then she cannot be my heir."

She turned back to meet her handmaid's gaze. Natalya smiled gently, her eyes warm. "So, then it must be Anastasia."

"Yes," Tatiana said. "Though she is a whole host of other problems. I do not see how anyone can have gone through what we've gone through and still have such immaturity about them."

"Everyone's ordeal is different," Natalya said, her voice going hard. Tatiana glanced up at her, suddenly remembering that Natalya was even younger than Tatiana's youngest sister. "Anastasia will grow up because she must. We all do."

"I have already lost my parents, my brother, and one of my sisters. I cannot lose another by passing her over for the succession. I will if I must, for the good of Russia, but . . ." Tatiana broke off.

Natalya reached out and covered her empress's hand with her own. "I quite understand," she said, her voice gentle. "You must protect her, but you do not want to alienate her."

"Yes!" Tatiana flipped her hand over and squeezed Natalya's fingers in gratitude. "That is exactly it."

Natalya nodded, and inhaled slowly through her nose. "Well," she said slowly. "She *is* a Grand Duchess of Russia. What if she were to marry?"

Tatiana blinked. Enough people had begun dropping pointed hints about *her* marriage that she hadn't really even thought about the prospect of her sisters' nuptials.

"A political alliance?" Tatiana said slowly, almost tasting the words. "One that takes her out of the succession, but ties another powerful family to our cause . . ." Then she blinked again and straightened as an idea struck into her brain and ran down her spine like lightning. "Natalya," she gasped, "I have it! Look at this!"

Tatiana reached for first one, then another of the piles in front of her. She rifled through it until she found the letter she wanted, and shoved it at Natalya, making the paper rattle.

Natalya took the page, her eyes quickly scanning the letter. It wasn't long, after all.

"What a pompous old man," she said quietly. "Meaning no disrespect to your royal cousin, of course, Tatiana."

"No, no, the King of Great Britain *is* a pompous old man," Tatiana said, waving away her friend's apology. "As if I would run to him while I've a war to fight! But that's not important. What is important is the invitation. And he's right about one thing. He does have the best Navy in the world ... and a bit of a wastrel son. I'd wager that Cousin George might be keen to get Cousin David settled down ... and who better to be Princess of Wales than an Imperial Grand Duchess of Russia?"

"Do you think he would be persuaded to help us in the war effort?"

"He'll be cagey about it, but there is a possibility. And even if Maria isn't suitable to be Tsarina, she *is* a dedicated royalist who hates the Reds as much as any of us. She'll be persuasive."

"So you will send Maria to Britain to marry the Prince of Wales?"

"Well," Tatiana said, pursing her lips. "Not *explicitly*. In fact, I think that would be a mistake. Maria wouldn't enjoy feeling managed like that. But our grandmother was born in Britain ... perhaps I can send both Maria *and* Anastasia, too. It would certainly be safer than keeping them here, and Grandmama is still at risk down in Crimea."

She looked down at the letter, and then up at Natalya with a grin. "Yes, Grandmama must be my ally in this, I think. *She* will understand how to best hint that Maria and David make a match of it, and Maria can have no better guide ... Yes. That is what we will do. I must write to Cousin George and Grandmama immediately."

"What about Anastasia?" Natalya glanced at the door through which the youngest sister often came in her role as Tatiana's secretary.

"I will think on that a little more. For now, this is enough to get started. Thank you, Natalya."

Natalya pushed her chair back and stood up, letting out a little laugh. "For what, your Imperial Majesty? I did very little."

"You did exactly what I needed, my friend. Except for breaking my rule about using my name when we're alone!"

"After I've properly greeted you once."

"Well, you just used my title for the second time, but I won't hold it against you." Tatiana grinned up at the girl who'd become her closest friend. "I will see you later for dinner?"

"Of course! I wouldn't miss it."

Interlude

The newspaper project in Kiev fell through, so Max and his family packed up again and moved to Odessa. His wife and children enjoyed the summer beauty of the seaside town, and he started working at *Juzhnoe Slovo*, a local newspaper edited by Ivan Bunin, among others.

I'd miss doing this kind of work, thought Max, *miss it terribly.*

It was never easy starting over in a new place, particularly not during wartime. The conflicts around Odessa had died down enough for them to move there, but the normal trials of moving took on even more difficulty due to wartime scarcities.

Still, Max had a job, and so they did all right. The ongoing civil war continued to concern him. The Bolsheviks had not come this far south, and a man named Denikin held the town. But there were still enough soldiers in the streets that it worried Ekaterina. Max had promised her that he would keep abreast of current events—it was his job, after all—and that they would be ready to move again if it became necessary.

Ekaterina hadn't greeted his assertion with enthusiasm. Resignation, yes. But not enthusiasm. And how could a man blame her?

Today, though, as Max hurried home through the wind-whipped streets of the seaside town, he had something interesting to share! A bit of news had come in that would go out in the morning edition, but Max didn't intend to wait before confiding in his wife.

"Max, welcome home—" Ekaterina called out as she stirred a pot on the stove. Max didn't know where the children were, and for the moment, he didn't care. Perhaps better if he told their mother alone, first.

"Ekaterina, I have something important to tell you," he said as he let the front door close behind him and strode through the tiny foyer into their kitchen. The house they'd rented in Odessa was smaller than what they'd had in Saint Petersburg, a condition which he knew Ekaterina disliked.

She turned from the stove, dismay pinching her face for just a breath before she smoothed it out and hid her feelings under her usual practical stoicism.

"What is it?" she asked. "Must we move again?"

"Not just yet," he said. He leaned in to kiss her on the cheek in what he hoped she would interpret as reassurance. "But something significant. We knew that some of the Imperial family was rescued, but not much beyond that. Apparently, Tatiana has crowned herself Tsarina, and is fighting the Bolsheviks with the very forces that rescued her!" Max couldn't keep the thread of excitement out of his voice as he spoke, even as he watched his wife's eyes remain blank and shuttered.

"What is that to us?" she asked, ever the practical one.

"I don't know. Maybe nothing, maybe everything. Denikin holds this city, and he has imperialists in his forces, yes. But he has socialists and democrats as well. I do not know if he will throw in with the young empress. Nor do I know how *we* will fare if he does. But it is interesting, is it not?"

"If you think it is interesting," Ekaterina said, a hint of tartness entering her tone. "That is all very well, Max. I am happy to listen to you. But unless you have something else to tell me that requires my immediate attention, I'm going to return to what I was doing so that our dinner doesn't burn, and we don't starve."

Max ducked his head as she turned back to the stove. "I am sorry, Mother. I just thought you would like to know. This... this could change everything. We may be able to return home someday."

"Someday, yes. But not today."

"No, my love. Not today."

Chapter Eighteen

Anastasia and Maria

Imperial House, Tobolsk, Russia

This place, thought Tatiana, Empress of all the Russias, etc., looking around at the walls and bookshelves of her father's old office, *may not be the home we were born to, but it's more home*-like *than perhaps any place I've ever lived before. If we win the war, I think I'm going to have someplace like this built, and just use the palaces for official functions.*

But, for now, business.

She forced her hands to lie still in her lap, instead of twisting fretfully as they wanted to do.

You know, I think I might be more scared of this conversation than I was before the battle. Sergeant Panfil was right. During the battle, I was too busy to be scared. Now ... I can only wait.

That thought made her turn and look out the window at the slowly thawing landscape. For just a moment, she felt again the sickening ripple inside her belly and chest from the impact of the enemy's shells nearby.

All right, all RIGHT; so Daniil wasn't wrong in both thinking it the dumbest thing he'd ever seen or heard of and then chewing me out over it. All-bloody-RIGHT!

A door opened, and a slight cough recalled her to the present. She turned to see Maria slipping through the door, Anastasia close on her heels. Tatiana summoned up a smile for her sisters and beckoned them forward to her little table.

"Your Imperial Majesty," Maria said. She stopped short of the table and sank into the perfect curtsey that Tatiana knew she'd practiced for hours back in Tsarskoye-Selo. Tatiana knew that, because she'd been right there beside her sister. Practicing the same technique, over and over until her legs ached.

And for what? Some archaic gesture of respect and adherence to rigid protocol that ... in the end ... didn't matter at all?

"Rise, Maria, Anastasia. Please. There's no need for this kind of formality when it's just us. You know that."

Anastasia, who'd followed her older sister's lead, straightened right away, but Maria remained where she was for another heartbeat. When she did rise, Tatiana couldn't miss the soft sigh of disappointment her middle sister let out.

"Maria?"

Maria glanced up to meet her sister's eyes for just a moment before looking away.

"Sister, what's wrong?"

"It's just that ... we've lost so much. Mother, Father, Alexei, Olga ... our whole *life*, Tatiana! It's all gone. So different from before. I just wish ... I miss ..."

Antastasia stepped forward and wrapped her arms around Maria in a hug. Tatiana leaned forward, started to stand, but Maria patted Anastasia's arms and stepped away.

"Forgive me, sister," Maria said. "You wanted to see us."

"There is nothing to forgive, dearest," Tatiana said. "I miss them too."

"We all do," Anastasia put in, and rather than rebuking her for interrupting, Tatiana merely nodded.

"I know," Maria said. "Just as I know that we are fighting—*you* are fighting to regain some of what we lost. It's just that, even the little things matter sometimes. The courtesies, the flourishes that I never even noticed when we were little. They now feel like a distant dream of home."

In the back corner of her mind, a tiny, dry voice pointed out that when they were little, their parents had placed them on a strictly disciplined regimen—at least for royal children. They'd made their own beds and mended their own clothes, so she wasn't entirely sure what fantasy past Maria had built up in her head . . . but in the end, it didn't matter.

It didn't change what Tatiana had to say, or what she needed her sisters to do.

"Please join me," she said, gesturing to the unoccupied chairs at the table. "We have things to discuss."

While Maria and Anastasia arranged themselves at the table, Tatiana took a moment to pour tea for all of them and consider how to begin. She took a deep breath, set the teapot down, picked up her own cup and sat back in her chair.

"I've had word from Britain," she said. "Our Grandmama, Maria Feodorovna, has been recovered safely from Crimea by the British Navy, and at my request, intends to establish a residence in London—"

"Oh, that's good!" Anastasia said, and then fell silent as both of her sisters looked a rebuke at her for the interruption. "I'm sorry," she said, "but it *is* good, isn't it? At least she won't be in danger of being captured like poor Aunt Ella!"

"Yes," Tatiana said, "She is safe, and that is good. But that is not the only reason I wish her to remain in London. I asked her to set up a residence there so that her household may support you both when you go."

Maria, who had been looking down into her tea with a dejected slump to her shoulders, suddenly straightened. Her blue eyes sparkled with interest.

"Go? To London?"

"Yes," Tatiana said. "Our cousin the King has offered, and I have accepted on your behalf. You and Anastasia will journey there as soon as travel can be arranged. Perhaps via the United States. It will be longer, but the trip may be safer . . . in any case, it has become apparent that despite our troubles here at home, Russia cannot remain sequestered from the world stage for much longer. We must cultivate and strengthen the international friendships we have, and perhaps seek to make new ones. There are many ways of doing this, of course, but as Grand Duchesses, you are both ideally placed for one particular and time-honored method."

"Marriage," Maria breathed.

Anastasia wrinkled her nose and flinched. "Marriage? Tatiana, really? We're still so young—"

"Not so young as all that!" Maria snapped. "And if we can help our sister *and Empress* in this manner, then our duty is clear!"

Tatiana raised a purely mental eyebrow, *And it's not like you would be all that upset to have a man, and all that . . . ummm . . . comes with one of your own, would you, sister, dear?*

She set down her teacup and reached out to take both of her sisters' hands. "Understand me, sisters," she said softly. "I love you both with my whole heart. I may be your Empress, but I will *never* compel you to marry where your heart does not lie. Your happiness is as important to me as my own. I have made no arrangements other than for you to visit. I would just like you to . . . see. Go to London. Be feted and celebrated for the beautiful survivors that you are. Tell our story, for ultimately, it may sway others to our cause.

"And if you should happen to fall in love with a handsome prince . . ." Tatiana trailed off and allowed herself a slightly conspiratorial smile and a wink as she used to do back in their carefree days as children. "Well. Then we shall go on from there."

A slow smile spread across Maria's face, lighting her up and bringing back the radiant beauty she'd been praised for as a child. She squeezed Tatiana's hand and the Empress found herself blinking back sudden tears.

She hadn't seen joy like that in Maria since Papa's abdication. It seemed a lifetime ago.

Tatiana squeezed her sisters' hands once more before letting go. "As

I said," she went on, picking up her teacup again. "We are still making arrangements, but I would like you both to begin preparations. Grandmama will be an invaluable guide to you during this process. Follow her instructions as you would mine. You must make no promises without her assent. She will correspond with me and ensure that the actions you take are favorable to our interests."

Maria, still smiling, set down her teacup and stood. She leaned forward to press a soft kiss to Tatiana's cheek.

"I will not fail you," she whispered, and then straightened and, eyes dancing in something a little like mischief, sank into a curtsey once again. Tatiana found herself so cheered by her sister's joy that she actually laughed.

"Come, Anastasia," Maria said as she straightened. "We have much to do."

"You do," Tatiana said. "But I must speak with Anastasia a moment longer. I will send her to you directly. You are free to go, Maria."

Anastasia, who had been about to follow Maria out, froze and turned back. Tatiana lifted her teacup to hide the smile that threatened to peek out. Judging by the stiffness of her limbs and the narrowing of her eyes, Anastasia expected a reprimand—likely about her habit of interrupting—and was feeling mulish about it. When Maria swept past their youngest sister with a self-righteous sideways glance, Tatiana barely held back the giggles that threatened to shatter her composure.

"Yes, Tatiana?" Anastasia asked, her tone civil . . . barely.

"Come sit back down, *shvibzik*. I have a few other things to say to you."

"I already apologized—"

"This is not about your interruption, although you do need to stop doing that. In private I care less, of course, but . . ."

Antastasia let out a delicate snort as she returned to her chair. "I know better than to interrupt you in public, whatever Maria thinks!"

"Does she scold you often?"

"Constantly. *You* tell me that you prefer the informality of sisters, and so I use your Christian name in private as you've requested. But *she* seems to think that now that you are Tsarina, we must be as formal in private as we were at your coronation!"

"She is grieving," Tatiana said, her voice gentle.

"So am I, but you don't see me trying to recreate Tsarskoye-Selo here in Tobolsk!" Anastasia sat back and crossed her arms over her chest, looking disgusted as only a teenaged girl can.

"And that is why we are having this conversation." Tatiana let her voice go from soft to steely, and straightened her spine as she set down her tea again.

"Anastasia Nicolaevna, you are my sister and I will always love you as my sister. But right now I must speak to you not as sister to sister, but as Tsarina to subject.

"No, not subject. Heir."

Anastasia's eyes widened, and her arms dropped slowly down to her sides. She, too, sat up straight, albeit slowly.

"Your Imperial Majesty..."

"For now, at least," Tatiana went on as if the girl hadn't spoken. "I hope that in time I shall secure my own successor, but my marriage will be an even more political and delicate matter than Maria's or yours. And with the war... well. We simply do not have time. So I must name one of you *the* Tsarevna."

"But Maria is older."

"Yes," Tatiana said. "But Maria grieves our parents too much to see the folly of their ways. I love her with all my heart, but she would be a disaster for Russia. You... I still have hope for you."

Anastasia's brow furrowed, and Tatiana stifled the urge to smirk as her younger sister puzzled her way through such a backhanded statement.

"So you will go with Maria to London, but I do not think you will stay there long. I spoke truly. I will never *compel* either of you to marry where your heart does not lie. But I must and will *prevent* both of you from marrying if the match will be a detriment to our cause. So while I quietly hope that Maria marries into a royal family... you must not. Or at the very least, if you feel an attachment to someone, he must be willing and able to forsake his native land to come to Russia as your consort if need be."

Anastasia swallowed and nodded, her face pale. "I—I do not think I will find someone," she said, her voice barely a whisper. "I am only seventeen."

"Grandmama was only nineteen when she married our grandfather," Tatiana said. "But I agree, you must take your time. Maria's objective is marriage. Yours is to remain safe, and to observe and learn, and prepare yourself. For even if I survive long enough to marry and produce my own heirs, you will forever be a mainstay of this court. I do not see how I could bear to lose you both to foreign marriages..." She trailed off and blinked furiously as the dratted tears threatened again.

Anastasia reached out and took both of Tatiana's hands in her own. "I won't leave you," she promised. Tatiana smiled and shook her head.

"You will," she said. "You must, for all the reasons I've stated. But you will come back, either as my heir or my close advisor. Heed what I told Maria, and follow Grandmama's instructions. She knows of my plans for you. Maria...does not. Yet."

Anastasia nodded.

Tatiana let out a sigh. "You have been our *shvibzik*, and the source of much joy, littlest one. But I am afraid that you are about to have to grow up very quickly. I fear it will be quite difficult at times."

"You did it. You had to grow up quickly when you became Tsarina. Before that, even," Anastasia protested.

"That is how I know, dear one. That is how I know."

Interlude

Anastasia:

And so my usefulness is reduced to staying alive and hanging around, in another country, until I am—maybe...someday—needed.

How depressing.

Of course, I cannot complain to my sister; she has enough to worry about already. So I will suffer in silence and do my duty. In England.

Stuffy England. Wet England. England where the lazy-as-dirt royalty may go an entire lifetime without ever once drawing the curtains on their windows for themselves.

Mother, Father; I never appreciated you enough for making us do our own chores, clean our own rooms, make our own beds...and even take cold baths. I am alive only because you insisted, Mother, that we sew jewels into our clothing, *ourselves*.

Maria is going to love it, of course, just love it. But I will not, not in the slightest. I am going to be bored and depressed and *useless*. In England.

Chapter Nineteen

Quentin Roosevelt and the Squadron Pooch

95th Aero Squadron, Saints, France

Quentin Roosevelt, son of the twenty-sixth President of the United States, had become an early riser. He'd also grown up a good deal.

It wasn't that he didn't feel tired. God knew that the rigors of war ground a man down day after day. Most nights, he fell like a sack of potatoes into his bed back in Maupertuis and was asleep before he'd even heard his roommate Ed's soft "good night, Q."

No, it was his job to be up early, but he had come to enjoy the quiet in these pre-dawn moments. None of the muffled booming of distant artillery, nothing but the soft shushing of the wind and the delicious thrill of anticipation curling deep in his belly.

Anticipation, because he knew that in a few short hours, that quiet would give way to the buzzing roar of his Nieuport 28 and the popping rush of his twin Vickers "Balloon Buster" aircraft guns. Despite the frigid cold, the dirty stink of exhaust, the constant spray of unburnt oil that had his guts twisting in a perpetual case of the runs . . . despite it all, Quentin loved flying.

Looking out over the moonlit grass strip, leaning against the rail in front of the squadron headquarters' main entrance, Quentin's reverie was interrupted by a stern greeting: "Lieutenant."

"Good morning, sir." Quentin stood suddenly straight as he sketched out a quick salute and winked as he grinned into the solemn gaze of his commander, Major Davenport Johnson. Major Johnson's heavy eyebrows slammed together in a frown of disapproval. Quentin stifled a laugh as the old man turned away.

Not that Major Johnson was that much older than Quentin himself. Flying was a young man's game. Some of the mechanics in their squadron might have been over thirty, but by and large, most everyone around was just like himself—young, eager, and aggressive.

But Major Johnson was the commander. The commander was *always* the "old man." And this old man was nearly always cranky. Quentin didn't fully know why. When he'd first arrived here at the 95th Aero Squadron last month, he'd heard some rumblings of rumor about Major Johnson. Something about leaving his wingman to be shot down by enemy fighters. As the son of a former President not always beloved by all, Quentin tended not to give much credence to rumor, but it made sense to him that the old man would adopt a stern demeanor to counter such stories.

Quentin reached out to open the door of the operations building that had been his destination and held it open while Major Johnson walked through, his heavy-browed frown intact. Through the slowly gathering light of false dawn, Quentin could see the shapes of two more men approaching, and so he continued waiting while Ed Buford and James Knowles hustled to enter.

"Morning, Q," James said, while Ed just nodded hello. Quentin grinned at them both and followed them in. Ed wasn't at his best until he'd had coffee.

Coffee was, thankfully, pretty readily available at Saints Aerodrome. With sorties going out every morning, the mechanics working on the

Nieuports and newer, better SPAD XIIIs often worked at night, turning wrenches under the glow of shielded electric lights. Quentin figured he owed the mechanics his life several times over. Not just because they maintained the aircraft his life depended upon, but also because they kept the coffee pots hot and full.

The three aviators followed their commander to said coffee, poured their mugs with little discussion, and then found their way to the map room at the center of the long, low-slung building. Two more men joined them after a few minutes, and then three more. By the time the old man stepped up to the large map on the central table, most of the squadron had arrived.

"Gentlemen, today's mission is patrol." Major Johnson's deep voice rumbled over the assembled group, stilling any remnants of conversation. "We are looking for German observation and reconnaissance vehicles. Our intent is to deny any useful information to the enemy. As you know, the *Boche* observation balloons tend to be heavily defended, including by that new Fokker, according to some reports. The Germans are cooking up another big offensive, we know that, so they're hungry for information. Let's make them starve.

"Your formation and aircraft assignments are posted, gentlemen. Good hunting."

Quentin stood to attention with the others as the commander left, and then joined the fray at the bulletin board to see what he'd be flying, and who would be on his wing.

"Looks like it's you and me, Q." Ed Buford slapped Quentin on the back of his shoulder as the two men looked together at the posted sheet.

"Yes, with Buckley and Sewall as the lead." Quentin smiled at Buford and then turned his grin on the other two aviators who would round out their formation. Lieutenant Sumner Sewall, however, was already turning away, waving for the other three to follow him up to the large map in the center of the room.

"All right," Sewall said on a sigh, in a peculiar mannerism that had become something of a joke amongst the others. "Let's look at our routing..."

By the time the sun broke over the Eastern horizon, Quentin had his prop spinning, his guns loaded, and his blood up and ready to go. The buzz of the Gnome-9 engine vibrated through his body with an almost sexual feeling as he nudged the throttle forward and coaxed the Nieuport-28 into a taxi across the dew-wet grass of the airfield. With his feet, Quentin stood on first the right rudder pedal, then the left as he maneuvered the airplane into takeoff position. She moved like a slow, ungainly turtle on the ground, but Quentin knew that was temporary. Once he got her into the air, she would be as responsive to his touch as the highest-priced courtesans in the Paris brothels...

Not that he'd know anything about that. Not as far as anyone, particularly his fiancée Flora, knew. Never mind about the small booklet in his locker. If pressed, he'd insist that one of his buddies had given him the copy of *The Pretty Women of Paris* on a lark.

Buford's airplane in front of him shuddered, and the noise from his engine built as Buford pushed the throttle up to takeoff power and started skimming down the grass runway. Quentin forced his mind to forget about Paris brothels and focus on the here and now as his wingman rotated and leapt into the air.

"Our turn, sweetheart," Quentin said, as he stroked his thumb forward on the throttle. As promised, the Nieuport responded, her buzzing roar heightening as she started forward on her own takeoff roll. Quentin inhaled, tasting the burnt-dirt scent of fuel and oil coating his tongue as he pulled back on the stick, tilting her nose up and sliding into the dawn-pinkened sky.

The windsock stood steady out of the southwest, so Quentin put in a little bit of a crab as he performed his after-takeoff checks. His two Vickers machine guns waited, loaded with the 11mm Balloon Buster rounds, ready for him to drop the lever that would engage the firing mechanism and synchronize the guns to fire between the turns of his prop. He banked right to follow Sewall and Buford as they turned west in order to head back north. Out of the corner of his eye, he caught the glint of the rising sun flashing off Buckley's spinning prop to the rear of the formation.

Quentin breathed in deeply again, grateful for the silk scarf that shielded his nose and mouth from both the cold and the oil spray. Some always got through, of course, but that stopped the bulk of it. And it was damn helpful when some of the oil got on his goggles, obscuring his vision. He reached up with his left hand and wiped one such spatter away. It smeared a little bit, but it wasn't bad.

Dawning sunlight flowed over the land below, highlighting the pockmarked hellscape that four years of war had created out of the once-lush French countryside. If it hadn't been for the oil and exhaust stink, he might have even been able to smell the charnel house miasma of shit, mud, and decay that sometimes arose from the old lines. He knew his brothers were down there, somewhere, and the thought dampened his flight-fed exuberance for just a moment. He wasn't entirely sure about religion as a whole, but he sent a quick prayer skyward to whoever might be inclined to watch over fools and aviators and then doggedly turned his mind back to his task.

Patrol flights were all about visual detection. See the enemy before he sees you and sneak up on his ass. Quentin trained his eyes just above the horizon, starting the methodical scan he'd been taught. Up ahead, Sewall banked to the right again, and Quentin followed, keeping back pressure steady on the stick to counteract the Nieuport's tendency to dive in a right turn.

As soon as he rolled out, Quentin felt the extra push from the direct tailwind. The ground below slid by faster and faster as the formation arrowed toward the German lines and whatever they would find there.

They flew for about forty minutes at an altitude between five and six thousand feet. Quentin kept a periodic check on his fuel gauge, knowing that the help they were getting from the tailwind would be a hindrance if they had to hurry back home ... if, say, they were being chased by a flight of Fokkers.

Guess I won't go running home, then, Quentin thought, welcoming the savage edge to his thoughts. This wasn't his first dogfight. He'd downed one of the *Boche* fighters four days ago, and nothing about that experience had changed his mind about one essential point: like his father, he was a hunter. Quentin Roosevelt didn't run.

Quentin Roosevelt attacked.

He didn't know at which point, exactly, they crossed over the lines into enemy territory. The ground below was even more pockmarked and riddled with trenches and shell craters. Plus, a small, scattered deck of clouds had started to form a couple of thousand feet below them. Quentin craned his neck upward to see that there were thin layers building above them as well: potential hiding places for enemy patrols. Adrenaline rocked through him, sharpening his focus as he turned his eyes back to the horizon.

They flew overhead some town ... Dormans, maybe? Whatever it was, by now they were solidly in *Boche* territory, so he wasn't exactly surprised when he saw the shadowy smudge of a formation coming at them from two o'clock high.

Quentin banked hard to the right, letting his Nieuport dive and accelerate as the first *poppoppop* of the Fokkers' guns raked through their formation. "Fuckers are coming out of the sun," he muttered through gritted teeth as he pulled out of the dive and rolled back left. He pulled back on the stick, trading some of his newly acquired airspeed for a tight, climbing turn as he threw his firing lever forward and pulled himself around to engage the closest of the five aircraft currently ambushing his friends.

Feldwebel Christian Donhauser was twenty-two years old. He stood five feet, four inches tall in his stocking feet and weighed in at a whopping ninety-four pounds. He was the smallest aviator in the Imperial German Air Force, which unfortunate fact had earned him the hated nickname "*Milchbubi.*"

He'd also earned the Iron Cross First Class for bravery after being wounded in action, and had a kill under his belt for taking out an enemy fighter while on a recon mission. "*Milchbubi*" Donhauser was no innocent child. Small in stature he might be, but behind the stick of a Fokker D.VII?

Christian "*Milchbubi*" Donhauser was deadly.

Due to some last-minute shuffling and assignments, Christian led a smaller formation of five, rather than the standard seven D.VIIs into a diving attack on the French—*No, not French. American,* he realized as the sun behind him illuminated the kicking mule insignia of one of the American Aero Squadrons.

Not that it will matter much. Whether flown by French or American pilots, the Nieuport-28s weren't half the machine his D.VII was. Christian allowed himself a little smile as his twin Spandau 08/15's barked out in rapid succession and the formation in front of them broke apart ... just as he'd planned.

There! Quentin's eyes locked on the tail flash of two enemy aircraft banking around to come up hard on Buckley's tail. He raked his fire across the aft fuselage of one of the Fokkers, feeling more than hearing the *pop-tink* of his rounds hitting the enemy plane. That *Boche* pilot banked right and sliced down through the air, a growing smoke trail in his wake.

The other *Boche*, though, stayed hard on Buckley, matching him turn for turn until Buckley dove down into the scattered cloud deck. Quentin broke off as more enemy fire raked his own lower right wing. Buckley would lose his guy in the clouds, leaving Quentin free to defend himself.

He pulled up hard, letting his airspeed bleed off as he gained altitude and came up almost inverted. As he saw the ground start to come back into view "above" his head, Quentin rolled hard to the right, knowing that the Nieuport's diving tendency would help him make up the airspeed he'd traded for the potential energy of altitude. She responded beautifully, snapping around in a tight little aileron roll that had him back in position and firing on the enemy that was now about to cross his nose a few hundred feet below him.

Adrenaline and savage glee shot through Quentin as he hit his firing lever again, engaging the two Vickers guns mounted on the fuselage just forward of his cockpit. Because he was firing Balloon Busters, he could see the line of tracer rounds bright against the grey-and-green background of the cloud-streaked vista below. As he pulled up out of his dive, he saw that the *Boche* pilot he'd engaged had maneuvered out of the stream of fire and was coming up and over the top, rolling inverted as he fought to get back to Quentin's vulnerable tail.

Quentin laughed and raised a hand in a wave as his eyes met the *Boche* pilot's. The *Boche*'s eyes widened, then narrowed in a glare.

Quentin slammed the stick to the right, once again letting the nose-down diving tendency of the Nieuport build his speed before racking it back up and to the left in a high, climbing left turn. The aircraft shuddered as she pulled against the gyroscopic forces of her own prop ... but Quentin traded off that little bit of extra speed, and she stayed controllable.

C'mon sweetheart, almost there ...

Christian didn't get angry when he fought. Personally, he thought that anger was a relatively useless emotion. He preferred the icy calm that settled in his being whenever he flew. Calm collectedness enabled him to be precise. Anger caused mistakes.

So when the Ami pilot raised his hand in a mocking wave, Christian didn't get angry. He just tightened his turn and pulled his beautiful D.VII over and around just a little harder. Not hard enough to damage her wings, but enough to get his nose and his guns back on the arrogant ass's tail...

Except he wasn't there. Christian looked wildly around, craning his neck to the right. The Nieuport-28 the Ami was flying was French trash...everyone knew they snapped down in a right turn and foundered like a whale in a left turn. So, they *always* turned right when in a dogfight. So where—

Pop! Poppoppop! Poppoppop!

"*Scheisse!*" Christian howled as he whipped his aircraft to the left, passing underneath the nose of the firing Ami. Somehow he'd gotten his trash airplane up and to the *left!* And come around firing, raking a line of rounds down the left side of the D.VII from just aft of the wings to the tail. The Ami missed the cockpit, but as Christian rolled out, he could smell the acrid stink of fuel intensify. He glanced up in his mirror, and horror opened up a pit in his belly. Flames licked the side of his fuselage, meaning that one of the Ami's damned tracer rounds must have impacted his tank. He had maybe minutes to put the damn thing out before it exploded.

Without even really thinking through it, Christian's hands flew through the emergency shutdown procedure for the engine while he lowered his nose to dive through the wispy scud layer gathering below. He'd have to dive to try and put out the fire, then dead-stick it in.

Quentin felt his lips stretch in a savage grin as he watched the *Boche* break away and dive down, smoke trailing from his wounded Fokker. He lowered the nose to follow the dive through the bare remnants of clouds, but almost immediately pulled up as the *Boche's* smoke trail thinned and disappeared.

What the...? Oh my God. He just shut down his engine! This magnificent bastard is actually going to try and dead-stick it in!

Despite himself, Quentin couldn't help but feel a surge of admiration for his enemy's dogged courage. Gliding an aircraft in was no mean feat on its own, but to do it in a shot-up machine, with no real runway in sight...

Well. The baby-faced kid he'd seen in the Fokker had balls. Quentin would give him that.

He was never sure, afterward, whether it was admiration or morbid curiosity that had him pull up out of his attacking dive to circle over the gliding Fokker. Probably some combination of both?

Crazy Boche. *I see you going for that road. You're damned sure to ball it up, though, as chewed up as this area is. Still. Hats off to you for having the guts to try.*

Christian passed through the clouds and saw the terrain spread below. Normally, it would have been an inviting land of soft, ploughed fields perfect to land in. Now, however, the mud-churned, shell-pocked landscape offered no such luxury. Christian checked back to see that his dive had successfully put out the flames, then turned his scan outward.

There!

Up ahead, shining in the sunlight, a thin ribbon of road ran straight for a stretch of nearly a mile. If he could make it there, he should be able to put the crippled D.VII down on that length.

He exited the shadow of the clouds overhead and angled for that straightaway, limiting his bank so as to conserve his speed and height until he could be sure he'd make it.

A shadow passed over him. He looked up to see the belly of the Nieuport, about five hundred feet above, S-turning over his flight path. Watching him? Wanting to confirm his kill?

Christian shook his head and put his enemy out of his mind. If the Ami wasn't shooting at him, then he wasn't his biggest problem. He banked gently to the right in order to line up with the straightaway. It ran roughly east-west, so he headed for the eastern edge, in order to line up into the wind for landing.

One chance, Christian, he told himself. *You get one chance to do this right.*

As he passed below a hundred feet, Christian eased back on the stick to flare off his airspeed and assume a landing attitude. His tailwheel hit first, the impact jolting through the frame of the aircraft. His main gear slammed down next, his right main falling into an unfortunate rut that ran the length of the road. The D.VII's right wing tilted toward the ground, and despite all that Christian could do to keep her level, his left main lifted back up into the air.

Christian shoved all ninety-four pounds of his bodyweight as hard to the left as he could. It wasn't enough. The D.VII's right wingtip snagged in another rut on the side of the road, and his speed sent the entire thing cartwheeling through the air. Christian saw a dizzying spin of white, blue, and gray before hearing a deep, muffled *snap.*

The world blinked black for a split second before coming rushing back with startling clarity.

For just a moment, Christian sat panting, wrapping his mind around what he'd just done. He hung half-inverted in his seat under the crumpled, almost tent-shaped wreckage of the D.VII's lower wing struts. It took a second for him to process this orientation. His brain didn't seem to want to make sense of it. Something was wrong, but he couldn't quite put his finger on it.

The buzzing scream of an aircraft in a dive penetrated his muddled thoughts, followed by the *pop! poppoppop!* of enemy fire.

The Ami, Christian thought, his body like jelly. For the first time during the whole sequence, he felt anger ignite in his gut and he looked skyward to see the Nieuport approaching on a strafing run, his bullets kicking up the dried mud of the far end of the pocked field next to this treacherous stretch of road.

Christian didn't think. He wasn't conscious of unfastening or cutting his straps, but somehow he was free of them and pulling himself down and out of his seat. His legs didn't seem to work right, but he could hear the Ami's trash airplane's scream getting louder.

"No time," Christian whispered to himself through gritted teeth. "No time, no time." He used every ounce of his upper body strength to pull himself free of the wreckage, and then crawled laboriously, arm over arm, to the side of the road, over the small berm at its edge, and into the dubious cover of the ditch beyond.

Poppoppoppoppop . . . BOOM!

A blast of heat hammered into him, and deadly stinging splinters of wood and flaming fabric rained down into his ditch, pelting Christian as he buried his face in the shit-stained mud and tried to protect his head with his arms.

A roaring sound rushed up from within him on a wave of pain-filled nausea. He managed one last inhale of hot, stinking air before the blackness rose up from the edges of his vision to engulf him and sweep him under.

✛ ✛ ✛

I should go back. I should go back and kill him.

Quentin looked at his fuel gauge and tapped it, but the story it told didn't change. One of the *Boche* rounds must have nicked a fuel line. If he didn't head back now, he'd never make it to the aerodrome with that headwind. That was a good enough reason, surely?

But why didn't I shoot him when I had the chance?

The truth was, he shouldn't have had to. That *Boche* pilot not only had balls of steel, but some deity somewhere was watching out for him. The fire in his engine should have made the Fokker explode midair—it didn't. He shouldn't have been able to put the fire out—he did. And then to try and dead-stick a landing on a rutted-out, shell-pocked road through an old battlefield?

When the enemy balled it up on landing, Quentin rolled in for a strafing run, figuring that he might as well destroy the wreckage past the point of repair. But as he'd started firing, he saw movement in the cockpit. The magnificent bastard had survived!

Shock had him pulling up off his run early, so even though he'd destroyed the wreckage, he hadn't been able to adjust and fire on the young man crawling for whatever shelter he could find.

In his heart of hearts, Quentin was secretly glad. Because suddenly, it seemed terribly wrong to kill such a brave, skilled aviator on the ground. Somehow, deep in his gut, Quentin knew that this *Boche* deserved better.

So even though a tiny part of his conscience screamed at him that one dead German meant several of his friends might not have to die, Quentin had waggled his wings in salute and turned for home. Thanks to the fuel leak, he was at bingo fuel anyway. Hell, he wasn't even going to make it home. He'd have to point toward friendly lines and hope for the best.

"Godspeed, you crazy bastard," Quentin whispered as he turned his thoughts toward finding a suitable landing field. "That was a hell of a fight."

Interlude

My Dearest Quentin,

I can hardly write for the tears. I've just had the most dreadful row with my family. I received your letter Thursday last, and as usual I pored over every line. Oh, my darling, though you are a man, and have that sex's infuriating tendency to be irritatingly sparse and understated in detail, I must tell you how your latest account was most thrilling to read. Such derring-do, like something out of a story! I even decided to read it to Papa, since I know that he appreciates courage and strength, and you have that in spades, my darling. You always have.

I do not know what happened. Your father must have said something or done something to infuriate mine, and through the worst of luck, I chose the same day to share your story. All I know is that Papa's face got darker and darker, until I faltered in my reading. I asked him what was wrong, but he merely shook his head and grumbled. I pressed him—what a fool I am! But you know how much I love my Papa, and how I have always been close to him. I thought surely, I could break him out of whatever terrible dark cloud he'd wrapped himself in. I was wrong.

He got so angry with me that he ordered me to leave off and never speak your name to him again. When I replied—rather tartly, it must be said—that it would be difficult to obey since we were to be married, he snarled at me and ripped your letter from my hand!

I've never seen him in such a rage!

I am so sorry, my darling, but he crumpled the letter and threw it into the fire, and then he said the most unforgivable thing. He thundered that it would be better for the whole country if the German fighters had killed you! He said that perhaps then your father would go into mourning and stop mucking around the country.

At that point, I realized what must have happened. We always knew that my father hated your father's politics . . . I suppose it was only a matter of time before it turned personal between them.

I tried to withdraw quietly, but the damage had been done. Papa had gotten his blood up, and he demanded that I end our engagement or be disinherited. Entirely.

"I will not see one penny of Whitney or Vanderbilt money pass into the hands of a son of that uncouth, conniving, jumped-up, nouveau riche excuse for a politician!"

Can you imagine?!

I wouldn't do it, my darling. I wouldn't give in, not for anything . . . but then he insisted that I would never speak to Mama or my brother and sister again and I . . . oh, I'm heartbroken.

I agreed.

And he announced it the next day. Mama was only just able to keep it out of the papers, but everyone knows.

My love, oh, my brave love, please forgive me. For I fear that I shall never forgive myself.

>Yours in agony,
>Flora.

Chapter Twenty

Imperial House, former Governor's House, Tobolsk

Tobolsk, Siberia

Tatiana shivered and pulled her robe closer, holding it closed just below her chin as she leaned forward to place her forehead on the frosted glass pane of the window.

"You wouldn't be so cold if you didn't insist on standing there for hours every night."

Natalya's words were biting, but her tone was gentle. Tatiana looked over her shoulder to see the young baroness standing in the doorway of her office. Natalya still wore her evening clothes.

"What are you doing up?" the Empress asked her friend. "It is late."

"I am checking on you, of course, Your Majesty."

Tatiana let out a sigh. "What is it, then? Barring a first greeting, you only call me 'Your Majesty' in private when you are annoyed with me."

"I am just wondering how long you plan to torture yourself—and him?"

Tatiana didn't pretend not to know whom Natalya was talking about. Instead, she turned back to the window and her study of the rain falling through the lights onto the street below. "I'm not sure what you would have me do," she said after a long moment.

"I suppose I would have you talk to him. Or scream at him. Or cry to him. Anything to stop this ongoing heartache you suffer, Tatiana. This is not healthy."

"I cannot speak to him. He will not see me."

"Oh, really? And here I thought you were the Empress of All the Russias, able to summon *any* of your subjects to an audience? No? Hmm. My mistake. Why, exactly, are we fighting a war again?"

Tatiana spun from the window, anger rising in her—just as Natalya had planned, she realized, once she got a look at the small smile on the younger woman's face.

"I'm not my father, Natalya. I'm not an autocrat. I can't compel him to talk to me—"

"Perhaps not. But you *can* require him to attend upon you. You can ask him to his face if he will ever forgive you. Perhaps he will not. But at least then you would *know*. And then you can move forward. Surely anything would be better than this . . . this limbo you inhabit now?"

Natalya walked further into the room, passing through the shadows until she, too, stood next to the window, illuminated by the outside glow. She reached out and took Tatiana's hands in hers. Tatiana blinked as she suddenly realized that Natalya had grown taller in the last several months. She now nearly matched Tatiana in height. The young baroness had been through so much in her young life, Tatiana often forgot that she was younger even than Anastasia.

"Tatiana, you cannot go on like this. Let me send him a message, at the very least. Let us see if he will come when asked. Please. Your people need you healthy and strong, not weakened by heartbreak."

It was the last point that got her, Tatiana realized later. She had sworn to do everything in her power to put the Russian people first, and to never let her personal emotions get in the way . . . but Natalya was right. Until she spoke to Daniil, she could not know how to proceed.

For the truth was, she needed him. She needed him to command her army, to keep her safe, to win this war . . .

And she needed him for herself, as well. But if he would not serve in those capacities, then she needed to find someone who would. And though the back of her mind screamed in defiance at the thought of anyone replacing Daniil, ever . . . she knew that it was imperative she do so, if he would not return.

Natalya let go of Tatiana's fingers and gripped her gently by the shoulders. She peered into the Empress's eyes, forcing Tatiana to focus on her.

"Please, Tatiana?" she whispered once more.

Tatiana breathed in deeply, and then nodded her assent.

The following evening, Natalya slipped Tatiana a piece of paper during a council meeting. Tatiana accepted it with a nod, but did not unfold the paper or glance at it until after they had concluded their discussion and she'd dismissed everyone.

Then, finally, she unfolded the paper and read the words written there:

He is here. In the garden.

Tatiana refolded the paper with care, willing her suddenly pounding heart to slow its frantic beat. She inhaled deeply and pushed up to her feet.

"Baroness, I believe I will have a walk in the garden tonight before supper," she said, for the benefit of anyone listening. "Will you join me?"

"Gladly, Your Imperial Majesty," Natalya said. As Tatiana's waiting woman, she had remained within the council room after delivering the note, and no one would find it odd for the two of them to take a walk together.

While she waited for her maid to fetch her cloak, Tatiana continued to try to force her racing pulse to calm. To distract herself, she considered why, exactly, Natalya had chosen to be so secretive about this conversation.

Perhaps she is protecting my reputation in case he chooses not to remain, Tatiana realized. *Or in case he does, for that matter. Not that it would be unusual for me to meet with the commander of my army . . . but he is no longer that right now, is he? Oh! This is such a stupid tangle!*

Tatiana embraced the irritation that flowed through her, let it add steel to her spine and lift her chin in something midway between imperiousness and defiance.

Her maid returned with gloves and a cloak, which she settled over Tatiana's shoulders. As usual, Tatiana murmured a quiet "thank you,

Irina" to the young woman, but her mind already surged ahead as she geared herself up for battle . . . or a conversation.

In some scenarios, they were one and the same.

"Choose your words with care, Your Majesty," Natalya whispered as they started down the long hallway toward the French doors that opened onto the garden.

"I always choose my words with care, Baroness," Tatiana said, her tone nearly as icy as the air outside. The last rays of the sun slanted across the western horizon, and their breath rose in clouds of steam as they stepped onto the garden path.

"Yes, Your Majesty," Natalya said, "only, I meant . . . consider your end goal for this interview. That is all." Perhaps it was the cold, but she sounded strange . . . more diffident than usual. Tatiana glanced over at her, and saw that her friend and lady-in-waiting watched her face, something like trepidation in her expression.

Tatiana let herself soften enough to smile. She reached out and gripped Natalya's gloved hand.

"Thank you," she said. "For facilitating this."

"I only want your happiness," Natalya said, her eyes uncharacteristically wide and vulnerable. "For your sake, but also for all our sakes."

Tatiana squeezed the younger woman's fingers and then dropped her hand, folding her own arms inside the sleeves of her cloak before continuing out into the garden.

He was there.

Further along down the path, Daniil Kostyshakov stood in the puddle of light beneath the next light post. He wore civilian clothes, but his ramrod-straight spine gave him away. You could take the man out of uniform, but you couldn't take the soldier out of the man.

Tatiana felt, more than saw, Natalya fall back and take a seat on a nearby bench while she continued on down the path. As she drew close, Daniil dropped to one knee on the path.

He didn't meet her eyes.

"Please stand, General," Tatiana said, her words soft as the snowflakes that fell in the hushed air around them. "Thank you for coming."

"Your Majesty summoned me," he said. His voice was rougher than she remembered, more gravelly.

"Because I have things I must say to you," she said. "Will you please rise?"

Slowly, he stood, returning to the position of attention, his eyes caged straight ahead. He still wouldn't look at her.

Tatiana inhaled slowly and squared her shoulders.

"Foremost among them," she said. "I . . . I owe you an apology."

That startled him enough that he glanced in her direction. Tatiana tamped down hard on the jolt of electricity that shot through her gut and deep into the center of her body as their gazes met for just the briefest instant. She paused for a moment, then licked her lips self-consciously and pushed on.

"*Not* for joining the battle, exactly . . . I do believe that was necessary. But . . . I should have been honest with you. I should have openly declared my intentions. I should have insisted. You would have found some way for me to do it with less risk to myself . . . to everything that we are building here, everything we are fighting for. I was rash, and foolish, and wrong, and Daniil . . . I—"

Tatiana's voice broke on the tears that closed her throat. She pressed her lips together and squeezed her eyes shut. But it was too late. She felt the hot track of a tear run down her chilled cheek. She sniffed hard and opened her eyes.

"I apologize," she said, forcing her voice to be steady . . . or steadier, at least. "It was wrong to hide my plans from you."

Daniil didn't say anything for a long moment. Long enough that Tatiana half-feared that he *wouldn't* speak, but would just stand there in silence until she gave up and turned to go back inside.

"It isn't—" He broke off, his voice barely louder than a whisper. She watched him swallow, his Adam's apple bobbing up and down before he tried again. "Your Majesty must know. It isn't just the risk to our cause. Your safety . . . it means more than just that to me."

It was Tatiana's turn to wait, silently, until he found the words.

"You can't know what it was like, when I heard. My first thought wasn't for my men, or for our objectives . . . it was for *you*. Tatiana, I cannot *function* unless I know you are safe."

Her earlier rage roared back to life. She felt her eyes harden and heat.

"Then why did you leave me?" she asked.

"Your Majesty—"

"No!" She snarled the word. "You called me Tatiana just now. We have moved beyond formalities, Daniil. You say that for you it's more than just political? Did you think you were the only one? *It is personal for me, too! I made a mistake. I was wrong, I admit that, and I apologize. But you left me all alone! How am I supposed to do this without you?*"

Tatiana stared into his eyes as a night breeze rustled the leaves around them. His expression had gone carefully blank, his military bearing firmly back in place. For a brief second, she dreamed of doing something to shatter that professional mask...

But the moment passed. She was the Tsarina. She had her pride.

Tatiana nodded slowly, swallowing hard against the sensation of her heart shattering in her chest. She started to turn, pivoting on the garden's cobblestone path—

Daniil reached out and caught her hand, pulled her back around to face him.

"Tell me to go," he said, his voice almost a growl as he pulled her up close against his body. His other hand rose to her face, sliding under her jaw to cup the back of her head. "Or I'll never leave your side."

Need flared deep in Tatiana's body. She looked down at him, at the dark intent in his eyes and, without meaning to do so, wet her lips.

"Stay," she whispered. "Stay forever."

Daniil let out a groan and stretched upward slightly to meet her as she bent and to take her mouth in a tangled, heated kiss. All around them, the wind continued to rise, rustling the leaves in the otherwise silent garden.

Chapter Twenty-One

White Russian Cossacks

Novocherkassk, Krug of the Don Cossacks, South Russia

The thatched-roof wooden cabin was not as grand as its current owner, General Pyotr Nikolayevich Krasnov, would've liked. The simple wooden table that sat between him and the generals of the White Army in South Russia should've been a polished oak surface instead of the rough-hewn cypress affair it was. It was clear from the skeptical, outright annoyed looks they gave him, that they were not sufficiently impressed with his status as *Ataman*, leader of the Host of the Don Cossacks.

Krasnov was a man of no small ambition, with talent and cunning to match—even his detractors would admit that much. He had led Cossacks valiantly under fire in Manchuria in 1904 and against the Germans in the West throughout the Great War. More importantly, from his perspective, he had taken care to write his own press, ensuring that his leadership in each war was perceived as even *more* valiant and adroit than the reality. Krasnov's will to power and status had seen him through the uncertainty of the February, and then October Revolutions.

Seeking an opportunity amidst the chaos, Krasnov found himself among the Don Cossacks who were straining against the yoke of Bolshevik oppression. Seeing a discontented but largely leaderless population, he'd traded on his reputation to convene a council, the Krug, of the Don Cossacks.

That his electorate was less than ten percent of the actual adult voting population of the Don Cossacks because most of the region was still under Bolshevik rule didn't give Krasnov a moment's hesitation. He styled himself the rightfully elected ruler of the free and independent Don River Basin.

For what Krasnov possessed in drive and skill, he lacked in honesty and humility.

And where did honesty and humility land you, anyway? Krasnov examined the commander of the so-called Volunteer Army sitting across from him in his office. Anton Ivanovich Denikin was a stocky man of average height, with a graying beard and a round face, his normally kindly countenance marred by open frustration with Krasnov. Krasnov had known Denikin since 1905—they'd had a stimulating discussion on the Trans-Siberian Railroad en route back to service against the Japanese.

He'd found Denikin bright and observant, but when the round-faced peasant had taken exception to some of Krasnov's embellishments regarding his own exploits in Manchuria, the conversation had turned chilly. In the intervening years, Denikin, for all his workmanlike military competence, hadn't grown an imagination or even a hint of flair for the dramatic. Little wonder he was such an uninspiring leader. The other White Russian generals had probably defaulted to him as the "safe" option, for he was as uncontroversial as he was uninspiring.

Denikin oozed integrity. Denikin radiated responsibility. Denikin saturated any room he was in with his selflessness.

Denikin was a sucker.

"Your Excellency," Krasnov said, smoothing the pointed, waxed ends of his gull-wing shaped mustache. "Given that my Host outnumbers your Volunteer Army by a factor of five, I would not be serving the constituency which elected me were I to submit my men to your command as you suggest."

Denikin's nostrils flared, his face growing even more flush. Krasnov carefully restrained his private glee at needling the old bear so mercilessly. He maintained an apologetic smile for the sake of the room.

"General Krasnov, I respect your place as leader of the Don Cossack host," Denikin said, his voice brittle. "I would remind you that I am, properly, your commander. I am not *suggesting*."

Krasnov set his tea on the table between them and fixed Denikin with a glare.

"Your Excellency, the army we both served in is now defunct. The Tsar to whom we swore our allegiance is deposed—perhaps even dead. I am no longer your subordinate, General Denikin. I am the duly elected leader of five million free and sovereign people. The Don Cossacks do not submit to the Bolsheviks, and we do not submit to you, though we wish to be your allies."

A muscle under Denikin's eye twitched, but before he could respond, his chief of staff, Romanovsky, cut into the conversation.

"General Krasnov, surely you can see the need to put aside these petty squabbles of rank and station to defeat the scourge of Communism that threatens us all?"

Denikin cast a sharp glance at his subordinate, but allowed the question to stand without correction, so Krasnov deigned to answer it.

"You are right, General Romanovsky. We must have unity of command. Therefore, I propose this—I will provide six million rubles for the pay and provisions of the Volunteer Army, and you will place yourself under my command for the duration of the war."

Denikin's patience visibly shattered.

"This is outrageous, Krasnov," he shouted, leveling a finger at Krasnov's nose. "We are fighting for Russia's very survival and you are trying to make some opportunistic gamble for power. I will not turn my men into mercenaries for an adventuring braggart such as you!"

Krasnov set his tea aside and crossed his arms.

"You wound me, Anton Ivanovich. How is my requesting your subordination any more outrageous than you demanding mine? We need unity of command; I have proposed a reasonable course of action to secure it."

Denikin sputtered. Romanovsky again tried to salvage the situation.

"General Krasnov, you know the other factions will never accept you as supreme commander, please let us drop the matter. You will, of course, retain command of your host under General Denikin—with your Cossacks, the Volunteer Army and the Kuban Cossack regiments we already have, we can isolate and destroy the Soviet 10th and 11th Armies in the Kuban, clearing the path to Moscow."

Krasnov shook his head and stood up, turning to the giant map of European Russia hanging behind his desk.

"This plan is too cautious, my friends," Krasnov said he gestured at the city of Tsaritsyn astride the Volga River. "Tsaritsyn should be the objective of our first campaign. Securing this hub of rail and river traffic to Siberia will allow us to link up with the anti-Communist forces to the East. Reinforced by them, we can drive directly on Moscow this Fall. We can end the war before Christmas."

Denikin's indignant expression now gave way to incredulity.

"You would have us leave two full-strength armies in our rear areas while we attempt an offensive against the most urbanized and densely populated region of all Russia? Are you mad?"

"Every month we delay, the Reds recruit more men, they produce more weapons, they solidify their interior lines," Krasnov said. "Today we have a large qualitative edge on most of their formations, but Trotsky sharpens them day by day. Our differential will shrink and vanish if we do not end this soon."

The two generals across from Krasnov did not immediately reply. Though they had earned his contempt, Krasnov knew neither man was militarily stupid—they would see the logic of his argument.

"You have a point, General Krasnov," Denikin said. "But we are perilously short on both infantry and artillery to undertake such an endeavor. Our Cossacks are magnificent on the open steppe, but to take and hold Moscow and the other cities would require they dismount and fight street to street, house to house. We have our Volunteer regiments and a handful of Cossack infantry, but they simply aren't enough right now."

Krasnov tilted his head to acknowledge the objection, then stabbed a finger back at Tsaritsyn on the map.

"That is why linking up with reinforcements from Siberia is vital. There are anti-Bolshevik Russian units forming there as we speak, and the Czech Legion, some fifty thousand battle-hardened infantrymen, reportedly now controls the Trans-Siberian Railway."

Denikin sighed.

"If reports are to be believed, the Czechs only took up arms against the Soviets when the Soviets tried to disarm and detain them," Denikin said. "Being willing to fight to return to one's home is not the same thing as being willing to die by the hundreds or thousands in another country's civil war.

"No, General, we will finish the liberation of the Kuban and the Don. We will swell our infantry formations to the necessary size for such an offensive, and then, with help from our Allies, we will advance on Moscow."

Krasnov shook his head.

"Even now, the Allies are crumbling under the Ludendorff offensive. What makes you think they will have any spare men or resources for us beyond the trickle we are already receiving?"

Denikin leveled a finger at Krasnov's face.

"You are too quick to side with the German villains against our allies."

"And you are too quick to place the interests of those allies coequal with those of our own people," Krasnov said, raising his voice, but then he held up a hand and affected a chagrined expression before Denikin could shout his response. "Forgive me, Anton Ivanovich, I spoke rashly, as I'm sure you did. I know your loyalty is always and forever to a free and united Russia. Intelligent, honorable men may disagree even about the most important issues.

"Since we seem to have come to an impasse, I propose that we continue to pursue our own strategies. I will take Tsaritsyn while you clear the Kuban of Soviets," Krasnov said.

"We would be much more powerful unifying our efforts," Romanovsky said.

"We would," Krasnov agreed. "Unfortunately, we cannot agree on how best to do that, so let us, at least, not weaken ourselves with petty squabbling. As a show of good faith, and in appreciation for the reality that your operations protect our Western flank, I will still give you the six million rubles as a gift with no strings attached, as well as some of the equipment we have liberated."

They haggled on for a few more moments, but in the end, Denikin accepted the money and equipment and left with a grudging expression of gratitude. Once they departed, Krasnov slouched in his chair. It certainly wasn't an unalloyed victory, but he'd retained his independence.

Without the Volunteer Army—especially the crack Kornilov, Alekseev, and Markov infantry regiments—the campaign for Tsaritsyn would be more dangerous, but he still had his Host, and Cossack communities throughout the Don Basin held thousands more young men to recruit to the cause once they were freed. The Reds were still largely disorganized and fighting with half-trained, unindoctrinated conscripts—but Krasnov had meant what he said when he told Denikin that their lack of training and discipline would quickly change.

Moreover, what Denikin had not apparently heard, but Krasnov had, were the rumors of a surviving Romanov girl, Grand Duchess Tatiana. Krasnov had no special love for the Imperial family. Nicholas had been a damn fool, and his wife a pathetic neurotic who made decisions while impaled on that madman Rasputin's cock.

Regardless, if one of the Tsar's daughters lived, she was an important chess piece. Getting to her before Denikin, shaping her perception of events in European Russia, might help him garner support from the monarchists in the White Russian camp. To say nothing of the fact that the girl had, apparently, rallied a nontrivial force unto herself, a force, if rumors were to be believed, that had been transported to her rescue by a *German* zeppelin.

Perhaps, just perhaps, the girl, having been beneficiary of German help in her survival, might see sense. Where old men like Denikin clung to the skirts of the French and British, and now even the Americans, willing to wag their tails like faithful dogs for table scraps, Tatiana might see the value of forming a closer relationship with the state which was currently in the process of winning the Great War, rather than compounding Russia's woes by anchoring her to a sinking vessel of geopolitics.

Krasnov's train of thought was interrupted by his chief of staff, Bogayesky, entering the room. He looked at his subordinate in irritation. Bogayesky had pushed and pushed for unity with the Volunteer Army and the Kuban Host, even intimating, indirectly, that the Don Host might elect a different leader if Krasnov couldn't bring the White Russian forces in South Russia into alignment.

Given that Bogayesky was also an experienced cavalryman with a good reputation among the Cossacks, Krasnov had little trouble discerning who the veiled threat to his position was.

Keep your enemies closer.

"General, what news?" Bogayesky asked.

"We have reached an agreement," Krasnov said, standing with the pronouncement and smiling broadly. "Denikin and his forces will clear the Kuban of Reds and destroy the Soviet 10th and 11th Armies. We will press the attack on Tsaritsyn."

Bogayesky grimaced.

"General, that will divide our forces unnecessarily—"

"I disagree and so does General Denikin and his staff," Krasnov lied. "Both objectives are vital and time sensitive. Though it is risky, we have forces available for both objectives. Speaking of which—"

Krasnov handed Bogayesky a sheet of paper upon which he'd written down the six million ruble sum as well as a list of the arms and equipment he'd promised Denikin.

"To seal our alliance with the Volunteer Army and Kuban Host, see that the money and equipment listed there are transferred to Denikin's train before they leave."

Bogayesky accepted this order without protest.

"Yes, General. Will there be anything else?"

"I need a courier prepared to take a message to *Hetman* Skoropadsky in Kiev," Krasnov said, referring the puppet governor the Germans had placed in Ukraine. "He may be able to confirm or deny the rumors I'm hearing about German involvement in the Romanovs' rescue. Perhaps he can even convince Field Marshal Eichhorn to send us some troops."

Bogayesky looked unhappy, but he didn't protest the collaboration with the Germans.

"Yes, sir."

Near Costantinovka, South Russia

A tall man in a brown field uniform sat at ease in the front passenger seat of a lorry as it traversed the ruts and deformities of the dirt road on a suspension system that had seen better days. General Baron Pyotr Nikolayevich Wrangel was long since accustomed to travel over rough roads, whether by horse or by motor car. His large dark eyes scanned the terrain relentlessly as he considered his new command and its situation.

The dark brown steppe of the North Caucasus stretched out in every direction from the road, the mountains only faint green masses against the distant horizon. Fortunately, the roads had hardened, but were not yet choked with snow, so the lorry's wheels propelled it easily enough, if not smoothly. The command vehicle trundled past the mule carts heading toward the front with ammunition and reinforcements, and the streams of wounded and captured enemy personnel meandering away from it.

Wrangel wore his customary stoic, faintly disapproving expression. His neatly trimmed black mustache twitched in a faint smile to see the long column of Bolshevik prisoners shuffling despondently southward into captivity. His command, the 1st Cavalry Division of the Volunteer Army, was doing well in this war of maneuver against the Communists. Something alarming caught Wrangel's attention, though—there were damned few guards for such large contingents of prisoners.

Wrangel tapped the lorry's driver on the shoulder.

"Vladimir, pull over a second, I want to have a word with the commander of that detail."

"Yes, sir," Obolensky said.

His driver and aide-de-camp was Captain Prince Vladimir Obolensky. Like Wrangel himself, Obolensky was old nobility—his ancestors had once ruled Kiev before the days of Ivan the Terrible. Obolensky and Wrangel even looked a bit alike in their long faces and angular features. Obolensky was much younger and had served valiantly under Wrangel in the Tsarevich's Own Cossack Cavalry in the Great War. He was one of few subordinate officers from Wrangel's old regiment who had reunited with him in the 1st Cavalry.

Obolensky loved motor cars and airplanes, and all things new and fast. Thus, he insisted on driving while Wrangel's enlisted orderlies sat in the back of the lorry, rifles at the ready. Wrangel allowed himself a small, wry smile. Even with their homeland torn asunder by civil war, he suspected Obolensky was still savoring the chance for adventure, regardless of the tragedy, danger, and suffering all about them.

The young lieutenant commanding the prisoner detail snapped to attention and saluted as Wrangel approached. Wrangel returned the salute crisply, gratified to see that the boy's discipline wasn't as lax as he'd seen in other corners of the Volunteer Army.

"Good afternoon, General!" the lieutenant said, nerves clear in his too-loud voice.

"Good afternoon," Wrangel said. He cast an eye at the stream of bedraggled communist prisoners. He stepped closer and lowered his voice.

"Lieutenant, it seems you have an unfortunately small number of guards for this many prisoners."

The lieutenant's expression mixed chagrin and frustration.

"I agree, General, but there's just too many prisoners. We can't afford any more men off the line," he answered in an equally quiet voice. "I only drew this detail because I was wounded."

The lieutenant indicated a filthy bandage and sling around his left arm.

"It's the damnedest thing, sir," the lieutenant continued. "Some of these Bolsheviks fight like maddened bears, but others just throw down their arms in the thousands the minute things get tough."

"They're a composite force." Wrangel did not say aloud: *like us,* "Wide variance in morale is to be expected. What is your name, Lieutenant?"

"Vasily Gavrikov, sir."

"Well, Gavrikov, I will pray for your speedy recovery," Wrangel said. He turned to go, but then he noticed the lieutenant carried no rifle, nor pistol, nor yet even a saber. "Lieutenant, are you unarmed?"

"Yes, sir." Gavrikov looked sheepish now.

Wrangel considered that for a moment, nodded once sharply, then undid the buckle on his pistol belt and handed it out to Gavrikov.

"General, I couldn't possibly take your pistol," Gavrikov said, his expression aghast at the very notion.

"You've more need of it than I do, Lieutenant." Wrangel gestured to the lorry where Obolensky and his enlisted guards waited. "I have these rough characters to protect me."

Gavrikov accepted the pistol and belt as if they were the Tsarina's Fabergé eggs.

"Thank you, General," he said, fervently.

Wrangel made a deprecating gesture.

"There's a round in every chamber and twenty rounds in the pouch for reloads. Good luck, Lieutenant."

They exchanged salutes again before Wrangel turned on his heel and returned to his command lorry.

"Anything else you'd like to donate while we're here, General?" Obolensky asked, grinning.

"Continue in this vein, Vladimir Platonovich, and I'll give him your pistol as well," Wrangel said, deadpan. "Drive. I want to inspect our divisional artillery before nightfall."

Obolensky wound through the columns of supply wagons and prisoners with a deft hand. The rattle of small arms and the concussive blasts of artillery became louder and more distinct the further north and east they traveled. They reached the battery by sixteen hundred, according to Wrangel's wristwatch.

The autumn sun painted the 76mm guns of his divisional artillery battery in warm orange light. The guns were arrayed in a field surrounded on all sides by tall rows of corn, providing some concealment for the aging, but still invaluable artillery pieces. Because the White Army was ludicrously heavy on officers, each light field gun crew had at least one officer, and some had two or more. Their crew drill was sharp, precise, and professional.

On a hillock overlooking the battery stood the stocky figure of Colonel Toporkov, one of Wrangel's brigade commanders. Wrangel told his enlisted men to wait with the car while he and Obolensky went to have a chat with Toporkov.

As they ascended the hill, new vistas opened up over the stalks of corn. In the distance, a battalion of enemy infantry were emplacing in a hollow alongside with their own light artillery pieces. His own Cossacks wheeled about them, harassing the infantry with rifle and pistol fire, but the Bolsheviks held firm. Their cannons barked, and belched smoke; the volley flew over the heads of the Red infantry and White cavalry to detonate just two hundred meters short of Wrangel's own artillery.

Once they reached the top of the hillock where Toporkov had set up his field command post, Wrangel cut through all pleasantries and came straight to the point.

"What is your situation, Colonel?" Wrangel asked.

"Fluid, sir," Toporkov said without hesitation. "The Reds don't have much in the way of quality cavalry, but what they do have seems concentrated in our sector, so we cannot dance about their flanks as easily as we have in the past. It doesn't help that Pokrovsky's division seems more interested in raping and looting than it does in fighting the fucking Communists, it leaves our right flank exposed."

Toporkov stopped speaking, the realization that he might have gone too far in criticizing another division commander in front of his own general plainly visible on his face.

"I beg your pardon, General."

Wrangel waved his hand in a gesture of negation.

"I expect your candor at all times, Colonel. Go on."

"We remain short on rifle and machine gun ammunition, but we have enough 76mm to give the Reds some trouble. We're emplaced now, we'll signal the Cossacks out there to break off their harassment so our field of fire is clear."

Wrangel opened his mouth, intending to voice his concern that his division's precious artillery was so far forward without infantry support and only a screen of light Cossack cavalry.

"The cavalry!" one of Toporkov's officers shouted.

Wrangel's gaze shot back to the battlefield. The Cossacks were galloping back toward friendly lines, a mass of horsemen four times their number in pursuit.

"Where the hell were the Reds hiding a regiment of cavalry?" Obolensky mused out loud.

"It hardly matters now," Wrangel said, then turned to Toporkov. "There's no time to displace. Signal the Cossacks to wheel left, then treat the enemy to an enfilade."

Signal flags went up, waved in a specific pattern, and went down. Whoever was commanding the Cossack cavalry squadron still had his men under good discipline, for the galloping formation of cavalry turned wide as instructed, clearing the artillery's field of fire. Even as the hooves of the charging enemy shook the dirt and grass underfoot, the artillery answered with its own basso roar. Smoke filled the air for dozens of meters around Wrangel and his men.

Exploding shrapnel rounds tore men and horses to ribbons of shattered bone and severed sinew. Wrangel's artillery killed dozens and left still more screaming and clutching at horrific wounds as their blood poured onto the Russian steppe. It wasn't enough. The battery only managed one more volley before the Red Cavalrymen burst through the smoke into the midst of the cannoneers.

A saber flashed and an artillery officer fell, his life's blood spilling through his own fingers as he clutched at the gash in his throat. The man next to him, a lad who couldn't have been a day over seventeen, avenged the fallen officer. He clamped onto the boots of his commander's killer and forced the Red out of the saddle, slammed him into the ground and rammed a trench knife into the horseman's guts repeatedly, only to collapse to the grass himself as a pistol shot took off the back of his skull.

"General, get the hell out of here," Toporkov said, drawing his saber with his left hand and his pistol with his right. "We'll slow them down."

Wrangel's stomach clenched. Run while his men died covering him? No—

Obolensky grabbed Wrangel's arm with crushing strength, and shouted in his ear over the din of rifle and pistol fire and the screams of man and horse.

"General, don't be a damned fool, you don't even have a weapon, you dying here won't win the war!"

Wrangel snarled his frustration, but seeing the artillerymen falling as if they were the harvest of the field, no alternative occurred to him. He followed Obolensky at a sprint even as Toporkov shot a Red out of the saddle, deflected a saber cut with his own blade and hacked down a dismounted enemy before the man could stick a bayonet into him.

They were fewer than fifty meters from his command car when an enemy shell detonated mere inches from its right-front wheel well. The explosion sent up an orange, black and gray geyser, and fragmentation from the shell shredded the rubber of the front wheels and made a metallic hash of the engine compartment.

The concussion of the explosion was enough to knock Wrangel off balance in his headlong flight and he tumbled into the yellow grass. Ignoring the high-pitched whine in his ears, he scrabbled back to his feet, grabbed Obolensky by the shoulder and pulled him, stumbling, off the road into the tall stalks of corn. They ran hunched over, trying to stay below the line of sight of the pursuing cavalry—no comfortable feat given that Wrangel stood well over six feet tall. Wrangel led them south and west, into the setting sun.

Behind him the rattle and blast of gunfire and artillery, the death screams of his men pursued Wrangel relentlessly, ripping at his conscience. He gritted his teeth and sped up.

"What now, General?" Obolensky asked. Wrangel thought enviously that the younger man sounded far less winded than he felt. Wrangel tried to answer without huffing and gasping.

"We find that Cossack squadron, take it to go get two more like it and our infantry. Then we cut off this salient and continue the attack."

After two grueling hours picking their way through the fields, an ambulance car sped past them. Sped was a relative term, given the condition of the roads. Wrangel chased it at a full sprint, Obolensky followed. Wrangel willed his legs to pump harder and he managed to catch the speeding car and jump up on its running boards.

"Who the hell are you?" the driver, a man with a thick brow and heavy features demanded.

"General Wrangel, 1st Cavalry," Wrangel answered with exaggerated aplomb. "If you don't mind, soldier, drop me off at my command post on your way to the aid station."

It took most of the night, but by dawn Wrangel had rallied a brigade of his Cossack cavalrymen. He and Obolensky secured mounts for themselves rather than try to find another truck or motor car. Wrangel rode at the head of the main body astride a beautiful black mare. Obolensky had convinced him that the division commander couldn't exercise proper control of his command out forward with the scouts. The scouts returned with news—the enemy was gone and so was their battery of light artillery.

It was an hour past dawn by the time they reached the battery's position, and the enemy was nowhere to be seen. The scouts' report had portrayed the grim reality accurately. The dead of both sides lay strewn about the field, largely stripped of clothes, as well as arms and ammunition. Two of the 76mm cannons were missing, two sets of parallel ruts in the grass indicating where the Bolsheviks had wheeled them northward. The rest of the guns had been destroyed with grenades or other explosives.

"They retreated, they fled before we could get here!" one of the Cossacks shouted.

"No, they never intended to hold this field," Wrangel said, glaring north with a stony expression. "This was a jab to give their main body time to retreat and reconsolidate to defend along the Ouroup rather than having to face our cavalry massed in the open field."

The officers gathered around him looked questioningly toward Wrangel. Before he addressed their worried looks, he pulled a blanket from his saddlebag and searched out Colonel Toporkov's corpse from among the fallen. The brigade commander had been stripped of his coat, shirt and boots. His revolver and saber were gone. Wrangel laid the blanket across his valiant subordinate's body and bowed his head, whispering a quick prayer.

Raising his head, he turned to regard his men.

"The fight will be harder—but the communists will pay no lesser a blood price than before. The road to Russia's salvation will take us through defeats as well as triumph, my friends, but we will follow it through regardless."

Interlude

From: Tatiana {etc.}

To: George V {etc.}

Our beloved cousin, we thank you for your letter of condolence on the loss of our Imperial parents. As you might imagine, this is a time of deep mourning and uncertainty for all of Russia. Civil war and famine plague our people, and the cancer of Bolshevism continues to eat away at the liberty and prosperity of our most vulnerable. To know that we have the support and affection of Great Britain is a great comfort.

We thank you, also, for the kind invitation to visit your fair land. An Imperial visit to the Kingdom of Great Britain would indeed be a beautiful statement of the solidarity of our family connection and would be most desirable to us personally as well. Alas, the dire circumstances described above will prevent such a dream from taking place for some time. We know that of all the inhabitants of God's earth, you most of all will understand. We can no sooner leave Russia in her time of need than you would desert your fair island in similar straits.

However, a thought occurs. We are fortunate to have two of our dear sisters remaining to us. The Grand Duchesses Maria and Anastasia would dearly love a chance to visit our beloved grandmother, the Dowager Empress Maria Feodorovna. It is our understanding that your Royal Navy has recovered her from the Crimea before the Bolsheviks could threaten her. For this, we thank you most sincerely. Perhaps we can arrange to send our sisters to you—and to our Grandmama—in the near future? Our sisters are most devout, most dutiful girls, but we confess that it pains our heart to see such lovely young women denied the gaiety and fun which should be theirs by right. Perhaps, under your care and that of the Dowager Empress, they might regain some of that ease? Perhaps they, too, may find joy and love in your court? Such a happy outcome would, if not heal, then at least ease the wounds in our soul left by the loss of our beloved parents, brother, and sister Olga.

301

We thank you, cousin, and keep you and your family in our daily prayers.

With love,
Tatiana Imperatrix

✣ ✣ ✣

To: The Dowager Empress Maria Feodorovna
From: Tatiana, Empress of all the Russias, etc.

Grandmama,

I received word that Britain's navy has plucked you from the Crimea before we could manage to get further word to you. We did receive your last letter, and I have taken every word to heart. I reread it almost every day. Your words give me courage. Thank you, Grandmama.

And now I must ask more of you. Cousin George has written with an invitation for us to all come to him in Britain. I suspect he feels guilty that he didn't offer sooner. I am going to shamelessly play on that guilt. I will not visit him, of course, but I will send Maria and Anastasia to you there in London unless you think it more advisable to meet them in New York, in America.

I should like Maria to marry. Into Britain's royal family, if possible. I think it would make her happy, and keep her safe. She is miserable here, Grandmama, and I suspect she will soon begin to hate Russia itself for what has happened to our family. I cannot afford that, as you well know, and so I need a safe, honorable way for her to be gone. So much the better if I can secure and reinforce allies in so doing.

I ask you to be my agent in this, not just for me, or Maria, or our family... but for the future of Russia herself. Until the war is settled, I doubt that I shall be able to make an acceptable marriage alliance of my own, and so I must name one of my sisters as heir. For the reasons stated above, I do not think Maria is suitable.

So, it must be Anastasia.

I know. Anastasia is the most mischievous and immature of all of us. But my hope is that she can be molded, forged, into a Grand Duchess and heir worthy of the Romanov name. I will send her initially to you, but I think she will not stay long in London. We are working out plans for her, which I will relay to you at a later date when they are more finalized.

Finally, I do have some good news. We have recovered Aunt Ella...
alive. She was badly abused by the Reds, may they burn in Hell for
eternity. But she is strong, as you know. She recovers even now. Her
reputation with the people of Russia will be a formidable weapon in
this war, especially once it becomes known how she suffered. Though
it is distasteful to me to use her personal tragedy in that way, I realize
that I can leave no advantage unused. She would say the same.

As would you, I know. I miss you tremendously, Grandmama. I
dearly wish I could have you here to guide me, but I think your
presence in London is the more critical at this juncture. If cousin
George can be persuaded of the Bolshevik threat, not just to me, but to
himself and his realm... I could dearly use his armed forces. I know
the time is not quite right to ask. But soon, I fear I will have no choice.

I need you, and to a lesser extent Maria, to prepare him, his court,
and the British government for such a question. Because when I ask, I
need them to agree.

I have all the faith in the world in you, Grandmama. You were an
exemplar of everything an imperial consort should be. And now I am
Tsarina regnant, and I shall adapt your example to my own situation.

With all of my love, and deepest hopes that I may see you in person
soon,

    Tatiana

P.S. Travel for my sisters is going to be catch as catch can. The Czech
Legion is going to secure the railway, but from Vladivostok there's no
telling how they'll cross the Pacific. They will wire you when they reach
America.

Chapter Twenty-Two

Shinyo Maru

Aboard the *Shinyo Maru*

Most of the passenger ships of the world, along with a good many of its freighters, were busy carrying troops, supplies, and equipment to the great war raging in France. Russia itself had only ever had a couple of passenger liners, and those, too, had been impressed by one ally or another. Even had they not been impressed, they'd been home-based on the Atlantic while the only safe route for the two younger grand duchesses had been across the Pacific.

Japan, however, still had one or two free, while a tramp steamer had been found at Vladivostok to bring the party to Yokohama. There they'd booked passage on the *Shinyo Maru*, a Nagasaki-built liner of some thirteen thousand, four-hundred twenty-six Gross Registered Tons. As a Japanese ship, the *Shinyo* was both spotlessly clean and yet lacking in creature comforts.

Anastasia shivered and pulled her cloak closer around her as she stepped out of her cabin. It wasn't the same fur-lined hooded cloak she'd had as a child when they'd go out on her father's yacht, but it was made of good wool and did the job. Though she'd meticulously tied her hair back, the ocean wind whipped around her, teasing strands free to float about her face as she walked.

They'd had a company of guards for the trip across Siberia to Vladivostok, a company and a great many men of the Czech Legion being dropped off to secure the railway. Now they had a few guards and Dostavalov, who had possibly been their dead sister's lover; none could say. Rather, of the two people who might have known, Dostavalov had, so far, kept his own counsel, while dear Olga was dead to a Red's bullets.

Underneath the girl's cloak, one hand fingered and caressed a slightly scarred piece of jewelry, built around a large blue sapphire, with the pearls of a choker emanating to either side. She could hardly put into words the affection she held for that bright blue, faceted stone. To call it a good luck charm was wholly inadequate.

This journey felt like it was stretching on forever. It had only been a few weeks since she'd last embraced her eldest remaining sister and departed on this next adventure. She'd been so excited to leave Imperial House, she remembered, for newly won Yekaterinburg where Tatiana would set up the new but temporary court, when she arrived, and where the two younger sisters could get passage east.

She couldn't forget the prison Imperial House had been. Nor how helpless she'd felt seeing her parents, her sister, her brother die at the hands of Bolshevik murderers . . .

Anastasia shook her head and pushed such dark thoughts away. She turned and focused her blue eyes on the steely gray horizon and the white-streaked water all around them. The *old* Anastasia had been a helpless child. She was no longer that girl.

She could not afford to be that girl.

Antastasia fought off another shiver that had nothing to do with the temperature and squared her shoulders. *This* Anastasia was more than just a mischievous princess. She was her sister's heiress, though it had not been publicly announced yet. If, God forbid, something happened to Tatiana, Anastasia would be Empress, and the weight she'd noticed on her sister's shoulders would be hers to bear.

"Dreaming of a handsome prince, Nastenka?" Maria's voice, light and playful, drifted over on the breeze. Anastasia smiled and turned to her fellow "little," where "little pair" and "big pair" had, in days past, referred to her and Maria, on the one hand, and Olga and Tatiana, on the other.

She slipped the sapphire and pearls into an interior pocket of her cloak.

"Not exactly," Anastasia admitted. "I was watching the sea and thinking about adventures."

"You're still such a little girl." Maria's gentle tone and ripple of laughter took any sting or rebuke out of the words, but Anastasia felt her usual mulishness begin to stir anyway. She held herself stiffly as Maria joined her at the ship's rail and threaded her arm through Anastasia's.

"But that's all right," Maria went on. "For you *are* only seventeen."

"You're only two years older," Anastasia shot back.

"Yes, and I'm the same age Grandmama was when she married."

"Tatiana said the same thing." Anastasia let out a sigh and leaned her head down to rest on her taller sister's shoulder. "She said I should have to grow up quickly."

"The *Tsarina* speaks truly," Maria's emphasis held the gentle note of disapproval that had become something of a constant whenever she spoke to either of her sisters. "We are all alone in the world without our sainted parents. We must conduct ourselves as grown women and Imperial Grand Duchesses ought."

"We have Grandmama," Anastasia pointed out. She felt herself smile at the thought of their grandmother. They'd not spent a lot of time together when Anastasia was a child, due to the fact that the Dowager Empress and the Tsarina were often at odds. So while Maria Feodorovna was not a complete stranger, Anastasia had only had vague memories of glittering jewels, kind hands, and beautiful eyes.

However, in her letters, Maria Feodorovna communicated a quick intelligence and deep, passionate loyalty to the cause of Imperial Russia. She'd given them some preliminary plans and provided some basic— though sometimes quite cutting and funny—dossiers on the individuals they would meet in Britain.

"I think it very likely," Grandmama had written in a joint letter to Maria and Anastasia, "that His Majesty King George nurtures a hope that the Prince of Wales might form an attachment to one of you two girls. Our families are closely related, it is true, but such an arrangement might very well suit everyone involved. His Highness is a handsome, intelligent man, to be sure, and he could not do better than a daughter of Imperial Russa as his future queen."

Maria had gasped and clutched the papers to her chest when she'd read the letter out to Anastasia in the privacy of their shared cabin. Her eyes had shone with tears and hope, and she'd been unable to think or talk about anything except "Cousin David" since.

Anastasia didn't say anything to dissuade her sister from her increasingly fervid obsession. If Tatiana wished to strengthen ties with Britain by making Maria Princess of Wales, then it wasn't her place to object. But still, in the back of her mind, Anastasia couldn't help but wonder if His Highness was really the paragon that the news reports and Maria's fantasies made him out to be.

"Shall we take a turn about the deck?" Maria suggested, recalling Anastasia's thoughts to the present. "You will want to keep up your exercise, lest you become too pudgy to receive any attention in London at all!"

"I am a Romanov Grand Duchess," Anastasia said, her tone dry. But she let Maria pull her into motion. "I could be an absolute warthog and I would still receive attention."

"That would have been true if Papa were still alive," Maria said. "But you must know that our situation is much reduced. You will want to look your best if you're to attract a powerful husband."

"I'm sure you're correct," Anastasia said, though privately she disagreed. People would be interested in her for the novelty, if nothing else. And as Tatiana's heiress...

Well. Perhaps it was better not to think too much about that at the moment.

"Besides," Maria went on, "the *people* will love you more if you're beautiful. The newspapers do not like to comment on ugly princesses, but they will spend paragraphs on a beautiful girl's gown. Grandmama would agree. You saw how she wrote of the importance of making a good first impression, not just on your husband and his family...but on his *people* as well. If they love you, they will support you. Think how our people loved her and our dear mama!"

Only they didn't love Mama. Anastasia stumbled as the thought impacted her with the force of a slap. They loved Grandmama, but Mama was too withdrawn and shy...and she took too long to have Alexei.

Anastasia had loved her mother, of course, but she'd always known that she had been a disappointment to her shy, sickly, withdrawn parent. Alexandra Feodorovna had rarely spoken to Anastasia except to scold or correct her . . . rather like Maria since their rescue. But while Maria was still gentle and loving in her corrections, Mama had been more and more waspish as years of strain and illness had taken their toll on her fragile nerves.

And the people hated her, Anastasia realized abruptly. *They hated her and they hated Papa enough to give the Bolsheviks a foothold for their "revolution." I cannot—We cannot be the same. The Russian people must love us if we're to survive.*

That's why Tatiana defied everyone to fight in that horrid battle. That's why her coronation regalia included a rifle and a helmet! The Russian people will—and do!—love her for her courage.

How can I make them love me?

Once more, Grand Duchess Anastasia Nikolaevna Romanova turned her eyes to the unrelenting emptiness of the ocean. While her sister chattered on about gowns and hairstyles and the importance of proper deportment and propriety, Anastasia realized something. It wasn't a husband she needed to woo. It was a population. More than one, perhaps.

Somehow, she needed to make not just one man, but the entire world fall madly in love with her. Enough that they would send men and weapons and money to support Tatiana's war against the Bolsheviks.

Enough that her sister, her family, their dynasty would survive.

And she was only seventeen.

Interlude

To Alice Roosevelt, Sagamore Hill, New York
From 2LT Quentin Roosevelt, 95th Aero Squadron, Saints, France

My Dear Sister,

I received your letter late last week and only now have a moment to sit and write. We have been flying every day, save only when bad weather grounds us, as today.

I wish you would not write such things about Flora. Despite her ending our engagement, I bear her no ill will and quite understand her position. Not every young woman has as indulgent a father as you have, you know! Flora always knew her duty to her family, and while I will make every effort to return home from this war, as we all know there are no guarantees. I cannot fault her for acceding to her father's wishes, and neither should you.

As to the matter of Mr. Roderick Tower, I really have no opinion. I trained with the man at Mineola, and he seemed to me to be a competent aviator. If he makes Flora happy, and can provide her the security and familial peace that I cannot, well, then I wish them every joy.

Let that be an end to the matter, Sister. I beg you. I shall keep my mind better occupied here in France. I daresay you must be very busy as well! I have heard of your tireless efforts to oppose our entry into Wilson's fool's league. Only take care that you guard your tongue, lest you find yourself banned from Washington altogether, instead of just from the White House!

Please give Mother my love, and reassure her that I am very well rested and cared for here in France. And tell Father I shall write to him soon with what news I may send.

Yours always,
Quentin

Chapter Twenty-Three

Lobby of the Palace Hotel, San Francisco, United States

San Francisco, California, USA

They arrived in San Francisco in the middle of the night.

Despite the grinding fatigue that dragged at the edges of her mind, disappointment twisted deep inside Anastasia. After all of the interminable delays in leaving Russia, the wait for passage in Japan, and the endless-seeming two weeks crossing the emptiness of the Pacific Ocean, she'd been quite excited about her first glimpse of America. But as soon as they disembarked, Anastasia and Maria found themselves ushered quickly into a closed motorcar which roared through the darkened streets of the city to a hotel. Someone had mentioned the name, but Anastasia had forgotten.

She did try to look out the windows at the buildings, especially whenever the car stopped, but she couldn't see much, and so she flopped back onto her seat with her arms crossed firmly over her chest and the familiar mulish stubbornness rising inside her.

"You needn't look like that, Nastenka," Maria said softly from her seat next to Anastasia. "We're all uncomfortable and exhausted. None

313

of us really want to be here in this dreadful backwater excuse for a city, but you will only make it worse with your childish temper."

"It's not that." Anastasia turned her frown on her sister. "I was just trying to *see*. We've never been to San Francisco before."

"There is nothing to see," Maria said, leaning her head back against the headrest and closing her eyes. "Everyone knows that American towns are dirty and ramshackle. The sooner we get to New York and can sail for London, the better. I am half afraid that the war might have us stuck in America forever." She shuddered, and Anastasia fought the urge to roll her eyes in sarcasm at her sister's increasing snobbery.

Tatiana was right, you have changed, Anastasia thought as she looked at her sister's profile. *You've always been beautiful, but something ugly has grown in you, dear sister. We were taught to know our worth, but not to look down on others! Certainly not those less fortunate! More and more I understand why she is sending you away . . . but I do hope that we don't live to regret the woman you will become in Britain.*

With these thoughts, Anastasia's mulishness settled into a pensive sort of discontent. She pursed her lips, but decided to let the matter drop and turned her gaze back outside the window when the motorcar rattled to a stop. Unseen, her hand slipped into an interior pocket of her cloak.

"We have arrived."

It was the guard, Dostovalov, who spoke, his words clipped and short before he exited the front seat of the motorcar and came to open the door for them. Since Olga's death and that of his friend, Chekov, he'd been their family's constant shadow. Whereas he once kept them prisoner, he now served as one of their assigned guards . . . and he appeared to take his duties incredibly personally.

Did he love poor Olga? Anastasia wondered. She'd overheard a whisper or two that led her to speculate. *Not that it matters. Olga is dead, Maria is changing, Tatiana is Empress and I am here in America. What a strange life we lead, do we not, Feldfebel Dostovalov?*

Anastasia gave him a smile as she accepted his hand out of the motorcar. Dostovalov remained stony-faced as ever, but his touch was gentle and his hands sure as he kept her from tripping over the uneven cobblestone street.

"Welcome to the Palace Hotel!"

The man who greeted them spoke English with an odd, flat accent.

He sounded as if he smiled broadly, but Anastasia couldn't really tell. He wore some kind of gauzy mask over his nose and mouth while he gestured expansively with both hands, as if he were a showman revealing some marvel or wonder. Anastasia smiled at him, but Maria contented herself with inclining her head slightly in acknowledgement.

"Right through here, ladies," the man said, opening up the door and ushering their party through to an airy lobby constructed of soaring arches and inlaid marble floors.

"Why is he masked?" Anastasia whispered to Baroness Buxhoeveden as they followed him inside.

"There is illness in the city," the baroness murmured back. "At the port, they informed me that hoteliers and their staff are required to remain masked to slow the spread. It is recommended for everyone, but ladies may substitute veils instead."

What an odd requirement, Anastasia thought as the American man continued to chatter on. Their party filed in as he gave them details about the construction of the hotel, its history, and some of its more notable guests.

A Hawaiian King, hmm? Anastasia followed Maria's straight back through the lobby and toward what the man said was one of four "rising rooms." The lobby was beautiful enough, to be sure, but no one who had grown up in the Tsar's Imperial court was going to be impressed by opulence.

Not that this man knew who they were. It had been decided that for their protection, they would travel discreetly. Baroness Buxhoeveden acted as the leader of their party and chaperone to the two younger women on an educational tour of the United States of America.

A thin lie, if this is all we're ever to see of America. Anastasia's thoughts turned back to her frustration. *A beautiful hotel not one quarter as splendid as some of the palaces at home, and a train ride. I do hope there is a delay in getting our train tickets. At least of one day!*

As it happened, Anastasia got her day. Baroness Buxhoeveden required that long to make suitable arrangements for them to travel by rail from San Franscisco to New York City, where they were to meet with Grandmama and the other representatives of His British Majesty's government.

Consequently, late morning found Anastasia wandering through the hotel's much-vaunted Garden Court, Dostovalov close at her side. She wound her arm through his and stifled a smirk at his stiff posture, but he refused to protest as he had upstairs in their suite.

"I am not traveling as Grand Duchess Anastasia Romanova here, my friend! It will look odd and attract attention if you are hovering behind my shoulder like some kind of bodyguard. It is better if we walk side by side as old, familiar friends. No one will notice us then," she had told him.

"It would be better if you would not insist on leaving the suite," he'd said, his voice a deep, annoyed rumble.

"I will not if you can honestly tell me that you do not think I will be safe with your escort." Anastasia had put her hands on her hips and arched her eyebrow in challenge. "If that is truly how you feel, I will remain here with Maria."

Dostovalov had let out a sigh and simply shaken his head in defeat, and so soon the two of them commenced to explore the public areas of the beautiful, grand American hotel.

Anastasia looked around with interest, taking in the veined golden marble of the ionic columns that defined the Garden Court. Daylight filtered in through the glass ceiling, reflecting off the cut crystal chandeliers in jeweled fire. A soft murmur of voices filled the space, providing a pleasant backdrop of sound punctuated by the occasional laugh or clatter of a morning teacup against a saucer.

"What do you think?" Anastasia asked her long-suffering escort as they took a full turn around the outside of the courtyard.

"It's very pretty," Dostovalov said, sounding as if he hated to admit it. "But places like these are what give the Reds their ammunition."

"What do you mean?" Anastasia asked, tilting her head to look up at him as she turned this thought over in her mind.

Dostovalov snorted softly and shrugged. "I've never been in a place this fine," he said. "If I had shown up here without you and your sister, I doubt they would have let me in the front door. Places like these are only for the elite, Your H— miss. And those as aren't welcome resent it. The Reds feed on that resentment and use it as fuel for their recruitment."

Anastasia narrowed her eyes and nodded slowly in contemplation as they continued to walk. But before they'd gone more than halfway down the length of the court, she shook her head again.

"I think I partially disagree with you, Anton Ivanovich."

"As Your . . . As you like, miss."

"No, listen. I think you're right to an extent. My family owned hundreds of rooms every bit as elegant and ornate as this one, and no one ever saw them but . . . well, you know who."

"I assure you, miss. I have no idea who was invited into your family's rooms."

Anastasia fought the urge to stomp her slippered foot. "But you know what I *mean*," she insisted. "No one was allowed in those rooms except those who were invited. But I look around at all of these people . . . All of these Americans, with no titles, no bloodlines to speak of. And they all just walked in here. The only requirement is money."

Dostovalov snorted. "Spoken like someone who has never felt the lack of money," he said.

Anastasia felt her spine stiffen, and a chill flood through her. She stopped and turned to stare up into his face, her eyes cold and hard. "We didn't have any money in Tobolsk, when we were prisoners there," she said softly. "As I think you well remember."

Dostovalov swallowed and ducked his head.

"I do," he said softly. "You are right. I apologize."

Anastasia stared at him for a moment before squeezing his arm that she still held.

"I forgive you," she said softly, pulling them into motion again. "And I understand what you are saying. Money is not easy to get when you don't have it, I do know that. But my point is that it *is* something one can get if one doesn't already have it. It might be difficult, or dangerous—"

"Or illegal."

"Or that," she nodded. "Yes, that too. But unlike the right family name or bloodline, money *is* a commodity that is nominally available to everyone. And here in America, if you have enough of it, you get to enjoy places like this. No matter who you are."

"Unless you're Chinese or Japanese or Negro," Dostovalov pointed out as they passed by the lobby and saw several people of each persuasion in servants' dress helping to stack the luggage of new arrivals.

"Perhaps that is because this is not China or Japan or Africa," Anastasia said. "Though I suspect if the Emperor of Japan or the King of one of the African nations arrived here, he'd be a welcome guest. The man last night said they'd once hosted a King of Hawai'i here."

"But once again, they are royalty."

Anastasia huffed out her breath and fought the urge to stomp once again. "Yes," she said with exaggerated patience. "But they are also rich. I am suggesting that their wealth matters more, here, than their bloodline or their rank, and I think that's an interesting concept, don't you?"

"If you say so, miss."

Anastasia gave in to the urge and stamped her foot. "Ooh! You are the most irritating man," she ground out softly between gritted teeth. "I do not understand what Olga saw in you."

As soon as she said the words, Anastasia wished them back again. While she didn't know what, exactly, had been between her late eldest sister and this man, he had mourned her loss to the extent of nearly taking his own life.

"Anton Ivanovich . . . I-I am sorry—"

His arm shook underneath her fingers. Anastasia glanced up to see his lips pressed together, his eyes filled with tears, yes, but as she watched, he let out first one, then several chuckles.

"Anton Ivanovich?"

"To be honest, miss, I have no idea!" He said this on a wave of further laughter. Laughter so infectious that Anastasia found herself first grinning, and then giggling along with him as he chose mirth over tears.

After a few minutes of this, Anastasia swiped one gloved finger under her eye to catch the tears that had gathered there and drew in a deep breath.

"You know," she said softly, pulling them over to a conversational grouping of chairs and out of the path of the perambulators. "Perhaps I do know what she saw. Clearly, it was your sense of humor!"

"And my good looks!" Dostovalov added, which sent them off into another laughing fit. Not because he wasn't handsome—he was, in a rugged, farm-boy sort of way—but because the whole idea was so absurd. A Grand Duchess and a common soldier? Impossible. And yet, it had happened.

Anastasia collapsed into one of the chairs, holding one hand tight to her middle and clasping the other over her mouth to keep from guffawing like a donkey. Dostovalov took the other chair and leaned forward, his own tears of mirth—and perhaps sadness—streaming down the planes of his face.

When they once again fell silent, Anastasia glanced around to see if anyone had noted their lack of decorum. Apparently not; all of the hotel and restaurant patrons seemed completely absorbed in their own conversations and business. Indeed, one of the tables nearby erupted into loud laughter of their own, and Anastasia felt her smile deepen.

"I don't know what she saw in me," Dostovalov said softly, bringing Anastasia's attention back to him. "But she was the most beautiful angel. Every time she smiled at me, I felt . . . I don't know. Like I could do anything."

"She had that effect." Anastasia nodded, still smiling. She reached out and laid her hand over his on the arm of his chair. "She could always make one feel special."

"Yes," he said, nodding, his eyes far away. "That's exactly it."

"She would be very proud of you, I think, Anton Ivanovich."

Dostovalov's eyes cut up to Anastasia's face. "Do you think so?"

"I do," she nodded. "She would not want you to grieve her in misery forever, or . . . well. She would want you to live, and to try and find happiness and purpose again."

"That is what the Emp—your sister said also. Or words to that effect. That is why I am here, why I protect you."

"And you do a fine job of it." Anastasia squeezed his fingers. He remained still for a long moment, then gave her the briefest of squeezes in return.

Anastasia pulled her hand back. It wasn't at all usual for her to have any kind of physical contact with a guard, unless in the course of his duties. And certainly to touch his hand in such an intimate, emotional moment was not the done thing . . . but this man had loved Olga, and lost her. And they were here, in this strange new country of America . . . well. Touching the man's hand to give him comfort seemed the least she could do.

"Did you and she ever—" she half-whispered, before she had even really decided to articulate the question that haunted her mind.

"No," he said softly. "Never." It was the first time he'd denied it because it was the first time he'd been directly asked.

"I wish you had," Anastasia said.

"Me too." He dropped his gaze to the floor. "If I had known . . ."

"If any of us had known," Anastasia said. "We would have found a way to make sure you could have had that together. She deserved—"

"She deserved more than me," Dostovalov scoffed.

"She deserved to be loved." Anastasia let her voice take on a slight edge. "And you loved her. *That* is what is important, Anton Ivanovich."

Dostovalov swallowed hard and nodded. Then finally looked up and met Anastasia's eyes. She saw grief and loss there, yes, but also gratitude. He nodded again, and smiling, so did she.

"Well," she said then, standing up and brushing off the front of her skirts in a brisk motion. "Shall we continue? I suppose Maria is wondering where we've gotten off to!"

"As you like, miss." He stood, glancing around in his professional manner, and offered his arm.

Anastasia smiled up at him and took it.

The following morning, they boarded a transcontinental railcar for New York City, by way of, among other places, Omaha, Chicago, and Pittsburgh. Anastasia suppressed a smirk at the way the signage proudly proclaimed that they would be crossing almost three thousand miles in just eighty-three hours. The distance from San Franscisco to New York City was a mere fraction of the length of the Trans-Siberian crossing they'd already made, to say nothing of sailing the entire width of the Pacific Ocean!

"It's endearing, really, don't you think?" she murmured softly to Maria as they carefully climbed aboard the luxuriously appointed First Class Pullman. "These Americans are so very proud of the size of their little nation."

"I do not care what they are proud of," Maria said. "I do not give a fig for America. I wish we were comfortably in London already."

Anastasia inhaled through her nose and fought the frustration that rose within her at her sister's words. Instead of snapping at her, she reached out and took Maria's hand in hers.

"Is your headache still bothering you?" she asked softly. "I can see if Baroness Buxhoeveden has a powder."

"A little," Maria said, squeezing Anastasia's fingers. "I am being grumpy, am I not? I apologize. I am just so tired of traveling!"

"It has been a long trip," Anastasia agreed. And, indeed, it had been.

They had departed Tobolsk for Yekaterinburg in mid-August—making the arrangements, not least getting the Czechs to secure the full length of the railroad, had taken months—and here it was thirty-nine days later. They would be four days on the train to New York, and then an unknown time there while the British government made arrangements for the final leg of their journey to London. By the time they were done, they would have circumnavigated over three fourths of the globe since being carted off from Tsarskoye Selo!

But unlike Maria, Anastasia found that she actually *enjoyed* the travel. San Franscico had been fascinating, even though she'd only really seen the Palace Hotel. This rail trip promised interesting scenery, and perhaps even new people to talk to, depending on how sequestered they ended up being from the other passengers. And since they enjoyed the most comfortable travel means that money could buy, Anastasia found herself slightly unsympathetic to Maria's complaints.

True to form, Buxhoeveden had secured a series of luxurious, private cabins for their use. Maria headed directly for her sleeping cabin to lie down, but Anastasia wasn't tired, and so she took a seat next to a large window in the lounge car. Ever vigilant, their chaperone, Baroness Buxhoeveden, had looked inquiringly at Anastasia. She was fierce of visage even when not trying.

"Anton Ivanovich has asked me to teach him English," Anastasia said quietly, even though he'd done no such thing. Behind the captain's shoulder, Dostavalov lifted an eyebrow in inquiry, but said nothing.

"We thought it best to sit in here, where the light is better," the girl explained. "And it was more proper than having a young man—even a guard—in the private sleeping car."

Buxhoeveden pursed her lips but nodded and continued to follow through the lounge car toward the sleeping cars. Dostavalov, playing his part, slid into the seat across from Anastasia.

Anastasia felt a sudden lifting of her spirits. *To teach Dostavalov English? To have a job, finally, and to feel useful, again? Be still my heart.*

"I don't recall wanting to learn English."

"You should," she said, rather tartly. "Since that is the language that is spoken both here and in Britain. Surely you would like to hear if someone behind you is saying that they are about to shoot me, no?"

"I suppose that depends on how well you've been behaving lately," he said, with a tiny smile.

Anastasia snorted and shook her head. Then she raised a hand to attract the attention of the Negro porter who strode up the aisles, asking if there was anything the customers wanted.

"Might we have today's newspaper, please?"

"Yes, miss," the porter said. "I've the *Chronicle* right here. Will that do?"

"Perfectly, thank you, Mr. . . ."

"You can call me George, miss." The porter smiled, his teeth very white against his dark complexion. "We're all called 'George.' It's part of the job."

"Well, then, thank you, George," Anastasia said with an answering smile. The porter handed Dostovalov a folded newspaper, and Dostovalov paid the man—plus a tip when Anastasia nodded significantly at him.

"My pleasure, miss. You just let me or any of the other Georges know if you need something else, now," the porter said, closing his hand around the tip.

"I'll do that, thank you, George."

Dostovalov watched the porter walk on, checking in with the other passengers in that same friendly, folksy, yet deferential manner. After a moment, the big Russian snorted softly.

"What?" Anastasia asked.

"I saw that man at the station, while the baroness was buying tickets. He was having a smoke with some other fellows. He didn't talk or act that way with them."

"No? That's interesting. How did he act?"

"Like a normal working man. To me, it sounded like he and his mates were grumbling a little, maybe about the passengers, but nothing to make me think he's a threat. Just . . . I think he must have dealt with some difficult people in the past."

Anastasia shrugged. "It's likely," she said. "People can sometimes be rude, especially to servants and the like."

"It's like he's playing an act."

"And so he probably is." Anastasia reached over to pull the newspaper from where Dostovalov still held it. "It sounds as if the character of 'George' is, as he said, part of the job. He probably gets paid more if he acts a certain way."

"So, it's back to money again?" Dostovalov asked, turning his attention back to Anastasia and letting her pull the newspaper out of his grasp.

"So it seems," she said. "Most things are about money, I suspect."

"I suspect you're right, miss," he said.

"I usually am. Just as I'm right about you needing to learn English. So now listen to me. I'm going to read you this article, first in English, and then in Russian . . ."

Though she was no stranger to rail travel, Anastasia found herself entranced by the varied scenery and landscape they traversed. Though it was wintertime, the tracks remained clear.

"These mountains are breathtaking," she said to Dostovalov one morning as they wound through a pass through the Rockies. The sun rode high in a crystalline blue sky, and the light glittered off the snow drifts and frost-covered trees that lined the track. That bright light disappeared for a moment when they passed through one of several short tunnels, but when it returned, it illuminated a picturesque mountain valley off to their right, complete with a jewel-blue lake in the center.

"Oh!" Anastasia gasped, her fingertips flying to her smiling lips. "Look, Anton Ivanovich!"

Dostovalov looked up from yet another newspaper. He had seized upon Anastasia's scheme of learning English with vigor. Every morning, he would ask one of the Georges for a new paper, and he and Anastasia would pore over it as he practiced reading and speaking the local tongue.

"Pretty," he said, and turned back to his study of the American gossip and entertainment page.

Anastasia rolled her eyes at Dostovalov's laconic appreciation and leaned forward to see what held his attention. He really had come a remarkably long way with his English, though his pronunciation remained terrible.

"What's that you're reading?" she asked.

"I am trying to figure that out," he admitted. He swiveled the paper towards her on the table that they'd somehow claimed as "theirs" for the trip and leaned back, rubbing his eyes.

"Oh, it's about an actress. Marion Davies. The author is quite enamored of her. The entire thing reads like an advertisement for her films..." Anastasia trailed off, her eyes flicking over the lines of newsprint.

"I did not realize. I saw the picture of the woman, and I thought she must be someone important," Dostovalov said. His cheeks pinkened slightly, and Anastasia smirked as she looked up at his face. She doubted it was Miss Davies' "importance" that had drawn his attention.

"I think, in a way, she is," Anastasia said, returning her attention to the article. "Oh, not important the way my sister is, or not the way Maria would define it, but look at how much space they devote to her! They write about her films, her shows... even her gowns! They speak of her as people at home used to speak about my grandmother, like she's some sort of... character in their dreams."

"She could be a character in my dream."

Anastasia snorted, then looked up at Dostovalov with laughter in her eyes.

"Don't let Maria or Baroness Buxhoeveden hear you say such things in my hearing, Anton Ivanovich. You'll get in trouble."

"I don't see them around, do you?" he asked, using English.

She smiled at him and shook her head, replying in the same language. "That will do you no good, my friend. Maria spoke English in the cradle, just as I did. But you are progressing very well. Let us continue..."

They crossed most of the Great Plains at night, but Anastasia woke early enough to spy the seemingly endless rows of ploughed fields stretching to the horizon on either side of the track.

For just a moment, resentment boiled in her gut, souring the mouthful of coffee she'd just swallowed. She'd seen similar fields in Russia, but too many of them lay barren, with no men to tend them, no crops to plant, nothing but war and death on every horizon.

"Good morning, miss. Just coffee for now? Or would you like to try one of our fresh-baked pastries?"

Anastasia blinked and looked up into the smiling face of the porter. She answered with her own weak smile.

"Just coffee will be fine, thank you, Geo... your name isn't really George, is it?"

"No, miss, it isn't, but you can call us George if you want to. It's part of the job."

"I'd like to know your real name, if that's all right with you."

The man's smile widened, and for the first time, actually included his eyes.

"My name is Henry Southam, miss. I am pleased to meet you."

"I am Ana Nicolaevna," she said. "The pleasure is all mine, Mr. Southam. Thank you for taking such good care of us."

Henry Southam drew himself up proudly and gave her a nod as he refilled her coffee cup. "That's what we do, miss." He smiled down at her once more, and then turned to serve another table.

"What was that all about?" Dostovalov, who had been sitting across from her and studying his newspaper, asked quietly in Russian.

"I am not sure," Anastasia admitted. "Only, I suddenly felt that it was important to know the man's true name. He did respond favorably to my asking, did you see that?"

"Of course he did," Dostovalov said. "You're young, pretty, and rich. What man wouldn't respond favorably to personal attention from someone like you?"

"That is a fair point, I suppose," she said. "Though I'm not nearly so pretty as my sisters."

"Definitely not," Dostovalov agreed, which made Anastasia scowl at him. He let it hang there for a moment before relenting with a small smile. "But you are the most fun."

Anastasia reached out and smacked him lightly on the bicep, and then sat back with her coffee, still contemplating the farmlands out the window as they slid by.

This country is swimming in wealth, she realized. *But they're like I was before Papa's abdication. They have no idea how quickly all that bounty can disappear.*

Eventually, as the rumble and clatter of the train rolled on, they started to pass through larger cities with shorter intervals of rural farmland in between. Here, in the bustling towns of Chicago, Pittsburgh, Philadelphia and the like, the contrast between old and new world stood out even more starkly to Anastasia's eyes.

Everywhere she looked, scaffolding and girders stretched upward as these young cities grew. New roads cut pale lines in the surrounding landscape, and commerce blazed around every corner. Even the most humble dwellings seemed to be advertising vegetables or handcrafted goods for sale.

"Ugh, finally!" Maria said on the last day, when the train's conductor made the announcement that they would be arriving in New York that evening. "I thought this awful train ride would never end."

"It wasn't nearly as long as the one back home," Anastasia pointed out. It had taken her all four days of the trip to persuade Maria to join her in the lounge car, and she didn't want to send her sister scurrying back to her private cabin. "Before we took ship for Japan."

Maria looked over at her sister, her eyes dark with annoyance. "I know," she said. "This one just *seems* longer. I am so tired of traveling."

Anastasia pressed her lips together before she could point out that her sister had hardly made any effort to enjoy the journey. Her entire objective in coaxing Maria out of the cabin had been to try and liven her up, not to start an argument in a public space.

"Are you excited to see Grandmama again?" Anastasia asked instead. "Baroness Buxhoeveden says she intends to meet us in New York."

"It will be wonderful to see her." Maria did smile. "I *am* looking forward to that, yes. Perhaps once she is with us, we can let go of this farce of poverty and actually travel as people of our rank are *meant* to travel."

"Maria!" Anastasia lowered her voice to a hiss and leaned forward over the surface of the table between their seats, lest anyone else hear her sister's snobbery. "You're being unreasonable! We've traveled in the most luxurious accommodations this country has to offer!"

"Hmm. Yes. *This country.*" Maria arched her eyebrows and returned Anastasia's censure glare for glare. "This backwater, uncivilized, upstart of a country. I fear you are in danger of forgetting who we are, Nastenka. Our father—"

"Is dead."

Maria closed her mouth with a snap and pressed her lips together. Her eyes filled with tears. Anastasia reached out to take her hand, but Maria pulled away and turned to stare out the window.

"Maria—"

"I think I will return to our cabin," she said, holding her body stiffly. "I find that headache still plagues me. I will rest until we arrive in New York. Do be quiet if you come in there, please."

Anastasia closed her eyes as her sister stood up and brushed past her to the central aisle. When she opened them, she saw Dostovalov nod, and one of their other guards stood up from his seat nearby and followed Maria as she exited the dining car.

By the time they reached the hotel in New York City, it was quite late. They had disembarked at a crowded train station, and all had been confusion and chaos for several moments while Baroness Buxhoeveden and one of the guards collected their baggage and secured transportation to the hotel. Anastasia remembered falling into the back seat of a long, shiny black motorcar, but then she must have dozed off. For the next thing she knew, they had arrived and a hotel valet stood next to the open door with his hand extended to help her out.

Like the Palace in San Francisco, the Plaza Hotel exemplified what Anastasia had begun to think of as "American elegance." From what she could see, the decor borrowed heavily from French stylings. Gilt glinted off the light fixtures and sparkled from crystal chandeliers. Cut flowers filled silver vases on tables here and there throughout the foyer. Thick carpets muffled the sounds of their footfalls as they made their way to their reserved suites.

When Dostovalov opened the door to the suite the sisters would share, Anastasia followed Maria in. She had to stifle a groan of relief at the sight of the merrily crackling fire in the grate and the turned down beds in the room beyond. Anastasia had enjoyed the train trip, but she didn't mind admitting that she was looking forward to a night's sleep in a proper bed. The Pullman cots had been comfortable enough for what they were, but the crisp bed linens and fluffy pillows of the Plaza's bed called to her fatigued body like a siren luring a sailor to a watery grave.

"Good night, Your Imperial Highnesses," Dostovalov called softly as he backed out, closing the door behind him. Anastasia heard the *click* of the lock as she turned to remind him that he was not supposed to use their titles.

"At last," Maria said, heaving a sigh and turning to Anastasia with a smile. "We can be ourselves again. I feel as if we're finally close to returning to civilization."

Anastasia returned her sister's smile, even though Maria's snobbery continued to bother her. But rather than start another argument, she walked over and wrapped her elder sister back up in an embrace.

"I hope you will be very comfortable in London," she said softly.

Maria squeezed her back. "I feel certain I shall," she said, and Anastasia could hear the smile and excitement deepen in her tone. "Mama loved it there when she was a girl."

Anastasia nodded, and then stepped back as a yawn overtook her. "Goodness! I suppose we should get some sleep. I hope we will hear from Grandmama about her plans tomorrow."

"I think we will! Perhaps she is already in the city!" Maria said, turning toward the washroom with a bounce in her step that Anastasia hadn't seen since . . .

Well. Since she didn't know when. *Since Papa's abdication, perhaps? Surely it can't have been that long!* And yet, try as she might, Anastasia couldn't truly name a time since then that she had seen Maria with such a look of happiness and excitement.

Has she been so unhappy? And what does that say about me that I am only now noticing? Oh, my dear sister, have you needed me and I just haven't paid attention?

"Come, Anastasia, you're right," Maria sang out, still with that joy in her voice. "We must get some sleep! Come wash your face and let's lie down. Tomorrow, I hope we will hear from Grandmama and then . . . wouldn't it be wonderful if we could leave within the week? Just think of it! We could be in London within a fortnight!"

But I don't want to go to London.

Anastasia blinked and actually paused in her progress toward the washroom as this thought slammed into her.

I don't. I don't want to go to London and find a noble husband or any of that. I want . . . I want to stay here longer! This country is so strange and yet, there is something wild and wonderful about the people. They reject royalty, yet they create their own "royalty" out of actresses and society stars. They almost worship money . . . and they are swimming in it. Maria yearns for London, but this is now the greatest city in the world.

"Anastasia? Are you quite well, dear?"

Anastasia blinked and gave herself a little shake, then looked at her elder sister with a smile.

"Oh! Yes, I am sorry. I am just so tired, I suppose I was miles away. Thinking of Tatiana."

This time, it was Maria who came forward to wrap her sister up in a hug. "I miss her too, and I worry! If only she had come with us, but I suppose I see why she did not. She is very strong, our sister. And she has the whole of our army to protect her."

"Yes," Anastasia said. She returned Maria's hug and then turned resolutely for the washroom. "And that will be enough. I have faith that it will."

Especially if we have people like these Americans on our side.

Chapter Twenty-Four

General Anton Ivanovich Denikin

Kislovodsk, Southern Russia

Whose side is God on? Anton Denikin wondered. *I know who the Devil fights for.*

General Denikin covered his nose and mouth with a kerchief and forced the nausea rising from his belly to still. It would not do for the commander in chief of all Southern Russia to vomit in front of the soldiers he commanded, the civilians who were counting on him to deliver them from the depredations of the Marxist savages.

The open mass grave reeked of voided bowels and bladders and dead, rotting flesh. The incongruously picturesque countryside, the golden domes of St. Nicholas's Cathedral, and the inviting wood frame homes of the spa town made the remnants of the Bolshevik's most recent atrocity all the more horrific in contrast. Men, women, and children were piled unceremoniously together in the wide, shallow hole. Expressions of surprise and terror were etched in rictus upon those faces visible through the mass of carnage.

"They wouldn't let us even fill it in," the mayor of Kislovodsk said; his voice quavered and tears slid out of his unblinking eyes. He had the unhealthy, pinched look of someone who had rapidly lost a great deal of weight—and not due to exertion.

It was a look that had never been exactly rare in Russia, but was rapidly becoming the default. The war consumed the means of transportation for vital foodstuffs, interrupted their flow as the Reds and Whites battled for control of the railways. Soldiers and bandits forestalled or destroyed the harvests, and appropriated what *was* harvested to feed one army or another.

"They will pay for this," Denikin said. "We will crush the Marxists and execute the men who did this."

If the mayor heard Denikin's words, he gave no indication, his empty gaze remaining fixed on one thousand five hundred men, women, and children murdered for being, "enemies of the Revolution."

"When your cavalry arrived, we thought we were saved, we welcomed Colonel Shkuro as a savior, opened our homes, fed him and his men only the best, then he rode away with his men, and the next day—" The mayor closed his eyes, and sank to the ground, his head falling forward into his hands.

Denikin knelt down and grasped the sobbing man's shoulder. He prayed silently over the man. He stayed until the mayor's wife, looking just as thin and harrowed as her husband, came to collect the mayor and take him home. After their departure, Denikin stood and walked back to the cabin where his staff had set up his command post. His chief of staff, General Romanovsky, was waiting for him in the dining room where they laid out the largest maps upon the massive teak table and did their primary planning.

"General, are you well?" Romanovsky asked. Denikin hardened his expression, realizing his grief must have been apparent.

"I am not. Fifteen hundred men, women, and children murdered for giving that fool, Shkuro, food and lodging, damn him."

"Sir, Colonel Shkuro is one of our best cavalry squadron commanders. His raids have sown chaos in the Bolshevik's rear,"

Romanovsky's tone was mild, but it was clear to Denikin that he felt his commander was being too sentimental.

"I'm aware that Shkuro has his uses," Denikin said. "I won't relieve him just yet, but we are supposed to be fighting the Communists to protect the Russian people, not to expose them to more atrocity and death."

"Atrocity and death are inevitable until we have conquered the Reds, General."

Denikin frowned. Shkuro wasn't here and he had days, perhaps even weeks before he would have a chance to discipline the impetuous cavalryman, so he saw no reason to dwell on the matter. He changed subjects.

"Any news while I was out?"

"Pokrovsky and Wrangel are both still advancing against the enemy's rear guard, though Wrangel lost his battery of 76mm guns and has requested replacements. We don't have any in reserve, so if you want to accommodate him, we will have to cross-level from another unit. Their front line is about here, along the River Ouroup."

"Slower than I would have liked," Denikin said. "Do they give any explanation for the delays?"

"A combination of stiff resistance and counterattacks from the Reds in some places, and the need to process large numbers of prisoners on the other. The raw number of enemy surrendering has actually imposed a hefty logistical and security burden all along the front."

Denikin snorted and shook his head.

"What a problem to have, eh?"

"It is, indeed," Romanovsky said. "Unfortunately, the Reds don't seem to be running short on manpower despite the surrenders and the casualties we've been inflicting on them."

"Inundating your enemy with prisoners is certainly a new approach in the annals of tactics. Anything else?" Denikin asked.

Romanovsky's expression clouded, and he visibly steeled himself to deliver the next bit of news.

"Wrangel has lodged a complaint against Pokrovsky. He claims that Pokrovsky's division has become distracted with looting and abuses of the local populace. In his words, their behavior both shames our holy cause and endangers our military mission."

"Abusing" the local population almost certainly meant that

Pokrovsky's men were taking liberties with the local girls in addition to stealing food and valuables. A certain amount of that behavior was tragically inevitable in war. An officer dealt with it by finding the looter, the rapist, and hanging or shooting them to reassert discipline. But if that sort of behavior was so common in Pokrovsky's division that it had come to another division commander's attention—that was something else entirely.

"Is it true?" Denikin asked.

"Pokrovsky's division is advancing at roughly the same rate as Wrangel's according to both their reports, but have his troops been looting and raping?" Romanovsky paused and removed his spectacles, rubbing the bridge of his nose. "Yes, sir, I think it's true. Our own staff couriers have returned with similar reports and Pokrovsky has been unresponsive when we've queried him on the matter."

Hanging a rapist or five was one thing. If Pokrovsky's whole command had rotted through with this behavior—could he bring a whole division to heel without shattering cohesion? In the Imperial Army, Denikin's Iron Division had never seen such indiscipline, and if it had, he would have had the villains shot without delay or fanfare. The Great War had been a brutal, grinding, and bloody business, but at least he hadn't worried about his army disintegrating out from underneath him if he imposed basic discipline.

It was like trying to win a fencing match with one hand while trying to keep your trousers from falling around your ankles with the other. Denikin found himself constantly beleaguered by herding conscripts, squabbles between his officers, and complaints from the various civilian political leaders that made up the disparate White Movement.

In name, Denikin was Commander in Chief of the Armed Forces of Southern Russia. In reality, he was the poor schmuck tasked with unifying the efforts of monarchists who wished to restore the empire, socialists and democrats who wanted some form of representative government in Russia, though they did not agree on exactly what that looked like, and the Cossacks, who, more than anything, wanted to be left alone. The only thing the various factions shared was a hatred of the Bolsheviks, and so they cooperated, to various degrees, in a patchwork army.

The Armed Forces of South Russia drew most of their combat power from the Volunteer Army and the Kuban Cossacks. The

Volunteer Army included most of the veteran officers of the Imperial Army who chose to side with the White factions over the Bolsheviks, as well as other volunteers from the Monarchist, anti-Bolshevik Socialist and Democratic camps. The Kuban Cossacks provided a large, well-trained and highly motivated cavalry force indigenous to the region.

With so many officers having joined the Volunteer Army, Denikin was not short on combat-experienced leaders for billets from company to regimental command. He was terribly short on trained enlisted men. The only experienced troop formations were the Kornilov, Markov, and Alekseev infantry regiments and his Cossack cavalry and infantry. His hardened infantry formations were a dwindling resource—indeed they were currently manned at ten percent of their initial strength. The Cossacks were still a tribal people tied strongly to their land. Once the Kuban was free of Bolsheviks, Denikin suspected the magnificent horsemen might not fight with such fervor in parts of Russia that meant little to them and theirs.

The Cossacks of the Don River Basin were allegedly allied with the South Russian Armed Forces as well as their Kuban cousins, but Krasnov had refused to subordinate himself to Denikin, even purely militarily, and so several thousand excellent cavalrymen galloped about the Don carrying out whatever idiocy Krasnov thought up for them, unavailable to the greater mission.

Denikin glared out the window as the weight of the task pressed on him. Of humble origins, son of a soldier and a Polish woman, no one would ever mistake the stocky, unassuming Denikin for an aristocrat, but he'd been a fine division commander in the Great War. He'd risen to his exalted rank without a patron, without family connection or noble blood, purely on merit—a rarity in the Imperial Army! He knew, he *knew* that he could lead the White movement to victory were it not for all the pestilential self-seekers like Krasnov and divisive political nonsense that beset him at every turn.

If he declared his intent to restore the monarchy, the republicans and socialists might splinter away from his cause. If he declared for democracy, the monarchists, who now saw any electoral process as an invitation to anarchy, might likewise leave. The peasants who provided the bulk of his rank and file pleaded for land reform, but the very reform that would win them over might alienate the kulaks who provided his food and the nobles who still made up many of his best field commanders.

Daily he walked the tightrope, ensuring his words and actions led no one to believe he had any defined aim beyond defeating the Communists. Thus no faction left the coalition—but the problems were never resolved, the arguments and resentments festered. Denikin himself was so busy ensuring he maintained the good graces of each faction that he was never allowed to concentrate fully on winning the war.

"General?" Romanovsky asked, piercing Denikin's frustrated reverie.

"We will think on the issues in Pokrovsky's division. Naturally, we should not countenance such atrocious behavior, but neither can we risk mutiny and the disintegration of the army by ill-considered action."

Raised voices from the hallway interrupted their discussion. Romanovsky left to see what the bustle was about. He returned a moment later with a Cossack in a filthy uniform. The Cossack grinned from ear to ear, but Romanovsky looked grim.

"Sir, it appears that Shkuro has taken Stavropol," Romanovsky said.

"What?" Denikin shot up from his chair, glaring between the two men.

"Yes, your excellency," the Cossack said. "It was a grand feat—the colonel told the Bolsheviks that we would shell them to dust with our heavy artillery if they didn't leave the city."

"Colonel Shkuro has no heavy artillery," Romanovsky said, his voice flat.

"No, but we'll be long gone by the time the Communists figure that out." The Cossack grinned. Denikin's heart sank as he considered the hundreds of dead innocents rotting less than half a mile from where he stood.

"Get me a courier, we need to tell Wrangel to alter his axis of advance, he needs to reach Stavropol before the Communists can retake the city. And you, private, get cleaned up, have a bath and some wine. In the morning you will return to Colonel Shkuro and tell him to hold until relieved."

"I thank your excellency!" the Cossack said, revealing yellowed, crooked teeth with his grin.

The Cossack departed. Romanovsky turned on his commander with a tight expression.

1919: THE ROMANOV RISING

"General, taking and holding Stavropol strains our lines of supply at this phase of the operation—there is too much rail line between here and there for us to patrol effectively. Wrangel will be at the end of a very thin thread."

Denikin met his chief of staff's eyes levelly.

"Wrangel is one of our best field commanders, he can handle it."

Romanovsky opened his mouth, apparently willing to argue the issue further, but Denikin cut him off with a glare and a slashing motion of his hand.

"General, we are supposed to be the guardians of the Russian people, and now one of ours has put innocent lives in peril, essentially on a lark. We will not abandon those souls. My decision is made."

Romanovsky shut his mouth on his protest, his expression closed up into an unreadable mask of discipline.

"Yes, sir."

West Bank of the Ouroup River, South Russia

Two weeks of bloody fighting finally yielded results. The Reds counterattacked across the River Ouroup at the junction of Wrangel's 1st Cavalry and Pokrovsky's division. Their attempt to force a wedge between the two units failed and cost them much of their ammunition and arms in the process, leaving insufficient defenders against Wrangel's counterattack.

Wrangel's cavalrymen forded the Ouroup River as the artillery and machine gunners provided a base of fire against the thin line of Red infantry holding the north bank. Withering under intense fire, staring at the mass of fearsome horsemen splashing across the river toward them, the Red infantry broke. Wrangel led his men in headlong pursuit for several miles, right to the outskirts of the village of Ouspeskaia. To the dismay of his Cossacks, Wrangel halted the charge of his cavalry short of the village.

"No, lads," he shouted over their jeering objections. "Clearing towns is the infantry's work. Colonel Dara, take one half the brigade and seal off all western approaches to the town; send the other half to close of the eastern approaches. Engage targets of opportunity with machine guns and our new cannons. I will bring up our infantry to clear the village."

"Sir, remember you are a division, not company, commander when we begin the clearance of this village," Obolensky said as they trotted back to join the infantry battalions.

Wrangel merely sniffed.

He surveyed his infantry with some dissatisfaction. He had an undermanned battalion from the Volunteer Army—this was ridiculously rank-heavy, with majors and even colonels in command of the companies and every platoon and squad led by no less than a captain. He had the cadres for a Cossack infantry division as well, which amounted to only another two companies of infantryman.

Fortunately, what they lacked in number, they possessed in skill and motivation. The veterans and Cossacks marched straight into the attack on the village. Battle-hardened officers blooded at Galicia or in the Italian Alps ensured their men fanned out in an orderly formation, but not too orderly, optimizing their own angles of fire while presenting the enemy with more difficult targets.

A hodgepodge collection of machine guns including Madsens, Chauchats and Lewis Guns kept the buildings on the edge of the village under steady bursts of fire as the riflemen closed. Enemy fire began to slacken as his men advanced. Wrangel could feel it in the air—the point of decision was near.

A gray-haired major, moving with a celerity belying his years, sprinted to within ten meters of a small house whose windows were sparkling with enemy muzzle flashes. He slid into a small depression; enemy fire kicked up geysers of dirt all around him. The major paid no heed and tossed a hand grenade in a beautiful arc right through the window of that house. It detonated in a muted orange-gray flash.

The destruction of their central machine gun nest eviscerated the volume of fire the Reds were able to pour forth from the village. The Volunteer and Cossack infantrymen charged, only a handful falling from enemy fire.

"Come, Vladimir," Wrangel said to Obolensky. "The enemy will break soon and we must be there to cut off their retreat."

They galloped off to rejoin the Cossack cavalry waiting on the flanks of the battle. Mere minutes after they rejoined the horsemen, the Red infantry began to flee the village.

"Hurrah, men! Take them!"

The Cossacks cheered as Wrangel spurred his horse, leading a galloping mass of Cossacks into the flank of the fleeing Red infantry.

With a vicious downward sweep of his saber, Wrangel himself felled a Communist officer, a deep gash severing the flesh and bone of his left shoulder. Hundreds more of the Reds died under lance, saber, and shot before the rest flung their weapons to the ground and held up their hands. Completing their charge through the Red lines, Wrangel signaled for his formation to wheel about, circling the surrendering Reds.

Infantry surged forward to take the prisoners' weapons and corral them. Wrangel raised his saber and galloped across his lines, eliciting a cheer from his men, the elation of victory chorusing from their ragged throats. The standard bearer raised high the guidon of the 1st Cavalry from a roof in the village and waved it back and forth. Wrangel favored his men with a rare smile as he galloped back and forth, accepting their adulation and shouting his pride in them.

Now he had formed a real fighting division.

That evening, Wrangel sat on the porch of the largest hut in Ouspeskaia as the sun sank low on the horizon. Its owner, a gray-bearded old man, had offered him lodging with an almost embarrassing air of servility—Wrangel was used to deference as both an aristocrat and a general officer, but the people of this hamlet were overjoyed to see Wrangel nearing the point of absurdity. It had taken him several minutes just to convince the man's stooped wife that he needed no service, no food at the moment, merely a few minutes of quiet to think.

He stared at the broad horizon, lost in thought as his men saw to their horses, saddles, and weapons, and counted the captured rifles, machine guns, and artillery pieces this defeated regiment of Reds had gifted to their captors. Wrangel's joy at his division's successful attack had worn off and now he considered his situation soberly once again. His division had performed well—absolutely. He had replenished his artillery, thankfully, and had several caissons of ammunition for each caliber of piece they'd taken. The fact that the Reds had allowed this much artillery to fall into his hands confirmed the chaos and disorder he'd sensed in their ranks. His cavalry brigades were likewise healthy, but he still sorely lacked infantry.

Yes, he commanded a cavalry division, and mounted warfare was his stock in trade, but even a man as saddle-worn as Pyotr Wrangel knew that a divisional element needed its own infantry. Infantrymen were necessary to root out enemies in urban areas, swamps, rocky hills, and thick woods, or to hold key pieces of terrain around which the mounted warriors could pivot. As surely and unerringly as the trinity of Father, Son and Holy Ghost in Heaven, the trinity of war on the ground remained Infantry, Cavalry, and Field Artillery. All responsible officers understood this.

"General Wrangel." Obolensky approached with a young captain on his heels. "A messenger from General Denikin."

The young captain snapped to attention and saluted crisply. Wrangel returned the salute.

"What word from the supreme commander, Captain?"

"Sir, General Denikin commands that the 1st Cavalry Division alter its axis of advance." The captain held out an envelope for Wrangel. "Your new objective is Stavropol."

Wrangel maintained a neutral expression, even as his heart thudded painfully in his chest. Stavropol was no mere hamlet, and it was at the end of a very long line of supply. How in the hell did Anton Ivanovich expect him to take a city in his division's current state?

There was no use arguing these points with a messenger.

"Captain, you've had a long trip, get some food, get cleaned up as best you can and get some rest. I will summon you after I've read the orders," Wrangel said. "Vladimir, see that he's set up."

Wrangel retreated into the straw-floored hut and lit an oil lamp to read Denikin's missive. As he read of the massacre at Kislovodsk resulting from Shkuro's actions, and his similar ploy at Stavropol, Wrangel let out an uncharacteristically vehement stream of profanity. Obolensky caught the tail end of his outburst as he entered the hut.

"What is wrong, sir?"

"Vladimir Platonovich, that fool, Shkuro, is what's wrong." Wrangel handed over the letter. "I told Denikin that he wasn't to be trusted with independent command."

Obolensky read the letter quickly, then looked up.

"General, how are we to take and hold Stavropol without so much as a full regiment of infantry?"

Wrangel glared out the window. He understood Denikin's impulse; he shared it. They were guardians of the Russian people, and the Communists had proven willing to slaughter anyone who showed even the slightest allegiance to the White Movement.

The humanitarian impulse didn't change the fact that this was militarily foolish. A refusal of the order, or perhaps a *request for clarification and confirmation* began to draft itself in his mind. He quickly discarded it. Sentimental or not, even foolish or not, Denikin was the Supreme Commander. Denikin was also tetchy about his more aristocratic subordinates, and sensitive to anything that might vaguely resemble insubordination from those born of higher social station.

There already existed enough tension and acrimony between the leaders of the White Movement, and while Wrangel privately thought Denikin was not the optimal choice for supreme command, he also had to admit there were far worse candidates. He wouldn't throw his men's lives away just to avoid an argument, but perhaps there was a way—Wrangel's glare landed on a corral of Red prisoners, huddled together against the chill of the late autumn night.

The NCOs and officers were separated from the rank and file, of course, and there were disproportionately fewer leaders than troops among those who had surrendered.

Perhaps...

"Follow me, Vladimir Platonovich, we have an unpleasant task ahead."

The officer commanding the guard on the prisoners was, to Wrangel's surprise, the same young man to whom he'd given his revolver. They exchanged salutes as Wrangel approached.

"Gavrikov, is it not?" Wrangel said.

"You honor me, your excellency," Gavrikov said. "Do you need your pistol back?"

The young lieutenant made to retrieve the weapon from its holster.

"No, I do not need my revolver back," Wrangel said. "And sadly, I do not honor you tonight. There's butcher's work needs doing, Gavrikov. It will be neither glorious nor honorable, but it is necessary. Find me twelve of your coldest men."

The rifles fired, their actions clicked and clacked, they fired again, *click-clack-click*, again, and yet again. The Bolshevik leaders fell to the ground, most dead near instantly, but some still screaming their pain to the cold, unfeeling stars, only to be finished off by a single round from Wrangel's old revolver in the hands of a grim-faced Gavrikov.

Wrangel marked that the young man appeared to take no pleasure in the killing, but did not flinch from his duty.

Wrangel maintained a stern mien as he oversaw the summary execution of more than three hundred men. Whatever gnawing his conscience intended for his soul, it was private, and the soldiers he'd ordered to commit the deed with their own hands deserved to see their commander resolute, assured of the necessity and justice of their acts.

When the last Bolshevik NCO was dead, he summoned the rank and file prisoners to witness the massed bodies of their leaders. They shuffled in, bayonets at their backs, machine guns positioned obliquely to mow them down without hitting the other guards if they became unruly. He mounted his new horse, the beautiful black mare, and cantered back and forth in front of the bedraggled prisoners. Their expressions were mostly exhausted and terrified, and he saw very little defiance.

As he had surmised when they surrendered—these were not Communist true believers.

These he could use.

"You have all committed treason against Mother Russia," Wrangel shouted at the top of his lungs. "You have sided with Godless Bolshevik scum against all that is good and decent on this Earth. By rights, you should share the same fate as your leaders."

Wrangel let the sentence linger in the chill autumn air for several seconds. Realization that they might *not* be lined up and shot like their officers and NCOs began to dawn on many of their faces.

Wrangel continued, "Fortunately for you, I love God and our Lord Jesus Christ nearly as much as I love the *Rodina*. It is for this reason, and this reason alone, that I extend you an echo of the gift He gave us all with His holy sacrifice upon the Cross. I offer you the chance to repent and redeem yourselves."

Hope bloomed in a thousand pairs of eyes, the chance of survival dangling like an oasis before them. Wrangel had set the hook, time to draw in the line.

"You were led astray by lying dogs such as these." Wrangel waved a hand at the massed bodies lying in the center of the hamlet. "But by divine providence you have been placed in my hand to spare or to slay. Rather than end your lives in your current miserable state, I bestow

upon you an honor I expect you to spend the rest of your life earning—
you will serve under my command."

Shock, relief, and confusion rippled audibly through the assembled
prisoners. Wrangel brought his horse to a halt in the middle of their
ragged formation. A deep, hoarse voice from the back of the formation
called—

"The Bolshevik drafted most of us anyhow, your lordship. Give me
a rifle and I'll gladly shoot some of the bastards for you!"

There was a ripple of humor and general agreement throughout the
prisoners. Wrangel did not smile.

"I'm glad to hear that, soldier, because there is no cheap grace.
Christ's forgiveness is unearned, given upon the moment of your
repentance. My forgiveness you will earn in blood, sweat, and agony.
Your officers will drive you, forge you into true soldiers, not the
glorified bandits the Bolshevik rabble intended."

The mass of them listened intently to his every word; he need only
reel them in over the point of no return.

"Together, we will stop the Reds' predation upon our people. We
will establish a sane and just rule for all Russia. You will follow me into
death, and fire, and victory, for the Glory of God, and the *Rodina*!"

The cheer started as a ragged, quiet, thing, but it gained in
momentum like a tidal wave cresting, the dull roar becoming a
cacophony of assent.

"Excellent," Wrangel said as soon as the cheer had died down. "In a
few minutes, your new chain of command will come to organize you
into squads and platoons and rearm you. Stay where you are until then."

Obolensky and his senior officers were waiting on the porch of the
hut in which Wrangel had taken residence. Wrangel dismounted and
allowed one of his orderlies to lead his horse to the impromptu stable
they'd established at one of the barns. Both his aide and his brigade
commanders regarded him with incredulous expressions.

"General, how do you intend to maintain control of the Reds once
you've rearmed them?" Dara asked in a low voice. "We haven't the
manpower to watch them all."

"We watch them the same way we watch our lads, with officers and
NCOs," Wrangel said.

"Our lads are not Communists, sir," Dara insisted.

"Neither were these a few weeks ago. We've given them an

honorable option to avoid their leaders' fate and they've taken it. Besides, Ivan Sergeivich, if their loyalty to Marxist ideas was more than theoretical, we would never have captured so many of them."

Dara looked ready to chew railroad spikes and spit out nails, and even Obolensky appeared worried, with furrowed brows over dark eyes.

"Gentlemen, we exist in a state where no safe, sensible options exist. We need more infantrymen; I have found them. Divvy them up among the Volunteers and the Cossacks, try to keep the well-acquainted away from one another, but make it fast. We march tomorrow at first light."

Chapter Twenty-Five

Maria Feodorovna (Formerly Dagmar of Denmark)

New York City, New York, USA

To Maria's dismay, it was a few more days before their grandmother arrived in New York. But arrive she did, and Maria's cry of joy rent Anastasia's heart with guilt. The two sisters had struggled not to snap at each other since arriving in New York, a situation not helped by the fact that the weather had turned nasty gray and rainy.

But Maria Feodorovna, Dowager Empress of Russia, swept into their hotel suite on a morning when the sun streamed through broken clouds to light up their hotel room. The sisters' collective mood brightened at the sight of their grandmother.

"Oh, my darlings!" said Maria Feodorovna, once known as Dagmar of Denmark, as she threw her arms around her granddaughters. Her words came out strangled and strained with the tears that ran unheeded down her elegant features. Anastasia's own eyes filled, and she wrapped her arms around her grandmother's waist and inhaled deeply the scent of her lavender and rosewater perfume.

"Grandmama!" Maria sobbed. "Oh, Grandmama!"

For just a moment, Anastasia let herself drift back to the child she'd been not so long ago. Only two years, but it felt like a lifetime had passed.

Anastasia dropped her arms, sniffed back her tears, and straightened up with a watery smile for her grandmother. While Maria sobbed on, Dagmar comforted her and petted her hair, but her eyes snapped to her younger granddaughter with interest.

"It is good to see you, Grandmama," Anastasia said, wiping her eyes to regain her composure. "Beyond good. Wonderful."

"Indeed," Dagmar said. "Wonderful is a good word for it. I am so grateful to our Lord God for preserving you girls. You have been at the center of all my prayers ever since—" She pressed her lips together and closed her eyes, then bent to kiss the top of Maria's bent head.

"Come now," the Dowager Empress went on, "but let us not wallow in the sadness of tragedies past. We are together, and you are both coming with me to London as soon as it is safe to travel! We shall have a very gay time there, you can be certain."

"Do you have any idea when it will be safe?" Anastasia asked, as Maria hiccupped and pulled back, trying to still her flood of tears.

"Not too much longer, I think." Dagmar let go of her embrace and reached out to take her granddaughters' hands in hers. "A few weeks, perhaps. Maybe a month or two. With the Americans fully in the war now, the rumors are rampant. The *Boche* cannot hold out much longer. Rather, they cannot *believe* that they can hold out for much longer, and that's the same thing.

"So, we will stay here in New York for a short time, but do not despair! There is something like society here, and some pleasures to be had. Indeed, perhaps tomorrow we shall go look at one of their museums. These bourgeois American upstarts are absolutely greedy for art, and they've managed to amass a decent collection here in New York. You'd like that, wouldn't you?" she asked the still-weeping Maria, who sniffed and nodded.

"There are some people here you should meet as well. The British Ambassador, of course, a few others. You will see. We will have quite a merry time of it here in the wilderness!"

This is hardly the wilderness, Anastasia thought as her grandmother squeezed her hand. But she smiled back and nodded, and then hugged Dagmar again, and then the still-weepy Maria. While her older sister tried to put on a brave face at the thought of staying in New York for up to two more months, Anastasia found herself thrilled. The opportunity to further explore this fascinating new country beckoned, and a curl of excitement burned within her chest.

That excitement wasn't lessened when the news came that Germany had asked for an armistice.

The Metropolitan Museum of Art was quite a substantial building.

Anastasia shook her head and quickly divested herself of her hooded cape as they hurried to get inside the tall, arched doorways. The rain continued to pound down, filling the New York streets with streams of water and mud and painting the stately buildings a darker gray or brown.

"Well, that was quite an adventure, wasn't it, Grandmama?" Maria said brightly as she, too, doffed her outerwear and handed it to the woman waiting nearby for that purpose. Anastasia smiled a thanks at the woman, but Maria didn't even seem to notice her presence It wasn't unusual. They'd been raised not to see the ever-present staff that made palace life possible. But in this country with its egalitarian ideals, her sister's lack of manners made Anastasia feel rather uncomfortable.

Dagmar, at least, also thanked the woman in a low tone, which earned her a smile and Anastasia's gratitude. She then turned and looked toward someone approaching from further inside.

"Your Majesty."

Anastasia turned toward the familiar sound of crisp British English and found herself looking at the top of an elegant woman's head as she bent her neck and her body in a formal curtsey.

"Lady Rice," Dagmar said, a smile in her voice. "It is so good to see you."

The British woman rose with a smile. "Welcome to New York, your Majesty," she said. "The pleasure, and honor, is all mine."

"Maria, Anastasia, may I present Lady Rice, wife of Sir Cecil, the British Ambassador to the United States. I have known her for many years, since my sister was first married. Lady Rice, Grand Duchess

Maria Nicolaevna and Grand Duchess Anastasia Nicolaevna. My granddaughters."

"Your Imperial Highnesses," Lady Rice said, dipping once more into that deep, formal curtsey. She was both the daughter and the wife of British diplomats and knew the ropes well.

"Please forgive an old friend of your grandmother's the impertinence, but it is my very great honor to meet you both. Tales of your stalwart bravery under the most horrific circumstances have traveled around the world . . . and . . . I am so sorry for your losses—"

"Thank you," Anastasia murmured, while Maria sniffled as if she were about to tear up yet again. Dagmar reached out and put a quieting hand on her friend's wrist.

"Yes," Dagmar said, "thank you . . . but we are not here today to speak of our family's great tragedies. Quite the opposite, in fact! I have brought the girls here to see the great American collection of art pieces."

"It is rather good, for a colony," Lady Rice said, with a dry smile. "I was delighted to get your note. My husband is one of the benefactors of the museum here—well, you know the family has a large collection, and it was helpful to his business interests to have some of the colonists owe him a favor, so we've lent them several pieces. Consequently, I'm allowed the privilege of giving you a private tour, though I do think the museum board is rather hoping I'll convince Your Majesty to become a benefactress as well."

"Perhaps I shall," Dagmar said. "Please relay my thanks to the board and curator. Shall we proceed?"

"Right this way, Your Majesty . . ."

Anastasia found herself rather liking Lady Rice. The woman's curious mix of supercilious formality and wry humor amused her, and appeared to satisfy Maria's sense of self-importance to the point that her older sister actually relaxed and looked around with enthusiasm. Lady Rice informed them that the building itself was often considered part of the Metropolitan Museum of Art's collection, as it had been designed by a well-known American architect and finished by his son in what Anastasia learned was called the "beaux arts" style. She let most of the information that followed those tidbits flow over and around her as she wandered through the admittedly beautiful columns and arches of the space, losing herself in the paintings and sculpture exhibited in each of the various rooms.

Anastasia didn't know how long she'd been lost in her thoughts and contemplation when her grandmother gently touched her shoulder to pull her attention from one particular piece.

"What do you think, Nastenka?" Dagmar asked, her lips curving in a gentle little smile. "It's not a bad collection, is it?"

"It's wonderful," Anastasia said, shaking her head slightly.

"Really?" Dagmar raised her eyebrows in surprise. "I would have thought you would have been more cynical. It's not as if this is the first time you've seen fine art, after all."

"Yes, we had lots of 'art' in the palaces," Anastasia said, waving a hand in a tiny gesture of dismissal. "But I always thought it lacked... something. Almost as if it were only for show. Even the treasures acquired by multi-great grandmother Yekaterina seem designed to give the *appearance* of opulence and culture." She lifted her hand and indicated the painting in front of her, a simple piece depicting a young woman in blue sitting by the sea. "This isn't art for royalty; *this* is art for the people, and most of it's a good deal finer than what graced the walls of our family's palaces."

Dagmar half-turned her body to study the piece anew, even tilting her head to the right as she regarded it. "Auguste Renoir," she said, almost sounding as if she was tasting the artist's name. "A French painter. One of those who experimented with nontraditional methods... *Impressionists*, I think they call them."

"I find so *interesting* how she is so clear, her face and body... and yet the background is a blur, a mere suggestion of light and color and movement." Anastasia stared at the painting, unable to look away.

"I suspect that was the idea," Dagmar said with a smile in her tone. "To draw the viewer's attention to the girl's beauty. It *is* a lovely piece."

"Yes," Anastasia said, and then blinked, breaking the painting's spell. She turned to her grandmother and smiled back. "Thank you, Grandmama, for bringing us here. This is an amazing place, and the American people are fortunate to have it. I wonder if—" She broke off, unsure if Dagmar would approve of what she was about to say.

Dagmar's smile widened, and she threaded her arm through Anastasia's, gently pulling her back toward the central part of the museum. "You are thinking that once we recover our palaces and our own collections, that perhaps we, too, should have a museum like this, where anyone may come and enjoy the art? It isn't *all* ostentatious and shallow, you know."

Anastasia chuckled. "That is fair," she said. "Even if our ancestress did not have the most refined artistic taste, there have to be one or two pieces with a soul tucked away somewhere!"

Dagmar joined her in soft laughter, and then sighed. "Darling Nastenka. How quickly you are growing up! I think that allowing our people access to our family's art collections is a wonderful idea, provided..." She trailed off and stumbled just a little.

"Provided there is anything left after the war...and the Reds," Anastasia finished for her, her tone grim. She shivered, though it wasn't exactly cold.

Dagmar didn't answer. The two of them held tightly to one another as they sought to rejoin the rest of their small party.

Anastasia would look back on that moment and see it as the point when everything changed. She didn't know it at first, obviously. It wasn't until years had passed that she could see how that conversation in front of the painting of the woman in blue shaped the course of her entire life going forward.

At the time, however, it had simply been an afternoon's diversion concocted by her grandmother to amuse them and pass the time while they waited for word that it was finally safe to cross the Atlantic.

Dagmar had arranged several such diversions for them—one the very next evening. They were to attend a dinner party with some prominent American citizens. Like the museum trip, the whole thing had been arranged by Lady Rice, who, despite being British, was clearly a linchpin of American society, not just in Washington but here as well.

The party was held at a mansion on New York's Fifth Avenue. Maria hadn't wanted to go, and had pleaded a headache to remain in the hotel. Thus, Anastasia faced the stares and curiosity of New York's elite with only her grandmother at her side. Dressed to the nines, she wore a bit of jewelry, slightly damaged, as a brooch.

Well, Anton Ivanovich was there, too, but he tended to fade into the background, as a good bodyguard must. While he was never out of Anastasia's sight—nor she out of his—no one even seemed to notice him.

No one, that is, until Anastasia's dinner companion.

The gentleman was older, with a mustache and bushy eyebrows that peeked out from behind wire-rimmed glasses. He appeared to have some kind of recent leg injury, for he limped as he approached her before dinner. But he smiled kindly, and politely and properly asked Lady Rice for an introduction.

"Your Highness, may I present the Twenty-Sixth President of the United States, Mr. Theodore Roosevelt. Mr. President, Her Highness, Grand Duchess Anastasia Nicolaevna of Russia."

Lady Rice spoke in a perfectly modulated tone, yet Anastasia would swear that every other conversation had stopped and everyone swiveled to look as the (former, she was given to understand; Grandmama had said that the current fellow was someone named "Wilson") President very properly shook her hand. Not as a commoner greets an aristocrat, but as a gentleman greets a lady of equal social status.

Anastasia flicked her gaze to her grandmother's, who stared back with her polite court mask firmly in place. No help or guidance there.

This is a test, Anastasia realized abruptly. *The Americans are testing me!*

Suddenly very glad that Maria had chosen not to come, Anastasia took a deep breath before speaking, and hoped her voice sounded clear and confident, rather than displaying her nerves and awkwardness for everyone to see.

"Mr. President," she said. "It is a pleasure to make your acquaintance."

Dagmar's eyebrows shot up, but the man in front of her squeezed her fingers and gave her a slowly widening, almost conspiratorial grin.

"Your Highness," he said in a soft, clear voice. "The pleasure is most assuredly all mine."

Conversation resumed around them, and Anastasia felt a great sense of relief. Mr. Roosevelt smiled at her again and presented his arm for her to take. She did so, exhaling softly.

"Well done," he murmured under his breath as they joined the general perambulation of the party guests toward the dining room. "Well done indeed."

"So you *were* testing me, sir?" Anastasia couldn't keep her tone completely devoid of tartness. But Mr. Roosevelt just chuckled deep in his chest.

"You're a quick one, Your Highness. I hope I didn't make that too uncomfortable for you, but I had to see what kind of Imperial Princess you really are."

"Not a very good one, according to my sister."

"The Empress?"

"No, my other sister."

"Ah. Well. On that, she and I disagree. You're in a new place, surrounded by new people. It's good to see that you've yet got a flexible mind, despite growing up in the dark heart of traditional European autocracy." He spoke as if he enjoyed the rhythm of his words, as if he were trying out phrases before writing them into a book. Despite herself, Anastasia began to smile.

"'Traditional European Autocracy' as you put it, sir, has not served my family particularly well of late," she said as they approached the table. "On that point, the Empress and I agree."

Anastasia felt, more than saw, the former President turn to stare at her for a moment in apparent surprise. She did not look at him, but rather allowed herself to be seated and relished the point that she seemed to have scored.

As the meal progressed, Anastasia was slightly surprised to find that she was thoroughly enjoying herself. The food was delightful, and Mr. Roosevelt was a fascinating dinner companion. Despite serving as President, the man had fought in a war against Spain, owned a cattle ranch, and had written books on the subjects of conservationism and life on the American frontier. She had not known any of this before dinner, of course, but found out during the course of the conversation.

Had he been anyone else, Anastasia would have suspected him of bragging, but he didn't simply list these accomplishments for her to admire, but rather mentioned them naturally, offhandedly, as they came up within the general context of the topic at hand.

It was during their discussion of his experiences while fighting the Spanish that Roosevelt mentioned Dostovalov.

"You've got a good man watching your back, there," he said as the staff cleared the latest course. "I had one or two like him in the Rough Riders. Trusted them with my life."

"As I trust him with mine," Anastasia said. "Anton Ivanovich is dedicated to my family."

"A member of one of your household's guards from before, then?"

"Oh no!" Anastasia startled herself with a laugh. "Quite the opposite, actually. He was ... well, he was one of our guards, but it was while my family was captive in Tobolsk. Only he and another fellow became familiar with us, and they helped our forces rescue us ... most of us ... some of us."

"I am sorry for the loss of your parents and siblings," Roosevelt said. "It is a hard thing, I know. You're a brave young woman."

"Thank you," Anastasia said. "But I am not half as brave as my sister. She ... well. You say it is a hard thing to lose one's parents, sir, and so it is. But it is even harder to come to the realization that perhaps one's parents, beloved as they may have been, were not quite correct in everything that they did."

Roosevelt put down the water glass he'd picked up and turned his head to look more fully at Anastasia while she spoke. She drew a deep breath and continued on.

"Tatiana ... Tatiana has done this. Has looked that truth in the face and forced me and others to do the same. I loved my parents, sir, and they loved us above all else. But while they were the best of parents, my sister and I have come to know that they failed as leaders, as rulers. They couldn't protect our family, just as they couldn't protect millions of Russian families all throughout our land ... and that, sir, is the worse tragedy."

Anastasia glanced to the side to find Roosevelt smiling at her, something like affection dawning in his eyes.

"I quite agree," he said. "So, then what, pray, does your sister the Empress intend to do about it?"

Anastasia let out a short, humorless laugh.

"You would not ask me if you knew her, sir. Tatiana keeps her own counsel. She will take inputs and advice, but she gives no sign of what she intends to do until it is time to do it."

"Not a bad policy," Roosevelt said. "Especially for someone in such a precarious position. But given what you know about her, what do you *think* she intends to do?"

Anastasia lifted her wineglass and took a long sip in order to buy herself time to properly frame her answer.

"I think," she said slowly, lowering the glass back to the table. "No ... I *know* that she means to save Russia from the evil of Bolshevism. And she means to preserve our country for all its people.

Those things I know. As to the *how* of it . . . ? Well, there is a war to be won, first. And as I said, she is not forthcoming until she means to be."

"And what would you do?"

"Me, sir?"

Roosevelt smiled. "Yes, you. As you said, there is still a war on in your country. I suspect that's part of the reason you're here. If something—may heaven forbid—were to happen to the Empress, what would *you* do?"

"Well, Maria is the elder," Anastasia said softly, mindful of Tatiana's admonition not to tell anyone about her plans for the succession. "But if it *did* come to me, I suppose I—I would look here, if I am perfectly honest."

"Here? What do you mean? You would abolish your monarchy entirely?"

"No, not exactly," Anastasia said. Frustration surged within her as she fought to articulate the thoughts swirling in her head. "I just . . . would change it. Autocracy cannot work in the modern world. Russia deserves better. Her people deserve better. They deserve a world where anything is possible. Where art and culture and science are available for all. Where a man's birth or station isn't a barrier, but rather just a starting place. Where all are equal under the law . . . and that law is clearly stated and understood by all citizens."

"Do you really think that is possible in a monarchist nation, Your Highness?" Roosevelt continued to smile, but the tone of his voice said that he clearly did not think so.

"I—I think so. Because, well . . . your country has its laws, doesn't it? And you were the leader for a time? Did not your laws delineate your role as President?"

"They do. Our Constitution does, which is our highest law."

"Yes! Well, I think perhaps we could have a constitution, too. One that firmly states the role of the monarch and how she—or he, in the future—interacts with other parts of the government. The elected parts. The Duma, for example."

"A constitutional monarchy? That's a difficult line to walk, Your Highness."

"What does the difficulty matter, if it's the right choice for Russia? They *need* Tatiana right now. She is the symbol of resistance to the Bolshevik evil. Without her to unite the various factions under one banner, the Reds are almost certain to win. Russia needs its Tsarina, and a constitution both."

Roosevelt's smile grew, and he lifted his glass and tapped it against the rim of hers. "Well said, Your Highness. Well said. You're a remarkable young woman."

"If not for my birth, sir, I'd be like every other young woman. I'm surprised to have to remind *you* of that!"

"No, not quite. Not every other young woman could have survived what you have survived," he said quietly. "Nor come out of those experiences with your spirit and optimism intact. I said before that you were brave. But at the time, I don't think I knew the half of it. It has been my honor to meet you tonight." To Anastasia's shock, Roosevelt inclined his head to her in a very proper gesture of respect that would have fit perfectly at court in St. Petersburg.

"The honor has been mine, sir," she said quietly as the staff began circulating with the next course.

"How long will you stay in New York, Your Highness?" he asked a few moments later.

"I don't exactly know, sir," she said. "My grandmother is to take us to London by ship once she determines that it is safe to do so."

"I wonder if you would like to come for a visit to my home of Sagamore Hill. I should dearly like for my wife and daughter Alice to meet you."

"I am sure I would love it," Anastasia said with a smile. "Though I don't know what Grandmama has planned, it may be that I cannot come."

"I understand," Roosevelt said with a smile. "Perhaps I shall bring Alice here to meet you. She's a bit older than you are, but I think you would like her."

"I am certain I would, sir."

At that, Roosevelt laughed. "I wouldn't be too sure. Alice is one of a kind! But I *do* think you might get along famously. There is a chance, at least, that you would."

Interlude

Russian Princesses In New York!

Imperial Romanov Princesses, Grand Duchesses Maria and Anastasia of Russia, were spotted attending a private showing at the New York Metropolitan Museum of Art alongside their grandmother, Former Tsarina Maria Feodorovna, and the wife of the British Ambassador. The princesses were famously imprisoned by Bolshevik forces in Siberia following their father, the Tsar's, abdication last year. Rumors persist that their sister, Tatiana, has claimed the throne as Tsarina.

Reports coming out of Russia have been contradictory, due to the ongoing civil war. It appears certain that the former Tsar and Tsarina, Nicholas II and Alexandra, are deceased, along with at least one and possibly two of their children. At least one Bolshevik report has it that the entire Imperial family perished, but the presence of Maria Feodorovna with the girls in New York City would seem to contradict that claim. (pg. 6)

Chapter Twenty-Six

General Baron Pyotr Wrangel,
known to the Reds as the Black Baron

Ekaterinodar, South Russia

To his staff's surprise, when Denikin received Wrangel's report and acknowledgement of orders, he not only approved of Wrangel's impressment of former Bolshevik troops, he ordered the rest of his subordinate commanders to begin screening Bolshevik prisoners, to see who might be useful in swelling their ranks. Wrangel was an aristocratic ass, but unlike other noble-born cavalry commanders

Denikin could name, the man didn't take foolish risks merely to satisfy his substantial vanity. Despite their differences, Denikin wouldn't refuse a good idea when he saw one.

Really, there was no practical way Denikin could override Wrangel even if he'd wanted to. With the telegraph and telephone wires usually cut and the railways contested, communication with the front was intermittent at best. Reports and orders were most often conveyed by couriers on horseback or motor car. He'd considered making use of his tiny, seven-airplane air force in the role, but they were too valuable and their fuel range too limited to make it a practical option. Trying to manage Wrangel, or any of his subordinate commanders too closely, was a fast way to ensure defeat in the field.

Denikin leaned back in his chair and closed his eyes. He'd never thought he'd be nostalgic for the early, terrifying days of the civil war. The Bolsheviks had stripped him of decorations and pushed him through a jeering crowd of soldiers brainwashed by Marxist propaganda. After a harrowing prison break and headlong flight to the North Caucasus, he and his fellow senior officers had seized a Bolshevik armored train through guile and daring, then rallied other volunteers, creating, almost as an act of sheer will, the Volunteer Army.

Kornilov had been in overall command then, Alekseev his chief of staff. Though facing overwhelming numerical odds and increasingly desperate logistical shortages and personal hardship, Denikin had been content with his duties. All that had been expected of him was that he led his men well and bravely. Sound tactical judgment, and good character—these things were meat to Denikin.

Now Kornilov was dead from a communist artillery shell. Alekseev's ailing health had finished him mere weeks ago.

Once, Denikin had led his army—now he merely commanded it. He longed to leave his headquarters in Ekaterinodar and go to the front, to be with his men. Denikin longed to share their danger and use his own judgment to direct the battle. But if he left the reins of state unattended too long, the consequences could be just as dire as any lost battle.

The survival of the fractious coalition of Cossacks, monarchists, and democrats rested on Denikin. He knew there were some anti-Bolshevik forces in Siberia, but if communication was difficult with his own front lines, it was nearly nonexistent with the eastern expanse of his country. News had reached him of the death of the Romanovs, of the Czech Legion's rebellion against the Reds, as well as American and Japanese troops operating in Siberia, but these, ironically, had come the long way via the Western Allies, and the news was always weeks or months old.

As far as Denikin knew, the Armed Forces of South Russia, which he commanded, were the only native, organized resistance to Bolshevik rule. Not only that, they were the only conduit for the military and economic aid that had finally started to materialize from their allies in Britain, France, and America. He despised his political duties with nearly the same level of vitriol he normally reserved for Germans and Communists, but there was no one else to assume them.

It was late at night, and fatigue was opening the door for melancholy, melancholy Denikin could ill afford to indulge as he made decisions that affected the lives of millions. He stood up, prepared to return to his quarters. His young wife, Xenia, would hopefully have gone to sleep already. She was pregnant with their first child and it hadn't been an easy carriage so far. Still, crawling into bed with her would impart a modicum of peace until the dawn.

An orderly knocked at his door. It was Corporal Timonov. He was a handsome lad with thick black hair and bright, alert eyes. The boy was shy a hand—taken by a malfunctioning grenade. Timonov had lost his parents to the Reds and thus had been motivated to continue the fight despite the loss. Since he was literate, intelligent and had recovered from his amputation due to a surprisingly resilient constitution, he'd wound up working as first one of Alekseev's, then Denikin's, enlisted orderlies.

"Your Excellency, the English colonel, Poole, is here to see you," Timonov said.

Denikin did not allow himself an audible sigh. Poole was his liaison from the Allied Expeditionary Force in Crimea. If the Englishman wanted to see him this late, it was likely something important. Poole was much more serious and steady than the French officers Denikin had been saddled with earlier in the war.

"Send him in," Denikin said.

Poole marched in and saluted crisply. Denikin returned the gesture.

"Good evening, General," Poole said in horribly accented Russian that was, nonetheless, far superior to Denikin's almost nonexistent English. "I'm terribly sorry to bother you so late, but I've just received a spot of news I thought you should know without delay."

"Not at all, Colonel, I appreciate your devotion to duty at all hours, please have a seat." Denikin took the seat at the head and gestured to one of the cushioned dining room chairs to his right. Once Poole was seated, Denikin asked: "What news, Colonel?"

"General, it concerns the former Imperial Family."

Denikin's back straightened and his fatigue vanished.

"What about them, Colonel?"

"The Tsar and Tsarina are dead, murdered back in March by the Bolsheviks in Tobolsk. The Tsarevich and Grand Duchess Olga died with them. I'm sorry, General, I just received the news today."

The confirmation settled on Denikin like a leaden mantle. Though politically progressive, Denikin was still a Russian and he'd seen, firsthand, what the magnificence of the Romanov Dynasty had meant to the people even a few short years ago. He'd never met the Imperial Family personally, but he'd seen the Tsar and Tsarina, and the Grand Duchesses at a military parade in Petrograd. They'd been such lovely, vibrant girls, their murder would be a travesty even if they'd possessed not a drop of royal blood.

Travesty, it seemed, might be Russia's most prolific crop for some time to come.

Whatever the Tsar and Tsarina's faults, and he could list many, it was ill fortune for Russia.

"You say the Emperor and Empress and Alexei and Olga have been murdered—what about the other girls, they survive?" Denikin asked, leaning forward.

"Yes, Maria we have invited to stay in England, though she hasn't arrived yet. Anastasia is in America. I know Your Excellency does not read English." Poole produced a newspaper from within his coat. "But that is the Grand Duchess in their New York City."

The large picture on the front page showed Anastasia in an immaculate dress, smiling while talking to some old men in suits.

"And Grand Duchess Tatiana?" Denikin asked.

Poole hesitated, then, visibly steeling himself, answered the question.

"She remains in Russia with the rescue force that freed her and her sisters. The Czech Legion and other native White forces have rallied to her and—" Poole paused again before plunging ahead. "She has crowned herself Empress of All Russia."

Thick, tense silence settled over the room. It lasted for several excruciating seconds while Denikin tried to process the news. Tatiana was how old? A teenager, still, or *perhaps* twenty? And women were forbidden by law from assuming the throne—an act of spite by Catherine the Great's son that hadn't been challenged in the intervening centuries.

Realistically, though, what was legal or not was of little concern— the real question was could she back her claim to the throne with more than words? Denikin stared intently into Poole's eyes.

"Is your government going to recognize her legitimacy? Will the French and Americans?"

Poole shifted uncomfortably in his seat. In the months they'd worked together, Poole hadn't been prone to hesitation or equivocation; his discomfort hinted at his answer before he started talking.

"It is possible, General," Poole said. "Thus far, none of the Allies have recognized her, and the fact that her rescue force was aided by the Germans is a mark against her as far as our governments are concerned. But as you can see, the Romanov girls are garnering public support rapidly, especially at home and in America."

Denikin scoffed.

"They are teenage girls," he said, leaning over the table. "The Americans are a young people, but surely Englishmen are not so easily taken in?"

"They are orphaned royalty who survived a terrible ordeal at the hands of vile Communists. They are now fighting bravely for their homeland against those Communists," Poole said. "While we English may be more staid and steady than our unruly cousins across the pond, even we are not immune to such an effective drama. It is not lost on us, either, that these are the great-granddaughters of Victoria herself, appealing to us for aid."

Denikin chewed on that—could the Romanovs be the key to increased allied support? How, though? He had always heard that the American isolationists had used Russia's monarchy as a reason to *avoid* entering the war despite ludicrous provocation from the Germans— that since it was not truly a struggle to support democracy against authoritarianism, but merely a struggle of old European empires over territory and pride, it was none of their concern.

Were the Americans so fickle that now the Russian monarchy was supposed to be a good thing?

It didn't matter. The murder of the Tsar and his wife and children was a tragedy, but it did not change the fact that Russia had to move forward into the new century, not backward to the last one. The societal cracks that the Bolsheviks had so adeptly levered to splinter Russia against itself must be sealed, not widened. Denikin kept his opinions to himself to appease the monarchists, but he knew in his soul that the status quo antebellum was dead.

But if the girl was charming the Allies, and if she'd already rallied anti-Communist forces in Siberia—opposing her openly might also weaken the war effort.

"We have several crates of the Em—of Tatiana's propaganda," Poole said. "Here, I brought you some."

Denikin accepted a small pile of leaflets.

"May I have the rest?" he asked.

Poole looked even more uncomfortable.

"I'm sorry, Your Excellency, but no."

Denikin nodded, and smiled sadly.

"In case your government decides to support Tatiana over my objections."

"Just so, sir."

Denikin exhaled mightily and leaned back in his chair.

"Thank you, Colonel Poole, you have given me much to consider. We'll talk again soon."

"Thank you for your time, Your Excellency, good night."

The next morning, Romanovsky read the pamphlets with a concerned frown. Denikin observed his chief of staff's expression from across the map table. The rest of his staff bustled about their duties, sending and receiving messages from couriers, updating ledgers and maps, and steadfastly ignoring the palpable tension between the two seniormost officers in their army.

"The girl has gone mad," he muttered.

Denikin laughed sharply.

"If she has, perhaps we could use some of her particular insanity.

Her forces have already won some impressive victories—and her sisters are wooing the allies far more effectively than I could on my best day."

Romanovsky looked up from the pamphlet.

"Your Excellency, you can't seriously be considering bending the knee to this child?"

When his commander failed to respond rapidly, Romanovsky sputtered.

"She is twenty-one years old, and Nicholas's daughter—if you cast our lot with hers, the democrats and socialists will desert in droves. We might lose half our army."

"And if we don't throw in with her, once it becomes common knowledge that she's calling herself the Empress, we risk losing the other half—to say nothing of the arms, ammunition, food and money we need from our Allies."

Romanovsky waved a dismissive hand at the American newspaper Poole had left on the table the night before.

"A passing fancy, as ephemeral as the plot of one of their moving pictures," Romanovsky said. "Even the Americans are not so naïve as to make policy based on a fairy tale."

"Perhaps, perhaps not. Regardless, we stay the same course for now," Denikin said. "We will express our profound relief that Tatiana and her sisters are alive, our rage at the Communist villains who murdered Nicholas, Alexandra, Alexei and Olga, but we will make no comment on her status as Empress. If pressed, say we are waiting for a chance to confer with her."

Romanovsky was silent for several seconds; his expression still conveyed irritation but his voice was calm when he spoke again.

"I understand your reasoning, Your Excellency. I hope you understand that our lack of a firm position is *also* a liability."

Denikin nodded.

"I do, Ivan Pavlovich, believe me I do. Who would have ever thought we'd long for the blood and marshes of the Great War, if nothing else, but for their simplicity and unity of purpose? I am a soldier, not a politician, but to whom would I give this task but myself?"

A knock at the door drew Denikin's attention. Timonov stood in the doorway, holding a letter in his hand. The boy was smiling broadly.

"I beg your pardon, Your Excellency, but we've just received word from General Wrangel via train—he's taken Stavropol."

Denikin smiled.

"Excellent news. Ready my personal train car—I'm going to Stavropol to congratulate General Wrangel personally."

Stavropol, Southern Russia

The people of Stavropol lined the avenues for miles, throwing flowers at the feet of the parading soldiers. Jubilant shouts echoed off the buildings. Girls and women of all ages darted out to kiss soldiers on the cheeks and put flowers in their lapels. Denikin, marching at the head of the column, smiled at the joyous chaos. His men had certainly fought hard and they had seen precious little of the hero worship they deserved.

Worry still ate at the back of Denikin's mind. Their offensive had culminated before they were able to fully encircle and destroy the Soviet 11th Army. At least a division had retreated northeast, toward Tsaritsyn. He'd sent couriers to warn Krasnov. While he despised the ambitious, petty tyrant, he still had designs to bring the Don Host fully into the fold someday. He only hoped the couriers could make it through in time.

Pushing these worries aside, for he could do nothing else about them, Denikin continued the parade up to a hastily constructed reviewing platform, upon which stood General Baron Pyotr Nikolayevich Wrangel, resplendent in a tailored, black full-dress uniform and flanked by his brigade commanders and senior staff officers. As Denikin mounted the steps to the stand, it occurred to him how tall and regal Wrangel looked in comparison to his own unassuming stature.

Just as the thought began to blacken his mood, Wrangel saluted Denikin with knife-edge precision and announced in a clear, ringing voice: "Your Excellency, I present to you the liberated city of Stavropol!"

The crowd screamed their approval, the earth itself seemed to shake under their stomping feet and the air wavered amidst their shouting and clapping. Denikin returned Wrangel's salute and waited a full minute for the adulation to die down enough that he might be heard.

"General Wrangel, in recognition of your outstanding and courageous achievements, I hereby promote you to the rank of Colonel General and name you the commander of the Cavalry Corps," Denikin shouted.

The crowd roared again, and Wrangel allowed his aristocratic restraint to crack just a sliver, his eyes widening at his sudden promotion. Denikin smiled, gratified that in this, at least, he'd been ahead of the confident cavalryman. Then he took pride of place on the reviewing stand. Wrangel stood a half-step behind and to his right, as was proper, to watch the remainder of the conquering heroes paraded down the streets of free Stavropol.

Denikin's shouting was audible even outside the front door of the governor's mansion. As he entered, Wrangel couldn't make out all the words, but it was evident the Supreme Commander of the South Russian Armed Forces was very displeased with someone. The guards at the large wooden doors saluted crisply and hastened to usher Wrangel in. In the antechamber, an officer with thick blonde hair and a bristly mustache to match emerged from Denikin's office and stalked toward the door.

Recognition was only a few seconds delayed; Wrangel knew this man.

"Colonel Shkuro."

The younger man stopped, meeting Wrangel's eye. Shkuro stiffened to attention.

"General Wrangel, sir, it's a pleasure to see you again."

"Colonel. What brings you to the Supreme Commander's office?" Wrangel kept his tone carefully neutral. Shkuro made a scoffing noise.

"Apparently Denikin doesn't appreciate the initiative that is expected of us cavalrymen. He took exception to my raids on Amira, Kislovodsk, and of course," Shkuro waved a hand at the city surrounding them, "Stavropol."

"*General* Denikin understands that initiative should always be tempered with discipline and good judgment," Wrangel said. "Your raids resulted in thousands massacred by the Red Army when we were unable to take and hold the cities that welcomed you."

"I am to be accountable for what the enemy does when I am not even present, then, General?"

"You are accountable for the reasonably predictable consequences of your decisions, Colonel," Wrangel said. "And were I you, I would speak with more respect of our Supreme Commander."

Shkuro's expression conveyed not an ounce of contrition or regret, but he inclined his head as if acknowledging a good point in a debate.

"Of course, I meant no disrespect to *His Excellency*. If you will excuse me, General, I must see to my duties."

Shkuro fled the building.

Wrangel proceeded into Denikin's office. It was well appointed, with dark brown wood cabinets, a desk to match and red leather chairs—it was a wonder these hadn't been burnt or stolen by the Bolsheviks in the time they'd controlled the city. Denikin was brewing his own tea, a look of frustration plastered on his blunt, bearded face.

"Your Excellency, General Wrangel reports to the supreme commander, as ordered," Wrangel announced.

Denikin nodded acknowledgement and appreciation of the formality, then waved Wrangel to a chair.

"Please, Pyotr Nikolayevich, have a seat. Would you like some tea?"

"Yes, Your Excellency, thank you."

Wrangel settled into one of the red chairs. Denikin finished steeping the tea, then poured it into two ceramic cups, each with a saucer. He walked one of these to Wrangel, then settled, not at his desk, but in the chair next to Wrangel's.

"I passed Colonel Shkuro on the way in," Wrangel said. "He seemed perturbed . . . and insolent as ever."

Denikin frowned and sipped his tea before answering.

"I'm aware you aren't very fond of Shkuro, but he is one of my better cavalry commanders—though clearly not my best." Denikin raised his teacup in a small salute to Wrangel, who reciprocated the gesture before pressing on.

"Personal fondness or lack thereof has nothing to do with this, Your Excellency. Shkuro is ill-disciplined and nearly as bad an adventure seeker as that fool Krasnov. His gallivanting has already incurred tragedy, why leave him in a position to do more harm?"

"I have spoken to him about his poor judgment." Denikin's earlier welcoming tone vanished, replaced by something much frostier. "I believe he still has a contribution to make."

"With respect, speaking isn't enough," Wrangel said, setting his tea down. "Shkuro isn't the only issue, nor even the worst. My God, Pokrovsky's men went through a Jewish village raping everything on two legs and in a skirt and killing anyone who objected, we saw the aftermath with our own eyes. This isn't anti-Bolshevism, it's

Godlessness. You must bring him to heel, we cannot afford for the Russian people to associate the White Army with atrocities."

"Atrocities like shooting three hundred defenseless prisoners?" Denikin asked.

Wrangel's mouth snapped shut, rage sending a thrill down his spine. His knuckles went white on the arms of his red leather chair.

"Three hundred and twenty-seven to be precise," Wrangel replied. "I executed three-hundred and twenty-seven traitors to Mother Russia to salvage a thousand infantrymen, a thousand infantrymen I needed to carry out the orders you gave me, Your Excellency. And if you don't see that difference between that and forcing some poor farm girl to lie beneath an entire platoon before slitting her throat because she happens to be a Yid, then perhaps this conversation is pointless."

The two generals glared at one another for several heartbeats before Denikin exhaled heavily.

"Of course there's a difference," he said, then he smiled ruefully. "Pyotr Nikolayevich, you are my most valuable subordinate. Do you know why? Where another man, promoted from division to corps command, might feel an impulse to thank his commander, your candor demands you open the conversation by criticizing my command decisions and accusing me of failing to instill discipline in my army. Where else would I find such honesty?"

Wrangel's fingers relaxed, and he picked up his teacup, taking a sip to cover his chagrin at the back-handed compliment.

"I beg your pardon, Your Excellency, if I have offended," Wrangel said, his tone carefully neutral. "I maintain that we must address these issues, as harshly as is necessary to quash them."

Denikin's expression clouded.

"I am as horrified by the crimes of our men as you are, but can we realistically bring them to heel? The Cossacks have always supplemented their income with plunder, and the Tsars rewarded them for their brutality against Jews and rebels. We cannot snap our fingers and force two centuries of learned behavior to evaporate. Among the volunteers, almost every regiment has lost its strength many times over, we've just discussed the kind of mobilization we are forced to conduct just to replenish our ranks. Sadly, many of the men we press into service will not be of the highest moral fiber. Their pay, when we can arrange for it, is anemic. It's little wonder they turn to looting."

Wrangel leaned forward in his chair.

"Perhaps we cannot halt all petty thievery, but the rapes, the murders—surely we can do something about that? This is not mere sentimentality on my part, Your Excellency. Every murdered child is a set of parents sympathetic to the Communists, every raped wife is a husband who will happily shoot at us for Lenin, whether he gives a damn about politics or not."

Denikin took a sip of his tea before setting it down.

"I am placing Pokrovsky's division along with the remainder of the Kuban Cossacks under your command in the cavalry corps. They will be yours to discipline. I recommend you make examples of the worst— as publicly as possible, for the encouragement of civilized behavior among our troops and to assure the populace that we intend to protect them. But have a care, Pyotr Nikolayevich—we need these units intact and ready to fight in the spring."

Wrangel pondered this development for a moment—he should've known that by bringing the problem to the commander's attention, he was also volunteering to concoct and implement a solution. Such was an officer's life.

"Of course, Your Excellency," Wrangel said.

"If anyone can bring the miscreants in line and keep them battle-ready for our drive on Moscow, it's you, Pyotr Nikolayevich." Denikin refilled both their cups before continuing. "There is another matter, some news that is both joyous and potentially dangerous."

Wrangel's eyebrows furrowed for a moment as he considered what might constitute joyous and dangerous simultaneously. The answer dawned on him rapidly, and he leaned forward.

"The Imperial family?" he asked. "Is it true? They survived?"

Sorrow pulled at Denikin's round face as he answered.

"Three of the daughters did; Tatiana, Maria and Anastasia are all alive. Tatiana sent Maria to the United Kingdom where she has been received at the court of King George. Anastasia is in America, apparently being entertained by the Roosevelts, and Tatiana is still in Siberia with a rescue force from the Kexholm Guards and some other troops who have rallied to her banner."

The news gave Wrangel several seconds' pause to assimilate. That three of the girls had made it *was* joyous news, but—

"The Tsar and Tsarina are dead? And Olga and little Alexei?"

"I'm afraid so. I'm sorry, Pyotr Nikolayevich, I know you knew them well."

Wrangel's throat constricted. He would shed no tears in public, but his sorrow turned in his chest like a spitted animal. Near the end of the Great War he'd served as Tsar Nicholas's military aide. The man had been a military incompetent who never should have attempted command of an army at war, but he had been unfailingly kind and decent, and his children had been sheer joy. The way all four sisters formed a shell of love and protection around their sickly little brother had touched his heart.

Olga had been such a lovely, generous girl, not unlike a younger version of Wrangel's own wife, also named Olga, who even now worked tirelessly as a nurse in an ambulance unit for the Armed Forces of South Russia. That the Bolsheviks had so callously murdered an innocent teenage girl alongside her parents and poor, broken little Alexei . . .

"We must crush them, Anton Ivanovich," Wrangel said, his voice low and deadly, his aristocratic reserve erased with a snarl of hatred. "We must crush the Communists, wipe all traces of their existence from the Earth so that none ever mutters the name of Lenin or Marx ever again in Russia."

Denikin leaned back in his chair, visibly taken aback by Wrangel's uncharacteristic outburst. But then he leaned forward, grasped Wrangel's hand in a brotherly grip and nodded.

"We will, Pyotr Nikolayevich, we will."

Wrangel took a deep breath and recomposed himself.

"You said the news was dangerous as well as joyous. How so, Your Excellency?" Wrangel asked.

Denikin stood, and walked around his desk, he opened the top drawer and retrieved a pile of leaflets. These he handed to Wrangel as he returned to his seat.

"Tatiana has declared herself Empress of Russia," Denikin said. "Her rescuers are backing her claim. It appears the Czechs are cooperating with her and if she has not already made arrangements with the Americans in Siberia, it's only a matter of time."

Wrangel's eyes scanned a leaflet that was an account of the Romanovs' captivity and attempted murder, and another which outlined Tatiana's call for a constitutional monarchy, land reform, and the extermination of Bolshevism. He said nothing while his mind processed this development.

"I have never spoken to Tatiana, or any of the Romanovs, I've only seen them at parades," Denikin said. "Tell me, Pyotr Nikolayevich, what are your thoughts on Tatiana Romanova?"

Wrangel ran a finger over his short, tightly trimmed mustache.

"Tatiana, though not the eldest, was always the most serious, the most responsible. The other children called her 'the Governess,' for she kept them in line for her parents. She was a bright girl, but never particularly outgoing."

Denikin gave an ironic tilt of the chin.

"Our reports are mixed, but they indicate she has delivered many fine speeches since her liberation, rallying many to her cause. Our English friends think it likely that the Western Allies will recognize her as the legitimate monarch."

Wrangel's eyes absorbed another recruiting pamphlet.

"Truly, the printing press has revolutionized war far more than the machine gun or the combustion engine," Wrangel muttered.

Denikin waited in silence for several seconds as Wrangel read, then, with an exasperated sigh, continued.

"Pyotr Nikolayevich—I need your advice. We both know I am no politician. I have kept this coalition together by saying as little as possible as to what shape the government should take after the final victory, but this twenty-one-year-old girl now forces my hand."

Wrangel exhaled through his nose and nodded agreement.

"It is an extremely perilous situation, Your Excellency."

"In my shoes, what would you do?" Denikin asked.

"Tatiana might make a far better monarch than her father; her ideas as outlined in her propaganda certainly make sense. She is, though, still a young woman, and has been much more insulated from the vagaries of Russian politics than any girl of her class should've been. Granted, the veil of separation her parents had erected had just been ripped violently away."

"This pamphlet," Wrangel held up the paper he meant, "details a plan for land reform, and a new, constitutional monarchy. Something similar to the what the British have, but with more teeth retained by the crown. It might be the path we need to forge ahead without further destabilizing our entire society."

"Perhaps, but can we then sell that to the monarchists and democrats?"

"Maybe." Wrangel's mind worked furiously. "Here is what I would do, Your Excellency—allow her propaganda to circulate, but make no comment on it, at first. Let the English distribute it, but have our officers listen to the reaction in the ranks, in the bars, in the streets. Her story is compelling, her ideas sound, and her list of victories so far, impressive—let them do the work for us. If they resonate, we will take advantage; if they divide, well, we'll have to chart another course."

Denikin tapped absently on the rim of his tea saucer with his middle finger.

"You think it will work?" He asked.

"I don't know, Your Excellency," Wrangel said. "But right now we have every advantage over the Reds save numbers and unity of command. Perhaps this can solve the latter."

"And if her messages do resonate and we then have to subordinate ourselves to a twenty-one-year-old girl as our Empress?" Denikin asked. "What if her leadership itself becomes a liability?"

Wrangel smiled.

"Young she may be, but she is clearly no fool. I do not think she will repeat her father's mistake of trying to do her generals' work for them."

"But you do not know."

"No," Wrangel admitted. "Still, she has survived a harrowing ordeal these last months and made decisions that have seen her power and influence grow despite all adversity."

"A facility for adventure is no guarantor of an ability to rule wisely," Denikin said.

"No, it isn't. You know as well as I, Your Excellency, that all is calculated risk in war, certainty is only ever a deceiver in our profession. I think Tatiana may prove to be a sound wager."

Denikin visible pondered Wrangel's proposal for several seconds before he sighed, stood up, and nodded.

"All right, Pyotr Nikolayevich," Denikin said. "We will try it your way. Let us see how the men and the people respond to Tatiana's appeals. If they do, then we'll discuss how best to align with her. If not, we'll have to persuade the Allies not to throw in with her—somehow."

Chapter Twenty-Seven

"I WANT TO BE SURE THAT ISN'T THE GUN THAT KILLED CASH HAWKINS."

CECIL B. De MILLE'S Production "The SQUAW MAN"
© FAMOUS PLAYERS-LASKY CORP. 1916.

Lobby card found on the street

New York City, New York, USA

I've been to grand balls in some of the most glittering palaces in Europe. Why does this feel so much more exciting? Anastasia thought.

That question hovered behind Anastasia's eyes as she watched the lights of Manhattan slide by outside the limousine's tinted window.

"Are you excited, my dear?" Alice Roosevelt asked, reaching over to squeeze Anastasia's hand. True to Alice's father's predictions, Alice and Anastasia had quickly become close. Anastasia's grandmother was not particularly fond of the association, but as the daughter of a former President, Alice was *just* respectable enough that Grandmama Dagmar had no *real* cause for complaint. And so, for perhaps the first time in her life, Anastasia had a bosom companion who was *not* one of her sisters.

"I am, I find," Anastasia replied with a smile. She returned the affectionate hand-squeeze. "I was just thinking that while I am no stranger to high-profile affairs, this will be my first American film premiere. I hope your press will be kind."

"Oh, they'll love you," Alice said with a wave of her free hand. "A beautiful Russian princess joining the New York social scene? That's exactly the kind of thing they love!"

"I hope so," Anastasia said again. "It's lovely that your youngest brother could join us."

"Yes!" Alice said, her enthusiasm ratcheting her voice up an octave. "It is so good to have him home! We were, of course, worried sick about him and Archie and Ted and Kermit. All four of the boys! This damned war . . . such a terrible thing."

"War generally is," Anastasia said softly, turning back to her study of the lights outside. "But it's not the worst thing."

"Oh! Darling, I'm sorry—"

Anastasia turned back to Alice with a smile and a quick shake of her head to indicate that she was neither offended nor hurt by the comments. She didn't have time for more, however, as their limousine was slowing to a stop outside the theater's lit marquee.

Alice squeezed her hand once more before sitting forward on the seat and pulling the collar of her evening coat close to her neck. An attendant of some kind came up and opened the limousine's door and extended a hand to help Alice out.

Shouts and pops of photographers' flashes rose as Alice stepped onto the red carpet that extended from the car to the front doors of the theater. Anastasia moved closer to the door, ready to step out as well. A quick peek reassured her that Dostovalov stood next to Quentin, who was currently kissing his sister on both cheeks under the photographers' strobing lights. Quentin had arrived in the car ahead of them. Dostovalov had ridden alongside the driver in their own car.

Anastasia was expecting the attendant, but instead Quentin turned and reached down to her. Anastasia blinked, but her childhood court training reasserted itself quickly, and she gave Quentin a smile with the proper degree of warmth and laid her fingers lightly in his.

As she stepped out, the noise erupted into a roar. People shouted her name and her title. One particular flash went off close by, leaving her stunned and blinded by its intensity. She blinked again, hoping that her eyes didn't tear, and looked to the side for Dostovalov.

"Here, miss," he said, his voice a soft, reassuring rumble just behind her shoulder.

Anastasia felt her smile deepen with relief at Dostovalov's solid presence nearby, and so she turned her attention back to the front doors of the theater as Quentin tucked her hand into the crook of his elbow.

The doors swelled, and then bulged out toward them as light spiked around the doors like a corona. Anastasia had a split second to wonder at the cost of such a pyrotechnic effect before the concussion hammered into her, picking her up and flinging her back toward the street as if she were no more than a child's doll.

Somehow, Dostovalov had his hands on her, shoving her down beneath the shelter of his body. She felt the thin silk of her gloves snag on the concrete of the pavement as he rolled her under himself and cradled her face to the side, away from the blast. Heat and noise roared over them, singeing the air as Anastasia fought to inhale with Dostovalov's weight on her back. Sound disappeared, replaced by a high, incessant whine that stabbed through her skull and throbbed behind her eyes.

Anastasia squirmed. The beads on her dress pressed into her neck unpleasantly, and she desperately wanted to *see*. Dostovalov held her firmly in place, however, and she lay there unable to do anything but watch as a charred, flaming bit of the theater's fabric marquee fluttered to the ground an arm's length from her nose.

Dostovalov's weight shifted, then disappeared, and finally Anastasia could drag a full breath into her lungs. The air tasted of burnt wood and metal, and the faint underlying scent of cooked meat.

"—ighness! Are you all right?! Your Imperial Highness!"

Faint sound returned as Dostovalov gripped her shoulders and hauled her up to her feet, his face white and wild with fear. She shook her head to try and dispel the remaining ringing and blinked away the ashy dust that clung to her eyelashes.

"Yes," she gasped. "Yes! Anton Ivanovich, I am fine! I am well! What happened?"

"Anastasia!"

At the sound of her given name, she and Dostovalov both turned to see Quentin holding Alice up by her shoulders. Alice's face twisted in pain and a ragged gash marred the side of her face. Blood dripped from this wound down onto the bosom of her beautiful gown, and she leaned heavily on her brother.

"Alice!" Anastasia cried, and took a step towards her friend.

"Your Highness, we have to get you out of here!" Dostovalov's grip on Anastasia's shoulders tightened, and then suddenly released as he dropped his hands, his face looking, if possible, even more horrified at having manhandled her.

"In a moment," Anastasia said. She reached out and gripped Dostovalov's arm. "Please! I must see Alice!"

Dostovalov nodded, and reached out to help Anastasia as she carefully navigated her way over to the two Roosevelt siblings.

"I am all right," Alice was saying. "It's just a little scratch..." But she trailed off as her knees buckled. Quentin caught his sister, and then bent and hauled her up into his arms, holding her as if she were a small child.

"Sir!" someone shouted behind them, back toward the street. "Sir, over here!"

Anastasia shook her head again as a high warbling started once more. But unlike last time, this sound grew louder and louder, and soon a pair of motorcar headlights cut through the dust-coated gloom.

"Sir!" a man in a police uniform shouted as he ran up beside them. "That's the ambulance. Is she hurt? I'll take her!"

"I'm fine..." Alice started to say, her voice weak.

"You're not, Sister," Quentin said. "Lead the way, man. I'll bring her. You've got her Highness?" He said this last over his shoulder to Dostovalov, who nodded once and presented his arm to Anastasia.

She felt purely ridiculous as she took it, but the truth was that her own legs were none too steady as they picked their way through the rubble and bits of flaming debris towards where the ambulance screamed to a stop. Quentin took Alice to the back and set her down while the medical crew began to clean and examine her head wound.

Anastasia looked around in dismay as clarity started to return to her thoughts.

The once beautiful theater had all but collapsed. The marquee, the postered windows, the box office... none of it remained. Instead, there was only dust and rubble, and—

"Help! Please!"

It was faint. So faint Anastasia thought at first she'd imagined it. But then the cry came again, from beneath a pile of debris. Anastasia took one tentative step toward it, then another.

"Your Highness, what are you doing!?"

"Help me, Anton Ivanovich!" Anastasia cried as she reached the pile. She fell heavily to her knees and began pulling at the shattered bricks and splintered wood. Her poor, abused gloves snagged and tore, but she barely noticed. The cries were getting louder.

"There's someone alive under here, Anton Ivanovich!" Anastasia said, panting with exertion as she continued to dig. "Help me, please!"

"You need to leave!" Dostovalov's voice was raw and rough as he nearly spat the words in Russian. But he, too, crouched beside her and began digging. "I need to get you out of here, now!"

"Please, just let us help this one person first!"

Before long others joined them. Anastasia didn't notice whom. Other voices called her name, called Dostovalov's name, but she kept her focus on the faint cries beneath her hands. Faint . . . and growing fainter.

Finally, Dostovalov pulled aside a broken piece of concrete to reveal a small cavity. Inside, a woman lay, her eyes half-closed, her face pale. For one heart-stopping moment, Anastasia thought she was dead, but then she let out a small moan. Dostovalov muttered something that was either a curse or a prayer and bent to try and pull her free of the sliding, unstable mass of debris.

"Here. Let me help."

To her surprise, Anastasia looked up to see Quentin on her other side.

"Alice?" she asked quickly.

"Our driver is taking her to the hospital," he said, grunting a little as he helped Dostovalov lift the woman's body free. Her legs hung at odd angles, and something seemed wrong with the shape of her pelvis, but she was breathing.

Once more, the three of them trekked back over the treacherous ground to the ambulance in the street. They turned the unfortunate woman over to the medics and stepped back.

Anastasia closed her eyes for a moment and whispered a prayer for the woman.

"Your Highness, I really must insist that you leave now."

Anastasia opened her eyes and looked up into Dostovalov's face. He was no innocent farm boy, but there was an earnestness about the hardened soldier's expression, and she realized with a jolt to her gut that he had truly been afraid. Not for himself . . . but for her.

"Anton Ivanovich," she said softly. "You saved me. Again."

"It is only my duty, Highness. But now we must *go*."

Anastasia shook her head. "We cannot go now."

"Your Imperial Highness—"

"No, listen. We *cannot* go now. Look around you! This place is chaos. There are others buried under the rubble, and we haven't even begun to think about who was inside the building! It would have been us, my friend. It *should* have been us, had the motorcars not been delayed by the traffic in the streets uptown."

"That is why you need to leave. It's entirely possible that this was a plot to kill you!"

"And that is exactly why I *cannot* leave." Anastasia pulled her spine straight and her shoulders back and stared into the furious eyes of her faithful protector. "I will *never* let it be said that a daughter of Imperial Russia runs away scared from a threat. There is work to be done here; we can *help* these people. But I need you beside me. I need you to watch my back and keep me safe. Please, Anton Ivanovich, in the name of my sister, whom you *could not* save . . . please help me save these people!"

Dostovalov swallowed hard, his face going, if possible, even paler in the flickering light from the remaining flames. He stared right back at her, his eyes boring into hers with an intensity that may have, in that moment, carried something of hatred in it.

But slowly, slowly, he nodded.

Anastasia pressed her lips together, closed her eyes and breathed a "thank you" in Russian. Then she reached out and squeezed his arm.

"Thank you," she said in English, for Quentin's benefit, for he stood very near.

"It's about to get quite chaotic," he said. "The police are on their way, and the fire department, but—"

"Anton Ivanovich and I are staying," Anastasia said, her voice firm. "I have seen war before and nursed soldiers at their bedsides. We can help these people."

Quentin looked from her to Dostovalov, and then back to Anastasia before giving her a tiny, approving smile.

"Her Highness help," Dostovalov broke in then, his English as rough as his voice. "I guard her back."

"Good man," Quentin said. "All right, then, Princess. Let us begin."

It got worse.

They didn't find another survivor, though they found quite a few mangled bodies in the rubble. True to Quentin's prediction, it became quite chaotic as more and more bystanders rushed to help. Anastasia found herself playing the role of coordinator, making sure that they searched each section of rubble thoroughly, literally leaving no stone unturned.

Not long after they started their search, a fire broke out, and Anastasia suddenly had the unpleasant realization that she knew exactly where the scent of roasting meat originated. Still, she shoved that thought to the back of her mind and set to as part of the hastily formed "bucket brigade." She'd never heard the term before, but when Quentin said it with a jaunty grin, she had to admit that it fit.

Despite his protestations, Dostovalov did, indeed, assist with the search and recovery efforts. He would not, however, leave Anastasia's side. Several times, she looked over at him to find him peering into dark corners and puddles of gloom, his hand resting softly on his hip where she knew he concealed a pistol.

"He worries about you," Quentin said at one point, while the two of them worked together to clear yet another pile of debris.

"He is my *telokhranitel*. My . . . bodyguard. He considers my safety a matter of honor."

"Sure, but it seems more than that. Almost . . . familial? He looks to you the way I look to Sister."

Anastasia pressed her lips together and glanced over at Dostovalov. He met her gaze, his eyes asking if she was all right. She gave him a reassuring nod and a smile before turning back to Quentin.

"If things had been different, he might have been my brother of a sort. If I had been a different girl, from a different family. Or he a different boy . . ."

"Different how?"

Anastasia fought the sudden, completely inappropriate urge to laugh. It wasn't funny. Nothing was funny about their current situation, and yet there it was.

"I know you are American, Quentin Roosevelt, but you cannot be that naïve. My sister was the daughter of a Tsar. Anton Ivanovich Dostovalov is a common soldier."

"And yet he loved her."

"And she, him. I think."

"This was Olga? Your eldest sister."

"Yes."

Quentin's hands stilled for just a moment. Anastasia glanced up at his face.

"I am very sorry, Princess, for your losses."

Startled, Anastasia blinked, and then gave him a half-smile. "Thank you," she said. "Thank you for saying that, but others have lost much more than I."

"Still. I see what my father meant when he said that you were older than your years."

That *did* make Anastasia laugh, a bitter, hollow sound.

"War has that effect, sir, as I'm certain you would agree."

"So it does," Quentin said, returning her half-smile. "So it does."

A shout of warning went up from another group as more flames surged. Quentin and Dostovalov reached out at the same time and grabbed Anastasia, both pulling her back from the fire.

She caught her heel on a broken piece of brick and nearly fell. Just as the two men held her up, a blinding flash exploded in her face and she gasped. Another explosion?

"Your Highness, over here!"

Another flash burst in front of her eyes and all of a sudden, Anastasia realized what was happening. The press had arrived.

Many of them, anyway. Most of the bodies they pulled from the rubble had been buried with the smashed remains of cameras.

"Let me stand," she said softly, first in English and then in Russian. Then she turned toward the voice crying her name and raised a hand to block the flashes that resulted.

"What is your name?" she called out into the blinding light, as the wavering siren of yet another fire truck or ambulance rent the air.

"My name, Princess?"

"Yes, you! The one with the camera! What is your name?"

The flashes never stopped, but a voice called back. "I'm Sam, Your Highness!"

"Sam. There are several of your fellow countrymen and women here! Please, come help us rescue them!"

"I'm a reporter, Princess, I can't get involved."

Anger surged through Anastasia, making her lift her chin and stomp her slippered foot on the uneven ground.

"Sam, I am a Grand Duchess of Imperial Russia! Anton Ivanovich Dostovalov is a soldier and my bodyguard. Lieutenant Roosevelt is an aviator and war hero and yet we do not hesitate to get involved! These are your fellow reporters, man! I promise you, if you put down your benighted camera and get to work, I will grant you an interview myself . . . after!"

The flashes finally stopped.

"You mean it? An exclusive interview?"

"I did not say exclusive . . . but yes. I will grant you an exclusive interview *if you help us help these people!*"

"Oh, masterfully done," Quentin breathed behind her, so softly that Anastasia could barely hear. She didn't acknowledge his compliment, but simply blinked as her temporary flash-blindness faded and she got a look at the tall, thin man approaching.

"I'll help, for an exclusive," the man—Sam—said. He pushed his hat back on his head and looked around. "Where do you want me?"

"Get on the bucket brigade," Quentin said. "And help us enlist the help of any other reporters who show up."

"Holy smokes . . . You're the President's son!"

"You're a quick one, Sam. Now grab those buckets!"

By the time it was over, Anastasia couldn't remember ever being so tired. Her body ached from head to toe, though she couldn't really say if that was from the work or from Dostovalov hurling her to the ground and covering her from the blast. Her poor silk gloves had been shredded, and hung in ragged ribbons from her wrists, and her beautiful beaded gown was torn in four places. Fortunately, none of the tears were enough to compromise her modesty, but she was certain that Sam's photographs would show her a disheveled, battered mess.

Grandmama will be appalled, she thought tiredly as she leaned her head back against the seat of the Roosevelts' motorcar and closed her eyes. It was long past midnight, and the police and fire department had finally gotten the theater blaze contained enough to dismiss the bucket brigade and send them home. Anastasia was certain they'd found everyone who could be found in the wreckage...

Mostly certain, anyway.

"Your Imperial Highness, we have arrived," Dostovalov said from the front seat. Anastasia opened her eyes and looked around in confusion. This was not the Plaza entrance!

"I had Cole bring us to the back entrance," Quentin said quietly from the seat beside her. "I thought you might want to avoid any further scrutiny, at least until you have had time to rest."

"Oh, *thank you*," she said. "You are exactly right, Que—Lieutenant Roosevelt."

Quentin smiled at her misspeak. During the chaos at the theater, they'd certainly used first names with each other. But even though they were but a few blocks away from the scene of the disaster, they'd entered an entirely different world—one where propriety reigned supreme, and young men and women in the public eye must tread a careful line.

"I will call tomorrow, if I may?" he asked as Dostovalov exited the motorcar up front and walked around to open Anastasia's door. "To check on you?"

"Perhaps not tomorrow," Anastasia said. "The day after might be better. I will have much to explain to my grandmother."

"Of course."

"If you would be willing, though..." She trailed off as a thought occurred to her.

"Anything."

"Well, I thought perhaps we could talk to that reporter together. Sam."

"Sam. Works for the *Times*. That's a good idea. My father knows some people, too. I'll have him check out old 'Sam' as well. You're going to try and spin the interview?"

"I think I must, if I understand your term 'spin' properly. It is obvious that the story cannot remain out of the public eye. Therefore, we must control the story."

Quentin let out a little laugh. "You sound like a politician."

Anastasia gave him a wintry smile. "I am a daughter of Imperial Russia. It is the same thing."

Quentin's laugh stilled, and he looked intently at her for a moment, and then grinned. "It was an honor to labor beside you tonight, Your Imperial Highness."

Surprised, Anastasia blinked. "Thank you, sir," she said. "The honor was mine."

"*Feldfebel* Dostovalov, I was proud to work beside you tonight as well. Keep taking care of her Highness."

"With my life, Lieutenant," Dostovalov said from his post beside the door.

"Good man. Goodnight to you both," Quentin said. Anastasia nodded at him and turned to let Dostovalov hand her out of the vehicle. He closed the door behind her and they both waited until Cole, the Roosevelt driver, pulled the car away before turning.

"I could almost have you carry me, Anton Ivanovich," Anastasia groaned. "Everything hurts."

"Shall I carry you?" Dostovalov paused, as if he would sweep her up into his arms as Quentin had carried Alice.

"No. But thank you. I think I will need to be on my feet when I speak with Grandmama."

Dostovalov didn't say anything . . . which meant he agreed.

Chapter Twenty-Eight

Anastasia, on her own, New York City, New York

"Your Highness. Your Highness..."

Anastasia opened her eyes to the sound of her maid's soft voice. She blinked and pushed herself up to a seated position, stifling a groan as her abused muscles protested. Next to the bed, the maid she shared with Maria dipped into a curtsey.

"Your Highness asked to be awakened when Her Imperial Majesty rose."

"My grandmother is awake?" Anastasia asked, pitching her voice low so as not to wake the sleeping Maria on the other side of the bedroom.

"Yes, Your Highness. She is taking breakfast in the small parlor just outside."

"Thank you. I will join her. Have you a day dress ready?"

"I have the light blue—"

"That will be perfect, Yelena. Thank you."

Yelena dipped into another curtsey, and then helped her mistress stand on aching, sore legs. Anastasia stretched her arms up over her head, letting out a hiss of pain as she spared a moment's longing for the hotel's well-appointed bathing chamber and the deep claw-footed tub therein. A soak in hot water sounded like pure heaven . . . but not right now.

She had more important things to do. Like face her grandmother.

Yelena had her dressed and coiffed in a matter of minutes. Anastasia flinched when Yelena's skillful fingers brushed over a bruise in her hairline.

"Are you all right, Your Highness?" Yelena asked, her voice threaded through with worry.

"I'm just finding new bruises. You heard about the explosion at the theater last night?"

"We are all grateful to God for Your Highness' safety."

"Yes, well. Grateful to God and to Anton Ivanovich Dostovalov, perhaps. He shielded me, but he could not exactly be gentle in the process. Does my grandmother know?"

"I believe she does, Your Highness."

Anastasia took a deep breath and squared her shoulders. "Well, then. I suppose I must speak with her. Thank you, Yelena, I think that is the best you will be able to do with my hair today. I appreciate your help."

Yelena dropped down into another curtsey and Anastasia rose to her feet. She took one more look in the vanity mirror, noting the slight purpling above her temple, and pursed her lips. Then she smoothed her face, steeled her spine, and turned to go and face her grandmother.

"Good Morning, Your Majesty," Anastasia said formally as she entered the "small parlor" that sat at the center of their suite of rooms. She kept her head high as she walked over to the table where her grandmother sat and dropped into a curtsey of precisely the correct depth and reverence for a Grand Duchess addressing a Dowager Empress.

"Oh, my dear," Maria Feodorovna said. Fabric swished and rustled as she came to her feet, and Anastasia found herself caught up in her grandmother's perfumed embrace.

She let her own arms come up around her grandmother's shoulders and cling.

"My darling," Dagmar said into her granddaughter's hair. "Are you all right?"

"I am, Grandmama," she said. "Thanks to the grace of God and the quick reactions of Anton Ivanovich Dostovalov."

Her grandmother pressed the third finger of her right hand against the corner of her eye, blinked rapidly, and resettled herself in the chair she'd been using.

She gestured to the chair next to her, and Anastasia took the invitation to sit down. Nerves kept her spine ramrod straight, however, and she mostly perched on the edge . . . but it was better than standing.

"What I do not understand," Dagmar went on as one of the attendant footmen stepped forward to pour steaming, fragrant coffee into the mug in front of Anastasia, "is why he did not *immediately* return you to this hotel once the explosion happened."

"Because, Grandmama, I asked him not to."

Dagmar arched an elegant eyebrow at her granddaughter. "Perhaps you had better start from the beginning . . . and leave nothing out."

Anastasia smiled her thanks at the footman and took a sip of the coffee. Normally she preferred tea, but she needed something to brace her nerves, and the strong, bitter flavor would do. She lowered the mug, took a deep breath, and then looked up to meet her grandmother's piercing gaze.

"As you know, Alice Roosevelt invited me to accompany her to the film premiere. She did warn me that it was public, and that there would likely be press there, so *Feldfebel* Dostovalov came along as my *telokhranitel*. On the way to the theater, our motorcar was held up by a traffic snarl on a side street, so we arrived a few minutes after we'd intended to do so. Lieutenant Roosevelt had just helped Alice and me out of the motorcar—"

Dagmar held up a hand. "Lieutenant Roosevelt?"

"Lieutenant Quentin Roosevelt. Alice's youngest brother."

"The President's son?"

"Yes. He was an aviator in France during the war. He's returned home. The press call him a war hero."

"I imagine they do." Dagmar lifted her own mug, her tone cynical. "He was with you and his sister?"

"He took a separate motorcar that arrived just before ours, but yes. He was there."

"And you were photographed with him?"

"Well, with him and Alice . . . and *Feldfebel* Dostovalov, I suppose. We were all standing together as Alice and I exited the motorcar."

Dagmar nodded. "And then—?"

Anastasia felt her pulse accelerate. She inhaled slowly through her nose to try to compensate.

"And then," she said. "The front of the theater exploded. Somehow, Dostovalov managed to shield me under his body, but the force was powerful enough to blow what had to be tons of brick and stone into the air. Alice was thrown into the motorcar and injured. Quentin—Lieutenant Roosevelt—rescued her and sent her to the hospital in the motorcar with his driver."

"He did not go with her?"

"No, Grandmama. He stayed, as did Dostovalov and I, to help find any survivors and to try and find the bodies of those who did not survive."

"This is the part I do not understand, Anastasia. Why would you do such a reckless thing?" Dagmar leaned forward, her cheeks flushed with something that may have been anger.

"I had several reasons, Grandmama," Anastasia said. She'd rehearsed this argument in her bed as she waited to fall asleep, and her voice felt high and tinny as the memory of the scent of scorched dust and roasting meat teased at her, making her stomach twist.

Dagmar lifted a hand in an invitation for her to continue.

"First," Anastasia said, "I heard someone calling for help. Under a large pile of rubble and debris. So, I started to dig them out and Dostovalov and Lieutenant Roosevelt helped. It was a woman, and she was badly injured. We put her in the ambulance, but I do not know if she will live. But I couldn't just leave her there to die in agony, buried alive."

Dagmar swallowed, but her eyes remained hard. "And then?"

"Then," Anastasia went on, "there was the issue of appearances. You see, the press was already on scene. Most of the victims were their own coworkers, there to photograph the people arriving for the premiere. They'd *seen* me . . . and they would see me and take note if I showed any sort of cowardice."

"It is not cowardice to protect oneself."

"No, but I had my *telokhranitel* and an American war hero with me.

And we *were* able to help, Grandmama. Not just that first woman, but in general. It was chaos, but Lieutenant Roosevelt and I . . . perhaps we are used to command, I don't know. But I know that when we began telling people how to organize themselves, they listened. We were able to search the rest of the wreckage for survivors. When the fire started, we were able to form a bucket brigade to keep it from spreading until the Fire Department could arrive with their equipment . . . and the press saw all of it."

"You do not think it will damage your reputation to be seen working like a common laborer?"

"Grandmama, this is not our world. This is America. They *pride* themselves on working! They *love* to work and, frankly, despise those who don't work. The richer they are, the harder they work. I do not think it will damage my reputation at all. On the contrary, it will *make* it!"

Anastasia couldn't have planned for better timing if she'd tried. At that exact moment, a member of the staff came in with the morning's folded newspapers on a tray. Dagmar raised her eyebrows in challenge as she turned her upper body to pick up the morning edition.

"Let us see, shall we?" she said. She flipped open the paper to the section she wanted and smoothed it down on the surface of the table. Anastasia held herself entirely still, refusing to fidget even as nerves and nauseating memories tangled deep in her gut. Dagmar's eyes scanned the tiny print of the news sheet, her face composed and showing nothing.

When she was finished, she folded the newspaper again and turned back to regard her granddaughter.

"This says you promised an interview?"

Anastasia swallowed and nodded. "Yes, Grandmama."

"You did not think to consult me first?"

"I did not have time, it was the only way I could get the reporter to put his camera down and actually *help* us. Besides, it seems obvious that since we cannot control the press directly, we must . . . what did Quentin call it? 'Spin' the story to our advantage."

"And you think you have the skill to do that?" Dagmar asked, her eyebrows rising up toward her hairline again.

"I think that if you help me prepare, I will," Anastasia said. "I know that this troubles you, Grandmama, but I genuinely see an opportunity here. The United States is a young nation, yes, but they are wealthy, and they have resources that could be incredibly helpful to our cause. Tatiana said it herself, if we are to survive, Imperial Russia must grow and change with this new century. We will need new allies as well as our traditional friends . . . for where were those friends when my father needed them?"

"The United States would not have intervened to save my poor Nicky," Dagmar said, her dark eyes narrowing in pain at the reminder.

"Perhaps not, but if I can win the hearts of their people, they may intervene to save his daughter. Tatiana *needs* men and materiel, Grandmama. More than I truly understand, if I am honest . . . and after the way the war has wrecked most of Europe . . . well . . . the United States may very well be our best chance."

"But they are different, these Americans," Anastasia went on. "I have been studying them since we landed in San Franscisco, and they do not think in old ways. They claim to eschew aristocracy, and yet they elevate their own pseudo-royalty in their newspapers and follow them with obsessive interest."

"Actresses and businessmen!" Dagmar said with a dismissive snort.

"Yes," Anastasia said, "And politicians. And remember, Grandmama, these politicians are elected by the will of the people. If we can make the people love us . . . love our cause . . . we may perhaps maneuver their government to the point where they do not dare to refuse our pleas."

Dagmar sat silently for a long moment, her dark, unreadable eyes boring into her granddaughter's.

"And you think you can do this?" she asked again, but this time her tone was less dismissive, more solemnly inquiring.

"If you help me, if you teach me, then yes, Grandmama. You are the best in the world at wooing a populace. You had our common folk eating out of your hand when you were Tsarina. Everyone says so. If you teach me, then yes. I not only think I can do this, I *know* I can."

"You will have to remain here. You will not be able to come with us to London as we had planned."

Anastasia nodded. "Alice has invited me to stay with her family for as long as I like. I believe she did so at the behest of her father, the former President."

Dagmar pursed her lips. "From what I've learned of her, I do not like Alice as a companion for you," she said. "She is too vain and self-centered. She thinks only of her own pleasure and not enough about the effect of her actions on her family."

"I think that was true several years ago, Grandmama, but she is no longer a young, wild woman. And more importantly, the American press love her . . . in part because of her wild past."

Dagmar tilted her head to the side, as if to acknowledge that Anastasia had a point.

"It is unorthodox, to be sure, but a former President of this country is probably of adequate status—barely—to host a daughter of Imperial Russia for a visit. Roosevelt is popular with the people, yes?"

"He is," Anastasia said. "More so with the working classes than the rich, I believe, but he is popular enough that he intends to run for another term."

"And when would this election be?"

"Next year. 1920. They have them every four years."

"Hmm." Dagmar lifted her coffee to her lips, her eyes staring at Anastasia over the rim as she sipped.

Anastasia waited. Her instincts told her that her grandmother would not be pushed or manipulated. So, she waited and let the dowager empress come to her own conclusions.

"You are determined to do this?" Dagmar asked.

"I am," Anastasia said, hoping that her grandmother wouldn't hear the nerves in her voice.

"Very well. If this is what your conscience says is the best way for you to help your sister, then I will help you. I do not relish being parted from you, my dear Nastenka, but it may be that you are correct about these Americans."

Anastasia tamped down on the flare of triumph that surged within her chest. She leaned forward and reached out to take Dagmar's smooth, long-fingered hand in her own.

"Thank you, Grandmama," she said quietly. "Thank you for believing in me."

For just a moment, Dagmar gripped her fingers with surprising strength that spoke of her own well-concealed emotions. Then she let go and straightened in her chair.

"So. Here is what you must consider, then," she said, turning to butter a piece of her toast. "You have already begun to do this, I believe, but you must continue to study the American character. Find out what they love, what they applaud. It will not be all the same things that I emphasized during your grandfather's reign, but many of the same principles will apply. Above all else, you must understand this: every person, whether man, woman, or child, common or noble, wants to *matter*. I could never make your dear mother understand this, may God bless her."

Anastasia swallowed hard and nodded. She had loved her mother, of course, but she could understand her grandmother's point. Mama had been shy at best when dealing with people outside their own circle. It had not made for an easy—or successful—tenure as Tsarina.

"We will begin with this interview of yours. Tomorrow?"

"Yes, Grandmama. I have asked Lieutenant Roosevelt to come, too. So that he can contribute his perspective. I could ask *Feldfebel* Dostovalov, but I do not think he would be comfortable being interviewed in English."

"Hmm. Yes, and let us not draw attention to his role as your *telokhranitel*. That will be better for your safety."

"As you say, Grandmama."

"I will sit in on the interview. You must ensure that what you say is completely above reproach. If you are going to do this successfully, Anastasia, you must be *pristine* in the public eye."

"Grandmama, I would never—"

"I know you think you would never do anything to damage your reputation as a daughter of Imperial Russia, but you must take extra care. If you are attempting to influence public opinion, you will need to draw attention. That means that there can be no cause for reproach . . . not even an imaginary one."

"Yes, Grandmama."

Dagmar lifted her cup again. "I will think further on this. I must write to Her Imperial Majesty, of course. We will need to take further precautions for your safety, especially if, as you hinted, the bomb was targeting you."

"It could have as easily been targeting the Roosevelt children—"

"I don't think so," Dagmar said, shaking her head. "Perhaps if their father had been attending. Elections do bring out the worst in people; they're a terrible idea, really. But nothing in recent American history suggests that his children would be considered political targets. If, however, the damned Reds have people here . . ."

"They do," Anastasia said quietly. "They'd almost have to. And such rhetoric is legal here . . . all rhetoric is legal here."

"Yes. Another flaw in the American system, to be sure. We will have to augment your security. I have a thought, but I must see if . . . well. I have a thought. I will think on it further."

"Grandmama," Anastasia said, her throat growing suddenly thick with emotion. "Thank you."

"For what, dear child?"

"For . . . trusting me. For believing in me."

"Oh, my dear." Dagmar set down her mug and her food and turned toward her granddaughter, opening her arms in invitation. "I have always believed in you," she said as Anastasia leaned forward to accept the embrace. "I always knew you would do great things, I just wish that your parents were here to see it."

Anastasia sniffled in a most undignified way. "Me too, Grandmama," she said. "Me too."

Interlude

✠

**IMPERIAL RUSSIAN PRINCESS
PROBABLE TARGET OF THEATER BOMBING!
EXCLUSIVE INTERVIEW INSIDE!**
By Samuel Graymount

Her Imperial Highness, Grand Duchess Anastasia Romanov was attending the New York City film premiere of *The Squaw Man* when an explosion rocked Manhattan on Thursday night. Despite being the probable target of the bombing, the Princess was unhurt, though her friend and companion Alice Roosevelt (daughter of former President T. R. Roosevelt) suffered minor injuries. Most remarkable of all, though, was the Princess's reaction to the destruction. Alongside war hero and flying ace Lieutenant Quentin Roosevelt, who has recently returned from the war in France, the Princess leapt into action, working to free the few survivors trapped in the rubble, and search for the remains of those unfortunates who lost their lives. New York police are investigating the cause of the bombing, but as the Princess is the sister of the beleaguered Tsarina of Russia, Tatiana I, it is not hard to guess who and what was behind the dastardly crime. (pg. 4)

Chapter Twenty-Nine

The Ipatiev House,
now the seat of Government of the Russian Empire

Ipatiev House, Yekaterinburg, Russia

While Tobolsk had been safer than Yekaterinburg, safety—security—is a defensive measure . . . and wars are not won by defense. Then, too, here was what amounted to the newly reformed Imperial Treasury. Here was industry, both in terms of extraction of raw materials and potentially the processing of those same materials into arms and supplies.

Here was where the seat of government, for the nonce, had to be.

Here, too, was a comfortable house, a mansion, really, the Ipatiev House, commandeered from Ipatiev by the Reds, now rented by the Imperial Government, with the rent being held in escrow on Ipatiev's behalf.

Bochkareva's former command, now under Princess Tatuyeva, had had a serious job scrubbing out all the blood left by their assault when Mokrenko had retaken the city for the empress. There was still the stump of a broken bayonet stuck in the wooden stockade wall.

Lastly, and perhaps most important of all, here was Aunt Ella, whom Guard Captain Turgenev had also suggested, and in the strongest possible terms, ought not be moved any distance after her ordeal. Turgenev hadn't explained the precise nature of the ordeal— perhaps he didn't know all of it and hadn't wanted to ask—but from what he had seen and relayed Tatiana still had a pretty good idea of what had been done to her aunt.

"She needs you now more than you need her," Turgenev had wired.

Ella herself, and such as had survived among her party, had a private wing of the local *lazaret*.

Tatiana lowered the newspaper clipping and let her eyes return to the handwritten note from her sister. Anastasia assured her in the strongest language that she was well, and begged Tatiana's leave to remain in New York while Maria and their grandmother continued on to London.

"Send General Kostyshakov in, please, and ask my aunt if she's up to coming here for a visit," Tatiana said, her eyes not leaving the page. She heard the page's footsteps rapidly retreating, and a moment later, a soft cough told her that Daniil had arrived.

"Yes, Your Majesty?"

"Whom can we spare to send to New York?"

"Truly, no one. But Bochkareva should arrive there any day. Why do you ask?"

"My sister has decided to stay there and try to promote our cause with the Americans. It is a good thought, and a good plan ... but there has already been an incident of violence. She is safe, thanks in part to Dostovalov, but—"

"I will find a contingent."

Tatiana drew in a deep breath and shook her head. "No," she said. "You are right. We need every man here, and with the addition of Bochkareva's forces, the Guards we sent with my sisters should be enough. Perhaps Bochkareva can stay with Anastasia while Maria goes on to London ..."

Daniil took another step towards where Tatiana sat at her correspondence table.

"If Your Majesty needs me to send more men, I will send more men." He spoke softly, in the tone she knew was hers alone.

"No," she said again. "There is no need. It was just my first impulse.

I—I sent them away so that they would be safe! But it appears that nowhere in the world is safe."

"We fight every day to change that, Your Majesty, you know that."

"I do," Tatiana said with a sigh. "I am just tired. And worried. Thank you, Daniil."

"Anything you need." He bowed at the waist and then as he straightened, he brushed his fingertips across his chest in a gesture that only they knew.

My heart, he said, *is yours*.

Tatiana nodded and touched her own fingers to her breast under the guise of adjusting her shawl.

"There's one other thing, Daniil. If your duties permit, I'd like you to pick up and escort my aunt here this evening after dark."

Nodding understanding, his eyes held hers for a second, and then he turned and left the room.

The Tsarina looked back down at the letter from Anastasia and smiled.

Despite the night's chill, Tatiana stood outside the Ipatiev House's stockade, waiting. She interlaced her fingers, keeping her hands clasped tightly at her waist so that they would not tremble. Her knuckles shone white in the paltry light from the entryway behind her.

"Your Majesty, please," her guard said, his voice pained. "It is cold, and you are terribly exposed. We will alert your staff as soon as they have arrived—"

"There is no need," Tatiana said, her voice as icy as the wind that whipped through the narrow space between buildings. "They are here."

She pointed down the lane to the left, where a pair of headlights knifed through the gloom as a lone vehicle navigated the last turn before pulling slowly up to a stop before the entrance. Her guardsman muttered a soft curse that Tatiana ignored as she allowed him to push her behind the dubious shield of his body as he stepped forward, his rifle at the ready.

"It's all right, Nagorny. I can see that she has not been content to wait inside where it is warm and safe." Daniil's voice, pitched low but clear, carried across the small space between the vehicle and Tatiana as he exited.

"It would not have been safe, neither for you, nor for your aunt. Now, I beg of you, *go inside*. We will be right behind you."

"But—"

"Every moment Your Majesty delays is another moment both you and your aunt are in danger. Please get inside the stockade."

Tatiana raised her chin and glared at Daniil from behind her erstwhile guard.

"Very well," she said, her voice going even colder. "Bring her in." She turned on her heel and stepped through the stockade gate, then strode back to the main door, thence to the small parlor that she'd been using as a sitting room.

Tatiana stepped into the room and strode toward the large fireplace where a footman was busy stirring the coals to life. He nodded deferentially as she murmured a quiet "thank you" before turning to look expectantly at the heavy wooden door.

She didn't have to wait long.

Another footman pushed open the door and stood to the side, allowing her to see Daniil waiting in the darkened hallway beyond.

"The Grand Duchess Elisabeth Feodorovna," the footman said. "And Major General Daniil Kostyshakov."

"Thank you," Tatiana said again, though she wasn't really paying attention to the niceties of her serving staff. She only had eyes for the veiled figure behind Daniil. She watched, swallowing hard against pain and tears as he led this figure forward into the room, then stepped back out of the way and closed the heavy door behind himself.

"Aunt Ella?" Tatiana whispered.

The woman in front of her lifted the veil that obscured her face and removed it from her hair; hair that had once been the same rich chestnut as her sister—Tatiana's mother.

It was now a snowy white.

"My dear girl," Ella said, her voice hoarse and trembling. She held out her arms in invitation.

Tatiana reached, tears blinding her eyes as she rushed to embrace her aunt. As her arms went around Ella's ribs, the older woman stiffened and let out a soft sigh. But she wrapped her own thin—far too thin!—arms around Tatiana and held her close in a trembling, almost desperate embrace.

"Thanks be to God you're alive," Tatiana whispered. "I had so feared—"

"Thanks to God and your soldiers," Ella murmured, letting go and stepping back. "I was—it was a very near thing."

Tatiana swallowed against the thick emotions rising in her throat and nodded. Then she looked up and met Daniil's eyes. "I must speak with my aunt in private. Please leave us."

Daniil held her gaze with his own somber one for a long moment and then nodded, gesturing to the guard to follow him as he turned to leave.

"And, General," Tatiana called. Daniil paused and turned to look back at her.

"Thank you."

He nodded and left the room, closing the door behind him with a soft *click*. Tatiana took a deep breath, then faced her aunt and took hold of her slim, slender hands.

"Come, let us sit," she said, and led Ella over to a low, comfortable sofa beside the fire. Ella followed, as docile as a child, and said nothing while Tatiana saw her seated and covered with a warm, crocheted throw blanket.

"Your majesty is fussing," Ella said, a thread of humor winding through her tone as Tatiana poured tea for them both before sitting down next to her. Tatiana gave her a small smile and a tiny, one-shouldered shrug.

"I don't know what else to do. These things are small comforts, perhaps, but I fear they are all I have to offer right now."

"Dear girl," Ella said, putting her tea down on the low side table and reaching out to take Tatiana's hand in both of hers again. "In that you are most grievously mistaken. What you have already done has given me the greatest comfort of my life."

"Aunt, I'm so sorry," Tatiana whispered. "I—I read the report. I know roughly what happened... before you were rescued. I am so sorry my men didn't find you sooner—"

Ella smiled, and while a vestige of dark, screaming horror flickered in her eyes, the expression felt genuine to Tatiana.

"You must not think that way," she said, squeezing Tatiana's fingers. "What was done... what those men d-did..." She trailed off, swallowed hard.

"Aunt Ella—"

Ella held up her right hand, closing her eyes and bowing her head in a silent plea for a moment.

"God gives us trials so that we might build our faith, child. I . . . those men were angry and ill-used. They had been misled into rejecting God, rejecting decency. Their minds had been clouded by sin and violence. They h-hurt me, and my fellow sisters and brothers in God's service . . . but we prayed for help, and help came. Because of you, my dear. Because *you* chose to fight back, for our family, and for Russia and her people."

Ella opened her eyes, and they glistened wetly in the flickering firelight. Tatiana felt her own eyes fill and a hot line of tears ran down the curve of her cheek. She sniffed in a decidedly unladylike fashion, but one hand held her teacup and saucer, and she wouldn't have pulled the other one from her aunt's grasp for all of her ancestors' fortune put together.

"My body will heal," Ella said. "Has mostly healed, in fact. With prayer and faith, the nightmares will fade in time. I-I may no longer lead my order, but I know that God has work for me yet to do. For while I pray daily for the strength to forgive those men . . ." She turned to stare into the fire for a long moment.

I suspect, thought Tatiana, *that so far God has answered your prayers with a resounding "NO! Some things are never to be forgiven!"*

Tatiana sat quietly, letting the tears run silently down her face as she bore mute witness to her aunt's pain and struggle. Ella had famously forgiven her husband's murderer, but Tatiana couldn't imagine praying to forgive the men who had violated the sanctity of her own body. The very thought made bile burn in the back of her throat, and she swallowed several times quickly to keep that sudden nausea at bay.

"There are others like them," Ella said, her voice low, and harder than Tatiana had ever heard it. "Others will suffer at their hands if God's order and law are not restored. He has called you to restore them, my dear girl. And I am told that you wish me to stand by your side."

"Yes," Tatiana said in a half-whisper. "I said that, but that was before . . . I wouldn't dream of pushing you. If you're not ready—"

Ella smiled. "Who is ever ready? That is not the point. The point is that you have called me, and God has called you and I . . . I live to serve God. The men who raped me cannot take that from me."

Tatiana blinked against the sudden flood that obscured her vision. She pressed her lips together and nodded, breathing through her nose in an attempt to keep her composure. She closed her eyes and continued nodding, even as Ella took the teacup and saucer from her hand, setting them down with a *clink*.

Then her aunt's thin arms wrapped around Tatiana again, hard as iron bands. She returned the embrace, and felt Ella's body start to shudder with silent sobs of her own.

She didn't know how long they sat there: two women holding each other and weeping for all that they had lost, all that had been done to them and those they cared about. But before too long, Tatiana found herself drawing in a ragged breath and sitting upright.

Then she laughed, as she and Ella both reached up to wipe beneath their eyes in the exact same mannerism at the exact same time.

"You are so strong," Tatiana said. "I pray that I can be a fraction as strong as you."

"On the contrary," Ella said. "I am, of myself, quite weak. It is God who is strong. Lean on your faith, my dear. He will never lead you astray."

"Well, and now that you're here, you can help keep me on the right path." Tatiana offered a watery smile with this tiny attempt at humor. To her great satisfaction, Ella let out a soft, delighted laugh, and for just a moment, Tatiana saw the echo of the beautiful young girl her aunt had once been.

"I shall do my best, Your Majesty."

Interlude

"So, the little Russian bitch is going to address both houses of Congress, is she?" President Woodrow Wilson folded the newspaper he held and stared over it at "Colonel" House.

"I'm sure she means to beg for troops to save her sister. She got Roosevelt to set it up. She's probably warming his bed along with his son's. Hard to blame the old man, she's a pretty enough girl." House shrugged and swirled the whiskey in his lowball glass.

"Can't fuck her way into an army, though, can she? Though one might almost admire her dedication if she tried!" The president smiled at his own joke, and House obligingly guffawed in appreciation.

"Still," Wilson went on. "I wonder if we should aid the chit. Bolshevism has an annoying tendency to encourage the lower classes to get uppity. And we can't have that."

"You think we should send men to Russia?"

"I think we should see what effect her speech—or her sexual gymnastics—has on Congress, and then decide. There are many pieces in play on this particular board, my friend. It's important to keep them all in view."

Chapter Thirty

President Theodore Roosevelt

Washington D.C., USA

Anastasia drew in a deep breath and let it out slowly. Roosevelt patted her softly on the shoulder.

"Have courage," he murmured under his breath. With a wink, he added, "Remember they're just a bunch of old men."

She was sorely tempted to scowl up at him for that comment, but the heavy wooden doors in front of her were already opening, and someone she couldn't see was announcing her name and "recognizing" her.

They'd been planning this moment for over a month. Anastasia had done the preliminary groundwork in the newspapers to get the public interested in her cause. Roosevelt had pulled the strings and called in the favors to get her here. And now the time had come. She straightened her spine, forced herself not to look at the American leader who had become her mentor and father-figure, and proceeded to walk slowly forward to take the podium at the center of the room.

Roosevelt had explained to her the stylized and formal rules that went along with making an address to the United States Congress. In a way, it wasn't terribly different from some of the court appearances she'd learned about as a child. Only instead of appearing to beg for the favor of an autocrat, she had a much more difficult task.

She had to convince a roomful of old men that it was in their interest to help her.

Remember who you are, she told herself. *Remember who Tatiana needs you to be.*

With every step she took, light glinted off the crystal beads scattered across the surface of her gown. She knew that if she moved just right, the gems in her jeweled tiara would throw rainbow fire in a halo-like effect around her head. The grand sapphire nearly the size of her palm sat in the hollow of her throat, the centerpiece to a five-strand pearl choker. Her long satin gloves covered her arms up to the elbow. She presented a perfect picture; a picture of the Imperial Grand Duchess she'd once been.

That was the starting point.

"Gentlemen of the United States Senate," she said, once the formalities had been observed and it was time for her to begin. "I thank you for the honor of your welcome and I appreciate the opportunity to speak with you today."

One of the men, a rangy, skinny fellow with a sallow face and a frown, stood. The man in charge—she couldn't remember what he was called, though Roosevelt had told her—recognized him, and he leaned forward.

"Before you start, Duchess," the sallow-faced man said, his voice almost, but not quite a sneer, "you should know that it doesn't matter how much you beg, this assembly will *not* vote to send American resources to take sides in your civil war!"

Anastasia met his eyes as coolly as she imagined Tatiana would have done.

"Thank you for that information, sir," she said. "But I assure you. I have not come here to beg at all. I have come to tell you a story."

"We're not children, to need to listen to stories—" sallow-face began, but the leader of the assembly rapped a gavel on the bench before him.

"We are obviously going to listen to what the Grand Duchess has to say," the leader said, his deep-timbred voice quelling in tone. "That is, after all, the purpose of this inquiry. However, it will take much longer than it should if we do not let her begin. I move that any further commentary or questions be held until after she has said her piece."

"Seconded!" another man called out from the gallery. This led to another round of formalities: voting, counting... Anastasia stood motionless and silent through it all. Roosevelt had warned her that something like this might happen. Not all of the men in the crowd were friendly to her cause. Maybe not even most of them.

Finally, however, the leader of the assembly recognized her once again and invited her to tell her story. He stated that none of the men there would interrupt her. She inclined her head with a tiny smile toward him in thanks.

"Gentlemen," she said, her mind working quickly. "I find I have even further reason for gratitude, especially toward you, sir." She made eye contact with sallow face, who scowled back at her. "What a wonderful demonstration of the inner workings of your republic! Thank you for allowing me to see the mechanisms by which you resolve disputes in a wise and civil manner.

"I had planned to begin my address to you tonight by telling you of how I have been studying the documents of your heritage. The Declaration of Independence, and your Constitution. I *have* been studying them, for they are fascinating and inspired works... but I find that I would like to begin with something else, tonight.

"When I first arrived in New York City," she said. "I was taken on a private tour of the Metropolitan Museum of Art. If you have visited there, you know that it is a treasure trove of beautiful masterworks from many lands and many eras. I confess, I was quite affected by the art I found there. Now you must understand, I grew up surrounded by beautiful things. My many-times-great-grandmother, Yekaterina II, known to history as 'Catherine the Great,' collected art from all over Europe, as have several of my other ancestors.

"But what I saw in New York was different. It had something that those beautiful, ornate family treasures I once knew did not have. It had a *soul*. Its purpose was neither to impress, nor overawe, nor was it created in an act of sycophancy.

"The art I saw there was art for the *people*. It was created for the enjoyment not of one family, but for everyone who experienced it. It was not locked behind some guarded palace walls, but it was in a beautiful building that welcomed the people of New York City, and indeed the people of the United States, if they could get to it.

"I was so moved by this experience. I thought, surely, this is a unique place! But no. I have learned that right here in Washington D.C., there is a series of museums dedicated to art, history, and industry, which all are welcome to explore!

"And I thought back to my ancestors' treasures and thought, wouldn't it be wonderful if every Russian citizen could come and see these beautiful things whenever they liked?

"In the time that I have sojourned here in your republic, my eyes have been opened to so many new thoughts and ideas. Not just about art, but about government, and culture, and science, and economics! And I confess to you gentlemen, in every case there was one fevered, passionate thought that seared its way through my brain.

"*I want that for my people as well!* The Russian people are very like you Americans, you know. We are each a strong, proud people inextricably linked to our vast nations, with all of their diverse regions and resources. We are a people who value strength and laugh defiantly in the face of death. And we fight, oh, how we fight for what we believe to be right!"

Anastasia took another deep breath and cast her eyes theatrically down to her hands in front of her on the podium. She let her voice thicken slightly as she said the next words.

"My father was a good father, but he was not a particularly good ruler. He had the chance to make things better for our people, yes. But, the prejudices of his past haunted him, and he saw it as his duty to preserve his autocracy. He did not have, as you gentlemen have, the benefit of an inspired Constitution to guide him in his role. Perhaps if he had, things would have gone differently for him . . . but we will never know.

"Because a cancer has taken root in my beloved home, Gentlemen. The cancer of Bolshevism, which lies so contrary to the free market principles that I see in practice everywhere I go in America, has taken my home and turned it into a war-torn wasteland.

"The Bolsheviks have taken those treasures that once belonged to my family. They say that they are the property of the Russian people... but I ask you, where are they? Where are the priceless masterworks my ancestors collected? They have not been seen, they have not been *enjoyed* by anyone but the Red leaders squatting in my family's former homes while they burn and pillage and murder their way across the land they claim to be fighting for!"

Anastasia paused then, tilted her head to the side, and gave a small smile. A quick scan of the room showed that a good portion of the men's eyes were riveted to her. A few of them whispered among themselves or looked down at papers they held. Roosevelt stood across the room, near the door she'd entered. He gave her a smile and slow nod of encouragement. She inhaled and continued on.

"But none of that really matters," she said, shrugging one shoulder. "In the long run, of course, art matters a very great deal, but when one lives in a war zone, it is often not one's first concern."

A few dry, appreciative chuckles rippled through the audience from some of the older men. Veterans of the U.S. Civil War, two generations ago, perhaps.

Conscious that those whispering had stopped, and those doing their paperwork had looked up, Anastasia reached to the nape of her neck and unfastened the clasp of the choker she wore. It came loose in her hand, and she held it there, staring into the sapphire's depths for a long moment before she spoke again.

"Two years ago, my father abdicated his throne. Shortly after that, my family was taken into custody. For our protection, they said." Anastasia emptied her voice of all emotion as she said these words. She let her eyes go dark and cold, and she felt the effect ripple through her now-riveted audience.

"Little by little, they took everything we had. They moved us from our home in Tsarskoye Selo to a house in Tobolsk. They took our own guards and replaced them with angry men, evil men, who wanted nothing more than to harm us.

"My mother, who was, like my father, blinded by her love for us, bade us girls to take our jewelry and hide it, sew it into the fabric of our clothing."

She turned the sapphire over in her hand, letting it glint in the lights that focused on her.

"She thought we would be rescued, you see." Anastasia let her voice go wistful and sad, and she glanced up from the gem with a tiny smile that matched her tone. "She knew it would happen, and she wanted us to have some means of exchange when it did. I remember sewing this sapphire between the ribs of my stays, so that it sat directly over my heart."

In point of fact, it had been just below her heart, up hard against the ribs beneath her breast. She remembered feeling its bulk pressing against the bone.

"When the rescue did come, it did not come easy. My little brother—" She stopped, her voice and throat genuinely thick as she thought of Alexei's sweet, determined face. She closed her eyes, let one glistening tear fall, and then inhaled sharply and soldiered on.

"When the rescue came, the evil men who held us knew their time was short. They activated a grenade and tossed it into the room where they'd herded us for control. My brave, doomed little brother gave his life to save us. He said . . . he said that though he could not live like a boy, at least he could die like a man protecting his family as he threw his wasted body atop the thing to absorb the blast."

A ripple went through the crowd. Roosevelt had said that it would be a good sign if they reacted that way, but Anastasia couldn't think about that right now. She had to keep going, or she'd never finish the tale.

"Finally, the rescue force found us, but while they were preparing to extract us from the house, one of them, a Bolshevik spy, opened fire on my whole family, spraying bullets wildly from side to side. My father died instantly, mother too. My oldest sister Olga was hit in her beautiful face, but the rest of us . . ."

Anastasia lifted the sapphire high and angled it so it would flash blue in the light.

"Tatiana, Maria, and I lived. Saved from the hail of lead by the fortune in gems and jewelry we had sewed into our clothes. *This sapphire stopped the bullets that would have ripped through my heart!*"

She stopped, panting for breath after that last, passionate cry. No one moved, no one spoke, not a paper rustled as she slowly lowered her arm and laid the sapphire dead center on the edge of the podium.

"But how many little girls," she whispered without looking up, hearing the acoustics of the room carry her voice to the back corner.

"How many little girls did not have sapphires to wear as armor? How many little boys?" She circled the front facet of the gem with her forefinger and then stopped, frozen for one single heartbeat.

Then she looked up, letting all of her rage and fear and intensity blaze in her blue eyes.

"How many of *your* children don't have jewels to sew into their clothing? Because make no mistake, gentlemen of the United States. If we do not stop them, the Bolsheviks will not be content with raping Russia.

"They are coming for you as well."

Anastasia let that dire sentence hang in the air of the room as she let her fingers trail once more over the jewel's chipped facets. Then she stepped back and away from the podium before she spoke one single sentence more.

"A gift for you, and for your children."

Without another word, she curtseyed as she would to leader of a foreign nation . . . for wasn't that what these men were, collectively?

And then she turned, head held high, and exited the chamber.

Chapter Thirty-One

Alice Roosevelt

Washington D.C., USA

An exultant Teddy Roosevelt exclaimed, "My dear, that was a triumph. An absolute triumph!"

Anastasia dragged in a shaky breath and nodded, then closed her eyes and focused on inhaling and exhaling for a few minutes. Fine tremors started in her hands and worked their way up her arms and through the trunk of her body. She felt Alice's slender arms come around her shoulders and hold her close. Alice hadn't been in the chambers when she addressed Congress, but she had waited for them in the anteroom outside.

Now they were back at the Roosevelts' townhouse in Washington, and Anastasia felt the control that had sustained her throughout the performance drain away, leaving her reeling.

"Come, my dear, have some wine," Roosevelt said.

"Just give her a moment, Papa," Alice murmured over the top of Anastasia's head. "That cannot have been easy for her to do."

"No, I suppose not." Anastasia heard the sound of Roosevelt's cane as he limped away, then the sound of a decanter clinking against glasses. "But I must admit, she was magnificent!"

"Was I?" Anastasia asked, her voice muffled against Alice's shoulder. "I hardly know. I feel so . . . I don't even know what to call it."

"That's how you know it's a good speech," Roosevelt said with a chuckle in his words. "And yes. Magnificent. Superb. That bit with the sapphire at the end . . . masterful, my dear. Simply masterful. I will be amazed if you do not get a vote tonight, or tomorrow at the latest."

"Do you think they will vote to send aid?"

"I think it's likely. There are some hardline isolationist holdouts still, but you certainly made their task more difficult. Either way, my dear, you have done something extraordinary today. I am proud to know you."

Anastasia straightened up at that, and met Alice's questioning eyes with a tremulous smile. "Thank you," she said, speaking to both father and daughter. "Thank you both, for everything."

"Oh, my darling friend," Alice said. "Thank you! You've brought such color and . . . and purpose into my life! You've become part of our family, and I couldn't love you more if you were my own sister."

Anastasia smiled at her friend, content for the moment to bask in their love.

But somewhere, deep inside her mind, Alice's words sparked an idea.

The following day, they departed for Sagamore Hill. Anastasia would have preferred to stay and await the vote in Congress, but contrary to Roosevelt's optimistic prediction, there seemed to be yet more wrangling to be done.

And Roosevelt himself had fallen ill.

"It happens," Alice had said grimly. "More often than I'd like. It's a legacy of his dratted Amazon expedition. The only thing for it is rest at home."

"Then we should take him home," Anastasia had said. "It's not as if we can do anything from here other than wait anyway."

"That's what I think, too."

So, they left early and arrived in mid-afternoon. The sight of the Queen Anne-style house gladdened Anastasia's heart, easing a pressure she hadn't realized she'd been carrying in her chest. She found herself smiling, her shoulders relaxing as she stepped up onto the porch.

"Welcome home, Father, Sister . . . Princess."

"Q!" Alice shrieked, wrapping her arms around her brother's neck as he strode out of the house and onto the porch to greet them. He hugged Alice, and then his father, whom he helped to navigate the steps up and into the house where Mrs. Roosevelt waited.

Anastasia followed them in, returning Ethel Roosevelt's smile. She didn't say hello, though, as she didn't want to interrupt the woman as she was busy trying to make her sick husband comfortable.

Quentin and his mother took Roosevelt back to his room, and Anastasia followed Alice back to the guest room she'd been assigned when she'd first come here. What a strange place this had seemed back then. She could hardly believe it had only been a few months ago.

It didn't take Anastasia long to settle her belongings and wash her face and hands. She thought about lying down to rest after the journey, but a wild kind of restlessness jangled along her nerves. So instead, she ventured back out onto the porch to watch the evening sky darken.

"Nice evening, isn't it?"

Anastasia turned with a smile as Quentin stepped out to join her.

"It is," she said. "I understand why you all love it here so much. There's such a sense of peace and serenity. How is your father?"

"He will be fine, the tough old bird. He just needs to rest."

"I am glad to hear it. He is a very special man."

"Yes," Quentin said, clasping his hands behind his back as he came to stand beside her at the porch rail. "He is."

They stood in silence for a while, side by side, watching dark silhouettes of birds as they hunted in the growing night. Gradually, the light from the windows seemed to glow brighter and brighter as the gloom deepened, until Anastasia felt hidden in the dark.

"Do you think they will send aid to your sister?" Quentin asked, his voice soft.

"I do not know. I hope they will. I hope that everything your family has done for me will not be in vain."

Quentin let out a short chuckle. "Anastasia, it would not have been in vain! Alice has loved having you here, and Father—he loves you, you know. Just as if you were one of us."

"I love him too," Anastasia said softly. "Though it feels terribly disloyal to my own father to say so. There could not be two more different men and yet...both absolutely devoted to their children."

"What was he like?" Quentin asked. "Your father. The Tsar."

Anastasia smiled, even though she knew her face was in shadow and Quentin likely could not see.

"He was very kind," she said. "And incredibly loving. I think my mother and our family was his entire world, and that's what led to his downfall. He could not see beyond his love for us."

"That sounds like a good quality."

"Not in the ruler of an empire, it is not."

"Not much of a romantic, are you?" Quentin said, that dry humor of his clear in his tone. Anastasia's smile grew and she shook her head.

"I cannot afford to be," she said. "For I am my sister's heir. I wasn't supposed to say that but, nonetheless, I am."

"That seems a harsh sentence, though. A life without love."

"I never said I would not love," Anastasia protested, angling her upper body to face him. "Just that I cannot afford to be romantic. I have always known that I would choose my marriage partner from a pool of politically suitable candidates. Nothing has changed in that respect.

"But I *will* be able to make that choice. My sister has given her word that she will not compel either me or Maria to marry anyone we do not wish to wed. But she also cannot afford to let us marry where it would be a liability to our cause. This is just reality."

"That sounds pretty loveless and cold."

"On the contrary! Why should I not *grow* into love with the man I choose?"

"You don't believe in love at first sight?"

Anastasia chuckled. "I am beginning to think that *you* are the romantic here, Lieutenant!"

"Not me," he sighed. "I don't believe in love at first sight either. Once, maybe. There was a girl...but her father didn't find me—what was it you said?—'politically suitable'? And so, she broke it off when I was in France."

Anastasia put her hand over his. "I am sorry, my friend. That must have been hard, especially while you were so far from home."

Quentin nodded; she could just make out the motion. "It was. Thank you."

"What a strange thing, too, that he should find you politically unsuitable. Here I have been thinking that you are quite the opposite."

Quentin froze. Then he, too, turned so that the light from the windows would more clearly let him see Anastasia's face.

"What do you mean?" he asked.

Anastasia's pulse began to race. It wasn't exactly the same feeling as she'd had before speaking to Congress . . . but it wasn't too far different, either.

"I mean," she said slowly. "If we could work out the details . . . I think you would be an admirable consort for a Tsesarevna."

"Are you proposing marriage to me, Princess?" Anastasia thought she heard a hint of a smile in his tone, but his eyes stared intently at her.

"I suppose I am," she said, ignoring the flutter of nerves in her stomach. "If you are interested. We already know that we work well together in a partnership. And the press would love it! The American people would be over the moon if I married an American man!"

"Gee, you really know how to make a fella feel good about himself," Quentin said, still laughing.

Anastasia shook her head. "I will not apologize for keeping our cause first and foremost in my mind," she said, allowing a hint of frost into her tone. "Not when failure to do so could spell disaster for what remains of my family, and my entire nation."

"No, no, you're right, of course," Quentin said, the laughter draining away from his words as he reached out to take her hands. "It's just . . . this is very much not the way I saw myself becoming engaged."

"But would you? Like to become engaged? To me?"

He looked at her, his smile softening. "I think . . . I would. If, as you say, we can work out the details. I assume your sister must agree."

"She already has," Anastasia said quietly.

"She has? How long have you been planning this?"

"Not long, but when I wrote to tell her I was staying with your family rather than continuing to London with Maria and Grandmama, her reply reminded me that I was supposed to be looking for a consort. Then she said that 'in a pinch, the son of an American President might do, but make sure he is rich, and of noble character.'"

"Did she truly?" Quentin threw back his head and laughed. "What a gas! Well, do my financial and character qualifications meet the Empress's standards?"

"I am confident that they will," Anastasia said. "Especially if you bring American aid with you as a bride price."

"*That* would be fine indeed." Quentin's smile faded. "Congress just *has* to pass the bill. It's just the right thing to do."

"I think you and I both know that people don't always do the right thing," Anastasia said.

"No, they don't... but that doesn't mean we can't stack the deck in our favor. I think you're right. If we announce an engagement this week, maybe with our old friend Sam from *The Times*, the resulting outpouring of popular support very well may have an impact."

"But only if you want to marry me," Anastasia said. "With everything that entails."

"What would it entail?"

"Leaving America, eventually. Becoming a Russian citizen, and a prince. Converting to the Russian Orthodox church, performing duties such as my sister will require... and changing your name."

"My name?"

"Well, not *your* name precisely. You will be known as Quentin Teodorovich. But you will be a part of the House of Romanov, and our children must be Romanovs."

"Roosevelt Romanovs, surely?"

"That is not our way, Quentin."

"I beg to differ, Anastasia. Is that not how 'cadet branches' of royal houses are formed? But it doesn't matter. I have three brothers to carry on the Roosevelt name if necessary. I suppose I can become a Romanov."

The fluttering of nerves became a slow tingle of excitement that spread throughout Anastasia's body.

"Do you mean it, truly?"

"I do, *if* you can answer one question for me."

"Ask."

"You said you hoped that you would grow to love the man you chose. Can you promise me, on your honor, that you will actively seek to love me? Because you are right. To my chagrin, I suppose I *am* a bit of a romantic. And I do not see how a marriage without love can endure."

Anastasia found herself once more smiling in the dark. "I give you my word," she said. "I will actively seek to grow more in love with you every day. Will you promise me the same?"

"I will," he said. And for the first time, Quentin reached up and trailed his fingertips across her cheek as he tucked a wayward strand of hair behind her ear. "I am half in love with you already, you know."

"I am, too," she admitted. "We do seem to fit rather well."

"I agree. So, if you're going to propose, you should probably be about it."

Anastasia laughed again and leaned into his caress.

"Lieutenant Quentin Roosevelt, will you do me the honor of becoming my husband and consort?"

"Why yes, Your Highness. Yes, I will."

American Princess!

Grand Duchess Anastasia Romanov to marry Quentin Roosevelt, son of former U.S. President Theodore Roosevelt! The couple announced their intention to wed in the spring in two ceremonies. One to be held in New York, and one in Russia! (pg. 6)

Chapter Thirty-Two

Pyotr Krasnov, *Ataman* of the Don Cossacks

South of Tsaritsyn, South Russia

The red brick walls and brass domes of the Cathedral of Alexander Nevsky dominated the hillside upon which sat the city of Tsaritsyn. To the North and East of the city, the blue-black waters of the Volga River flowed from here all the way onward to the horizon and Siberia beyond. The view would've been idyllic were it not for the battle raging about the city.

Amidst the buildings on the southern edge of the city, sparkles of muzzle flashes from rifles and machine guns, and the crack of their rounds zipping through the air, underscored the earth-shaking blasts and gray-orange plumes of artillery pieces firing southward.

To the south, yellowed grasslands and trampled crop fields stretched miles to terminate in forested hills. Krasnov's Don Cossack host was arrayed upon those fields. Thousands of men, now dismounted, advanced under murderous machine gun fire and lethally accurate artillery bombardment. The Reds had 105mm and 152mm pieces in the city. With fields of fire miles long, they were able to shell the attackers along their entire axis of advance.

Krasnov gritted his teeth. The Cossacks were still advancing despite the winnowing of their ranks. It was a bloody, slogging advance, but Krasnov could feel the defense of the city cracking. His own artillery was emplaced now—and they opened fire with a thunderous counterbattery barrage, giving the advancing Cossacks a modicum of relief from the voluminous enemy shelling.

The repetitiveness of the campaign for Tsaritsyn had worn on Krasnov and his men over the course of the summer and fall. In the open steppes approaching the city, his commanders had maneuvered deftly, enveloping Red formation after formation in the open field, securing railway station after railway station. Thousands of prisoners and tons of war materiel fell into Krasnov's hands.

Many had lamented the death of cavalry as a useful arm, but this campaign had proven them still very much relevant—under the right conditions.

Denikin's objection had proven warranted, though—while the cavalry still had its place, the taking and holding of cities was work for infantry and artillery. The river and terrain meant that his cavalry could not envelop or surround Tsaritsyn, at least not before it was reinforced by the Reds, and charging headlong into well-prepared artillery and machine guns astride a horse *was* indeed lunacy, especially in narrow city streets that created fatal funnels. Thus, they had reached the outskirts of the city once before and been driven back, only to surge forward again, today.

His Cossacks had long since learned the basics of dismounted skirmishing and assault in the course of the Great War. The idea being to move rapidly, utilize cover, and alternate between sprinting and crawling forward to make oneself a harder target. The issue was that they had done so in platoons and troops to eliminate machine gun nests and enemy strong points. The Don Cossacks had never conducted a dismounted attack as a massed, divisional-sized formation. Thus, they advanced across the plain in an uncoordinated lurch. When combined with the stark lack of cover and concealment leading up to Tsaritsyn, there was no way to take the city that wouldn't inflict a brutal butcher's bill.

This time, though, this time they had enough men, enough shells: this time they would break through.

The drumbeat of hooves pummeling the earth became audible even over the artillery duel playing out before him. Krasnov turned south. A man in the uniform of the Volunteer Army galloped toward his command post upon a great, gray horse.

"General Krasnov, General Krasnov!" the man shouted as he reigned in his horse a mere five feet from where Krasnov and his staff observed the battle. "I must speak to General Krasnov!"

Krasnov stepped forward and put a soothing hand on the horse's neck, calming the beast which was still tramping its feet after ending such a headlong sprint.

"You've found him, man. What message have you from General Denikin?"

"General, I am two hours ahead of a Soviet rifle division," he said, breathing hard and pointing southwest. "They've overcome your pickets and will threaten your rear shortly."

"No," Krasnov snarled, looking at the cracking defenses of Tsaritsyn, at the field full of Cossack bodies before him, then back south in the direction the messenger pointed. "No!"

"General, you must withdraw your forces, or else they'll be caught and butchered on this plain."

Yard by bloody yard his men advanced—but not fast enough. The defenders were losing their nerve—but not fast enough. Even if his assault reached the city, it was an impossibility that he could have his men reorganized and ready to defend it in two hours.

Pride and vanity flared in Krasnov's soul, demanding he make a valiant gesture, charge forward and lead his men to a seemingly impossible victory. But Krasnov's pride and vanity, though each great in their own right, were no match for his ambition and will to self-preservation.

"Sound the general retreat!" he shouted at his deputy commander, then grabbed one of his aides. "Run to the artillery, tell them to intensify their rate of fire to cover our withdrawal, melt the barrels if they have to."

Having made his decision, Krasnov wasted no time in issuing sensible orders, and by his cleverness and the skill of his Cossacks, the Host survived the day, retreating south and east into the Don River Basin, to fight another day.

Toward evening, having successfully broken contact with the Soviets, Krasnov boarded his personal train car to make the remainder of the trip to Novocherkassk. He did not sleep; his mind would not let him as it churned through every possible stratagem to shift the blame for this failure onto anyone but himself and maintain his role as *Ataman*.

Novocherkassk, South Russia

Though Russia's suffering seemed only beginning, the Great War was over. Word of the armistice had finally reached Southern Russia. Krasnov couldn't know, of course, but he assumed the Allies had carried word to the White forces in Siberia as well. Germany had lost. Worse—the Allies, no doubt informed by that sycophant Denikin, knew he'd courted the Germans before their defeat, invited them to greater influence inside Russia's borders.

When he'd reached out to the English to try and set up an independent line of supply for the Don Host, they'd told him bluntly to route any and all requests through General Denikin's headquarters.

In a final indignity, the second Krug of the Don Cossacks, now with the majority of the population free of Communist dominion and able to vote, had just this morning ousted him in favor of Bogayesky.

Where another man, having fallen so far, might look longingly at a round chambered in his revolver, Krasnov inhaled deeply and began packing his things.

Pyotr Krasnov had risen from nothing before. He would do it again. As always, on his own terms.

Denikin and Wrangel stood next to Denikin's personal train car, discussing the events of the Krug and other matters at play in the world. Obolensky stood at Wrangel's side, Romanovsky at Denikin's.

"Bogayesky seems eager to cooperate with us," Wrangel said. "It will be a great boon to have the Don Host at our disposal."

"It will, indeed," Denikin agreed. "What's more—we've received an advanced party from the Americans. If they are to be believed, they will be reinforcing us with a full division of veteran infantry and a brigade of their tanks. The floodgates have also opened for food, money, arms and ammunition. We'll have doubled our artillery strength by March."

Wrangel smiled at the news.

"It seems Grand Duchess Anastasia has done yeoman's work as a diplomat," Wrangel said, allowing his tone a bit of wryness.

Denikin inhaled sharply, a sour look crossing his face as he exhaled, but he nodded. "She has, indeed. And the troops and our people have responded to Tatiana's propaganda much as you predicted they would."

Wrangel chose not to say anything, letting the silence draw out and Denikin's contemplation to breathe.

"You were right, Pyotr Nikolayevich. I will write a letter to Her Majesty and inform her that the Armed Forces of South Russia stand ready for her," Denikin said. "And that we will make every effort to link up with those forces already directly at her disposal so we may unite our efforts to free Russia of the Bolsheviks and restore her to her rightful throne."

Romanovsky coughed.

"Your Excellency, it's true the socialists and democrats are not as hostile to Tatiana as they were to Nicholas," he said. "But that doesn't mean an open proclamation of monarchy won't divide us."

"As you've said, not voicing a position is a liability to us as well," Denikin said.

"And Tatiana's proposal would create the most democratic government Russia has ever seen," Wrangel added. "*Far* more democratic than the Bolsheviks, for example."

As they spoke of the consequences of recognizing Empress Tatiana as the rightful sovereign, Wrangel spotted a familiar figure walking under the weight of a heavy pack, bags in each hand. Denikin stopped speaking, turning to follow Wrangel's gaze.

"General Krasnov," Wrangel said. "Where the hell is he going?"

"General Krasnov!" Denikin shouted, waving at the man. Krasnov dropped his bags near another track, then marched over to join them.

"Good afternoon, Your Excellency," Krasnov said, then nodded at the rest of the group. "Gentlemen."

"Why are you packed, General, and where would you be going?" Denikin asked.

Krasnov smiled and gave an ironic little laugh.

"Well, as you may have heard, Your Excellency, I no longer have a position here," Krasnov said. "It appears I must seek my destiny elsewhere."

"Krasnov, there is still a war on, and you are a talented officer and administrator. Stay, we have need of you."

"Stay and serve you?" Krasnov said. "As always, Anton Ivanovich, you are too kind. But no."

"You would choose exile over service just to salve your wounded pride?" Wrangel said, unable to hide the sneer in his voice.

Krasnov turned to Wrangel, his ironic smirk still in place.

"I know His Excellency does not read English," Krasnov said, nodding at Denikin. "But I think you do, correct, General Wrangel?"

"I have some facility with that language," Wrangel said, stiffly.

"Have you ever read a Scottish poet named Milton?" Krasnov asked.

"No, I haven't."

"If you can find a copy, I recommend his *Paradise Lost*. Fascinating read. Good day, gentlemen."

Krasnov turned on his heel and left without another word.

"I have no idea what he was talking about," Denikin said, his eyes on Krasnov's retreating back. Wrangel nodded his agreement.

"I think I might," Obolensky said, the three generals turned their eyes on the young major, who seemed unfazed by their scrutiny. "We read *Paradise Lost* at Oxford when my parents sent me to study there. I believe General Krasnov is referencing Lucifer's words when he was cast down by God for his rebellion, 'Better to reign in Hell than serve in Heaven.'"

Wrangel shook his head. A man of no small ego himself, it disturbed him to his core to see someone as capable as Krasnov so twisted with his own ambition that he served nothing but himself.

"Well, if Krasnov wants dominion in hell, let him have it," Denikin said, his tone philosophical. "For our part, let's get back to work and make sure he has to go somewhere other than Russia to find it."

Epilogue

France

The AEF elected not to court martial William J. Donovan for refusing to attack the Landres-Landres et St. Georges line again. In fact, Donovan was awarded the Distinguished Service Cross for his leadership in the attack and for refusing to be evacuated until his men were safely out of contact. He was also promoted to full colonel and given command of the regiment when Mitchell was promoted out of the billet.

Sigmund, too, was awarded the DSC, with no small push from Donovan on the matter. General Pershing pinned Sigi and Donovan with their medals for actions in the Argonne on the same day in the same ceremony. General MacArthur even paused to offer Sigi a word of congratulations after the ceremony before sweeping off to loftier matters.

The 42nd's attack, while disastrous in many respects, had weakened the Germans significantly. Fresh American units broke the main German line in the Argonne but were halted before they could take the key road and railway juncture of Sedan so that the French could reconquer their city themselves.

Sigi and his men occupied relatively quiet sectors and ran routine patrols until the armistice was signed. For both the 165th and the AEF as a whole, the final victory came as more of a sigh and a collapse onto the couch than as a climactic crescendo.

With the war in the West decided, all eyes turned to Russia. Grand Duchess Anastasia's speech before Congress had galvanized public opinion. President Wilson, with the consent of Congress, held that the Bolshevik Revolution had been the act of an enemy state, Germany, against a sovereign allied nation and that alliance with the legitimate government of Russia in the person of Empress Tatiana necessitated a strong American response to the disease of communism.

Sigi hadn't even realized that America had dispatched troops to Archangel and to Siberia until after the armistice.

"Well, Sigi, it looks like we may be visiting the land of your fathers," Donovan had said after the regimental intelligence officer had briefed them on the capabilities of the nascent Red Army.

"I take it you don't mean Israel, sir."

"If only I did; we all could use a little heat."

Several weeks passed in garrison duty in, of all places, Luxembourg. Sigi found the locals cold and disingenuous, but he was too busy to do much sightseeing in any event. The 69th was nearly up to full strength again, but the army had filled their ranks with a combination of brand-new replacements and the survivors of other units that had been shattered beyond repair in the Argonne.

Each category of replacement posed their own type of command challenges. The survivors needed to be evaluated and acclimated to the 69th and its ways. If they were going to Russia, Sigi didn't want a shellshock case endangering his men; best they were identified and shuffled out.

The replacements had all the clueless naivete one could expect, plus the added bonus that many were foreign born and spoke English poorly, if at all. As a polyglot, Sigi ended up devoting a significant chunk of his time to helping Father Duffy run a basic English course for these immigrant recruits.

He was in such a class when the orders finally came down. The 42nd Infantry Division and all subordinate units would inventory and entrain all assigned personnel and materiel for the port of Le Havre, there to be sealifted to New York for a victory parade, refit and resupply, and one week of R&R, then another boat to the Panama Canal, the Pacific, and sunny Vladivostok.

Sigi read the order twice, then chuckled, shook his head, and handed it back to his superior.

"Well, sir, at least we get to spend a week at home first."

It was night in Le Havre. The moonlight played softly upon the water, creating an adequately romantic scene for anyone, but Hank Thornton wasn't peering out over the water with a local mademoiselle. Instead, he gazed upon the forty-two brand-new Renault FT-17s lined up on the dock and grinned. His tanks, that the men of his new command would man.

The first thing Colonel Patton had dropped on them upon his

return from the hospital had been their orders for Crimea. The second had been a passel of promotions, and the third a new table of organization.

The 1st Tank Brigade (Provisional) was now the 304th Tank Brigade. Sereno Brett still commanded the 344th Battalion, now sporting a lieutenant colonel's silver oak leaf. Major Compton command the 345th, which Patton intended to become a tank school for their Russian allies, and *Major* Henry C. Thornton commanded the newly formed 346th.

Hank touched his new gold oak leaves, then, realizing he'd done it, quickly moved his hand back to his side. The promotion was a brevet due to exigencies of operations, etc., all caveats amounting to a warm; *don't count on keeping it, kid*. He hoped no one had seen him fondling his rank insignia.

"Oh, Major Thornton, sir, your leaves are oh so shiny."

Hank would've recognized that Queens accent anywhere. He turned to see Sigi Abramovich approaching. Sigi now wore captain's bars on his collar and overseas cap, a Distinguished Service Cross and a Legion of Honor with Palm pinned to his chest. His Victory Medal bore two citation stars.

Sigi threw his friend a mockingly precise salute, which Hank returned with equal overstatement. Then the two friends laughed and pulled each other in for a back-slapping hug.

"I should've known you'd find a way to make sure you outranked me," Sigi said, ruefully.

"You know it's mostly my sunny disposition, Sig. Flies with honey, and all that. You should try being pleasant sometime."

"And take away your only advantage? I wouldn't dream of it."

"My only advantage? Are you sure you won't need me to give you a boost onto your ship when you're ready to go, shrimp? I can ask Colonel Patton for temporary duty to give you a hand."

Sigi laughed.

"So, do you at least get an R and R back in the States?" Sigi asked.

"I'm afraid not," Hank said. "We're sailing straight for Crimea with the French."

The two friends were quiet for a moment.

"Are you all right, I mean, going back to the motherland? I know your folks don't exactly feel kindly about the Tsars."

Sigi shrugged.

"Tatiana is not her father, let's hope she turns out better. Besides, you've read the papers. The Bolsheviks are worse than the Kaiser on his foulest day."

Hank nodded.

"Well, I see you ignored my advice to keep your head down," Hank said, pointing at Sigi's DSC.

"Me? You have two of them," Sigi retorted, jamming a finger at the oak leaf cluster that indicated a second award on Hank's ribbon.

"Well, you have more citation stars than me," Hank said, waving a hand at the silver star pins on Sigi's Victory Medal.

"These? These were for administrative excellence."

Hank laughed from his gut and slung an arm around Sigi's shoulder.

"I've got six hours until I've got to be back on this dock, what say you and me find a good bottle of wine and you can catch me up on all your adventures in administrative excellence."

"That plan is so good, I have a hard time believing you didn't copy it off of me," Sigi said.

Hank grinned and together they walked toward the part of town with all the restaurants designed to separate American GIs from their overly generous pay.

"I can't believe you're going straight from here to Russia," Sigi said. "I find it hard to believe we're going to Russia at all. Didn't we just fight the War to End All Wars?"

Hank snorted.

"You know, Colonel Patton is an *interesting* fella to work for sometimes," Hank said. "But he's no dummy. He said something during St. Mihiel that stuck with me, 'there isn't a War to End All Wars until Kingdom Come.'"

Sigi cocked his head and nodded.

"Well, at least we won't lack for employment."

Glossary

Arshin: AKA "Russian Cubit." An obsolete Russian linear measure, set by Tsar Peter the Great at exactly twenty-eight English inches.

Berkovets: Russian measure of weight, just over three hundred and sixty-one pounds.

Bozhe: Russian for God

Chetvert: An obsolete Russian liquid measure of a bit over a liter and a half. There was also a dry measure called the same thing, but differing vastly in value.

Desyantina: Obsolete Russian unit of measurement, for area. Roughly one hundred and seventeen thousand square feet. A bit over a hectare.

Dolya: Obsolete unit of Russian measure, roughly a sixth of a gram.

Draniki: A savory potato pancake

Erkenungsmarke: German dog tags

Ersatz: A German word meaning substitute or replacement, but with strong connotations of being an inferior product.

Euxine: Old name for the Black Sea

Feldfebel: Russian version of a German rank, Feldwebel. Roughly equivalent to a U.S. Army Sergeant First Class or a Marine Gunnery Sergeant.

First floor/Ground floor: Americans are unusual in considering the ground floor of a building to be the first floor. In most of the world, the first floor is the first *rise* above the ground floor.

Funt: Obsolete Russian measure, a bit under a pound.

Furazhka: Visored, peaked caps

Gospodin: Sir or Mister

Gulaschkanone: A mobile field kitchen, generally pulled by horse, capable of making both stew and hot drinks. It's called a "Kanone" because of the stovepipe.

Gymnasium: In European terms, a gymnasium is a school for those of higher intelligence and greater scholastic achievement, to prepare them for university. Boston Latin, in the United States, is a Gymnasium.

Hauptmann: German for Captain

Jagdstaffel: Fighter Squadron

Kapitaenleutnant: A German naval rank roughly equivalent to naval lieutenant or lieutenant commander. If in command of a ship, he is still *the* captain.

Kasha: One or another variant on porridge

Kolbasa: Russian for Sausage

Kontrabandisty: Russian for smugglers

Kremlin: Russian for fortress or fortress inside a city.

Kubanka: Also Papakha. A usually rather large, usually cylindrical but sometimes hemispherical, fur hat with one open end.

Kulak: Russian for a prosperous peasant farmer. A kulak owns more than eight acres.

Lewis Gun: An American-designed, British- or American-built light machine gun.

Lot: Obsolete unit of Russian measure, twelve and four-fifths grams.

M1910: A Maxim-style heavy, water-cooled machine gun

Mikhailovsy: A large theater in Saint Petersburg

MP18: A German submachine gun or, in their parlance, machine pistol

Mudak: Russian for shithead

Nemetskiy: Russian for German

Nemka: The German woman, a none-too-flattering term for Alexandra, the late tsarina.

Obermaschinistenmaat: Senior Machinist's Mate

Oberst: German for Colonel

Oberstleutnant: German for Lieutenant Colonel, though called "Oberst" out of politeness.

Pelmeni: Russian dumplings, much like Polish pierogi but with a thinner shell and never sweet.

Peezda: Russian for cunt

Pevach: First run of Samogon, q.v.

Pood: Russian measure of weight, 16.38 kilograms.

Portyanki: Foot wrappings. They serve in lieu of socks and are not without their advantages, though using them is something of an art.

Praporschik: A kind of Russian warrant officer

Prostul doarme; bate în cap: Romanian for "beat his head in."

Radovoy: Private

Rodina: Russian for Motherland or Homeland.

Salo: Unrendered pork fat, usually salt- or brine-cured, sometimes smoked or spiced, eaten cooked or uncooked.

Samogon: Self-distillate, hooch, rotgut, moonshine. It might be pretty good or pretty awful or downright dangerous.

Sapogi: Russian for boots

Shvibzik: Imp

Skufia: A soft-sided cap worn by Orthodox clergy

Solyanka: A thick, spicy and sour Russian soup

Soviet: Russian for council

Sterlet: A smallish sturgeon

Syrniki: A kind of dumpling made with cottage cheese

Taiga: Sometimes swampy coniferous forest of the northern latitudes

Telezhka: Cart

Te rog nu mă ucide: Romanian for "please don't kill me."

TNT: Trinitrotoluene, a high explosive (Yeah, yeah, we know, but *somebody* isn't going to know that.)

Tsarskoye-Selo: Tsar's village

Tsaritsyn: Volgograd, AKA Stalingrad

Tsar: Emperor

Tsarina: Empress

Tsarevich: Crown Prince

Ulitsa: Russian for street

Ushanka: A Russian fur cap with folding flaps for ears and neck.

Vedro: Obsolete Russian unit of measure, about three and a quarter U.S. gallons.

Vozok: A kind of enclosed sleigh with very small windows and sometimes some means of heating it.

Yefreytor: Lance Corporal or Private First Class, borrowed from German *Gefreiter*

Yekaterinoslav: Dnipr, AKA Dnepropetrovsk